LAURA GRIFFIN

LIAR'S POINT

BERKLEY
New York

BERKLEY
An imprint of Penguin Random House LLC
penguinrandomhouse.com

Copyright © 2024 by Laura Griffin
Excerpt from *The Last Close Call* copyright © 2023 by Laura Griffin
Penguin Random House supports copyright. Copyright fuels creativity, encourages
diverse voices, promotes free speech, and creates a vibrant culture. Thank you for buying
an authorized edition of this book and for complying with copyright laws by not
reproducing, scanning, or distributing any part of it in any form without permission.
You are supporting writers and allowing Penguin Random House to continue to
publish books for every reader.

BERKLEY and the BERKLEY & B colophon are registered trademarks of
Penguin Random House LLC.

ISBN: 9780593546758

First Edition: May 2024

Printed in the United States of America
1   3   5   7   9   10   8   6   4   2

Book design by George Towne

For Kevan

CHAPTER
ONE

THE BEACH WAS deserted again.

On sunny days it was the good sort of deserted, empty and peaceful like a postcard. But today's sky was cold and colorless, and the beach just felt bleak. The wind nipped at Cassandra's cheeks, and she wished she hadn't come.

Focus on the breathing, not the pain.

She set her gaze on the foamy waterline and tried to get into the zone. The tip of her nose felt frozen, and her knuckles were numb as she pumped her arms.

Almost there. Just a little more.

She should be used to this by now. She'd been coming here for months on her evenings off. The route to the lighthouse from her apartment was a perfect two-mile loop that was both scenic and invigorating.

Her mind shifted to the stress that had prompted her to come out here and freeze her butt off when what she really wanted to do was pour a fat glass of wine. Today had been crazy, even for a Saturday. Her classes had been filled to capacity, and then she'd had to pick up two classes for Reese, who was out sick.

Or so she'd claimed. Reese had a new boyfriend, and Cassandra had her doubts about that excuse. But she'd filled in anyway, without complaint, because she owed Reese a favor.

Pounding out her frustration on the sand, Cassandra focused on the lighthouse. Perched upon a grassy hill, it looked gray and lonely in the waning daylight. During the summer, the lighthouse was packed with people climbing to the top for a panoramic view of the island's south side. But the visitors' lot was vacant now—not a tourist in sight.

Up ahead, a little blue car was parked on the beach near the dunes. Cassandra scanned the shoreline for its owner but didn't see any walkers or wade fishermen. She looked out at the waves.

A low buzzing noise pulled her attention back to the beach. She glanced up, searching for the drone. She couldn't see it, but the menacing hum told her it was there. She halted and stared up at the sky.

A red-haired boy darted out from a sand dune, with an excited black dog bounding behind him. The kid looked up, and Cassandra saw that the noise wasn't a drone but a remote-control airplane. The plane did a series of rolls and loops. Then a man joined the boy and took over the controls to bring the plane down for a smooth landing.

Cassandra resumed her run. She focused on her breathing again, sucking in big gulps of air, then blowing them out. Like magic, the anxiety faded, and her limbic system began to settle down.

Just a dad and his kid. Don't be so paranoid.

The wind whipped up, making her eyes water as she neared the lighthouse. She sprinted the last twenty yards, then stretched her arms above her head and turned around. The boy and his dog were leaving now. The dad loaded them into a pickup truck and walked around to the driver's side. He drove in a circle on the beach and disappeared behind the dunes.

Cassandra spied the solitary blue car again. Something about it needled her.

She glanced around. Still no shell seekers or fishermen, and she gazed out at the churning surf. Had someone gone for a *swim*? It was freezing. But maybe that was the point. Cold water could grab you by the chest and squeeze the breath right out of you. It was terrifying but exhilarating, too, and she understood the allure.

Even so, this end of the island had a notorious rip current. You'd have to have a death wish to swim out here alone, especially at sundown.

Cassandra veered toward the car, unable to stay away. Jogging toward it, she studied the tinted windows, the dinged door. She caught sight of something hanging from the rearview mirror, and her heart lurched. A dream catcher. A small white feather dangled from the hoop.

She jogged straight up to the door and looked through the window. Someone was asleep in the front seat. Long brown hair, pale arms.

Cassandra's breath caught, and her stomach did a somersault. Panic gripped her as she noticed the flies.

N ICOLE LAWSON FELT naked.

It wasn't the minidress or the strappy sandals. It wasn't even the weird slit that left the entire side of her thigh on display.

It was the Smith & Wesson .40 caliber pistol—or absence

of it—that was making her feel exposed. She was so accustomed to those twenty-nine ounces riding on her hip, and the lack of weight was making her antsy as hell.

She checked her phone, then flipped it over.

Nicole glanced around the restaurant, which was wall-to-wall couples, of course. She'd never been in here before, and the decorations grated on her nerves. They were going for elegant, she knew—this was the Nautilus, after all—and it wasn't like the place was covered in pink balloons. The bloodred rosebuds on every table looked nice, actually. Ditto for the votive candles that emitted a soft glow. Really, it was the glitter that was giving her hives, all those tiny gold hearts sprinkled across her table like pixie dust. Just the sight was making her feel even stupider than she already did in this ridiculous dress.

She checked her phone again.

For the first time ever she had a date on Valentine's, and not just any date. Tonight was *the* date. She and David had gone out three times already. The last time had ended with intense kissing in his car, which definitely would have continued if he hadn't been called into work. Nothing like being summoned to an autopsy to kill the mood.

He wanted to make it up to her, though. Those were his exact words when he'd invited her to this expensive restaurant. And so Nicole had squeezed herself into a low-cut black dress that gave her the illusion of boobs, borrowed her sister's stilettos, and come here to meet him for dinner.

"Are we still waiting?"

Her server was back again with that pitying look that was almost as annoying as the glitter.

She smiled up at him. "We are."

"And would you like some wine, perhaps? Maybe a cocktail?"

"I'm good." She nodded at her half-finished water. "Thanks."

He walked off, leaving her to her silent phone. No text, no voice message. She'd even checked her email, but zip.

Nicole looked around, sure people were staring at her. God, the white-haired couple behind her was already paying their bill.

Her phone vibrated on the table, and she snatched it up.

"Hello?"

"Where the hell are you?"

Not David. She closed her eyes.

"I'm out. Why?"

"Didn't you get the call?" Emmet asked her, and she pictured him at the police station surrounded by the typical Saturday-night chaos.

"I'm off tonight."

"Not anymore."

Her phone beeped with an incoming call, and she checked the screen.

"Listen, that's Denise. I have to go." Nicole got off with Emmet and took the call.

"Hey, what's up?"

"The chief asked me to reach you. He needs you at a scene."

Damn it.

Nicole pushed her chair back and grabbed her purse. "Does he know I'm off tonight?"

"Yep."

She unzipped her little black clutch and left a ten on the table. They were going to have to bus it, even though she hadn't ordered anything.

"Well, what's going on?"

"One sec," Denise said, and cut over to another call. When things were busy, the Lost Beach PD receptionist doubled as a dispatcher. She was also the chief's right hand, doing everything from managing his calendar to deflecting reporters who called in from time to time.

The front of the restaurant was packed with waiting couples. Nicole scanned the bar and the area around the hostess stand but didn't see any tall, handsome doctors looking around for their date. It was 7:32. She'd officially been stood up.

"Nicole?"

"I'm here." She squeezed past the people and pushed open the door. A cold gust hit her, and she stepped back.

"He needs you at Lighthouse Point right away. And keep it off the radio."

"What's going on?" she asked again.

"I'm not sure."

"Well, what did he say?"

"He said, 'I need Lawson at Lighthouse Point ASAP. Keep it off the radio.' That's all I have."

Nicole hunched her head down, wishing for her leather jacket as she strode across the parking lot. It had filled in since she'd arrived.

"What's your ETA?" Denise asked.

"I'll be there in five."

"Roger that."

Nicole slid behind the wheel of her pickup and started it. Cold air shot from the vents, and she turned the heat to max. She set her purse on the passenger seat and backed out, still looking for David's black Pathfinder in case he was pulling in late. He wasn't.

She should shake it off. He had a demanding job, like she did. It was unpredictable. Maybe he got tied up at work and forgot to call.

But really, that only made her feel worse. She'd been looking forward to this all week. She'd planned her outfit and put on makeup and spent half an hour straightening her damn hair. This was why she didn't go out. She hated the bullshit. She was much happier at home binge-watching TV with her cat.

The lighthouse came into view, and Nicole's pulse picked up. Three, four, *five* emergency vehicles—four cruisers, plus a fire truck. No ambulance, which was a worrisome sign. Everyone was parked in the lot, but the action appeared to be centered on the beach where some portable klieg lights had been set up. Nicole whipped into a space beside the fire rig and scanned the crowd as she shifted into park.

She reached into the back and rummaged around. There was a flannel shirt, an LBPD windbreaker, and a rain poncho. No shoes, damn it. She had a pair of waders in the toolbox in back, but the mud boots she normally kept on hand were on her balcony at home, drying after she'd hosed them off.

She grabbed the windbreaker, then unzipped her little black purse and slid out her backup pistol. A tube of lipstick fell out, too, as if to taunt her.

She got out and pulled on the jacket, then tucked the gun into the pocket, along with her badge. Not that she needed her detective's shield. Even at a glance, she could see she knew everyone out here.

She crossed the parking lot, attempting to look confident, which worked fine until she reached the sandy trail leading to the beach. She considered kicking off the heels and going barefoot, but there might be glass on the beach, plus her sister had threatened her within an inch of her life if anything happened to her precious Jimmy Choos.

"*Don't* leave them at his house," Kate had said. "And if he has a dog, put them up high."

"I'm not going to end up at his house."

"Yeah, you will."

"I will not."

"When he sees you in that? You will, trust me."

Nicole strode across the sand to the group of men milling in the shadows near the klieg lights. A perimeter had been cordoned off around a small blue Subaru. The only person inside the yellow scene tape appeared to be their CSI, who wore a white Tyvek suit and a purple face mask. Miranda was just back from maternity leave and no doubt had plenty of things she'd rather be doing on a Saturday night. She crouched beside the car's open passenger door and snapped a photograph.

Nicole headed for the cluster of first responders. Adam McDeere saw her and did a double take.

"Whoa." He looked her up and down and seemed to get stuck on her cleavage. "Where were you?"

"Out. What's going on?"

He cleared his throat, still distracted. "We got an OD. A jogger called it in 'bout an hour ago."

Nicole looked at the car. "Where's the ME's team?"

"They came and went. It was pretty straightforward. No blood."

"Is it a suicide?"

He raked a hand over his buzz cut. "No note or anything yet. But who knows?"

"Lawson!"

She glanced up, and Brady was waving her over. She went to talk to him, and his brow furrowed as he looked her over.

"What do we have, Chief?"

"Drug OD," he said. "There's a bottle of pills spilled across the passenger seat."

"All right."

The other guys turned to look at her, and she felt their gazes moving over her bare legs.

"Any note?" she asked.

"Not that we know of. We don't have her electronics yet."

So, it was a woman. Nicole turned to check out the car again, where Miranda was still taking photographs. Emmet knelt beside the door now, shining his flashlight inside the vehicle. He glanced over and caught Nicole's eye.

"I need you to interview the witness."

She turned back to Brady. The chief wore his typical weekend attire of a barn jacket over a flannel shirt and jeans. He'd been off duty, too, but it didn't look like he and his wife of thirty-plus years had been out celebrating.

"We tried to get her statement already, but she was pretty hysterical. Having some kind of panic attack, she said."

"'We'?"

"Owen was the first one here."

She looked at Owen, who had stepped away from the group to talk on his phone. He stood in the shadows with his back to everyone, as though he wanted privacy.

So, Owen Breda hadn't been able to get a statement from the witness. Not exactly typical. Owen was one of their best detectives, and his easygoing charm put people at ease, particularly women.

"Where is she now?" Nicole asked.

"Over there." Brady nodded toward the water.

Nicole turned and suddenly noticed the figure seated on the sand about thirty yards away. The person was little more than a shadow, really—just a dark silhouette sitting still as a statue.

"What's she doing?" Nicole asked.

"No idea," Brady said. "Woman's a space cadet. We couldn't even get an address out of her."

In Brady's book, a "space cadet" could mean someone who was high or flaky or habitually out of it, for whatever reason.

Nicole looked at the woman again. "Is she local?"

"She works at the Banyan Tree."

Nicole turned to see Emmet walking over. "You interviewed her?"

"As much as I could." He stopped and gazed down at her, hands on hips as he took in her little black dress. "She kept having breathing issues."

"Does she need a paramedic?"

"I tried. She didn't want one. Said she just needed some space."

Nicole looked at the woman again, then back at the chief. "I'll go talk to her," she said, zipping her jacket.

"Find out if she saw anything suspicious," Brady instructed.

"I will."

"It looks like a suicide, but you never know. Ask her if she saw anyone else around before she found the car."

Nicole bit her tongue. Did he think she didn't know how to conduct an interview?

"And pin down her timing," Brady added.

"Got it."

She felt Emmet watching her and turned to look at him. He wore his usual leather jacket and jeans, but the hint of cologne told her he'd been on his way out somewhere when he got the call.

"Want me to go with you?" he asked.

"I'll handle it."

Nicole set off for the water, skirting around the glare of the portable klieg lights. In the distance, people were milling on the sand, no doubt wondering what all the fuss was about. It was the off-season, but the island still had plenty of snowbirds and full-time residents who liked to walk the beach at night, and all the first responders had caused a stir. No media yet, though, which was one bit of luck. But it wouldn't be long. Suicide or not, a death on the beach would at least be worth a news brief in the mainland paper.

The witness sat cross-legged on the sand, her posture ramrod straight. The dark braid down her back went all the way to her waist. Her hands rested on her knees, palms up, and Nicole stopped in her tracks. Was she meditating?

Stepping closer, Nicole picked up a faint hum. She *was* meditating. This was a new one. Nicole didn't know the etiquette here, but it didn't matter. Someone was dead, and the chief was counting on her to get something useful from this witness.

"Excuse me?"

The humming stopped. The woman's chest rose and fell. Then her head swiveled to face Nicole while the rest of her body remained stock-still.

"I'm Detective Lawson, Lost Beach PD." She pulled the badge from her pocket and held it up. Even in the dimness, she could see the woman's expression didn't change. "Mind if I ask you a few questions?"

A slight nod.

"I understand you came upon the car and called it in?"

Another nod.

She definitely was *not* hysterical. She seemed unnaturally calm, like maybe she was on something. She wore black leggings, sneakers, and a gray sweatshirt that looked a hell of a lot warmer than Nicole's thin windbreaker. She was sitting on a jacket, too, probably to protect her clothes from the wet sand.

Witness Interrogation 101: eye contact.

Nicole stepped closer and crouched down, tucking her knees under her jacket as her dress rode up.

"Cold out here, huh?" Nicole smiled.

"There's a front coming in."

"Do you jog out here often?"

"Three times a week. On my evenings off."

"And where do you work?"

She took a deep breath and blew it out slowly. "I teach yoga at a studio downtown."

"The Banyan Tree?"

She nodded.

"Sorry. I didn't catch your name."

Another deep breath. The woman's eyes looked almost black in the dimness. She had pale skin, and Nicole wondered how long she had lived here. Most full-time residents had year-round tans unless they constantly slathered on sunscreen.

"Cassandra Miller."

Nicole took the little spiral notebook from the inside pocket of her jacket. "Is that with a *C*?"

"Yes." She eyed the notepad with a wary look.

"And your home address, Cassandra?"

She rattled off the address of an apartment complex in town several blocks off the beach. Then she surprised Nicole by volunteering her cell phone number. With a twinge of satisfaction, Nicole jotted everything down. Already she'd managed to get more than Owen.

"So, you mind telling me about what happened? How you came upon the vehicle?"

The woman turned her face to the water and took another deep breath. Deep breaths seemed to be a big thing with her.

"I was nearing my midpoint."

"Midpoint?"

"I always turn around at the lighthouse."

"All right."

"I noticed the car when I first passed it."

"What time was this?"

"I don't know. About ten after six?"

Nicole made a note. "Did you see anyone inside?"

"No. I thought it was empty."

"Did you get a close look at it?"

She shook her head. "I was running. Then I reached the lighthouse and turned around, and that's when I got a weird vibe."

"A vibe about what?"

"Just, you know, a *feeling*. I knew something was off. Something about the car bothered me."

Weird vibe, something off, Nicole scribbled.

"I thought maybe someone was swimming or surfing. The waves are high today. But there's a rip current here, and there are warning signs all over the place. I started to get worried that maybe someone was out there alone."

She took a deep breath and blew it out for an eternity as Nicole waited, her pen poised above her notepad.

"And then?"

"Then I jogged over for a closer look, and that's when I saw the dream catcher." She glanced over her shoulder at all the cops. "I recognized it."

"Recognized what?"

She turned to face her. "The car. The dream catcher. All of it seemed familiar. I looked closer, and sure enough, it was her."

Nicole leaned closer. "You're saying you *know* the person who—"

"Yes. Her name is Aubrey."

CHAPTER

TWO

Emmet pulled into the parking lot and scanned the rows. No black Nissan Pathfinder, thank hell. He glanced up at the second apartment from the end. Her light was on.

He got out and climbed the stairs. As he reached the top, his phone vibrated with a text from his brother.

Buck's is dead tonight. We're headed to Finn's.
U coming?

Be there in 20, Emmet responded.

He walked down the open breezeway to Nicole's door and gave a few sharp raps. A shadow moved in front of the peephole. Several seconds ticked by and then the door swung open, and she sighed.

"Expecting someone else?"

"No," she said, moving back to let him in.

He stepped inside, and she glanced out at the parking lot

before closing the door and turning to face him. The mini-dress and heels were gone, but he could still smell her perfume. She'd changed into an oversized sweatshirt and leggings.

"Want a beer?" she asked.

"Sure."

He followed her into the kitchen, on alert for her skinny cat, who hated him.

"What's up?" she asked.

"I came by to update you."

The phone on the counter chimed, and Nicole grabbed it. Her brow furrowed as she read a text.

Emmet scooted around her and opened the fridge. He grabbed a Corona and watched as she tapped out a message to someone, probably David. He took a bottle opener from the drawer by the oven and popped off the top.

"So what's going on?" she asked, setting her phone aside. Her long auburn hair was back in a ponytail now, and she looked like herself again, except for all the eyeliner.

"I talked to my DPS contact," he said. "The prints match the ones on file from her driver's license. Aubrey Lambert, twenty-four years old. Houston address. Her parents live at the same location."

Nicole leaned back against the counter. "I thought she was local."

"Guess she didn't get around to changing her driver's license." He took another sip. "We called Houston PD. They're going to send someone first thing in the morning to notify next of kin."

"Why not tonight?"

"It's Houston." He shrugged. "They're slammed. I'm guessing conducting a death knock for us isn't high on their list."

Nicole rolled her eyes.

"Anyway, once the family's notified, I'll get in touch with them about logistics. We figured you'd want to handle the autopsy. The chief wants a rush on the lab work. If someone sold her some bad shit, maybe something laced with fentanyl, we want to know that sooner rather than later."

"Brady said it was prescription pills."

"Yeah, but you know how that goes. Could be from one of the pharmacies over the border."

She folded her arms over her chest. "Who is 'we'?"

"What?"

"Who decided I should handle the autopsy?"

"Brady. Owen and I were talking to him after you left the station house."

Her brown eyes flashed with annoyance. "Well, why'd he choose me?"

"He probably figured you'd want a chance to drop in on your boyfriend. What's the problem?"

"The problem is I hate autopsies."

Nicole's weak stomach was legendary. But Emmet got the sense there was more to it.

"Trouble in paradise?" he asked.

She opened the fridge and grabbed a bottle of water. "I just don't see why it has to be me on this one," she said, ignoring his fishing expedition. "It sounds like Brady's leveraging my personal relationship to work a case."

"People do it all the time. That's how the system works."

She twisted the top off and shook her head.

"I can cover it for you, if you want," he said.

"Good. You cover it. I'll reach out to the family about logistics."

"Anyway, suicide or not, a death on the beach is going to be news," he told her. "If it's fentanyl-related, even more so."

Emmet sipped his beer, watching her. She seemed anxious. She probably wanted him out of here in case her boyfriend showed up.

He glanced around her apartment. He hadn't been over here in months. Well, except for a few late-night drive-bys. He wasn't sure why he'd come tonight of all nights when he was likely to bump into David, and he could have easily handled this by phone. But making things easy wasn't in Emmet's DNA.

He checked his watch. "I'm headed over to Finn's to meet Calvin and Kyle," he said. "You want to come?"

"It's almost midnight."

"So?"

She shook her head. "I'll pass."

Her phone chimed on the counter, and she reached for it. A worried look came over her face as she answered the call.

"Lawson."

Emmet watched her shoulders tighten as she listened.

"Yes, sir." Her eyes met his. "All right. Well, I was talking to Emmet, and he offered to cover it." Her jaw tensed. "Okay." Another pause. "Yes, sir." She turned away. "All right, will do."

She set the phone down, and Emmet knew what she was going to say before she turned around.

"That was Brady." She crossed her arms. "I'm on the autopsy."

He smirked. He'd known Brady would insist on her going.

"Why are you gloating?"

"I'm not." He took one last sip of beer and set the bottle on the counter. "Thanks for the drink."

Emmet headed for the door. She reached around him to open it, and he wished there was something he could say to get her to come out with him.

He should just let it go. But he couldn't help himself.

"Sure you don't want to come out with us?" he asked.

"I have to be there at seven freaking a.m. I'm going to bed."

Right.

"Thanks for offering to trade with me," she said.

"No problem." He stopped in the doorway and gazed down at her.

She arched her eyebrows. "What is it?"

He stepped outside.

"Skip breakfast," he told her. "Maybe you won't puke."

CHAPTER

THREE

THE COUNTY JUSTICE center was busy with the typical Sunday traffic—detectives dropping off evidence, girlfriends bailing out boyfriends, and bleary-eyed deputies heading home after a long night of traffic stops. After waiting in line to get a visitor's badge, Nicole took the elevator down and navigated through the windowless labyrinth where the medical examiner worked.

"You looking for David?"

Nicole turned around to see Cynthia bustling toward her. The clerk had a clipboard in one hand and a giant coffee mug in the other.

"Is he in yet?"

"Honey, he's *been* in. I don't think he went home." She stopped at the big metal desk and set her mug on a stack of files. "Y'all got a case today?"

"Drug OD," Nicole told her. "It came in last night."

"Whew. We got flooded last night." She set her clipboard on the desk and ran a glittery purple fingernail down the list. "Must be the full moon. People actin' crazy. You're with Lost Beach PD, right?"

"Right."

She flipped a page. "Scheduled for seven a.m. but . . . I think he just finished."

"He did?"

"I saw him in the hallway a minute ago."

Nicole muttered a curse and headed for the autopsy suite.

"Upstairs," Cynthia told her. "He was on his way to the lab."

"Thanks."

Nicole retraced her steps to the elevator bank. How had David finished already? He would have had to start at five. Had he actually spent the night? That seemed extreme, even for a workaholic triathlete who operated on very little sleep.

She hit the elevator button. Irritation roiled inside her as she waited. She and David still hadn't had a live conversation. After reading his text message last night, she'd let his calls go to voicemail. Maybe she should just get over it. He was obviously buried with work. He had a high-pressure job.

But she did, too, and that didn't stop her from communicating with people and showing basic common courtesy. She hadn't heard from him until eight last night, a full hour after he was supposed to meet her. And it had been a text message. Just thinking about it pissed her off, and she jabbed the call button again.

The doors slid open, and David stepped out.

Nicole froze.

"Hi." He frowned. "What are you doing here?"

"I'm here for the post."

He wore blue scrubs that matched his eyes and well-worn

running shoes. He rested his hands on his hips and stared down at her with an intense look.

"I'm sorry about last night," he said.

"No biggie."

His frown deepened, as though he knew she was lying.

"I caught a double traffic fatality right as I was walking out the door," he said.

"I know. I read your text."

He glanced around, then touched her elbow and guided her toward an alcove with a pair of water fountains. She shook off his hand.

"I'm really sorry, Nicole. There was nothing I could do."

She tipped her head to the side. "Well, that's not *completely* true. You could have called me."

"I tried. You didn't pick up."

"I mean before I waited around at the restaurant feeling like an idiot."

"I'm sorry. By the time I got free—"

She held up her hand. "You know what? Forget it."

"No. Listen. By the time I got a minute to call you—"

"I said *forget it*." Her cheeks flushed, and she pictured Cynthia down the hall, eavesdropping on every word.

"Nicole." He took her hand in his. "I sincerely apologize."

He gazed down at her with those serious blue eyes, looking genuinely sorry.

The thing was, she knew that he *was* sorry. Their first date together, they'd spent the whole night bonding over their mutual frustration with their crazy work schedules and lack of time for a personal life. He'd told her he'd had this whole epiphany about it on his forty-third birthday, and he'd resolved to change things.

"Will you let me make it up to you?"

She rolled her eyes. He'd said that last time.

"Please?"

"I'll think about it." She tugged her hand away. "Anyway, I didn't come here to talk about this. I'm here about a case."

His remorseful look vanished, replaced by cool professionalism.

"The benzodiazepine overdose."

Nicole didn't know the clinical term for it. "She had a bottle of pills spilled all over her car. Did you finish the postmortem?"

"Yes."

She breathed a sigh of relief. "Well, was it Xanax? Brady wants a rush on the tox report. If there was fentanyl in her system, we need to know sooner rather than later."

He gazed at her for a long moment. "Come with me."

"Why?"

"I need to show you something."

He walked away, and Nicole's stomach filled with dread as she followed him down the cinder-block hallway. They passed Cynthia's desk—which was empty, thankfully—and he led her around the corner into a long corridor with garish fluorescent lighting. The temperature dropped noticeably as they turned another corner and neared the autopsy suite.

He stopped beside a door and entered a passcode.

Nicole's stomach flip-flopped. "I thought you were finished?"

"I am. I want to show you something."

Biting back a curse, she followed him into a narrow room with a row of stainless steel sinks on one side. He took a surgical mask from a box by the door and handed it to her before grabbing one for himself.

Nicole followed his lead and put on the mask, then pulled on a pair of latex gloves.

"Here." He turned and dabbed gel on her mask. Vicks. It was supposed to combat the smell, but instead it brought back memories of the last time she'd been here, and her stomach started to churn.

He held the door for her and ushered her into the exam room. The back of her neck began to sweat, despite the refrigerator-like temperature.

The room smelled of death and disinfectant. Two long metal tables stood in the center of the space. The far table was empty, but on the closest table was an ominous lump covered by a gray sheet.

Nicole looked at the room next door, separated by a big glass window. A couple of people in scrubs were hunched over an exam table under a bright white light. They had a radio on, and the faint sound of pop music carried through the wall.

Nicole turned her attention back to David as he approached the table. Bile rose in the back of her throat, and she swallowed it down. The mound on the table looked so flat, hardly big enough to be a full-grown woman.

"You okay?"

She glanced up and nodded.

He reached for the top of the sheet, and she looked away.

Skip breakfast. Maybe you won't puke.

She had skipped breakfast, but now her skin felt clammy, and the contents of her stomach were about to come up.

"Shit," she muttered.

"I know you hate this."

She clenched her teeth and eased closer as David adjusted the covering around the body, exposing only a slender white arm.

Nicole examined the inert limb, trying not to think about how it was attached to a dead body. A dead *person* who had recently been cut open, and dissected, and stitched back up again.

"Nicole?"

Her gaze snapped to David's. His eyes bored into hers.

"You see it?"

She looked down at the arm again and tried to block out everything—the cold, the stench, the obscenely upbeat music coming from next door.

Aubrey Lambert had a delicate green vine winding around her right forearm. The tattoo ended just below her elbow with a monarch butterfly that looked like it was tangled in the leaves.

David traced his gloved finger over the back of her arm, below the shoulder. "See?" He twisted the arm, and Nicole's stomach jolted.

"What am I looking at?"

"The contusion. See it?" He tapped a pale reddish blotch no bigger than a pencil eraser.

"You mean the bruise? What about it?"

"Here." He reached behind him and grabbed a magnifying glass off the counter. He handed it to her and then adjusted the overhead light. "Look."

Intrigued now, Nicole bent closer, studying the waxy white skin through the glass. In the center of the blotch was a dark brown dot.

"Twenty-three-gauge needle."

"So . . . she was shooting up when she ODed?"

He glanced at the ceiling, clearly impatient. "Nicole, *look.*"

She looked again, taking note of the awkward way he'd positioned her arm.

"That's a weird angle for an injection."

His eyes brightened. "Exactly."

A cold feeling swept over her.

"Most people are right-handed," she said. "But even if

she wasn't, this would be a nearly impossible angle for a self-injection. She'd have to be a contortionist."

"Right."

"Which means someone *else* injected her."

She watched David's eyes over the mask as he carefully tucked the arm beside the body and re-covered it.

"In my professional opinion, yes, that's precisely what happened."

"So, you're telling me—"

"I'm telling you what I'm putting in my report," he said. "The manner of death is homicide."

EMMET WALKED INTO the bullpen and went straight for the break room. He had a monster headache today. He fed some money into the vending machine, and a Red Bull thunked down.

"You're late."

He turned around to see Denise in the doorway. She wore her Sunday earrings, which looked like little silver hubcaps.

"How was church?" he asked, grabbing his drink.

"Why don't you come sometime and find out?"

"I will."

Denise taught Sunday school at Lost Beach Unitarian, where her husband was the assistant pastor.

Emmet popped the top on his drink and took a long swig.

"You'd better get in there," Denise said. "They started ten minutes ago."

"What, the staff meeting? What's the big deal?"

Her eyebrows tipped up. "You didn't hear?"

"Hear what?"

"The death at Lighthouse Point. The ME said it's a homicide."

"Seriously?"

She nodded.

Fuck.

Emmet pulled out his phone and checked it. Why hadn't someone told him? Specifically Nicole. The autopsy was hours ago, and she should have called him by now if there were any surprises. They made a point of keeping each other in the loop.

He drained the drink and pitched the can. Then he grabbed a notepad off his desk and entered the conference room, where he found the chief and every other detective seated around the table. Even Adam McDeere was there, and he hadn't even officially made detective yet.

Emmet took one of the few empty chairs and looked at the screen on the wall. He recognized one of Miranda's photographs from last night. It was a picture of the Subaru taken from the inside passenger side. Emmet had been crouched beside her, shining a flashlight through the windshield when she'd taken the shot.

"So, how do you explain the writing, then?" Owen asked.

Emmet glanced across the table. Owen sounded testy, and he had his arms folded over his chest. Maybe he believed the ME had gotten it wrong.

"Yeah, I thought she wrote 'Goodbye' across the inside of the windshield in lipstick," Adam said, gesturing at the photograph. "You're saying someone else wrote it?"

"I didn't say that at all," Nicole replied, clearly defensive. "I'm just sharing what Dr. Bauhaus told me. Which is that—in his professional opinion—this death is a homicide." She turned to Adam. "And anyway, it was ChapStick, not lipstick."

"Same difference," Owen said. "It reads like a suicide note. You know, 'Goodbye, world' or something like that."

"Well, maybe the message is more like 'Goodbye, bitch' instead of 'Goodbye, world,'" Nicole countered. "Maybe it was some kind of revenge killing, and the killer wrote it. Or, I don't know, the scene was staged."

"But it *was* a Xanax overdose, correct?" Owen said.

"That's correct," Nicole said. "According to the preliminary screening."

Owen leaned forward now. "Well, Aubrey Lambert's name is on the prescription bottle. Are you saying this revenge killer staged that, too?"

"I have no idea." Nicole looked at Brady. "I'm just relaying the pathologist's conclusion. Which is that we should be treating this as a *homicide*, not a suicide or an accidental overdose."

"Based on one tiny needle mark in the back of her arm, which she could have made herself?" Owen asked. "I mean, I'll grant you, it's a weird angle. But we're talking about someone who does yoga, right? Wouldn't we expect her to be flexible?"

Nicole jutted her chin out and crossed her arms. She didn't like people putting her on the spot. Or questioning her boyfriend's judgment.

Emmet scanned the faces around the table. All looked skeptical, including Brady, who typically put a crapload of confidence in Dr. David Bauhaus. Everyone knew the deputy medical examiner was wicked smart.

The mood in the room got tense and quiet. No one wanted this to be a homicide investigation. They were just coming off a major case, and the entire department was running on fumes after spending the last ten weeks helping a multiagency task force close in on a sex-trafficking ring in the Rio Grande Valley. Operation Red Highway had been a major success and resulted in some high-profile arrests. But their understaffed detective squad had been working evenings and weekends, and people were tapped.

Emmet took in everyone's expression. Owen and Adam looked cranky, Nicole looked pissed off, and Brady looked grim as the ME's conclusion sank in.

The chief turned to Emmet.

"Glad you could join us."

He nodded. "Sorry I'm late."

"You talked to the family this morning? Her parents in Houston?"

Emmet nodded again. "Had a video interview with them at ten. They're in shock." He glanced at Nicole. "Said they can't imagine their daughter taking her own life."

The chief shifted his attention to the screen where the crime scene photo was displayed.

Crime scene. Emmet was already rethinking everything and wishing he could turn back the clock. He thought about the countless pieces of evidence they had already missed out on by making assumptions.

Never assume.

It was so basic. The mantra had been drilled into him, over and over, by every mentor he'd ever had, including Brady himself.

The chief studied the photo silently. He smoothed a hand over his gray buzz cut. Then he turned to Emmet.

"You're the lead on this one."

Emmet gave a crisp nod, despite the dread filling his stomach. "Yes, sir."

Normally, he would jump at the chance to lead a homicide case. But this one was off to a rough start.

"Breda, you and McDeere go back to the beach," the chief said. "Take a couple uniforms with you and do a grid search. Then we need to canvass the area. Interview joggers, walkers. All the regulars who frequent that beach."

"Got it," Owen said.

Brady turned to Emmet again. "Track down our witness. Take Lawson with you." He looked at Nicole. "You got her talking yesterday. See what else she knows."

"Will do," Nicole said.

"What about the car?" Emmet asked.

The Subaru was a glaring problem. It had spent the night at the impound lot when it should have been at the crime lab.

Brady pushed his chair back. "I'll handle the car." He looked at all the faces around the table. "Let's move quickly, people. This is now a homicide. Every hour matters, and we're making up for lost time."

CHAPTER

FOUR

Nicole walked out of the station house.

"Hey, thanks for the heads-up."

She glanced back at Emmet as he winced at the sunlight and pulled a pair of aviators from the pocket of his leather jacket.

"Would have been nice to get a call, you know, so I could have been here when the meeting started."

"It's not my job to get you to work on time," she said. "Anyway, Brady called me into his office the second I showed up."

She ignored Emmet's simmering look as she strode toward the parking lot. She refused to feel guilty even though, yes, she could have called him. But the encounter with David had rattled her, for numerous reasons, and she'd been distracted.

"We'll take my car," she said, popping the locks. She'd been the first one here this morning, so she'd had her pick of vehicles and had selected their newest unmarked police unit, which had a better radio and didn't smell like vomit yet.

Nicole slid behind the wheel and nestled her insulated mug in the cup holder.

Emmet got in the passenger side and immediately racked the seat back to make room for his long legs. He reached for her mug.

"This coffee?" He took a sip.

"Help yourself."

"Thanks."

She exited the parking lot and took the shortcut through town.

"You're thinking the Banyan Tree?" he asked.

"Yeah. Aren't you?"

He checked his watch. "Makes sense."

He picked up her coffee again, and she cast him a sidelong look. She couldn't see his hazel eyes behind the sunglasses, but she'd seen them in the meeting, and they looked bloodshot and tired. Yes, he'd managed to shave this morning—probably as a courtesy to the grieving family he'd had to interview—but she could tell he was dragging today.

She neared a stoplight and hit the brakes.

"Shit," he said, sloshing coffee.

"Sorry," she muttered, even though she wasn't really. Served him right for being out late drinking.

He grabbed a napkin from the floor and glared at her. "Let's just have this out now," he said, blotting the coffee.

"What?"

"You're pissed off Brady made me the lead."

"No, I'm not."

"Bullshit. I'm in charge, and you're mad because you think it should have gone to you."

"How would *you* know what I think?"

"You're competitive, Nicole. And you think I don't deserve to lead this one because I showed up late and hungover."

Frustration welled up inside her, mainly because he was dead-on. She glanced at him.

"I was the one who got up at the crack of dawn and went to the autopsy and found out this is a homicide," she said. "And I'm the one who's established a rapport with our only witness. So, yes, I think Brady should have made me the lead here."

"Good. We agree." He tossed the napkin on the floor. "But he put me in charge, not you, and you should be relieved. This thing is shaping up to be a shitshow and we're not even one day in."

She shook her head.

"What, you think I'm wrong?"

"No." She glanced at him. "Let's just move on. You're the lead. I'm over it."

"Fine." He sighed and looked out the window. "Okay, give me the rundown. Why homicide?" He looked at her. "It couldn't only be the needle mark. What else?"

Well, at least he was giving David some credit.

"We discussed this before you arrived," she told him. "There was something else he discovered at autopsy. Something with the livor pattern."

"Oh yeah?"

"He found discoloration on her skin that made him think she was on her back for a while and then moved into the driver's seat where she was found."

"How long? An hour? A day?"

"A few hours, he estimated."

Emmet looked straight ahead as they made their way through downtown. It was a typical off-season weekend. Not too many tourists, mostly locals. But the lunch places were starting to fill in.

"That's an important detail," Emmet said.

"Yeah, no kidding. It wasn't just about the needle mark." Her frustration was back again. "I don't know why everyone decided to shoot the messenger."

"It's not you. They're just mad." He shook his head. "We fucked up. No question about it. We never should have released the crime scene. And the car—it's sitting at the impound lot instead of the forensics lab."

She sighed. "What a mess."

"Tell me about it. Now *if* we manage to recover any good evidence from it, and *if* we make an arrest, and *if* the case goes to trial, some defense attorney someday is going to have a field day. Not to mention the prosecutor, who's obviously going to hate us."

Nicole's stomach clenched, and she set her hand on it. She'd felt queasy since her meeting with David, and not just because of her close encounter with a corpse. Emmet was right. They'd screwed up, and some mistakes were irreparable. If they never got justice for Aubrey Lambert's family, it was completely on them.

Emmet sighed and ran his hand through his sun-streaked brown hair. It was getting long again, and she hoped he wouldn't get around to cutting it. He looked over and caught her watching him. "What?"

"You know the other problem, right? Besides the car?"

"If she wasn't killed there, then we've got another crime scene," he said.

"Right."

"It's possible she was abducted from someplace or killed at another location and brought to the beach," he said. "Either way, the perp had to have been in or near the vehicle, so maybe we'll get lucky, and someone spotted him."

Luck. Sure. They'd had so much already.

"Where did she live again?" Nicole asked.

"That apartment complex near the wharf. Angler's Landing."

"Nice."

He looked at her. "Not really. You ever been over there?"

"No. But at least it's gated. And new." Unlike Nicole's place, which had been built in the seventies and looked it. "And where did she work?"

"Her parents said she waited tables at O'Toole's sports bar. But I don't remember seeing her in there. Do you?"

"No. But I've never been in there at lunch. Maybe she worked day shifts?"

"Maybe."

Emmet shook his head, and she knew what he was thinking. They needed to find out about the victim's work hours—and a million other details of her daily routine—so they could piece together her movements leading up to the discovery of her body at Lighthouse Point. It was a process that should have started yesterday. The first days of a case were critical, and they'd lost valuable time.

Emmet was right. This was shaping up to be a shit-show.

"Guess I was optimistic to think we might have a slow off-season," Nicole said. "First, we had the task force op, now this. Everyone's tapped."

"That's no excuse," Emmet said. "We need to rise to the occasion."

"I know." She took a deep breath. "Okay. Let's nail this interview."

She had gotten this witness talking before, and now she just needed to coax more information out of her. Surely the woman had seen *something* useful while she was jogging on that beach.

Nicole swung into the parking lot of the Banyan Tree

and had to drive all the way to the far end to find an empty space. The yoga studio shared the strip center with a martial arts academy, a dog groomer, and a doughnut shop that had a line out the door. The shop was known for its chocolate cake doughnuts, and Nicole's stomach rumbled just thinking about them.

She and Emmet got out and looked around.

"You used to take classes here, didn't you?"

She glanced at Emmet, surprised. "That was, like, four years ago. How do you remember that?"

"I remember things." He checked his phone and slid it into the pocket of his jacket.

"Yeah, I got a membership once." She sighed. "I was on a fitness kick. I went to just enough classes to realize I'm not cut out for yoga."

They crossed the parking lot, and as they neared the door, Nicole spied a slender woman in workout gear with a dark braid all the way to her waist.

"There she is." Nicole hurried after her, hoping to catch her outside. "Cassandra?"

The woman opened a glass door, and Nicole walked faster. "Cassandra?"

The door swung shut, and Nicole grabbed it. "Cassandra Miller?"

She turned around, and Nicole halted. "Oh, sorry. I thought you were someone else."

She smiled. "Cassie Miller?"

"Yes."

"She's in my studio next door."

Her studio next door.

"Oh. Thank you." Nicole walked out, and Emmet stood on the sidewalk. He pointed to the sign painted on the door.

"That's the martial arts academy."

Nicole glanced around. "Yeah. They've changed everything since I was here last."

"Damn, they're busy," Emmet said, pulling open the neighboring door.

Busy was an understatement. The lobby area was crowded with spandex-clad people, mostly young and mostly female. The scent of sandalwood incense hung in the air, masking the smell of sweat. Nicole darted a look at Emmet, who seemed remarkably unfazed by all the dewy young bodies. All the women turned to look at him—which was what always happened when Emmet entered a room. Nicole used to get annoyed, but she was used to it now.

Squeezing through the crowd, she made her way to the reception counter, where a thin, thirtyish man was ringing up a T-shirt sale. They'd opened a gift shop, apparently, and seemed to be doing a brisk business in yoga gear and aromatherapy.

"Excuse me. I'm looking for—"

"Nicole."

She turned around, and Emmet jerked his head toward the hallway.

Nicole spied Cassandra Miller in the corridor. She wore a formfitting lilac-colored outfit and had her hair in a long braid again. She hooked a white towel around her neck and reached for a glass door.

"Cassandra?"

She turned. A look of panic came over her face as Nicole approached her.

"Hi. Detective Lawson, remember?"

Cassandra's mouth dropped open but she didn't say anything. Then her gaze shifted to Emmet.

"And this is my colleague, Detective Davis. Is there somewhere we can talk?"

Her eyebrows shot up. "You mean here?"

Emmet smiled, turning on the charm. "We just have a few questions."

She swallowed. "I can't. Not right now. I've got a class starting and—"

"This shouldn't take long," Nicole said, although that wasn't true at all.

Cassandra started to say something, then seemed to change her mind. She glanced past Nicole.

"Reese? Hey, I need a favor."

A tall blond woman stopped in the hallway. She looked straight out of a Lululemon catalogue, right down to the stylish belt bag clipped around her waist.

"Could you get my twelve fifteen started? I have to handle something."

The woman cast a curious look at Emmet, no doubt noticing the holster peeking out from beneath his leather jacket. "Sure."

"This way," Cassandra said, and then led them down the hallway. She stepped into a side nook that was crowded with laundry carts heaped with white towels, and Nicole got the distinct impression the witness didn't want to be seen talking to police at her workplace.

"What did you need to talk about?" Cassandra looked from Nicole to Emmet and a worry line appeared between her brows.

Nicole smiled, trying to ease the tension. "The woman next door—I thought she was you."

"You mean Danielle? She teaches tae kwon do." Cassandra looked puzzled. "That's what you wanted to talk about?"

"No, I was just wondering." Nicole took out her spiral. "Is this *her* studio or—"

"She and her partner, Paula," Cassandra said. "They run the Banyan Tree and the martial arts academy next door. They expanded last year and bumped out the space."

Nicole opened her notepad, and Cassandra darted a look over her shoulder. "Listen, my class is starting. Is there any way—"

"We just have a couple questions," Nicole said. "About Aubrey Lambert."

Cassandra flinched at the name.

"We're investigating her death," Nicole added.

"Well . . . okay. I mean, I haven't remembered anything new since yesterday but—"

"Do you recall anyone else on the beach at the time?" Nicole asked. "Specifically, anyone near her car?"

She shook her head. "It was just parked there all by itself."

"Who else was around?" Nicole persisted. "The beach is never totally empty. Were there any wade fishermen? Beachcombers? Other joggers?"

"No. Well, just some guy with his kid."

"A guy?" Nicole eased closer. "Where was he?"

"He was farther down the beach." She cast a nervous look at Emmet. "Not near Aubrey's car or anything."

"And he was with a kid?" Emmet asked.

"Yeah. A little boy and a dog. I mean, I assumed it was his kid, but I guess it could have been his nephew or something like that. They were flying a remote-control plane together." She looked from Emmet to Nicole. "I'm sorry, why is any of this relevant?"

Nicole ignored the question as she scribbled notes. "What did they look like?"

Cassandra took a deep breath and stared down at her bare feet. "I don't know. The dad was like, dark hair, medium build. The boy had red hair."

"Were they in a vehicle?" Nicole asked.

She waited a beat and seemed to think about it. "A teal green pickup truck. They were leaving as I turned around to jog back."

"Was there anyone else at Lighthouse Point yesterday?" Emmet asked. "Maybe anyone who struck you as out of place?"

"No. There was no one. It was cold and windy." She looked at Nicole. "Again, what does this have to do with Aubrey's suicide?"

"As of now, we're investigating this as a homicide," Emmet said.

Cassandra's face drained of color. "You're—but I don't understand." She looked at Nicole. "I thought she ODed. What happened?"

"We're not in a position to share details right now," Emmet said.

Cassandra's eyes filled with tears, and she looked down at her feet.

"Are you all right?" Nicole asked.

Emmet stepped away, and Cassandra swayed slightly. Nicole reached for her arm.

"Do you need to sit down or—"

"I just need to center." She pressed her hand to her chest and took a deep breath.

"Here," Emmet said, offering her a paper cone filled with water.

"Thank you." She sipped the water and closed her eyes.

Nicole watched the woman's face as the word *homicide* seemed to penetrate.

"Sorry." Cassandra shook her head. "I just—I don't understand this. What about all the pills in the car? I thought she—"

"Ma'am, can you think back to the teal green pickup truck?" Emmet asked. "Did you happen to notice the license plate?"

"No."

"Or anything distinctive about it? Maybe a bumper sticker? Or a toolbox in back?"

"No."

"Was it a regular or extended cab?"

Cassandra shook her head. "I didn't notice. Listen, I need to get back to my class so—"

"What about the dog?" Nicole asked.

"The dog?"

"What kind was it?"

"I don't know. It was black, I think." She darted another glance over Nicole's shoulder. "I really have to go now."

"Just a few more questions," Nicole said. "Do you remember if you touched the vehicle?"

"What?"

"Aubrey's Subaru. Do you recall if you touched it when you jogged up and saw her in the front seat there?" Nicole asked. "Maybe touched the window or tried the door handle?"

"No. I told them this last night, I didn't touch anything. Look, I really need to get back to my students, so—"

"Here." Emmet handed her a business card. "We'll let you go."

A look of relief came over her face.

"Call us if you think of anything else."

She nodded.

"We'll be in contact," he added, and she walked off.

Nicole watched her rush down the hallway and duck into the restroom.

She shot a look at Emmet. "What was that? I wasn't finished yet."

"We can circle back."

"But I have more questions."

"Give her some time to absorb. Come on."

Nicole followed him as they retraced their steps through the hallway, which was less crowded now that the next class had started. They passed a glass door and Nicole saw

Cassandra's co-worker leading everyone through a series of standing poses.

Nicole and Emmett stepped outside, and she darted a look at him.

"That was bizarre," she said.

"What was?"

"Her reaction."

He shrugged.

"She definitely didn't want to talk to us," Nicole said as they reached the car, and she popped the locks open. "It was strange, don't you think?"

"Not really. The woman wears a crystal around her neck and teaches yoga."

"So?"

He slid inside, and Nicole got behind the wheel.

"So, she's a little out there," Emmet said. "Plus, we hit her with a shock. We just told her that her friend was murdered. How'd you expect her to react?"

Nicole shook her head. "My radar is up. She's hiding something."

E MMET GAZED DOWN at the young woman seated on the curb.

"And what time was it that you left here for work?"

She looked up at him with puffy pink eyes. Her makeup was smeared, and she'd obviously been crying. "Around one forty I think." She rubbed her nose with the sleeve of her sweatshirt. "My shift started at two. I didn't get back home until after ten."

Aubrey Lambert's roommate waited tables at a seafood place on the bay, and Emmet remembered seeing her there when he'd been in for po' boys. She had told him just now that she was twenty-two, but he'd always thought she looked more like eighteen.

"And she was at the apartment when you left?" Emmet asked.

"She'd come home around one. I didn't see her yesterday morning. I don't know where she spent the night."

"Where do you think she spent the night?"

She shook her head.

"If you had to guess?"

She bit her lip and looked down at her sneakers. They were on the sidewalk outside the victim's apartment while Miranda and a CSI they'd borrowed from the county crime lab scoured the place for clues.

"I don't know. She wasn't seeing anyone lately, so maybe her ex."

"Ex?"

"Sam Somebody."

Emmet wrote it down on his notepad. "You don't know his last name?"

She pulled her sleeves over her hands and crossed her arms. "I never met him. They weren't together very long."

"Okay. And did Sam ever come here to the apartment?"

"Not that I know of. I think they went to his place."

"Hey, Emmet."

He glanced up, and Adam was motioning to him from the door to the leasing office. Emmet held up a hand for him to wait.

"Did you ever see Sam?" Emmet asked. "Maybe out at a bar or something? Could you describe him?"

She shook her head.

"Do you know where he lived?"

"No."

"Well, do you know where they met?"

"I'm not sure. Maybe online?" She looked up at him.

"Do you think—" She put her hand over her mouth. "Do you think he had something to do with this?"

"We're just gathering information right now. We're trying to learn more about what Aubrey was doing in the days before she died. Do you know what she planned to do yesterday?"

"I'm not sure. She came home with groceries. And I think she mentioned something about a yoga class later? Other than that, I don't know."

"Emmet."

He glanced at Adam again.

"Listen, Lauren, it would really help us out if you could write down the names of Aubrey's close friends." He tore a page from his notebook and handed it to her with a pen. "Could you do that? And phone numbers, if you have them. I'd like to talk to more people who knew Aubrey."

She nodded and took the paper.

"I'll be back, okay? Write down as many as you can."

He left her to her task and crossed the parking lot to the Angler's Landing leasing office, where Adam and Nicole had been interviewing the property manager. The office had been closed today, and they'd had to call this guy in from his fishing boat.

"Anything from the roommate?" Adam asked, holding the door open.

"Aubrey spent the night out, maybe with an ex."

"Oh yeah?"

The lobby was furnished with white leather chairs and beach-themed art. Emmet spied a water cooler near the reception desk and went over to grab a cup.

"How's Miranda doing in there?" Adam asked.

"No evidence of forced entry." Emmet downed the cup and refilled it. "But the roommate tells me they're pretty lax about keeping the place locked."

"Seriously?"

"Sounds like he could have just walked in."

Emmet heard Nicole's voice in the back room, along with someone else's—presumably the property manager.

"And the roommate was out all afternoon?" Adam asked.

"She was gone at work from one forty until ten. She said Aubrey was here at the apartment when she left for her shift." Emmet pitched his cup in the trash and nodded at the back office. "What's she got back there?"

"Come look."

Emmet followed Adam into a dingy office that looked nothing like the outer lobby. A suntanned guy with a shaved head sat at a gray metal desk in front of a computer. Nicole leaned over his shoulder and looked at the screen.

"That's it. That's the date," she said. "Can you fast-forward to one p.m.?"

Emmet eased around the desk. "This is the surveillance vid?"

"From the parking lot." She glanced back at him. "What's Miranda finding in the apartment?"

"Not much."

"They've only got one security cam," Nicole said, "and it's trained on the main gate—*which*, unfortunately, has been out of order for more than a month."

"The gate or the camera?" Emmet asked.

"The gate," she said. "Anyone could come in or out."

"Okay, here's one o'clock." The property manager turned around and frowned at the crowd now gathered behind him. His mirrored shades were perched on top of his head, and he didn't look happy to be called in on his day off to deal with a bunch of cops.

"The roommate says she left the apartment around one forty," Emmet said, "so Aubrey had to have left sometime after that."

All four of them stared at the grainy black-and-white surveillance footage. The manager fast-forwarded the video until a white car moved through the gate.

"Wait, pause." Nicole grabbed her notepad off the desk.

"That's one of ours," the manager said.

"How do you know?" Adam asked.

He backed up the video and paused it. "All our residents have that black decal on the back." He pointed at the screen. "See?"

Emmet leaned forward to examine the sticker. He'd noticed one like it on the back of Aubrey's Subaru.

"Okay, white Kia sedan." Nicole jotted notes as the video continued.

A dark pickup came into view, and the manager hit pause again.

"And . . . a black F-150," Nicole said. "No decal here."

"Looks like a visitor," the man said, hitting play again.

Nicole's jaw tensed, and Emmet knew what she was thinking. The secure, "gated community" touted on the banner outside wasn't secure at all, and Aubrey's killer would have had easy access to both her home and her car.

"There. Pause it." Nicole leaned forward as another car passed through the gate. "That's Aubrey. And she's alone."

Emmet glanced at the time stamp in the upper corner. "That's one twelve, about a half hour before her roommate left for work."

"Maybe someone followed her home," Nicole murmured, leaning closer.

The manager hit fast-forward again and they watched the footage. A black Honda exited the property.

"That's Lauren, the roommate," Emmet said. "She drives a black Accord."

They continued watching as the manager fast-forwarded

through the next hour and several more cars entered the complex, all with parking decals.

"There." Adam leaned closer. "Isn't that her?"

A dark-colored Subaru neared the exit gate, and the manager hit pause. "This?"

"Yeah."

Emmet's pulse picked up as he studied the image. The time stamp was 3:22 p.m. "That's not Aubrey."

"Wait, wait, wait. Let me zero in." Nicole leaned closer and took over the mouse to zoom in on the car. The person driving wore a black hoodie and sunglasses.

"That's a dude behind the wheel," Adam said. "Where's Aubrey?"

Nicole's face looked grim. "I think he's got her in the back."

CHAPTER

FIVE

CASSANDRA DUCKED HER head against the cold wind and used her elbow to jab the crosswalk button. Shivering on the corner, she watched the cars whisk by as she waited for the light. When it turned green, she rushed across the intersection and past the sign for Grandview Villas, which—despite its name—didn't have much of a view. But its location within walking distance of the Banyan Tree had been a major selling point.

She clutched her grocery bags in one hand and her pepper spray in the other as she scanned the shadowy parking lot. The lighting on the property needed improvement, but Cassandra wasn't holding her breath. The landlord was cheap. He could hardly be bothered to fix a leaky faucet, much less make security upgrades for the safety of the tenants.

We're investigating this as a homicide.

Aubrey had been murdered, and Cassandra still couldn't get her head around it. Lost Beach was all about quiet.

Solace. Serenity. People came here specifically to escape the sort of crime that plagued big cities. And now someone had been murdered just footsteps away from the island's iconic lighthouse. Cassandra felt sick just thinking about it.

She stepped onto the sidewalk, then jumped aside just in time to avoid colliding with a kid on a skateboard. He glanced back at her without slowing, and she muttered a curse at his back—not that he could hear her with his Air-Pods stuffed in his ears.

Scanning the sidewalk for any more surprises, she walked to her apartment and dropped her groceries on the doorstep as she fumbled with her keys. Her gaze fell on a white FedEx envelope tucked behind the flowerpot. She snatched it up, and her stomach knotted as she read the Colorado return address. Could this day get any worse?

She grabbed her groceries and entered her apartment, then locked the door and went straight into the kitchen to dump everything on the counter.

Her head pounded as she stripped off her fleece jacket. She desperately needed a shower and an aspirin. But first she had to get something into her stomach. They'd been crowded all day again thanks to Danielle's "Bring-a-Buddy" New Year's promotion, and Cassandra hadn't even had time for a lunch break.

She switched on the oven, then toed off her running shoes and went into the bedroom to get out of her sweaty clothes. After pulling on her comfiest pj's, she put the groceries away and slid a veggie pizza into the oven.

As she poured a glass of wine, she eyed the FedEx package on the counter. Did they deliver on Sundays? It had probably come yesterday, but she'd somehow missed it, probably because everything after that 911 call had been a blur. The whole night had been awful, and she'd lain awake for hours, tossing and turning.

She sipped some wine to brace herself and then tore open the cardboard mailer. Inside was a plain white envelope with her name typed across the front. Opening the envelope, she found a folded invoice. It looked just like the last one she'd received, only the Due Date column was highlighted in pink and the words 60 DAYS PAST DUE appeared in red along the bottom.

Tears burned her eyes. What about the *services* that were sixty days past due? Where was the explanation for that?

A loud knock sounded at the door, and her pulse jumped. Who would that be? She wasn't expecting anyone. Maybe someone's food delivery had the wrong door? As the knock came again, she crept across the room and peered through the peephole.

Detective Lawson stood on her doorstep. She was alone this time, no sign of her hot partner.

Cassandra pulled her fleece jacket on over her pj's and slid the overdue invoice under a stack of mail. Then she returned to the door and took a deep breath before unlocking the door and pulling it open.

"Hi there," the detective said with a smile.

"Hello."

"Sorry to interrupt your evening. I just had a few more questions I wanted to run by you."

Cassandra stared at her. Answering questions was the last thing she wanted to do right now, but apparently she didn't have a choice.

"Questions about Aubrey?"

"That's right." Another reassuring smiled. "I called but you didn't pick up, so I thought I'd swing by. This shouldn't take long."

Cassandra stepped back and ushered the detective inside. With the exception of the police windbreaker, the woman looked completely different than she had on the beach last night. No high-heeled sandals, no minidress. Tonight she wore jeans and thick-soled hiking boots, and her auburn hair was pulled back in a ponytail.

"Nice apartment," the woman said, glancing around. "I had a friend who used to live over here."

"Oh?"

"Second-floor unit, one of the ones on the end."

Cassandra's living room furniture consisted of a single purple futon, so she led the detective into the kitchen.

"So." Cassandra leaned back against the counter. "How can I help?"

"Well, we've been interviewing people who knew Aubrey, trying to get a sense of her life. Do you know if she was having any problems with anyone? She ever mention anything like that to you?"

"No. But I really didn't know her very well. You should talk to her close friends."

Nodding, the detective took out a spiral notebook. "Also, we've been circling back with the witnesses."

"Witnesses?"

"People who saw Aubrey's car at Lighthouse Point yesterday. I just want to go over a few details with you." The detective flipped open the notepad. "At the beach last night you said you typically jog there on your evenings off. When is that, exactly?"

"My evenings off?"

She nodded.

"Tuesday, Thursday, Saturday," Cassandra replied. "I get home about five thirty and have time for a run. All the other days—like today—we have seven o'clock class and I don't get home till now."

The detective jotted something on her pad. "And do you run the same route every time?"

"From here to the point and back."

"That's what? Three miles?"

"Two miles round-trip." Cassandra watched as she wrote it down.

"And do you see some of the same people each time?" The detective looked up. "Fishermen? Surfers? Other joggers?"

Hadn't she been over this already? Irritation surged inside her, but she tamped it down.

"I didn't see anyone else on the beach yesterday," Cassandra said. "Well, except the man with the airplane."

"Yeah, but what about other evenings? Are there any regulars you typically encounter?"

Cassandra glanced down at her feet and thought about it. "There's a tall guy. Always wears black. I pass him some nights."

"What about last night?"

"No."

"Could you describe him a bit more?" Lawson asked. "Is he heavy? Thin? White? Black?

"Pretty thin," Cassandra said. "He's got a runner's build, and always wear a black T-shirt and visor."

"He ever have a dog with him?"

"No."

She flipped a page in her notebook. "Okay, and the guy with the airplane and the kid. Anything else you can tell me about him?"

Cassandra shook her head. "Really, I just saw them from a distance. They're not regulars or anything."

"Okay." She flipped another page. "And the timeline. You said you saw the car about ten after six. How sure are you about that?"

Cassandra's guard went up. "Fairly sure. Why?"

"Any chance it was later?"

"Well, maybe. I mean, I wasn't looking at a watch or anything."

"And after you saw the blue Subaru—for the second time—and approached it and saw that there was a person inside it who appeared to be unconscious, what did you do after that?"

"I called 911."

"Right away?"

"Yes."

"You didn't open the door or try to render aid or—"

"I've been over this already," Cassandra said. "I saw her in there and I called 911."

The detective glanced at Cassandra's hands, and she realized she was gripping the counter. Cassandra let go and folded her arms over her chest.

"I saw her in there. I realized she was dead. I called for help," Cassandra said. "I don't understand what the issue is."

"No issue, really. Just a discrepancy."

"A what?"

"Well, the call came in at six twenty-eight. So there seems to be a discrepancy." The detective's gaze met hers. "I'm just trying to pin down what time you saw the victim exactly."

"Oh." Cassandra thought back, but everything blurred together now. Mostly she recalled feeling like she couldn't breathe, like she was trying to suck air through a straw. "Well, I suppose it could have been a bit later. Like I said, I wasn't looking at a watch or anything."

A buzzer sounded, and Cassandra jumped. She stepped over to the oven and stopped the timer. "Sorry. One sec." She grabbed a dish towel off the counter and took out the pan.

"That should just about do it," Lawson said. "I'll let you get back to your dinner. Thanks for your time."

"No problem."

"Would you mind if I use your bathroom?"

"My bathroom?"

"I have another stop after this."

"Sure." Cassandra glanced down the hallway. "It's just there on the left."

"Thanks."

The detective tucked her notebook into her pocket and headed down the hallway as Cassandra stood there holding her pizza.

When the bathroom door closed, she set the pan down and dug her phone from her purse. Sure enough, she'd missed a call twenty minutes ago while she'd been at the store.

Cassandra eyed the stack of mail on the counter. Then she took a plate down from the cabinet and washed her hands with the lavender soap that was supposed to be *calming*. Right. As if soap could cure her frayed nerves and the anxiety of having a police detective in her house.

Closing her eyes, she took a deep breath and held it in for ten seconds. Then she blew it out and repeated the process. Her nerves began to settle.

But then she pictured Aubrey slumped across that seat, and her stress kicked in again.

"Nice dream catcher."

She turned around, and Lawson was back again, standing on the other side of the counter now.

"What?"

"Your dream catcher." She nodded at the window above the sink. "It looks like the one in Aubrey's car."

"Oh." Cassandra dried her hands on a dish towel. "Yes. We sell them in the gift shop."

"We?"

"Well, Danielle sells them. The gift shop has become a big revenue center."

Cassandra walked around the counter, ready to wrap up the interview.

"Thanks for your help tonight," Lawson said, moving to leave finally.

"No problem."

"I've got your number if I have any more questions."

Cassandra opened the door. "If there's anything else, just, you know, give me a call."

CHAPTER

SIX

THE SMELL OF French fries hit Nicole the minute she walked in. She ignored her grumbling stomach as she scanned the crowded bar.

"Nicole."

She whirled around.

"Over here."

Her sister and Siena were in a booth behind the hostess stand. Nicole walked over but didn't sit down.

"Hey, stranger," Siena said with a smile.

"You're just in time," Kate told her. "We haven't ordered yet."

Kate's hair was up in a loose bun, and she wore her favorite black halter top, despite the cold weather. She took in Nicole's sweater and jeans with a sigh. "Gee, you really dressed up for us."

"Give me a break. I just got off work."

"Speaking of work, Emmet is here," Siena said. "Along with Owen Breda."

Nicole turned around. "Where?"

"Over by the dartboard."

"Look, they're still doing their Valentine specials," Kate said, sliding over a little pink menu. "What are you drinking?"

"I don't know yet. One sec."

Kate frowned. "Where are you going?"

"I'll be right back."

Nicole walked over to the bar area and spotted Owen and Kyle playing darts. Emmet stood nearby beside a high-top table that had a basket of fries and a pitcher of beer in the middle. Nicole's stomach fluttered as she looked them over. Two cops and a firefighter, all in ripped condition and brimming with masculine confidence. Emmet, Owen, and Kyle were quite a trio, and had been since high school. As usual every woman in the bar had an eye on them.

Emmet glanced up and caught her eye as she walked over, and a rush of warmth went through her.

"Hey, Nicole, perfect," Kyle said. "You can be on my team. We're about to start a new game."

"Sorry, not tonight." She turned to Emmet. "What happened with the family? I thought you drove up to Houston."

"We're meeting tomorrow."

"Why?"

He looked her over as he picked up his beer. "You just get off work?"

"Yeah. Why tomorrow? I thought they wanted to meet tonight."

"They called and changed it. Said they prefer to come down here." He slid the pitcher toward her. "Want a beer?"

"No. Thanks." She glanced over her shoulder. "I'm meeting up with Siena and Kate." She turned back to Emmet, and he was watching her closely.

She didn't know what to make of the fact that he was

here tonight. If she'd been leading the case, she'd be at the station house right now, either running leads online or combing through everything that had come in today.

"Relax, Nikki."

"What's that mean?"

He set down his glass. "I can see what you're thinking, and I'm still working. I'm here to see Lainey."

She frowned. "Who?"

"Lainey Wheaton, Aubrey's manager." He nodded toward the bar. "The bartender tells me she's on her way in."

"Oh." Nicole crossed her arms, feeling bad now for thinking he was here wasting time. "You want my help with the interview?"

He smiled slightly. "Think I can handle it. Go hang out with your sister."

She glanced back at Kate and Siena. They had scheduled this meetup days ago, and Nicole knew they couldn't wait to hear all about her big date, but she was dreading talking about it.

She turned back to Emmet. "So." She snagged a fry and dipped it in ketchup. "I'm striking out on teal green pickups."

"Oh yeah?"

"There are only two registered in the county, and I checked both of them."

"Maybe the guy's a tourist."

"Great. Another dead end."

Emmet shrugged. "Not necessarily. We could try the hotels, see if they have a record of him."

"Or he could be staying at a rental. Or here visiting friends." She blew out a sigh. "I'm frustrated. I was excited about that lead. Green Pickup Guy was our only potential witness."

"Don't forget the yoga teacher."

Owen walked over. "Yeah, how did it go with her? You went to see her at home, right?"

Emmet looked surprised. "You did?"

"I wanted to follow up, see if she remembered anything new."

"Did she?" Emmet asked.

"Not really." She popped another fry in her mouth. "Once again, she seemed squirrelly."

"Squirrelly?" Owen asked.

"Yeah, evasive. I can't tell whether she's genuinely flaky or hiding something she knows, for some reason."

"Why would she?" Emmet asked.

"I don't know that yet."

"Well, we've got the phone dump working," Owen said. "Maybe that will give us something useful."

Emmet glanced over Nicole's shoulder. "Looks like Lainey's here."

Nicole turned and watched a woman stride through the bar. Tall, blond, killer body—she was exactly Emmet's type. She waved at the bartender and disappeared into the back hallway.

Nicole looked at Emmet. "Sure you don't need a hand?"

"I'm good." He took one last sip, then set his beer down and headed to the back of the bar.

"The chief put a rush on it."

She turned to Owen. "What's that?"

"The phone records. He called his contact and told him we need those ASAP. The guy said he thinks he'll have something by tomorrow. Maybe we'll get a lead on the ex-boyfriend."

"Let's hope." She looked Owen over. He seemed distracted—not his usual laid-back self.

"You okay?" she asked.

"Yeah."

"Where's Macey?"

"Los Angeles for a work thing," he said. "She's supposed to be out there all week."

Owen's girlfriend was a documentary filmmaker, and she traveled a lot for her job. So maybe he was grumpy because he knew he wasn't getting any for an entire *week*. Nicole had zero sympathy.

"Hey, how about one-on-one?" Kyle asked her, grabbing a beer glass off the table.

"Sorry," she said. "We're about to have dinner."

"Come back after?"

"Maybe."

She left them to their drinks and rejoined her sister and Siena in the restaurant.

"So, enough with the stalling," Kate said as Nicole slid into the booth beside her. "How was your date?"

"It wasn't."

Siena's face fell. "What do you mean?"

"He didn't show."

"Get *out*!" Kate exclaimed. "He stood you up?"

"He texted me after we were supposed to meet and said he had to work."

"*Texted?*" Her sister looked appropriately outraged. "Tell me he at least showed up later with some candy and flowers or something."

"Nope."

A server stopped at their table with a tray of frozen margaritas.

"We ordered for you," Siena said as the server set down the drinks.

Nicole reached for her margarita.

"Wait," Kate said, pulling the glass away. "No distractions

yet. Are you telling me it didn't happen at all? After the dress and the shoes and the freaking pedicure? Did you even see him last night?"

"No." Nicole grabbed her drink and took a cold sip.

"That sucks," Siena said.

"Well, did he at least apologize well?"

Nicole shrugged. "It was okay."

Her sister rolled her eyes.

"Well, this is disappointing," Siena said. "I was excited to hear about at least one of us having sex last night."

"I can't believe he had to work."

"I can." Nicole took another tart sip. "That's what he does. That's practically all he does. Miranda warned me— the man's a workaholic."

"I was so hopeful." Kate sighed. "What a waste of great shoes."

"*You* weren't wearing them," Siena said.

"Well, did you at least get a good guilt trip out of it? Maybe he'll make it up to you."

Nicole's stomach twisted at the irony. Last night was supposed to make up for the last time David had canceled. She was beginning to doubt whether he'd been honest with her when he'd said he wanted a relationship in his life. He'd seemed genuine, but his actions didn't back up his words.

"Think positive," Siena added. "So he works a lot—at least he has a good job, right? That's always a plus."

"Let's talk about something else," Nicole said, stirring her drink and looking at Siena. "How was *your* Saturday night?"

Siena was just out of a relationship and had been trying to meet people.

"Boring," Siena said. "I watched TV and had takeout for dinner."

Nicole turned to her sister.

"What are you looking at me for?" Kate asked. "You know I had no plans whatsoever. Well, besides being your wardrobe consultant."

"Whoa. Hold up," Siena said. "Who is *that*?"

"Where?" Kate turned around.

"In the bar with Kyle and Owen."

Nicole craned her neck, but it was too crowded to see.

Kate stood up. "Oh. Wow. That's Alex Breda." She shot Nicole a look and sat down.

Nicole glanced back again and, sure enough, Alex Breda now stood at the table with Owen and Kyle.

"*That's* Alex Breda?" Siena asked. "I haven't seen him in, like, ten years or something. Is he the middle brother?"

"The youngest," Kate said. "It goes Joel, then Owen, then Alex."

"Didn't you see him at Joel and Miranda's wedding?" Nicole asked Siena.

"No. I was there catering, not mingling with the guests."

"Anyway, he's a lawyer in Houston now," Kate said.

"Was," Nicole said. "I heard he's back."

"*Back* back?" Kate asked. "You mean he's back here for good?"

"That's what I heard. I think he rented an office downtown."

Siena and Kate stared at her as she took another sip of her drink.

"What?" Nicole asked.

Kate rolled her eyes. "You know what. Alex Breda is amazingly hot, not to mention successful."

"So?"

"So, you have the perfect in, as usual. You're friends with his two brothers."

The server reappeared, this time with a heaping platter

of nachos. She set it in the middle of the table and passed out appetizer plates.

"Anything else for y'all?" she asked.

"Thanks, that should do it," Kate said.

As soon as she left, Siena scooped up a nacho.

Kate elbowed Nicole. "Maybe if things don't work out with David, you should hit up Alex Breda."

"Right."

"Why not?"

"It would be beyond weird. I work with both of his brothers."

"So what?" Kate said. "What does working with his brothers have to do with anything? It's not like you work with *him* every day. I could see how *that* might be weird."

Nicole shot her sister a warning look at the not-subtle reference to Emmet. But Nicole would never go there because she didn't want to be one of Emmet's casual hookups. Plus, they worked together, and the fallout would be bad, especially for her. She'd spent her whole career trying to get the men in her field to treat her as an equal and take her seriously. The last thing she needed was everyone talking about her sex life. The guys she worked with—hot as they might be—were definitely in the look-but-don't-touch category.

"You have no idea how good you have it," Siena said. "You spend your days surrounded by attractive men. If I were you, I'd take advantage of the situation."

"It's not that great, trust me." Nicole picked up a nacho and pinched off a strand of cheese. "They can be annoying as hell. And too many badge bunnies."

Siena frowned. "Badge bunnies?"

"Women who chase cops," Kate told her. "It's a thing."

Nicole glanced across the bar to where Owen and Alex were now playing darts while Kyle flirted with a pair of women. Emmet was still in the back with Lainey the manager, presumably.

"Well?" Kate asked.

"Well what?" Nicole chomped into her nacho.

"If things fizzle with David, why don't you make a play for Alex?"

Nicole could see from Kate's smirk that she was just trying to needle her. And as usual it was working.

"I'm not going to *make a play* for Alex Breda," Nicole said. "I've got enough guy problems."

L AINEY STEPPED INTO the office where Emmet was waiting and dropped her purse on the desk piled with paperwork.

"Sorry about that," she said, setting her phone down. "Thanks for waiting."

"No problem."

She sank into the swivel chair and sighed. "Don't ever get married."

Emmet lifted an eyebrow. "Trouble at home?"

"My ex is a deadbeat."

Emmet and Lainey had gone to Lost Beach High School together. She'd married a real estate developer down from Austin and had two sons, if Emmet remembered correctly.

"How are the boys?" he asked.

"Crazy, as usual." She picked up a water bottle from the corner of the desk and twisted off the top. "But enough about me. What can I do for you? You're here about Aubrey."

Emmet nodded.

She took a gulp of water and plunked the bottle down. "I'm sick about it. I still can't believe it."

"What can you tell me about her?"

She slumped back in the chair. "God, she was great. One of my best people." She shook her head. "*Was*. That still sounds wrong to me. It hasn't really sunk in yet."

"How was she at work?" he asked. "Any issues?"

"None at all. She was on time. Reliable. No drugs, no bullshit."

"Did she seem depressed ever?"

Lainey shook her head. "Not that I'm aware."

"What about friends? Was she social?"

Lainey blew out a sigh. "She was friendly. But not overly social, I don't think."

"She have a boyfriend, that you know about?"

"Not that I'm aware of, no. I could ask the other servers if they know of anyone."

"That would be good. Or I could talk to them."

Lainey's brow furrowed. "The news brief I read said it was a drug overdose. Is that as in suicide?"

"We're still investigating." He watched her expression as she shook her head. "Why?"

"Just . . . I don't know. I didn't get that feeling from her."

"What feeling?"

"That she's someone who would do that." She took a deep breath, blew it out. "She seemed to be doing well. You know she was in recovery, right?"

"Recovery?"

"AA."

Emmet tried to mask his surprise. "She told you she was an alcoholic?"

"I guessed pretty quick after she started working here. Takes one to know one."

Emmet kept his expression neutral. He hadn't known about Lainey either.

"Kind of odd for her to work in a sports bar, don't you think? I mean, if she's a recovering alcoholic."

"Not really. I've been doing it for years." Lainey sat forward and rested her arms on the desk. "I saw her at meetings occasionally. But she seemed to have her shit together, you know? She was a hard worker. Always got here on time. Another thing—she'd asked me for a raise recently."

"Oh yeah?"

"I gave it to her. This was just last week." Lainey shook her head. "I didn't get the sense that she was in any kind of dark place where she might kill herself."

"Would you say you were close with her?"

"No. But I've been running a bar for ten years. You get good at reading people."

The cell phone on the desk chimed, and Lainey picked it up. She checked the screen and flipped it back over.

Emmet stood up. "I'll let you get back to work."

She pushed her chair back and stood. "Wish I could help more. I don't know much about Aubrey's background. She'd only been here eight months. I'll talk to the staff, though."

"Thanks." He reached for the door. "One more question. You have anyone working here named Sam?"

"Male or female?"

"Male."

"Nope. We had a Samantha last summer, but she went back to college in the fall."

Emmet pulled open the door and Lainey came around to stand beside him. "So, you're still investigating? Does that mean it might *not* be a suicide?"

"I can't comment."

She raised an eyebrow. "Of course you can't."

"Sorry."

"Well, you want my two cents' worth?" She put her hand on her hip and tipped her head to the side. "I don't believe Aubrey Lambert took her own life. Maybe she accidentally

ODed or something, but I don't think she intentionally killed herself."

"No?"

"No. Not that you asked me, but like I said, I'm good at reading people."

He pulled a card from his wallet and handed it to her. "My mobile's on the back there. Give me a call if you think of anything I might want to know."

"Sure." She tucked the card in her pocket, then folded her arms over her chest, giving him a view of her cleavage.

"Thanks for your time," he said.

"Of course."

He stepped away.

"Hey, Emmet."

He turned back, and she smiled slyly.

"You know, I'm sure single moms are your kryptonite. But you could call *me* sometime, too. I wouldn't mind at all."

He smiled. "Thanks again, Lainey. You take care."

NICOLE PUT DOWN the margarita glass and picked up her phone.

"I have to take this," she told Kate, and slid out of the booth.

"Is it David?" she asked.

"It's Brady."

Kate rolled her eyes as Nicole connected the call. "Lawson."

"They finished the car," the chief said without preamble. "I just got word."

"Okay."

"I need you to head up there first thing in the morning and see what they got."

Nicole wove through the noisy crowd of people. She pushed through the front door, and a gust of wind hit her full force. "All right. Is the whole team going or—"

"I've got Emmet doing something else, so it's you and McDeere. See what all they came up with—prints, blood evidence, whatever they have—and then we'll circle back for a meeting at oh ten hundred. You got that?"

"Yes, sir."

"See you tomorrow."

He clicked off, and Nicole stared down at her phone. Sometimes she wondered what it might be like to work for a large urban department where the police chief didn't have her programmed into his phone. Maybe she'd actually have a personal life.

A text from Kate appeared on the screen.

We're getting another round. Want one?

Nicole hesitated. She felt tempted. But she had to drive up to the county crime lab again first thing in the morning.

And, again, she'd probably bump into David.

The door behind her opened, and a trio of girls stumbled out. Nicole didn't recognize them, so they were probably tourists. She watched them as they made their way on wobbly high heels to the parking lot and got into a waiting Uber.

Not ready to go back inside yet, Nicole walked around to the side deck overlooking the beach. When the weather warmed up, people would gather around TVs out here to drink and watch games. Tonight, though, the deck was cold and empty. Nicole leaned against the wooden railing and gazed up at the moon, thinking about what Cynthia had said.

Must be the full moon. People actin' crazy.

Nicole looked out at the surf. The waves were up again, same as they had been yesterday, when Aubrey's body was found. More than twenty-four hours had elapsed, and they still had no real suspects. Not only that, they were bound to have missed key evidence by releasing the crime scene too early.

Because they hadn't known it was a crime scene.

Nicole gazed down the beach at the distant lighthouse. The lantern room at the top glowed brightly. The light was for decoration—something the chamber of commerce had decided would appeal to tourists. It hadn't been a working lighthouse in decades, but it attracted visitors, and Lighthouse Point was the most photographed spot on the island.

"Hey."

She whirled around as Emmet stepped through the door. He looked her over with a frown.

"What are you doing out here? It's freezing."

"Nothing." She turned back toward the beach. "Just taking a phone call."

"Brady?" He came up to stand beside her and set his beer glass on the railing.

"Yep. He called you, too?"

"Yeah, he's doling out assignments."

Emmet leaned back against the rail and folded his arms over his chest. He wore a short-sleeve black T-shirt that left his forearms bare.

She watched him closely. "So, how'd it go?"

His eyebrows arched.

"With the manager," she said.

"She didn't have much." He turned and looked out at the beach. "Except that she doesn't think Aubrey Lambert killed herself."

"We already knew that."

"Yeah."

Nicole looked at him in the moonlight with his wind-blown hair. It was so thick, and she always had the urge to run her fingers through it. He gazed out at the waves with a pensive expression, and she knew he was feeling the pressure of the case, even though he didn't let on.

"Anything on the ex-boyfriend?" she asked.

"She doesn't know him. No one named Sam works here."

Nicole sighed and rested her palms on the railing.

Emmet looked at her, and the corner of his mouth ticked up. "Told you you didn't want to lead this one."

"You were right."

His jaw dropped. "I'm *right*? Did I hear that correctly?"

She ignored the feigned shock. "I'm so damn frustrated, Emmet. All my leads are going nowhere."

"We'll be in better shape tomorrow."

"How do you know?"

"We'll have the car, the ME's report. Maybe some leads from the family." He nudged her with his elbow. "Hang in there."

She turned around and faced the bar. Through the windows she could see Owen, Alex, and Kyle laughing and playing darts. Emmet's brother, Calvin, was with them now, too, and she felt like she was in high school all over again, watching all the cool guys hang out together while she pretended not to notice.

She glanced at Emmet, and he was watching her with a look she couldn't read.

He picked up his beer. "So, what's up with you and David?"

She bristled. "What do you mean?"

"Seemed like something was wrong earlier."

She shrugged. "He's slammed at work. The usual."

He lifted an eyebrow, and she looked away. She didn't

want to talk about her love life, and especially not with Emmet. She was embarrassed at having yet another date get canceled.

Her phone lit up with another message.

Hello?? Another rita???

She sighed. Nope. I have to be up early, she texted.

Kate responded with a line of sobbing emojis.

"I should get home." She glanced up at Emmet. "You staying?"

"For a little while. Sure you don't want to hang out? Calvin's here," he added, as if that would change her mind. Emmet had always thought she had a thing for his brother. For a detective, he could be pretty clueless sometimes.

She pushed off the railing. "Yeah, I'm out."

"I'll walk you to your car."

"Why?"

"Because."

She laughed. "That's silly."

He took her elbow and steered her toward the parking lot, leaving his beer glass behind. The wind gusted up again, and she hugged her arms around her body.

"You okay to drive?" he asked.

"I had one margarita."

"I repeat—"

"I'm fine."

They crossed the lot to her pickup and she checked the shadows nearby out of habit as she dug her keys from her pocket. She opened the door and slid behind the wheel.

Emmet leaned his palm on the top of the door and looked at her, his hazel eyes serious. "Sure you're okay?"

"You want to Breathalyze me?"

He stared down at her, and she would have sworn he was tempted. What was his deal?

"I'll take your word for it." He stepped back. "Night, Nicole."

CASSANDRA DOUBLE-CHECKED THE lock on her front door, then padded barefoot into the kitchen and poured another glass of wine. The last one hadn't helped. Neither had the steamy bubble bath. She still felt paranoid, and every noise in the building was putting her on edge.

All those months of work she'd done to bring her anxiety down "within normal range"—whatever that meant—and now her nerves were sparking like a live wire.

Wineglass in hand, she checked the lock on the sliding glass door and shifted the curtain to peer out at the patio. The only thing out there was a collection of chipped clay pots filled with withered stems. For what felt like the hundredth time today, she wished she'd opted for a second-floor apartment. But when she'd subleased this unit, it had been the only thing available that was remotely in her budget. Now she wished she'd kept looking.

She returned to the kitchen and switched off the main light, leaving only the light above the sink. The dream catcher caught her eye.

She should have taken it down yesterday, but it had never occurred to her that the police would show up here asking questions.

It should have, though. She should have thought of it. Had Detective Lawson bought her story about the gift shop? It hadn't been a lie, really. They *did* sell dream catchers in the shop. But that wasn't where she'd gotten this one. It had been a gift from Aubrey.

Cassandra stared at the little white feather dangling from the hoop. Aubrey's smile came back to her, and she felt a sharp pang.

There seems to be a discrepancy.

Cassandra had known from the beginning that this ordeal had the potential to blow up in her face. And now it was. Which was why she'd hesitated before calling 911. She hadn't wanted to get involved.

She went into her bedroom and set her wineglass on the windowsill, then reached under the mattress for the phone she'd stashed there. She sat on the bed and stared down at it, debating. Finally, she powered it up.

Another minute ticked by as she considered the risks. Finally, she dialed. It rang and rang, and she was about to hang up when Jess answered. The sound of her best friend's voice put a lump in her throat.

"Hey, it's me," Cassandra said.

Silence. Then, "Hold on."

She heard shuffling. Then Jess's voice was back, low and urgent. "Where *are* you? Is everything all right?"

"No." She took a deep breath. "I think I have a problem."

CHAPTER

SEVEN

THE ME'S OFFICE was small and stuffy. Emmet sat in the hard plastic chair festering with resentment as he scrolled through his phone. He glanced around the room, noting the framed diplomas, the Phi Beta Kappa certificate, the pile of marathon medals sitting on the bookcase crammed with medical journals.

Emmet checked his phone again, and finally the guy walked in.

"Sorry. Had to take a call." David Bauhaus pulled the door shut and walked around the desk. He had on blue scrubs and worn running shoes that probably had a thousand miles on them. The doctor flipped through a stack of manila folders by his computer and then dropped one in the center of his desk.

"So. Audrey Lambert." He opened the folder. "You're with Lost Beach PD then, I take it?"

"Detective Emmet Davis." He gritted his teeth. "And it's Aubrey."

"What? Oh. Yeah." He scooted his chair in. "Aubrey." He slid on a pair of reading glasses, and Emmet felt a twinge of satisfaction as the guy peered down at the paperwork. He glanced up. "Your chief wanted the report expedited. I sent it over last night, so I assume—"

"I read it, yeah."

The pathologist looked at him over the tops of his glasses.

"I had a few questions," Emmet said. "The livor mortis, for one."

He flipped through the report. "What about it?"

"You included photos."

"Yes." He turned to his computer and used the mouse to click open a file. "Let me see. We can enlarge these. . . ."

Emmet winced as a row of autopsy photographs appeared on the screen. Aubrey Lambert's body whisked by in a blur of pale flesh.

"Here we go." He landed on a picture of the victim's back. She was positioned face down on the stainless steel table, and the photo showed the tops of her buttocks. The doctor zoomed in on the reddish patch of skin, evidently reading Emmet's mind.

"You're wondering about the whitish pattern here." He turned to Emmet.

"That's right. It looks like some kind of impression?"

"Maybe a hammer, a wrench, something of that nature that was underneath her when the blood pooled. Someone with the state lab might be able to help you. They have a tool marks examiner."

Emmet nodded. "And a time estimate? How long was she lying flat on her back?"

"Well, she wasn't. Not exactly. Based on the other livor marks, I believe she may have been on her back with her knees near her chest"—he pivoted in the chair and brought his knees up in a modified fetal position—"like so for several hours. It's hard to pin down the amount of time, precisely."

Emmet nodded. "And you did a rape kit."

"Yes." He flipped through the report on his desk again. "It's at the lab. No results yet. I can tell you I didn't find any defensive wounds."

"Any chance she was roofied?"

"The tox report just came back. Did you see it?"

"Not yet."

He turned to his computer again and closed out of the autopsy photos.

"This just came in"—he glanced at his black sports watch—"two hours ago. Let's see . . . ibuprofen, benzodiazepine—" He glanced up. "In other words, Advil and Xanax. Quite a lot of Xanax—about eight times the recommended dose for a woman her size. And a lethal injection of fentanyl."

"Fentanyl. You're sure?"

He nodded at the computer. "It's right here."

"No, I mean you're sure that she was injected? Maybe her pills could have been laced with something or—"

"I swabbed the injection site at the back of her upper arm. She was injected with it. And the location would have been highly unlikely, if not impossible, if she had injected herself."

He had *swabbed* the injection site. This guy thought like a detective. Emmet didn't want to like him, knowing he'd been jerking Nicole around for weeks. But he had to admit the man was good at his job.

"The other thing," Emmet said. "Your report mentions something about fibers on the body. Is that like carpet fibers or—"

"Not carpet."

"No?"

He shook his head. "Something else synthetic. I'm no expert, but the state has someone who could identify it. And the FBI. The feds have a huge database, actually. They'd definitely be your best bet."

Emmet scoffed. "Yeah, if I had a year to wait."

"Well, yes. There is that."

The phone buzzed on the desk. David flipped it over and frowned as he read a text message. He glanced up. "I'm needed down the hall. If you have any more questions—"

"I'll be in touch." Emmet stood up, and the doctor stood, too. "Thanks for the time."

"No problem." David stepped toward the door and stopped. "By the way, is Nicole Lawson with you? I'm guessing she's here about the victim's car? Our lab techs just finished processing it."

"Yeah, I think she's upstairs."

He checked his watch and opened the door. "Hey, tell her hi for me, would you?"

Emmet stepped through the doorway and looked back. "Tell her yourself."

N ICOLE FOUND MIRANDA in the women's restroom near the forensics lab. The CSI was twenty minutes late for their meeting, which was totally unlike her.

"Hey, there you are," Nicole said.

Miranda glanced up at her in the mirror, and her eyes were pink and watery. "I'm just finishing up." She grabbed some paper towels from the dispenser and dabbed her face.

Nicole stepped closer, eyeing the tote bag sitting beside the sink. "Everything all right?"

"Yes." She squeezed her eyes shut. "No. I don't know. Sorry." Miranda wiped her eyes. "I'm just having a day. My milk isn't flowing, my nipples are bleeding, and I dropped my bottle and spilled half of it down the sink."

Nicole noticed the baby bottle on the counter beside the tote bag—which she now saw contained a breast pump.

"Your nipples are . . . bleeding?" Nicole winced. "That sounds awful."

Miranda blew her nose. "It's no big deal, really. They're just chafed, you know? Well. You don't know. But it's okay. It happens to people a lot. I'm just strung out today. Janie has a cold, and we were up all night."

Nicole wasn't a hugger, but she reached over and rubbed Miranda's shoulder. "I'm sorry. Is there anything I can do?"

"No. Thanks, though. I'm fine, really. It's Joel I'm worried about."

"Why are you worried about Joel?" Nicole asked, although she could guess. Miranda's husband, who had once been a detective with Lost Beach PD, was now part of a multiagency task force working on drug and human trafficking throughout the Rio Grande Valley, including operations such as Red Highway. It was a hazardous job and grueling, too.

Miranda shook her head. "He hasn't had a day off in weeks. He's hardly been home except to sleep. He finally came in last night and crashed, and then the baby got sick and both of us were up all night. I tried to get him to go back to bed, but he's barely seen her, and he wanted to help." Miranda wadded the paper towels and tossed them in the trash. "It's her first cold, and I didn't know what to do. Turns out, there's nothing you really can do."

"How is she today?"

"A little better." Miranda pulled a phone from the pocket of her lab coat. "Our nanny just called and said she's napping peacefully, so maybe she's through the worst of it."

Nicole waited, not sure of what to say. She'd never seen

Miranda so out of sorts. Right up until her due date, she'd seemed completely Zen and appeared to have everything under control. Nicole had gone to visit her, and she'd had the nursery perfectly decorated and her freezer filled with casseroles.

Nicole watched Miranda as she washed her hands. She wore a lab coat over jeans and a button-down shirt, which probably worked well for nursing. Instead of her usual tidy French braid, her long brown hair was up in a messy bun.

"Well, enough of this, right?" Miranda dried her hands and loaded up her tote bag. "Let me just get this bottle into the fridge and I can give you the update. Has Ryan started?"

"He was waiting for you."

"Sorry."

"Miranda, please."

She shouldered her tote bag. "God forbid they might have a private room in this damn place so I wouldn't have to pop out a boob in front of all the men I work with."

"There's nowhere you can go?"

"Well, I could go to my car, but that just takes longer."

Nicole followed her down the hall. Miranda turned a corner and entered the garage where vehicles were processed. They paused beside the door to pull paper covers over their shoes. Then Miranda stepped over to the break area and stashed a bottle of breast milk in the mini fridge.

"There you guys are. We ready now?"

Nicole turned to see Ryan crossing the garage. The CSI wore white coveralls and had a pair of goggles perched atop his head.

"Yes," Miranda said, joining them.

"I was just showing Adam the trunk." He looked at Nicole. "You want to see?"

"Absolutely."

She followed him past a mangled Kia and two pickup trucks to the far side of the garage. At the end of the row was Aubrey Lambert's little blue Subaru.

Adam McDeere stood off to the side. Today he wore the typical Lost Beach detective uniform—navy golf shirt, brown tactical pants, and all-terrain boots—even though he wasn't technically a detective yet. Like Nicole, he had covers over his shoes, and he looked very studious holding a notebook and pen in his gloved hands. Adam was three weeks away from his detective's exam, and he'd been taking a lot of notes lately.

Ryan offered Nicole a box of latex gloves. She pulled out a pair and tugged them on.

"So, what did you find?" she asked.

"A lot," Miranda said. "Have you had a chance to see the autopsy report?"

"Brady emailed it to the team this morning."

Nicole had scoured it for clues and planned to study it more this afternoon.

"There were some small nylon fibers clinging to the body," Miranda said.

"Yeah, I saw the notes about that. What are those, you think?"

"These were tiny, thready-looking fibers clinging to the skin and hair, apparently." Miranda stepped closer to the trunk, and Ryan shined a flashlight into the cargo space. "We found similar fibers back here."

Nicole and Adam moved closer and peered down at the trunk.

"Not seeing anything," she said, glancing at Adam, who looked blank, too.

"Here." Ryan dug into the pocket of his coveralls and pulled out a pair of tweezers. He reached in and lifted a tiny blue thread about the size of an eyelash.

"I don't know *how* y'all find this stuff," Nicole said as Ryan placed the thread on Miranda's outstretched palm.

"We collected numerous samples and sent them to the state lab for analysis. At a glance, David thinks these are the same type of fibers he recovered from the body."

"So . . . you're thinking she was wrapped in a blanket or maybe, what? A tarp?" Nicole glanced at Adam.

"Could be a rug?" Adam ventured.

"My guess would be a duffel bag," Miranda said.

Nicole's stomach knotted. "Really?"

She nodded.

"So, maybe he killed her at her apartment and loaded her in here?" Adam asked.

Miranda nodded again. "It's possible. Of course, the lab will have to confirm the type of fibers we're dealing with, but that would be my best guess. If he *didn't* have the body contained in a bag or something like that, we would expect to find more evidence in the trunk. Hair, skin cells, maybe bodily fluids."

Nicole stared into the trunk. A chill came over her as she visualized Aubrey's killer zipping her into a *duffel bag* and stashing her back there like luggage.

"This dude's sick," Ryan said.

Nicole looked at him. The CSI had seen a lot—they all had—but this crime was particularly callous.

"Okay, let's move on to the front," Miranda said, lowering the trunk lid.

They walked around to the driver's side. The door stood open, and a box of plastic numbers sat on the concrete floor nearby, along with a metal ruler. The markers would have been used when Miranda photographed whatever evidence she'd found, and the ruler provided scale.

"We recovered the pill bottle on the passenger seat, as

you know," Miranda said. "Along with twelve loose pills scattered on the seat and floor."

"Do we know how many were in the bottle originally?" Adam asked.

"The label said thirty," Nicole said. "But who knows if she had taken any before that day?"

"The toxicology report should help you with whatever was in her system," Miranda said. "I'm just telling you what we found in the car. Which could have been staged, of course."

Nicole glanced at Adam. Her working theory was that the scene *was* staged, and she knew he and Emmet and Owen were all coming around to that.

Ryan crouched down and aimed his flashlight through the windshield. "Then you've got the writing," he said.

His light illuminated the word *Goodbye* written across the inside of the windshield in—what *appeared* to be—a woman's loopy handwriting.

The writing had bugged Nicole from the moment she'd seen it. It looked feminine, yes. But she had trouble picturing someone who was distraught enough to kill herself writing the word so artfully.

"Pink ChapStick," Nicole murmured. "Did we ever find it?"

"Strawberry." Miranda crouched down beside Ryan. "The tube was down here, just beneath the driver's seat."

Adam lifted an eyebrow. "Fingerprints?"

"Yes." She looked at Nicole. "The prints come back to the victim. But, of course, if the ChapStick was hers and someone wore gloves—"

"Or if he put it in her hand and wrote it," Adam said.

"Right." Miranda stood up. "The lack of someone else's prints on the tube doesn't really tell us anything."

Miranda seemed to be on the same page with Nicole about how everything went down.

"So, the nylon fibers, the pills, the ChapStick." Nicole looked at Ryan. "What about the exterior?"

He smiled. "We're not done with the inside yet. Tell them about the mirror."

Nicole looked at Miranda, shocked. Thus far their perp had been meticulous.

"You got prints off the *mirror*?"

Miranda shook her head. "We're not *that* lucky. But we did find something you're going to like."

EIGHT

NICOLE STRODE INTO the break room with her liquid lunch in hand. The chief had bumped the meeting to eleven, and she hoped it was because he had something new to share.

"Where's Brady?" she asked Owen, taking an empty seat between him and Adam.

"He and Emmet were meeting with the family," Owen said.

"Where?"

"They're staying at a hotel near Aubrey's apartment."

Nicole scooted her chair in, not envying Emmet right now. Talking to a victim's family was the hardest aspect of her job, even worse than observing autopsies.

"Any word on how it went?" she asked.

Owen shook his head.

The chief walked in and dropped a notepad at the head of the table.

"Okay, everyone here?" he asked, taking a seat. His attention landed on Nicole. "How was the crime lab?"

"Good," she said. "We got some new info."

"Let's hear it."

"You want to start?" She turned to Adam, who looked momentarily panicked. But if he was going to be a detective he needed to get used to briefing the chief.

"We went over the car." Adam opened his spiral and flipped through a few pages. "The Subaru." He cleared his throat. "The CSIs recovered some fibers from the trunk that make them think she was put back there."

Brady frowned. "What kind of fibers?"

Adam flipped through another page, and Brady looked at Nicole.

"Something synthetic. Not carpet," she said. "We need confirmation from the lab, but it looks like potentially nylon fabric. Miranda thinks the victim may have been placed in a duffel bag and loaded into the trunk."

Brady's frown deepened. "When?"

"Based on the video evidence, most likely at the apartment," Nicole said.

"Walk me through it."

She glanced at Adam, who looked all too happy to let her do the talking.

"We have surveillance video of her entering her apartment complex around one o'clock the afternoon of the murder. Her roommate left shortly after that, around one forty. Then at three twenty-two her car is captured on video exiting the complex with someone else at the wheel, no sign of Aubrey."

"Here." Owen pivoted his computer to face the chief. He had the video footage that they had copied onto a thumb drive pulled up on the screen.

Brady took a pair of reading glasses from his pocket and slid them on, then leaned closer to the laptop. "We're sure this is her vehicle?"

Owen nodded. "Correct."

"Can we enhance this?"

"We already did."

"This guy in the hooded sweatshirt and sunglasses—he's our guy." Brady looked at Nicole.

"We believe so. The car leaves the premises and never reenters," she said. "So we think Aubrey is inside it and unconscious or dead."

"In a duffel bag in the trunk," Brady stated.

"That's what the CSIs seem to think, based on the fiber evidence."

Brady leaned back and removed his glasses. "Shoot me that footage," he told Owen. "I have a contact with the FBI cyber crimes unit in San Antonio. I'll see what they can do to enhance the image. Maybe we'll get a better look at this guy. What else do we know?" He looked back at Nicole. "Anything more in the car?"

"No prints except the victim's. However"—she glanced at Adam, who still looked happy to let her take the lead—"the rearview mirror was adjusted for someone much taller than Aubrey, who's five foot three."

Brady's eyebrows tipped up. "He leave any fingerprints when he adjusted it?"

"No. We assume he was wearing gloves. However, the mirror could still give us a lead. Miranda swabbed it for touch DNA, which could have potentially been transferred to the gloves if he touched his face or something while he was wearing them. Miranda *also* recovered a single strand of dark hair in the driver's seat, which is potentially huge."

The chief stared at her without comment. Evidently, he didn't see the potential "hugeness" of Miranda's find.

"The victim has dark hair," Brady said.

"Yes. But this strand was about three inches long. Aubrey's is much longer."

Brady tapped his pencil on his notepad. "So, your theory

is that this guy slipped into her apartment. No sign of forced entry—" He glanced at Owen for confirmation.

"That's right."

"—and attacked her, had her ingest some sleeping pills, then injected her with a lethal dose of fentanyl, according to our tox report. Then he loaded her into a bag, put her in the trunk, and drove her to the beach to stage her suicide."

Silence came over the room as the chief looked around the table. His gaze settled on Nicole.

"That's the theory?"

She nodded crisply. "Yes, sir. Based on the evidence we have so far."

"Why?" Brady looked at Owen. "What's his motive?"

Owen's brow furrowed. This was the weakness, the aspect of the case for which they had zero leads thus far.

"We don't know," Owen said. "The lack of forced entry could mean that she knew him and let him in."

"So, you're thinking a boyfriend?"

"Her roommate thinks she may have stayed with her ex-boyfriend overnight," Adam said, chiming in at last. "She didn't spend the night at the apartment. We know that."

"So, what then?" Brady asked. "You guys are thinking some kind of jealous ex scenario?"

"Could be a crime of passion," Owen said.

Nicole shook her head. "Nope."

Brady looked at her. "You don't agree?"

"What jumps out at me about this crime is that it's passion*less*," she said. "I mean, this guy injected her with a lethal drug, zipped her into a duffel bag, then drove her to the beach in the trunk of *her own car*, and staged a suicide. He even faked her handwriting." She looked around the table. "That's the definition of cold and calculated, not passionate."

Quiet settled over the room. Nicole glanced at Owen, who seemed to be considering her theory even though she'd contradicted him.

Once again Nicole was struck by the callousness of it all, and the complexity. It wasn't the sort of crime anyone expected to see in their quaint little town.

But their town was changing.

"But again, motive," Brady said, pinning his gaze on Nicole. "Why would some stranger go to all that trouble?"

"I don't know," she admitted.

"I still think we need to look at the boyfriend," Adam said.

Owen nodded. "Agreed."

"Where are we on the phone dump?" Brady asked Owen.

"Supposedly, we'll have it by end of day today."

Nicole bit back a comment. Obviously, they needed the victim's phone records, but she was much more optimistic about the leads Miranda had found.

"I think we should focus on the forensic evidence," she said. "I think that's the key to this."

"The hair," Brady stated.

She nodded. "Miranda sent it to the lab."

"*One* hair."

"Yes. But the length doesn't match the victim. So, even though whoever drove her vehicle was wearing a hoodie and probably gloves, too, we might be able to get some DNA from the hair."

Brady didn't look convinced. "Did she say how probable it is we'll get usable DNA off this one hair?"

"Well, no. It's definitely not a sure thing. There's no evidence the victim put up a struggle inside the car, so the hair was likely shed instead of being pulled out. So, there may not be a hair follicle attached with DNA on it. Still . . .

if there is DNA on it, it could end up being our strongest lead."

T HE OFFICE OF Alex J. Breda, attorney at law, smelled like fresh paint and sawdust. Cassandra pulled the door shut behind her and glanced nervously across the waiting room at the dark-haired woman standing atop a stepladder.

"Hello?" Cassandra called.

The woman didn't turn around. She tucked a hammer into her apron pocket and adjusted the framed photograph she was hanging on the slate gray wall. The picture was a seascape at sunset—or was it sunrise? The black-and-white shot showed a tall sailboat silhouetted against an eerie sky with a storm front on the distant horizon. Looking at the scene, Cassandra was taken back to that gusty evening at Lighthouse Point. It was only a few days ago, but she'd been through so many cycles of stress since then that it felt like weeks. Cassandra tried to remember the opening she'd rehearsed on the way over here.

She cleared her throat. "Excuse me?"

The woman whirled around. "Oh! Hi." She plucked a pair of earbuds from her ears and slid them into her apron. "Sorry! Didn't hear you." She looked at the picture behind her. "Does this look straight to you?"

Cassandra ventured into the seating area. It was furnished with a glass coffee table and a suede sofa the exact shade of gray as the storm cloud in the photograph.

"Um . . . I think it's a bit crooked," Cassandra said.

"I knew it." The woman sighed and glanced around. "Where'd I put my level?"

Cassandra spotted it on the reception counter and picked it up. "Here," she said, taking it over.

Up close, she saw that the woman had vivid blue eyes and the kind of thick, wavy hair that Cassandra had always envied.

"Thanks." She placed the level on the top of the frame and shifted the picture until the bubble was centered.

"Looks perfect now," Cassandra said.

"Thank you." She climbed down from the ladder.

Cassandra took a deep breath. "Are you Alex Breda?"

She smiled broadly. "Close. I'm Leyla Breda. One sec, I'll get him." She strode past her and leaned her head into the hallway. "Alex! You have a visitor."

Then she returned to the seating area, tucking her hands into her apron pockets.

"Can I offer you a coffee?" She nodded at a granite counter along the wall. "Alex only has the Keurig, sadly, but there *are* some coffee pods."

"No thanks."

"You know, you look really familiar. Do you work at the Banyan Tree, by chance?"

"I do, yes. You've been in?"

She made a face. "Not in a while. I was doing those stretch classes with Danielle last fall, but then my schedule got crazy, and I fell out of the habit."

Cassandra smiled awkwardly, wondering how long she was going to have to make small talk. "You should come back, though. Get into the groove again."

"Ugh! This one's crooked, too." Leyla Breda stalked across the room and adjusted the picture beside the door. She took out the level again and placed it atop the frame.

Cassandra walked over to study the picture. It was a framed magazine article with a color photograph of a man and woman, both with their arms crossed and their backs to each other as they smiled for the camera. **Breda & Braxton Take On H-Town**, read the headline.

This man was Alex Breda? He looked like someone straight out of central casting.

Yes, we're looking for tall, broad shoulders, commanding presence. Perfect teeth and golf tan a must. Oh, and make sure he has blue eyes and ridiculously long lashes.

Cassandra's last lawyer had had bifocals and pattern baldness and was four inches shorter than she was.

The woman straightened the frame. "Doesn't that look nice now?"

"It does."

She glanced at the back of the office. "Sorry. One sec."

She walked to the hallway and disappeared around the corner this time. Cassandra heard a door open, followed by muffled voices.

"Alex, someone's *here*."

"Who?"

"I don't know. A client, I think. Get your ass out there."

Cassandra tucked her file folder under her arm and turned to look at the seascape again.

A moment later, the woman was back with a smile. "He's coming."

"Thank you."

A man strode into the room. In ripped jeans and a faded Rip Curl T-shirt, he barely resembled the magazine photo.

"Hi. Alex Breda." He thrust out his hand and smiled, and she caught the perfect white teeth.

"I'm Cassandra Miller," she said, shaking his hand. "I saw your sign out front. Are you open for business or—"

"Absolutely. What can I do for you?"

"Well. Uh—" She darted a glance across the room, where Leyla Breda was now arranging mugs near the coffee machine.

Alex cleared his throat. "Leyla?"

She glanced over her shoulder. "Oh. Right. I'm out!" She crossed the room and grabbed a tote bag beside the reception counter. "I'll be back in an hour with sandwiches." She hitched the bag onto her shoulder. "Alex, chicken pesto or portobello mushroom?"

"Chicken," he said. "Thanks."

She pulled open the door.

"*Wait.* Come on, Ley. Seriously?"

She turned around, and Alex was glaring at the framed magazine article by the door.

"What? It's perfect there." She gave him a pointed look and walked out.

The second the door closed, he stepped over and unhooked the frame from the wall.

"Sorry." He rolled his eyes. "Come on back."

Cassandra followed him down a corridor and into a semi-unpacked office.

"We've gone nine rounds over this thing," he said, stashing the picture behind the door. "She wants it front and center."

"Your wife seems proud of you."

He glanced up. "My sister. She's very helpful and also very opinionated." He removed a banker's box from a side chair. "Please excuse the mess. Here, have a seat."

He set the box on the floor behind a giant mahogany desk that matched the empty credenza behind it. Then he opened another cardboard box on the floor and fished out a legal pad.

Cassandra lowered herself into the side chair and settled her hands on top of her file folder.

"So." Alex dropped the legal pad on the desk and leaned back in his chair. He smiled, and she felt a warm tingle that traveled from her stomach to the tips of her toes. "What brings you in today?"

"Well." She fidgeted with the edge of her folder, then forced her hands to be still. "I wanted to inquire about wills."

"*Wills.*" The smile widened. "That wasn't what I thought you were gonna say."

"You don't do wills?"

"No. I do." He leaned forward and rested his tanned arms on the desk. "Just most of my will clients are, like, sixty. Or new parents."

He looked at her expectantly.

"I'm neither," she said, fidgeting with the folder again. "I've been pecking around online." She cleared her throat. "I think I have an idea of what I need? But I don't want to get it wrong. It's too important. You see, my brother has special needs. He lives in a group home in Arizona. I want to make sure he's taken care of."

He took a pen from the drawer and jotted something on his legal pad. "Age?"

"Me or my brother?"

"Both."

"I'm twenty-seven," she said. "Lucas is thirty-one."

He made a note and glanced up.

"I think I might need a trust? I don't know. You're the expert, obviously."

"Is it just you?" he asked.

"What do you mean?"

"Do you have a husband? Kids? Would this be for the entirety of your estate?"

"Oh. It's just me."

He nodded and made a few notes.

"As far as my estate . . . I don't have a lot of assets right now. Very few, actually, at the moment. But if I *were* to have some in the future—"

"You want to make sure someone is looking out for Lucas's best interests after your death."

"Yes. Is that something you can write up?"

"Sounds pretty straightforward." He set down his pencil and looked up. "My cousin has special needs, and I wrote a will for my aunt and uncle. I should be able to pull something similar together for you, no problem."

"And everything we discuss would be confidential, I assume?"

"Yes. Our conversations are covered by attorney-client privilege."

She nodded. Then took a deep breath. "And how much does something like this cost, typically?"

She held her breath, watching him, thinking about his Rolex watch and suede sofa. His storefront was simple enough, but she was pretty sure now that the black Porsche 911 parked out front belonged to him.

He was watching her closely, and she started to fidget again.

"Ms. Miller, what do you do for a living?"

Her stomach tightened. "It's Cassandra. Or Cassie. I'm a yoga instructor over at the Banayan Tree."

He rubbed his jaw and seemed to be debating something.

"Well," he said. "I've got a sliding scale for some clients."

Relief flooded her. "Really?"

He nodded. "And we can break things into payments, if we need to."

Tears burned her eyes as his words sank in. "That would be amazing. Thank you. I can't thank you enough." A tear leaked out and she brushed it away.

He looked down at his notes. "I'll just need some basic info about you and your brother."

"Sure. Yes." Another tear spilled out and splatted on the folder. She swiped at her cheeks as she handed him the file.

"Cassandra, are you all right?"

"Yes. Sorry. It's just . . . been a long week."

He gave her a crooked smile, and she realized it was only Monday.

"Thank you again. I truly appreciate it."

"Sure," he said casually. "I'm happy to help."

NICOLE PLODDED ALONG the sand, wishing she had stuck with that January spin class. But she hadn't. And the last time she'd been running was before Christmas.

A muscle cramped, and she clutched her side. Well, maybe it was before Thanksgiving. Either way, it had been far too long, and her body was loudly protesting her decision to jog on the beach in thirty-four-degree weather.

She scanned the coastline, looking for anyone even vaguely resembling the man who Cassandra had described. But not only were there no runners in black clothes this evening, there were no runners at all. The only people out here were an elderly beachcomber and a fisherman up to his knees in the surf.

She kept a steady pace as she watched the waves. She'd always liked it out here. The beach was wide and spacious. As kids, she and her siblings were strictly prohibited from swimming at this point because of the rip current, but that taboo had only given the place more allure. They had loved to come out here with their dad whenever he went fishing. Their mom would pack a thermos of lemonade, and Nicole and Kate and Kevin would dig holes on the beach and search for sand crabs. And when their dad was done fishing, he'd walk them to the old lighthouse, where they would race each other up the grassy hill and log-roll to the bottom.

That was before the lighthouse had been renovated, back when it was still boarded up and empty, and kids used to say you could see ghosts in the upper windows on windy summer nights. Later, Nicole discovered that it wasn't ghosts doing the haunting but teenagers looking for a place to make out and get high.

Nicole surveyed the lighthouse now as she jogged against the wind. She still found it strange that the crumbling old building from her childhood was now one of the island's top attractions. So much had changed in her hometown—more tourists, more traffic, more crime—and even though all that growth was the reason Nicole had a job, she couldn't help being nostalgic for the sleepy little beach town that was gone forever.

The cramp tightened, and Nicole slowed to a stop. Panting, she held her side and checked her watch. It was 6:25, the time Cassandra had said she liked to jog after work. But it was Monday, and she'd said she typically came out here Tuesdays, Thursdays, and Saturdays, so maybe Nicole should try again tomorrow.

She turned around and spotted a man jogging toward her. Her heart skittered. He wore a black sweatshirt, black shorts, and a black visor. Even his running shoes were black, with the exception of the neon green laces.

Nicole's feet started moving before her brain could catch up.

"Excuse me. Sir?"

His attention was focused on the horizon, and he didn't even look at her until she was ten yards away.

"Sir?" She smiled as his gaze settled on her. "Hi. You mind stopping for a minute?"

He halted. "What's that?" He swiped the screen of his phone, switching off whatever he'd been listening to.

"Hi." She smiled again, trying to visualize how she must look to this guy. Her cheeks were flushed, and her sweatpants were spattered with wet sand. This man was barely breathing hard, and his legs were sand-free.

"My name is Nicole Lawson." She pulled her badge from the zipper pack clipped around her waist. "I'm with Lost Beach PD."

His eyebrows arched as he looked at the badge.

"I'm investigating a recent incident here."

"Here . . . as in here on the beach?"

"That's right. I'm interviewing some of the regulars. You know, dog walkers, wade fishermen, people like that. Do you jog here routinely?"

He stared at her as if she were speaking a foreign language.

"Have you ever jogged here before?" she amended, giving him a question it would be harder to say no to.

"Uh, yeah."

"Are you here often? Like, several times a week?"

He glanced over his shoulder, as though she might be talking to someone else.

"I guess you'd say that," he replied. "Five or six times a week, usually."

"Great." She stepped closer and tipped her head to the side. "Then maybe you can help me. Were you here last Saturday evening?"

"I don't know."

"You don't know? I'm talking about this *last* Saturday. Just a couple days ago."

Something flitted across his face, and she could have sworn it was panic.

"Saturday, yeah. I think I was here."

She smiled. "You mind pinning it down for me? I'm talking about February fourteenth. Were you jogging on this beach that evening?"

"I was, yes." He nodded. "The fourteenth."

"Great, then. Can you tell me who else you might have seen out here? For example, did you see any other joggers or walkers? Any parked cars?" She nodded toward the exact sand dune where Aubrey Lambert's car had been parked less than thirty yards away.

"No."

"No . . . what?"

"No, I didn't see anyone else out here," he said.

She stared up at him, trying to get a read. His eyes looked nervous and slightly hostile, too. Fair enough, though. Who liked having their workout interrupted by a police interrogation?

"Are you sure?" She smiled, hoping he'd relax. "Did you notice any vehicles parked near any of the sand dunes here?"

"No."

"Anyone walking around who maybe looked out of place? Maybe they weren't dressed for the weather? It was cold and windy that day."

"I didn't see anyone out here."

"No one at all? Think back. Were there any people flying kites, maybe? Or people out with their dogs?"

He shook his head. "I told you. I didn't see anyone."

Nicole stared up at him. He looked hostile again, and again, she felt like something was off. Clearly, he wanted to end the conversation.

"All right." She tugged a little notebook from her pack. "Let me just get your contact info."

He gave her his name and number and then he took off toward the lighthouse at a faster pace than before.

Nicole zipped her notebook into her pack and watched him go. Then she retraced her route, scanning the beach for other potential regulars. But evidently she and Black Visor Guy were the only people crazy enough to be out jogging in this weather as the sun went down.

She replayed the interview as she made her way back. Finally, she reached the beach access road where she'd parked her pickup—less than half a mile away from where Aubrey Lambert's body had been discovered.

Nicole hitched herself into the driver's seat and held her feet outside the door as she pulled off her sand-caked sneakers. Her socks were sandy, too, and she dropped everything into a plastic bag and chucked it into the back to deal with later. Then she slid her freezing feet into flip-flops and reviewed her interview notes as she waited for the heat to get going.

The passenger door jerked open, and Nicole's heart lurched.

"Hey." Emmet jumped into the passenger seat.

"God. You scared me."

He smiled. "How'd it go?"

"How'd what go? What are you doing here?"

"Same thing you are." He pulled off his baseball cap and wiped his arm over his forehead. He was dressed for running, too, but instead of sandy sweatpants, he wore athletic shorts and a long-sleeved T-shirt.

"Aren't you *cold*?" she asked.

He grabbed her water bottle. "No. I just went running."

She shook her head as he took a swig.

"So, how'd it go? That was Cassandra's runner dude, right? The man in black?"

Nicole watched him, wondering how Emmet knew about the runner. But of course he did. He would have reviewed her report, if not memorized it. Emmet was thorough. And conscientious. His carefree, surfer-boy thing was just a persona he put on—probably because it appealed to women. But the real Emmet was a competitive workaholic, same as she was.

"His name's Chris Wakefield," she said, "and he said he didn't see anything."

"No?"

"No. He says the beach was empty."

"Hmm."

"I swear." She pulled off her baseball cap and tossed it in the back. "I can't catch a break with anyone. *No one* saw anything. I mean, how is that possible? This is one of the most popular spots on the island."

"Yes, but it's winter."

"Tell me about it. I've been out here for half an hour freezing my ass off." She put her fingers in front of the vent and felt nothing but cold air.

"Let's get something to eat."

She glanced at him. "What, now?"

"Yeah, I'm starving."

Her stomach fluttered as she watched him sitting there in her passenger seat, all slick and energized from his run. She hadn't seen him in shorts in a while, and now she was reminded of his muscular legs and how he'd played football in high school. He smelled like sweat, which should have been off-putting, but she didn't mind, really.

"Aren't you hungry?" he asked.

"Yes."

"So let's have dinner. You can catch me up on what you got today."

She bit her lip.

"Unless you have plans," he said.

"No. But I need to shower first."

He rolled his eyes.

"You do, too."

He pushed the door open. "Go home and change, don't shower. I'll meet you at the Shrimp Hut in twenty minutes."

"There's no way I can—"

"Twenty minutes, Nicole."

CHAPTER

NINE

EMMET WATCHED HER walk in. He'd known she'd shower, but she'd done something to her hair, too, and it fell in loose auburn waves around her shoulders. His pulse kicked up as she cut through the crowd. Nicole was beautiful, but she really didn't know it, and it was one of the things that had always amazed him about her. She had no idea the effect all that cool self-confidence had on men. Him in particular.

She stepped outside and spotted him at a picnic table.

"Hey," she said, taking the bench across from him.

He pointed his beer bottle at her. "You're late."

"Oh, whatever." She grabbed the menu tucked behind the condiment bottles. "You showered, too."

"Can I get you something to drink?"

She glanced up at the server. "I'll have a glass of red wine, please. Whatever you have." She looked at Emmet. "Did you order yet?"

"No."

She ordered a shrimp basket, and he did the same. When the server was gone, Nicole put the menu away and gazed out at the marina.

"I'm surprised you wanted to eat outside," she said, glancing back at the propane heater behind her.

"They're full tonight, so it was this or wait."

She zipped up her blue fleece and tucked her hands in the pockets. "Brrr."

"You want my leather jacket?"

"I'm fine." She leaned forward. "So, what's wrong? I can tell something's bothering you."

"Why do you say that?"

"Because. When was the last time you asked to meet me for dinner?"

He knew exactly when it was. It had been last July when his dad had heart surgery. Emmet had taken the day off work to sit with his mom at the hospital. The surgery had gone fine, but by the end of the day Emmet was completely wrung out—not to mention he'd reached his limit on small talk with relatives. So he'd called Nicole and invited her to dinner.

"Come on," she said. "What is it?"

He sipped his beer, then set it on the table in front of him. "Nothing, really. Just had a shit day."

It was the kind of day that made him question his life choices.

Nicole watched him, her deep brown eyes filled with concern. "You met with Aubrey's family, right?"

He nodded.

"That must have sucked. How were they?"

"How you'd expect." He shrugged. "Her mom was distraught."

"And her dad?"

"Pretty combative, actually."

"Oh?"

"I don't think he has much faith in our department."

Nicole sighed.

Because of the town's size, outsiders often assumed LBPD was a Podunk police department and no one knew what they were doing. But they were located close enough to the border to be on the receiving end of extra funding and training, and their department definitely punched above its weight. Operation Red Highway was a case in point, and Emmet was proud of the way they had out-worked other members of the task force—even a few FBI agents who had come down here thinking they were God's gift to law enforcement.

"So, how did you guys handle it?" she asked now.

"Brady gave him the usual. We're on top of the case, pursuing every possible lead."

The server was back with the wine. Nicole thanked her and slid the glass aside, still focused on him.

"Anyway, how was *your* day?" he asked.

"We were talking about you."

"I want to hear about the crime lab. What did they come up with?"

She took a sip of wine, and he knew he'd succeeded in changing the subject. "Well, I'm sure you got an update, right? You heard about the hair that Miranda collected?"

"Yeah, but I wasn't there. How did she seem about it?"

Nicole tipped her head to the side. "She seemed . . . optimistic."

"Yeah?" Emmet felt a glimmer of hope for the first time all day. Miranda was the best CSI he'd ever worked with. If she felt optimistic about the potential for DNA, that was a good sign.

Nicole's brow furrowed. "And you heard about the fibers, right?"

"Yeah, like she was zipped into a duffel bag."

She shook her head. "That's really sick."

"I know."

Just the thought of Aubrey's parents learning that detail made his stomach turn. He couldn't imagine how it would feel to know something like that happened to your daughter.

"The livor mortis pattern makes it look like the bag was sitting on something in the trunk," Emmet said. "You notice anything back there? I haven't had a chance to look at the car photos yet."

Nicole seemed to think about it. "There was a flashlight. One of those mini ones? It was in a case with batteries."

After meeting Aubrey's father, Emmet could picture him giving his daughter a flashlight to keep in her car for safety. He seemed like a protective dad.

"Anything else?" he asked.

"A tire iron. About, I don't know"—she held her hands up almost eighteen inches apart—"this long, maybe? Could that have been it?"

"Possibly. I'll have to take a look at the pictures and study the scale."

Nicole took a sip of wine. "So . . . the lab was okay, in terms of getting new info. The rest of my day was crap, though." Frustration sparked in her eyes. "Did I tell you I ran into Green Truck Guy?"

"No."

"Well, I thought it was him," she said. "It was this afternoon. I had to respond to a call in Sunset Shores."

"The golf cart theft."

"Right." She rolled her eyes. "Anyway, I had just taken the report and was leaving the neighborhood when I spotted this teal green pickup truck. It was a landscaping contractor, and his crew was planting palm trees at one of the houses there. This guy even had a black dog with him, too. I was sure it was him."

"And?"

"And I pulled over to interview him." She shook her head. "He had no idea what I was talking about. Said he wasn't on the beach that day."

Emmet watched her expression. "You don't believe him?"

She shrugged.

"Why would he lie?" Emmet asked.

"I don't know. That's the thing. But I could swear he was lying. I mean, he had a black dog in his truck with him. What are the odds?"

The server was back again, this time with two baskets heaped with fried shrimp and French fries.

"Anyway, it's just so frustrating." Nicole handed Emmet the Tabasco sauce, and he shook it over his food. "How is it possible I can't turn up a single decent witness on our most popular beach? Even in the dead of winter, people are back and forth there."

He picked up a fry. "We've got three potential witnesses, not none."

"Yeah, but why do I feel like I'm not getting a straight answer out of anyone?" She dunked a shrimp in tartar sauce. "Green Truck Guy says he wasn't there, but I can sense he's not telling the truth. And this runner says he *was* there but didn't see a damn thing—not a single car or person, nothing."

"What about the yoga teacher?" Emmet asked. "Anything new with her?"

"Nothing, really, just more strange vibes from her whenever I question her. She's being evasive for some reason." Nicole leaned forward. "You know, even her place was off."

"You mean her apartment?"

"Yeah. I did some snooping around—"

He laughed. "How did you manage that?"

"I said I needed to use the restroom and then poked around a bit. You know her linen cabinet was completely empty?"

"So?"

"And she barely had any furniture. She had, like, one futon in the entire living room."

"Sounds like my place."

She shook her head. "Your place is a bachelor pad. At least you've got a TV and, I don't know, *towels* in the bathroom, even if they're crumpled on the floor or whatever."

"I know how to hang a towel, thank you very much."

"I'm saying this place looked like a crash pad, not a typical woman's apartment. It didn't add up."

Emmet lifted an eyebrow.

"You think I'm off base, don't you?"

"That's not it at all," he said.

"Yeah, you do. I can tell."

"I think you're reading too much into it. This woman's a yoga instructor. So what if she doesn't have all the usual crap in her apartment? Maybe she's a minimalist."

Nicole sighed. "Maybe." She popped a fry into her mouth, and Emmet could tell she wasn't convinced.

Which told him she might be onto something. Nicole was observant. And she had good instincts about people. Sometimes too good. Good enough, for example, to have picked up on the resentment that flared inside him every time the subject of her boyfriend came up. It was the one thing he couldn't talk to her about. He and Nicole worked together. Full stop. Anything else would fuck everything up.

NICOLE WATCHED EMMET polish off every morsel of his food and her leftover fries, too. Despite his appetite, she could tell something was still bothering him, although he didn't want to talk about it.

But deep down he did, or he wouldn't have invited her here.

The server returned with their check, and they split it down the middle. Nicole's phone chimed as they were getting up from the table. She checked the screen and slipped the phone into her pocket.

"You need to get that?" Emmet asked.

"No."

The restaurant was crowded, so they exited the side gate that led directly to the parking lot. Nicole had created a parking space at the end of a row, and Emmet walked her to her pickup even though his was two rows closer.

She gave him a sideways glance. "I'm sorry you had a rough time with the family."

"It's fine."

"People have different reactions to grief."

He shot her a look. "I know."

Obviously, he knew. He'd been a cop for eleven years, and he'd dealt with plenty of people in terrible situations.

He stopped beside her truck. Dusk had faded, and the stars were starting to come out. He gazed out at the dark bay, his expression solemn.

"What, Emmet?"

He turned to her.

"Something's bugging you."

He shook his head and looked down.

"Is it the case?"

"No." He frowned. "Well, maybe." He ran his hand through this hair. "Have you ever thought you might have made a wrong choice? About something important, and it's too late for do-overs?"

She stared up at him, trying to read his eyes. "You mean the job or—"

"Yeah, I mean, sometimes I think I'm really not cut out for this," he said.

"No one's cut out for talking to grieving families."

"You are."

She drew back. "No, I'm not."

"Yeah, you are. I've seen you. You've got a knack for dealing with people. I get around people going through something, and I get uncomfortable. I clam up. People think I don't give a shit."

"No, they don't."

He shook his head.

"Emmet. Anyone who knows you *knows* you give a shit. This job defines you."

He looked at her.

"You're the most tenacious detective I know," she went on. "So, maybe you're not the best at hand-holding. So what? You never let up until you get answers, and that's what matters. You're amazing at what you do."

He gazed down at her, his eyes intense, and she started to feel uneasy.

She looked away, but she could still feel him staring at her. Maybe she'd said too much.

From a work standpoint, she'd never really told him how much she admired him—probably because they had always been so competitive with each other. But she figured he knew. She glanced at him, and the simmering look in his eyes sent a jolt of heat through her.

He'd walked her to her car again. Was he just being protective or was there something more? She stared up at him, searching his eyes, and the moment seemed to stretch out.

His phone buzzed, and he stepped back to pull it from his pocket. The name Lainey was on the screen. Not *Lainey Wheaton*, or *O'Toole's*—just *Lainey*.

It buzzed again.

"You need to take that?" she asked.

"Yeah." He glanced up.

"Thank you for dinner."

He looked confused. "Why? We split it."

"Well. Thanks for inviting me."

His phone was still buzzing as she opened her door. She got behind the wheel and watched in the side mirror as he walked away with the phone pressed to his ear.

Shaking her head, she pulled her phone from her pocket. She'd missed David's call, and he'd left a voicemail. She pressed play as she backed out of the space.

Hey. Me again. You're not picking up, so I'm guessing you're at work still. Or possibly avoiding me.

Nicole crossed the parking lot as the silence went on.

Listen, I really meant what I said. I'm sorry about Saturday. I want to make it up to you, so I was thinking, how about Wednesday night at Angelo's Bistro? I'd really like to see you, Nicole. Let me know.

She pulled onto the highway and glanced at the phone on the seat beside her. Then she trained her gaze on the road, and her nerves fluttered as she thought of Emmet's hazel eyes staring down at her just now. Once again, she was twisting herself in knots trying to read into his looks, his gestures, his unspoken words. And once again, she felt like she was grasping at straws. As long as she'd known him, his feelings had been a black box.

And then here was David—upfront, no games, just putting it all out there. That took guts, and maybe she wasn't giving this thing between them enough of a chance. She of all people understood how consuming his job was, and it wasn't fair to hold that against him.

She grabbed the phone and dialed him back. He answered on the first ring.

"David, it's me."

"Hi," he said, sounding surprised.

"So, I got your message, and I'm free Wednesday night."

EMMET CAUGHT LAINEY'S eye as soon as he stepped into O'Toole's. She held up a finger for him to wait.

He moved out of the traffic flow and glanced around. They were even busier than yesterday, and he remembered their Monday-night half-off pitchers, which always drew a crowd. He glanced at Lainey, who stood behind the taps talking to one of her two bartenders.

Finally Lainey looked at him again. She jerked her head toward the hallway in back, and he met her near the door to her office. She wore all black again today, down to the lace bra peeking out from her scoop-neck T-shirt.

"We're packed tonight," she said, steering him into an alcove stacked with kegs. "How's the case coming?"

"It's coming."

"This whole thing's really rocked the staff. I've got one girl who called in sick and another one who showed up a basket case. Apparently, she was good friends with Aubrey."

"Who is she?" he asked.

"Britta Phelps. She's on break in my office. I thought you might want to talk to her."

"I do. She's a server here?"

"Yeah. She's twenty-three, and she's been here almost a year."

Lainey crossed her arms over her chest.

"What?" he asked.

"Evidently, there's a rumor circulating that it *was* a murder, not a suicide. Is that true?"

The manner of death had been reported on the news tonight, so there was no use dodging the question now.

"That's true, yes," he said.

"Well, do you have a suspect?"

"I'm sorry, but I can't discuss—"

"Yeah, yeah, I know." Sighing, she stepped across the hall and reached for the door. "Listen, I'm happy for you to talk to her, but try not to drag things out, all right? I'm shorthanded tonight."

He nodded. "I hear you."

She turned and opened the door, then stepped back so he could go in. The young woman sitting at Lainey's desk looked up from her phone. She had long blond hair, and her eyes were swollen from crying.

"Hey, Britta," Lainey said in a softer voice. "This is the police detective I told you about."

Britta gave him a nervous look and set her phone down. She seemed upset, yes, but not nearly as undone as Aubrey's mother had been earlier.

"You need anything?" Lainey asked her. "Maybe some water?"

She shook her head. "No, thank you."

"We won't be long," Emmet said, mostly for Britta's benefit. "I just have a couple questions."

"Sure thing."

Lainey stepped out, leaving the door ajar behind her.

Emmet took the side chair he'd occupied yesterday, putting the witness in the power position, which he hoped would make her more comfortable.

"I'm Detective Davis." He pulled a business card from the pocket of his jacket and slid it across the desk.

She eyed it warily but didn't touch it. Like all the servers here, she wore a black T-shirt with the O'Toole's logo on the front. Aubrey had two identical T-shirts hanging in the closet at her apartment.

"Lainey tells me you and Aubrey worked together?" he said.

She nodded.

"I'm talking to some of her friends and relatives, trying to learn more about her." He paused. "How did you hear the news?"

She cleared her throat. "We have a text thread."

"We?"

"Some of us who work here. Me, Jill, and Chantal." She paused. "And Aubrey."

"Do you guys talk every day?"

"Not really. Usually just when someone needs a sub or someone to swap shifts with them."

Emmet pulled a spiral notebook from his pocket. "Mind if I take notes?"

She shook her head.

He took a moment to jot down the names of the other two co-workers in case he needed to follow up with them later. Then he looked at her. "So, do you know if Aubrey was having any problems with anyone lately? Did she mention anything?"

"No."

"All right. Do you know if she was dating anyone recently?"

"Not right now. Well, there was this one guy."

"Yeah?"

"But they stopped seeing each other. At least, that's what she told me."

"You know his name?"

"Sam."

He nodded. "You happen to know his last name?"

She shook her head. "I don't think she ever mentioned it."

"All right. And Sam—do you know where Aubrey met him?"

"Online, I think."

"And how long were they together?"

"It was only a few weeks or so. Maybe a month? But then it went sideways."

Emmet watched her eyes, waiting for more.

"Why did it go sideways?" he asked.

She bit her lip.

"She didn't really say," Britta told him. "But I think maybe he had a drug problem?"

"What makes you think that?"

"Aubrey mentioned something once about him blowing his parents' money on drugs. But I don't know if that's why she stopped seeing him. And I heard them arguing about drugs once."

Emmet's pulse picked up. "When was this?"

"It was on the phone." Britta rubbed her nose with the back of her hand. "We were on a break together outside. He called, and she stepped around the side of the building to take the call, and I heard her say something about how he needed to be in rehab."

"And you're sure it was Sam on the phone?"

"Yeah. Right before she answered it, she was like, 'Ugh. Sam. He keeps calling me.'"

"You remember when this was?"

She shook her head as she picked up her phone. "I think it was a few Fridays ago? We had the lunch shift." She swiped at her screen. "No, sorry. Thursday three weeks ago. That's the last time we worked lunch together."

Emmet wrote down the date, then looked at Britta. "Do you know if Aubrey had a drug problem at all?"

"Aubrey? No." She shook her head. "She didn't even

drink. She was totally into yoga and exercise and clean eating, stuff like that."

Emmet watched her expression, waiting to see what else she might say. Just because this girl didn't think Aubrey was into drugs didn't mean she *wasn't*. But so far everyone he'd talked had said pretty much the same.

Britta glanced at the door behind him. "Sorry, but . . . I think I should get back soon. Is there anything else you need to ask about?"

"Not right now." He put his notepad away. "Well, one more thing. You know if Aubrey was having any financial problems?"

"Financial?"

"Like, do you know if she was having any trouble with money?" He didn't mention that Aubrey had just asked for and gotten a raise. Lainey probably wouldn't appreciate him sharing that.

"I don't think so. If she did, she never told me."

Emmet nodded. "Britta, you've been really helpful."

Relief washed over her face as she stood up. "Thanks."

"Don't forget that." He nodded at his business card as he stood up. "Call me if you think of anything else that might help us."

She took the card and tucked it into her pocket. "I will." She stepped toward the door and then turned. "I just had one question."

"Yes?"

"I heard—" She took a deep breath. "I heard she might have been murdered?"

"As of now, we're investigating Aubrey's case as a homicide."

Her face crumpled and she looked away. "Do you think . . . it was someone she knew?"

"At this point, Britta, we don't know," Emmet said, hating that it was true. "But we intend to find out."

CASSANDRA'S PORCH LIGHT was out.

She cast a wary look at all the shadows along the sidewalk as she dug her key from her purse and unlocked her front door. As she pushed it open, something fluttered to her feet.

She switched on the hall light, and her pulse sped up as she saw the sealed white envelope on the doorstep. No address, no stamp. Just her name written across it in neat block letters.

CASSANDRA

She stared down at it a moment, heart pounding. Then she quickly locked the door and peered through the peephole.

The sidewalk outside was dark and empty.

She picked up the envelope and carried it into the kitchen with her take-out bag from Thai Ginger. She set the food on the counter and studied the envelope. She didn't recognize the handwriting.

Tearing it open, she found a gray card with a single white rose on the front and the words IN SYMPATHY printed across the top. She opened the card.

It was blank.

No message, no signature. She flipped it over. Who had left this at her door? Baffled, she stared down at the snowy white rose.

Her phone chimed, and she pulled it from her pocket. Reese. Probably wanting her to cover another evening yoga class so she could see her boyfriend. Cassandra set the phone on the counter without answering and looked at the card again.

It was just a card, nothing sinister. Anyone who knew

she was friends with Aubrey could have dropped it off—
maybe Danielle, or Reese, or one of her students.

Stop being so paranoid.

She set the card on the counter beside the ever-growing
pile of junk mail. Maybe Reese had left the card for her.
Reese was nice, actually, and Cassandra felt guilty about
dodging her.

Her phone chimed again, and this time she picked up.

"Hi," she said.

"Hello."

She'd expected Reese, but it was a man's voice. A glance
at the Colorado area code sent a dart of panic through her.

"Who is this?" she asked.

"I'm calling on behalf of Malcom."

Her pulse skittered. "Who is this? Where did you get
this number?"

"He'd like you to reconsider."

She gripped the phone as a bitter stew of fear and anger
churned inside her. She glanced at the front door, then
moved to check the slider. It was locked. Of course it was.
She never went anywhere without locking her doors. She
nudged the curtain aside and saw the patio was empty.

But some eyes were invisible. She knew that better than
anyone.

"Do you understand?"

Her temper flared. "Tell him he can forget it."

Low laughter on the other end.

"Don't call me again," she snapped.

"Malcom wants—"

"He can talk to my lawyer."

She hung up.

What the hell what the hell what the hell?

Heart thundering, she stared down at the phone. Then
she flung it away like a hot potato.

TEN

Emmet PULLED UP to the police station as Adam walked out with a cardboard coffee cup in his hand.

"Hi," Adam said, sliding into the passenger seat.

"Hey."

"You want some coffee?"

Emmet had been up since five and was already two cups in. "I'm good."

"So." Adam slid on a pair of mirrored sunglasses as they exited the parking lot. "What's the plan this morning?"

Emmet had called him to see if he wanted to work together today. Adam was set to take his exam in a couple weeks, and Emmet had been trying to spend some extra time with him before then to build his confidence.

"We're following up on the surveillance video," Emmet said.

"You mean from the victim's apartment? I thought Brady sent it to his contact in San Antonio."

"He did."

They hadn't heard anything back yet, and Emmet wasn't keen on waiting. No doubt the FBI had great resources when it came to enhancing video footage. But the man behind the wheel of Aubrey Lambert's car had been wearing a hoodie and sunglasses when he drove out of her apartment complex. So Emmet figured the chances of the feds being able to enhance the video enough to use facial recognition software or any of their other tools were slim. They were going to have to do some old-fashioned detective work.

Emmet wove through downtown toward Angler's Landing. He turned onto Eighth Street, a block away from the apartment's main entrance with the still-broken gate. Emmet pulled over beside a grassy utility easement directly behind the apartment complex.

Adam turned in his seat, looking out the back window. "Isn't that her building?"

"Yeah, and I was here earlier. I want you to see something."

"What?"

"Just watch."

Emmet adjusted the rearview mirror. Meanwhile, Adam sipped his coffee and checked the side mirror, probably wondering what they were waiting for.

He glanced at Emmet. "So, you took your exam what, four years ago?"

"Five."

Adam nodded. "You think it was hard?"

"It was okay." Emmet looked at him. "You nervous?"

He shrugged. "Written tests have never been my thing."

"Me either." Written exams had been the bane of his existence in high school and college, but he'd muddled through. "You been studying?"

"Yeah, and Nicole's been giving me some tips. She seems pretty squared away."

"She is."

Emmet hadn't known Nicole was helping him, but he wasn't surprised. She was generous like that, always offering to help train new people. Even without her help, he figured Adam would do fine on the test. As a former Marine, he was thorough and detail-oriented, plus he had a good memory.

Of course, there was more to the job than passing a test. People skills were critical—more so than Emmet ever would have imagined when he'd set his sights on being a cop.

So, maybe you're not the best at hand-holding. So what?

Nicole's words had been echoing through his head since last night. *You never let up until you get answers. You're amazing at what you do.*

The "amazing" part was her trying to cheer him up because he'd had a shit day. But she was right about his determination to get answers. It was burning a hole in his gut right now.

Emmet thought of Aubrey's parents again—her mother weeping and her father looking ready to punch something. Both had seemed broken, but in different ways, and Emmet couldn't shake the guilt that Brady had tapped him to lead this thing, and their team still had almost nothing to share with the victim's parents.

Movement in the mirror caught his eye. "Here we go."

Adam looked in the side mirror as a woman stepped through a wrought iron gate at the back of the property. She wore a gray sweatshirt and striped pajama pants, and she had a little white dog on the end of a leash.

"What are we—"

"Watch," Emmet said.

The woman turned and picked up something off the ground.

"What is that?" Adam asked.

"A brick."

"Is she propping open the gate?"

"Yeah."

She walked down the street to the utility easement behind them and stood there scrolling through her phone as her dog sniffed around.

"Think that's how the guy got in?" Adam asked.

"Yep." Emmet glanced back at the gate. "I was here early this morning, and it was propped open then, too. Some people don't even bother closing it when they come in and out."

"So, you're thinking he entered the complex on foot, not through the front gate."

"He was probably aware of the cameras. He wore the hoodie and sunglasses, remember?"

Adam nodded.

"So, looks to me like he came on foot, then exited in her vehicle."

Emmet put the car into gear and drove down Eighth Street. Two blocks later, he turned into the parking lot of a gas station. They were busy with morning customers, and Emmet pulled into a space beside the car wash.

They got out and approached the convenience store, and Emmet held the door for a young woman in workout clothes before stepping into the warm shop. It smelled of hot dogs already, and he got in line behind a pair of teen boys buying powdered-sugar doughnuts and Yoo-hoo for breakfast.

Emmet stepped up to the counter, where a young clerk with bushy red hair stood behind the register. Emmet flashed his badge, and the clerk's eyes widened.

"Morning," Emmet said. "You've got two security cameras outside. I need to review the footage."

The clerk stared at him wordlessly. Then he swallowed.

"I'll need to talk to my manager?"

"Sure."

"One sec."

He walked out from behind the counter and went to the back.

Adam stepped out of the store and gazed at the security camera mounted on the corner of the building.

"Looks pretty new," Adam said.

Emmet hoped so. Some of the businesses around here had cameras that barely worked and were mainly for show, as though some cheap-ass camera was going to deter an addict who was desperate for money.

A balding guy with glasses came out from the back, trailed by the clerk.

"May I help you?"

Emmet pulled out his badge again. "Detective Davis, LBPD. I'd like to see your security camera footage for the afternoon of February fourteenth."

The manager frowned for a moment, clearly not excited about getting involved in a police investigation.

"Which camera? There are two."

Emmet tucked his badge away. "The one facing Eighth Street."

"This past Saturday?"

"That's right."

The man heaved a sigh. "Come on back."

THE BULLPEN WAS strangely empty when Nicole walked in at lunchtime.

"Where is everyone?" she asked Denise.

"We just had a call," Brady said from his office.

Nicole stopped at the chief's door. Brady had his laptop computer open and a Tupperware container of salad in front of him. Nicole was pretty sure she'd never seen him eat anything green before, but she didn't comment.

"What happened?" she asked him.

"Injury accident downtown. Someone hit a utility pole."

"You want me to go?"

He shook his head. "I sent Emmet and Adam. I need you here with Owen. Our phone dump just came in, and we need to analyze it ASAP."

"I'm on it."

Nicole strode through the sea of empty cubicles. Their newest patrol officer sat at a desk, talking on the phone, but other than that the bullpen was empty. She found Owen in the conference room with his back to the murder board and papers spread out in front of him.

Nicole's gaze snagged on one of the grisly autopsy photos as she sat down.

"When did this come in?" she asked.

"Ten minutes ago," Owen said, not looking up. "I just printed it out. I haven't even had a chance to cross-reference anything yet." He slid a stack of pages toward her. "Here, look through those. That's November and December."

"How far back did we get?"

"Four months. Well, not even." Owen ran his hand through his hair. "November first through yesterday, so three and a half months."

Nicole wanted the more recent records, but Owen had first dibs, so she took the pages he'd given her and began combing through, starting with December. She immediately noticed a lot of 281 and 713 area codes.

"I've got a lot of Houston stuff," she said. "I assume that's her family?"

"Her parents, yeah. Here are their numbers." He slid a notepad toward her with some phone numbers written down.

"Then there are calls to O'Toole's, where she worked," he said.

Nicole spotted a phone number that looked familiar. Was it Cassandra's? She tore off a sheet of scratch paper and jotted it down. Then she noticed a different number that appeared six times in one day. The date was December 31.

"What's this 512 number on New Year's Eve?" she asked.

"You've got it, too?"

"Yeah, there's quite a few of these." She glanced up. "That's an Austin area code." She flipped through the papers. "A lot of these 512 calls are late at night."

"Same with mine." Owen pivoted to the laptop computer beside him. He tapped at his keyboard and looked over at her, making eye contact for the first time. "Thanks for helping."

"Sure."

"Anything new from Miranda today?"

She shook her head. "I was going to ask you."

Miranda was Owen's sister-in-law, but evidently he hadn't bugged her for an update on the lab work today.

"I haven't talked to her," he said.

"I'll send her a text, see what she's got."

"Thanks."

Nicole typed up a message to Miranda as Owen ran the 512 number through the database.

Miranda responded immediately. Nothing yet but I put a rush on that DNA analysis.

Nicole's pulse picked up. If the DNA came through, it would be a game changer.

What's your best guess on timing? Nicole asked.

IDK. Maybe by Friday?

Owen pounded his fist on the table, and Nicole jumped. "Jesus. What is it?"

"This number traces back to Samuel Pacheco." His eyes sparked with excitement. "Sounds like Sam, the boyfriend."

ALEX BREDA'S OFFICE looked dark and quiet. Cassandra checked her watch. She'd thought she might swing by for an update before her four o'clock Bikram class, but there was no Porsche out front, and it didn't look like anyone was there. Maybe Alex had gone home early for the day. Or maybe he'd never come in at all.

She eyed Alex's new sign as she crossed the intersection. So, was he a one-man show, no assistant? She might have made a mistake hiring an attorney whose practice was barely up and running.

Something about Alex Breda appealed to her, though, and it wasn't just his looks.

It was his eyes. They seemed trustworthy. And when he'd mentioned that he had a cousin with special needs, Cassandra was hooked. There was something about that, as though maybe fate had put this man in her path.

Cassandra reached the end of the block and rounded the corner. As she neared the strip center for the Banyan Tree, she spied the blue-and-white awning in front of Dee's Donuts. Just the sight of it made her stomach grumble. Her lunch today had been a kale smoothie, and a cream-filled doughnut sounded like heaven right about now. But she had to resist. One of her biggest struggles since taking this job was *looking* the part. People expected yoga instructors to be slender and lithe—like Reese—so cream-filled doughnuts weren't part of the plan. Cassandra's natural body type was voluptuous, not thin, and she had to watch her diet, especially now.

The strangeness of it all wasn't lost on her. Growing up in western Colorado, Cassandra never would have dreamed she'd one day teach yoga classes in a Texas beach town. She'd always wanted to move to a big city—maybe Denver or even Los Angeles. But then her mother had died, and she'd ended up working in the spa at a luxury ski resort, where she'd met her future husband. She would never forget that buzzy, totally-in-lust feeling. He had been so attentive and charming that in just one weekend, he had turned her life upside down.

And now, four years later, he was still doing it.

As Cassandra race-walked past Dee's, she noticed the people milling in front of the martial arts academy. Several moms stood near the door, along with half a dozen kids in their white tae kwon do uniforms.

A woman looked up from her phone and waved. "Excuse me. Reese, is it?"

Cassandra stopped in front of her. "I'm Cassie."

"Oh. Sorry." She removed her sunglasses and rested them on top of her head. "Do you know where Paula is? Our class was supposed to start fifteen minutes ago."

"I don't, sorry." Cassandra eyed the **Closed** sign hanging in the door. "Did you try calling or—"

"No answer. Just voicemail. Can you check and see what the deal is? If she canceled class, I would have appreciated a text alert. We drove all the way here."

"Let me see what I can find out." Cassandra walked around the crowd and tried the door to the yoga studio. It was locked, so she took out her key.

Cassandra let herself in and glanced around the dim lobby. The place should have been open by now. Danielle was very particular about having aromatherapy candles lit and the gift shop open for business as people arrived. Reese had a stretch class starting in half an hour, and Cassandra's Bikram class began soon after that.

Cassandra glanced down the hallway and spied a light on in the office.

"Reese?" she called.

No answer.

Cassandra switched on the light by the reception desk and made her way down the hallway. Had someone come in through the back? The office door was ajar, and Cassandra looked inside.

Reese's purple backpack sat on Danielle's desk.

Cassandra frowned. Where was everyone?

She headed down the hallway and pushed open the door to the restroom.

"Oh!" Reese jumped back.

"Sorry. I didn't—" She halted as she saw Reese's tear-streaked face. "What's wrong?"

"*Cassie.*" Reese threw her arms around her neck.

"What is it?"

She pulled away. Her eyes swam with tears and her cheeks were splotchy. "You didn't hear?"

Dread filled her stomach. "Hear what?"

"Paula just called. Danielle was in an accident."

Cassandra's blood turned cold. "Oh my God. Is she all right?"

"*No*, Cassie. She's dead."

OWEN LEANED HIS head into the conference room. "Still here?"

Nicole glanced at the clock. How was it nine already? "I'm about to wrap up."

Owen nodded. "I'm heading out. We'll tackle it again tomorrow."

Nicole rubbed her eyes. "You hear back from that co-worker? Jill?"

"No."

They had reached out to Aubrey's friends in case anyone had a lead on Samuel Pacheco's address.

"But if I do, I'll let you know," Owen said.

Nicole sighed and glanced down at her files. "Okay, see you tomorrow."

Her vision blurred and she rubbed her eyes again. She'd been through everything they had so far, including every single one of the autopsy photos, which made her sick to her stomach. She'd been hoping to spot something—anything—that would potentially generate a new lead.

Discovering the last name of Aubrey's ex-boyfriend had seemed like progress. But the guy wasn't answering his phone and his driver's license record showed an Austin address. Until they figured out where he lived locally, they were no closer to interviewing him than they had been before they had his full name.

"Detective?"

She glanced up to see their new patrol officer standing in the doorway.

"Hey, Neil, what's up?"

"We've got a gentleman here who wants to talk to you?"

A *gentleman*.

"He give a name?" she asked.

"No. But he has your business card."

Nicole pushed back her chair. "All right, thanks." She smoothed her hair and checked the clock again. Odd time for a drop-in, but she was curious. She'd passed out dozens of business cards over the past few days, so maybe somebody was coming forward with a tip. They could definitely use one.

Crossing the bullpen, she glanced through the glass divider and saw a tall man with his back to her. He wore a dress shirt and slacks.

He turned around.

Black Visor Guy. Only he looked nothing like the sweaty runner she'd encountered yesterday.

She opened the door to the reception area. "Hi."

"Detective Lawson." He nodded crisply. "Do you have a minute?"

"Sure." She held the door open. "Come on back."

She looked him over as he passed through the door into

the bullpen. He seemed nervous as he glanced at all the cubicles, which were empty except for a couple of uniforms typing up reports.

"We can sit at my desk or—"

"Would you mind if we talk privately?" he asked.

Yep, nervous.

"No problem," she said, and led him to an interview room with a table and two chairs.

She ushered him in and left the door ajar. This guy had her radar up.

"Have a seat," she said.

He glanced around before taking a seat in the chair closest to the door.

"So." She sat across the table from him. "What can I do for you, Mr. Wakefield?"

He cleared his throat. "I've been reading about the recent case. And I just wanted to correct the record."

"Record?"

"Or conversation yesterday. I may have given the wrong impression."

"Oh?" She tipped her head to the side.

He folded his arms over his chest, then unfolded them. His tanned skin contrasted with his starched white dress shirt. According to her research, this guy worked for a financial services firm.

"So, you asked me about Saturday." He coughed into his hand. "I had a chance to check my calendar. I had a meeting that afternoon, and everything got so busy that—"

"What is it you do, Mr. Wakefield?"

He looked surprised by the question. "Me?"

"Yes."

"I'm a certified financial planner. My office is in San Antonio, but I work remotely most of the week from our beach house here." He smiled slightly. "So, you know, a lot of video meetings and conference calls, that sort of thing."

"I see. So, that's you and your wife who live here part-time?"

A worry line appeared between his brows. "Yes." He nodded. "And our two boys. Twins, actually." He cleared his throat. "Anyway, what I was saying . . ." He frowned again, as though he'd lost his train of thought.

"Your afternoon got busy Saturday?"

"Yes. Right. So . . . when you asked me if I had gone running that evening, I thought I had. But, actually, I didn't make it over there."

"No?"

"No. I usually run on Saturday evenings. I run most evenings, except Sundays, like I said. But last Saturday, I ended up meeting a friend."

"A female friend?"

The skin of his neck reddened, despite the tan. He nodded.

"So . . . you usually go running on Saturday evenings, but not this *past* Saturday."

"That's right," he said. "I was mistaken when I told you I was jogging then."

"And your wife, too, right? That's what you told her?"

He just sat there for a moment. Then he nodded.

She leaned forward, looking him in the eye. "Just to make sure I understand, you have *no* firsthand knowledge of any people or cars that may or may not have been on the beach near Lighthouse Point on Saturday, February fourteenth. Is that what you're saying?"

"That's right."

"In other words, you lied to me."

His flush deepened, and he cleared his throat. "I wanted

to correct the record so, you know, your investigation didn't get off track or anything."

She stared at him, frustration welling inside her as she thought about how much time she had wasted not only searching for this man but going over his bullshit story to figure out how it aligned with established facts. She imagined slapping her handcuffs on the table and threatening to charge him with obstructing a police investigation.

He'd probably piss his nice pants.

She smiled and shook her head. Then she pushed her chair back and stood. "You know what? I appreciate you coming in, Mr. Wakefield. You've been helpful."

He stood up, looking confused. "So . . . that's it?"

"That's it. Thanks for setting the record straight."

EMMET WALKED INTO Finn's and scanned the crowd. Owen and Kyle were at a high-top table in back, and Kyle spotted him as he made his way through the bar.

"Hey, you made it," Kyle said.

Owen looked Emmet over. "You just getting off work?"

"Yeah. Where's Nicole?"

"I don't know. Home, I think."

"Have a beer with us," Kyle said.

Emmet checked his phone as he took an empty stool.

"Any luck with the roommate?" Owen asked him.

"No."

Aubrey's roommate, Lauren, had no idea where Sam Pacheco worked or lived, or if he even lived on the island. She claimed she'd never heard his full name before tonight.

Owen shook his head. "This case, man."

"I know."

They'd been working every angle, and they didn't even have a solid suspect. The best lead so far was some ex-boyfriend—who may not have even been on the island last weekend, much less anywhere near the victim.

"Any news from Miranda?" Emmet asked.

Owen shook his head. "No. She told Nicole it might be Friday before they get anything back on the DNA."

"I thought she put a rush on it?"

"She did."

A server appeared at the table and flashed a flirty smile. "Y'all want some drinks?" she asked, resting her tray on her hip.

"I'll have a Shiner," Kyle said.

"One for me, too," Owen said. "And one for my brother."

Emmet ordered a beer and glanced at Owen as the server walked off. "Joel's coming?"

"Joel? No way. He's neck-deep in task force shit. Alex is on his way."

As he said this, Alex Breda stepped over.

"I ordered you a beer," Owen told him.

"Thanks." Alex smiled and glanced around the table. "The detective squad's here. Where's Nicole?"

"Home," Owen said.

Alex took the seat next to Emmet. He and Emmet's younger brother, Calvin, had been good friends in high school. Alex was always the brainy one, though, and no one had been surprised when he'd gone on to law school and become a hotshot attorney in Houston.

Why he'd given all that up to come back here was a mystery.

"How's the move coming?" Emmet asked him.

"Slow." Alex ran a hand through his hair, and Emmet noticed his gold watch. "I'm still unpacking."

"Where are you again?" Kyle asked.

"On Main Street. Right next to that real estate office with the swing out front."

Kyle frowned. "Isn't that a title company?"

"Used to be. Now it's my office. Leyla's helping me get set up."

"Speaking of," Owen said. "A little bird told me you've already got a client. Cassandra Miller. You know who she is, right? A key witness in our investigation."

The server was back with a tray full of beers. She distributed the bottles. "Anything else for now?"

"We're good, thanks," Alex said with a wink.

She walked off, and Owen picked up his beer.

"The suicide on the beach thing?" Alex asked.

"Homicide," Owen said pointedly. "So, what gives?"

Alex picked up his bottle. "What do you mean?"

"What does she need a lawyer for?" Owen asked.

Alex shook his head. "No comment."

Owen's eyebrows shot up. "Seriously?"

"Yeah."

Owen looked annoyed. "Are you for real right now?"

"Yes." Alex crossed his arms and stared at his brother. "I can't talk about my clients."

Owen glanced at Emmet, then back at Alex. "But she *is* your client, though, right? Is she in some kind of legal trouble or—"

"Look, I can't go into it. But she came to see me about something routine, okay?"

Owen's phone buzzed and he flipped it over on the table. "Why didn't you just say so?" He picked up the phone and answered it as Alex rolled his eyes.

Emmet sipped his beer, observing the friction play out between the two brothers. It was going to be interesting watching Alex practice law in the same town where his two older brothers were cops.

"Hey, that's good." Owen looked at Emmet. "Nicole got a lead on that address."

"Oh yeah?"

"He's sitting right here," Owen said. "You want to talk to him?"

Owen handed him the phone.

"Hey," Emmet said. "What's—"

"I'm going over there," Nicole said.

"Where? You mean the boyfriend's?"

"The ex-boyfriend's, yes," she said. "Samuel Pacheco. I want to talk to him."

Irritation surged through him. He slid off the chair and stepped away. "You can't just go charging over there, Nicole. It's late."

"Yeah. *It's late.* On day four of our crappy investigation with *no* viable suspects or even a freaking person of interest. You bet your ass I'm going to talk to him. We need to get eyes on this guy, feel him out, see if he's a suspect."

"What are you planning to say to him?"

Silence.

"Nicole? Have you even thought this through?"

"I'll figure something out."

Emmet gritted his teeth. "Where are you?"

"Over near the marina. Why?"

"Swing by Finn's."

"Why?"

"Because I'm coming with you."

T HEY RODE IN tense silence, with Emmet drumming his fingers on the door.

"How old is this address?" he asked.

She glanced over at him as she drove through downtown. "June of last year," she said. "That's when he filled out the job application at Surf's Up."

Emmet shook his head and looked out the window.

Nicole tried to ignore her disappointment. She hadn't expected effusive praise, but he at least could have said *something* positive after she'd spent most of her day tracking this down. Nicole had talked to one of Aubrey's friends who recalled Aubrey mentioning that Sam worked at a surf shop. Nicole had contacted every surf shop on the island, and finally this evening one of the managers called back to tell her that, yes, she had had a Sam Pacheco on staff until he quit around New Year's. Nicole had persuaded the manager to drive to the shop and look up the employment application so she could get Sam's address.

It was a solid piece of detective work, even if no one bothered to acknowledge it.

Emmet glanced at her. "What?"

"Nothing."

He seemed stressed, even more so than yesterday, and she could see the case was weighing on him. His eyes looked bloodshot, and he hadn't shaved in two days.

He glanced at her. "Do you even know anything about this guy?"

"What do you mean? He doesn't have a record. I told you—"

"I know, I mean what else do you have? I can't believe you were just planning to go pound on his door when you know next to nothing about him."

Irritation bubbled up. "I already ran him. I told you."

"*I* ran him, too, Nicole. But that doesn't tell me jack shit. This guy could be violent, and I can't believe you were going to go over there alone."

She bit back a retort. He was right—just because someone didn't have a rap sheet didn't mean he wasn't dangerous. But still, Emmet's tone right now irked her.

"Well, he doesn't have a criminal record," she reiterated.

"And anyway, I was going to ask Owen to go with me. That's why I called him."

Emmet crossed his arms, looking only mildly placated. Maybe he thought she should have called him instead, since he was the lead on this case.

The turnoff for Sam Pacheco's neighborhood came into view. She slowed and put on her turn signal.

"Well, we're almost here," she said, "so we should figure out how we want to approach him."

She turned down the street and neared the apartment complex. It was a two-story building with moldy white stucco and a red tile roof. A spotlight out front illuminated a clump of dead palm trees and a sign that said **Seabreeze Apartments**. She pulled into the driveway. No gate or passcode or even a security camera out front.

"You been over here lately?" she asked.

"Yeah." Emmet shot her a look. "The meth bust three months ago."

"That was here?"

"Yes."

She swung into a visitor's space and parked. At least they were in her pickup right now, which was slightly more low profile than an unmarked police car. Emmet glanced at the unit on the corner where two men stood in the shadows.

"Pacheco's place is around back," she said. "He's in unit 149."

"Let's do some recon first."

"Don't you think that will tip him off?"

"Tip him off that what?" he asked. "That cops want to ask him questions about his dead girlfriend? Unless he's stupid, he already knows."

Nicole stared at the building, thinking. "He may not even be aware of Aubrey's death," she said. "Assuming he didn't kill her, that is. Have you considered that? It sounds like he doesn't run in the same circles as her and her friends."

"This thing has been all over the news. He'd have to be living under a rock not to know about it."

"Still . . ." She surveyed the building. The men in the shadows were gone now, and she noticed a woman staring down from an upstairs window. "I think we should just walk up and knock on the door, catch him off guard and get a read on his reaction."

"And I think we should scope it out first," he said.

"So, is that an order?"

He looked at her. "What's that mean?"

"Is that you calling the shots again because you're *lead*, and my opinion means nothing?"

"Nicole—" He shook his head.

"What? I don't appreciate your tone with me. And I don't like the way you're treating me different because I'm a woman."

He looked offended. "How the hell am I treating you different?"

"Giving me crap about coming over here. If I was Owen, we wouldn't even be having this conversation right now."

"That's right. Because Owen wouldn't rush off to interview a murder suspect half-cocked."

"He's not a suspect yet."

Emmet glared at her, and she regretted using such a weak defense. Of course Sam Pacheco was a suspect. Even if it wasn't official, Aubrey's ex-boyfriend was the closest they had at this point.

Emmet leaned in. "And we're having this conversation because even after you got your ass kicked last year, you still insist on going it alone all the time."

Her cheeks flushed. She didn't like being reminded of being jumped by two guys when she'd been touring a crime scene last year. Emmet had given her hell for going over there alone late at night, and she'd admitted it was a tactical error. But he never missed a chance to bring it up again.

"I *told you*," she said, "I was going to ask Owen to come."

"Right."

"I was!"

"Nicole, please. I know you. You were on your way over here by yourself, and if I hadn't insisted on coming, you'd be out here on your own again walking into who the hell knows what."

She stared at him, fuming. Why couldn't he just take her at her word? She *had* been planning to ask Owen to come out here with her. Maybe it wasn't the first thing she'd been thinking about when she called him about this lead, but she would have asked him. And if she hadn't, he would have suggested it.

She turned away as her eyes burned with tears of frustration. What the hell? Why was she getting emotional, and in front of Emmet, of all people? She hated that he refused to forget about her mistakes.

"Nicole."

She looked at him.

"Let's just do this together, okay?" His voice was softer now. "No more arguing."

"Fine."

"We're not in competition."

She started to disagree but stopped herself. She often felt like she was in competition with him. But maybe that was just her. She was the only female detective on the squad, and she constantly felt pressure to prove herself.

Silence settled over them as Emmet watched her. The only sound was the whisper of wind buffeting the truck, and the air felt charged suddenly. Emmet's gaze dropped to her mouth, and her stomach did a nosedive.

No.

No possible way was he thinking about this now.

He lifted his gaze, and a jolt of yearning went through her. Something in his expression made her think he felt it, too. Surely she was reading this wrong. But his eyes were locked on hers, and he was so close she could feel his body heat.

He turned and opened the door.

"Wait." She grabbed his arm, and he turned around. "We didn't decide on a plan."

He shook his head. "We'll scope it out and see."

He got out of the truck. Nicole did, too. She locked the doors from inside to avoid making a noisy chirp with her key fob.

Emmet stepped onto the sidewalk and looked at the building. His posture was tense, and his hands were loose and ready at his sides as they started down the path.

"It's just around back, two from the end," she said.

"How do you know?"

"I looked at a site map of the place." She glanced around, noting the rows of cars in the poorly lit parking lot. There was a guy parked on the end, sitting behind the wheel, his face illuminated by a phone. And she noticed a woman in a patch of grass on the corner. She had a phone in one hand and a leash in the other as her dog squatted near the sidewalk.

"No lights," Emmet said, nodding at the second door from the end, number 149.

The two windows that belonged to that unit were dark.

Emmet walked up the sidewalk of the neighboring apartment. He reached into the inside pocket of his leather jacket and pulled out a flashlight, then cut across the lawn and strode right up to the window.

What was he *doing*? She hissed his name, but he waved

her off. Nearing the window, he leaned close and peered in, as though he might see through the mini-blinds.

Great. Very subtle.

The little dog on the corner started yapping, and Nicole turned to look at it. Perfect, now the neighbors were watching. Their stealth approach was blown at this point, so she pulled out her flashlight and walked up to the other window.

"There's a gap in the blinds," she said, peering through.

Her heart sank.

"*Damn* it," she said.

"What?"

"It's empty. No TV, no furniture. Nothing but a bare mattress."

Emmet came over, and she felt him looking over her shoulder. "*Fuck*. I thought he lived here."

Her stomach twisted with disappointment. "Not anymore."

CHAPTER

TWELVE

A SHARP KNOCK AT the door made Emmet look at his watch.

"Hang on," he told Owen over the phone. "I think my food's here."

"I'll let you go. I just wanted to hear how it went. Sorry it was another dead end."

"We'll hit it again tomorrow."

Emmet left his phone on the coffee table and went to the door. He was surprised to find Nicole standing there.

"Hi." She looked him up and down and bit her lip. He'd changed into sweats and a T-shirt as soon as he walked in, but she was dressed the same as earlier in her LBPD windbreaker, and clearly she hadn't been home yet. "Is it too late?"

"Not at all."

"I wanted to update you."

He pulled the door back. "Sure. I'm watching the game."

She stepped inside. "So, I tracked down the superinten-dent at the building and—"

"Hang on," he said as a dinged white car pulled up to the curb. Emmet waited for the delivery guy to come up the side-walk, then tipped him and brought the pizza into the kitchen. He set the warm box down and opened the lid, and the smell of Italian sausage filled the room.

"Want some?" he asked.

She eyed the pizza and gave a little sigh. "No, thanks."

He pulled the slices apart as she stepped over to look at the framed picture on the wall.

"This is new." She studied the poster-size photograph of the Grand Canyon at sunset. "Where'd you get it?"

"It's from my trip last summer. Remember, I went raft-ing with Calvin and Kyle?"

She turned around, eyes wide. "*You* took this?"

"Yeah."

"I didn't know you were a photographer."

"I'm not. I took it with my phone." He handed her a plate with a slice of pizza on it. "Here."

"What's this for?"

"You look hungry."

He walked over to the couch and sat down in front of the basketball game. The Rockets were up two on the Lakers in Los Angeles.

Nicole shrugged off her windbreaker and draped it over the sofa. Then she set her plate on the coffee table and took the seat right beside him. It was either that or drag a bar stool over from the kitchen.

"So, what's the update?" He folded his pizza in half and took a bite.

"Oh! I forgot to tell you—" She touched his arm. "I talked to Chris Wakefield tonight, and I was *right* about him." Her eyes sparkled with excitement as she told him this.

"The runner in black."

"Yeah." She plucked a bite of sausage from her slice and popped it into her mouth. "He came by the station."

"When?"

"Tonight around nine? Turns out, he *wasn't* running on the beach at Lighthouse Point Saturday evening at six. That was his cover story for his wife. He was busy getting his Valentine from some other woman."

Emmet shook his head. "Sounds like you called it."

"I know." She sighed, and the light in her eyes dimmed. "But that wasn't what I came by to tell you."

He waited, watching as she made a pile of black olives on the side of her plate.

"So, I tracked down the superintendent of the building," she said. "This guy put me in touch with the property manager who told me that unit 149 is a sublet. An *unauthorized* sublet."

"The landlord wasn't aware of it?"

"Yeah, he's never heard of Samuel Pacheco." She took a bite of pizza, then licked sauce off the corner of her mouth. "But he gave me the name that's on the lease, so in the morning I can reach out to her and see if she knows where her tenant went after he vacated. I'm hoping she got a security deposit from him, so maybe he gave her a forwarding address to send a check."

"Nice work," he said.

"Thanks."

Emmet finished off his slice in two more bites, then offered her his glass of water.

"I'm good," she said, focusing on the pizza she'd said she didn't want. She had worked even later than he had today, and he felt a twinge of guilt—along with something else he didn't want to put a label on.

"You know, I was thinking about what you said." He set his empty plate on the table and looked her in the eye. "Sorry I got pissed earlier. You're right—if it had been Owen I wouldn't have reacted the same."

She nodded. "I know that."

"The thing is, you weigh—what?—a buck ten?"

"Um, no."

"Well, whatever. I didn't want you confronting some potentially violent asshole who's probably been sitting around all night drinking."

She set her plate on the table and slid a look at him. "You know, I did, in fact, attend the same police academy as you. And I did, in fact, learn how to handle potentially violent assholes like everyone else did."

"Hey, I'm apologizing."

"I accept." She thrust her chin out, though, and he knew she was still ticked off.

He got up to get another slice of pizza. "Want more?"

"No, thanks."

He stepped into the kitchen. Nicole had never been good at accepting apologies. She was so competitive all the time, especially with him.

His phone buzzed on the coffee table. He couldn't see the screen, but she leaned over to look at it.

"A pineapple is calling you."

He walked over and sent the call to voicemail, then sat down next to her again.

"You don't want to get that?"

"No."

"Sorry but have to ask." She smirked. "Why the pineapple avatar?"

"I don't know. She put that in there." He flipped his phone over.

Nicole lifted an eyebrow and looked at the game.

"What?" he asked.

"Nothing." She set her plate on the table and checked her watch. "You know, I should probably go."

She started to get up, and he put his hand on her knee. "Eat. What's the rush?"

"I don't want to keep you from your booty call."

"You're not," he said, getting annoyed. He started on the second slice of pizza. "Anyway, how's David doing?"

She tensed. "Why?"

"Just asking."

"I guess he's good." She shrugged. "I honestly don't know. I haven't seen him in a week and a half. Well, outside of work, that is."

Emmet watched her, trying to read her expression. "Why haven't you seen him?"

"Because. He cancels about fifty percent of our plans." She lifted a shoulder like it was no big deal, but it clearly bothered her. "Anyway, we're supposed to have dinner tomorrow at Angelo's, so . . ."

He waited for her to complete the thought. She didn't.

"Sounds fancy," he said, trying to keep his tone neutral. "So, what's the problem?"

Another shrug. "I don't know. We'll see if it happens. I'm slammed, too, right now. This job isn't exactly great for my social life." She wiped her hands on her jeans. "But that's what I signed up for, right? I knew this job was a liability. No big surprise there."

"It's not that bad."

She scoffed. "Not if you're *you*."

"What's that mean?"

"Nothing."

He leaned closer, forcing her to make eye contact. "What?"

"Nothing. It's just different for the rest of you."

"Rest of you . . . ?"

"Don't be dense, Emmet."

"What?"

She rolled her eyes. "It's just . . . this is why my mom didn't want me to be a cop. She said I'd never meet anyone and never get married. Oh, and she'd said I'd get shot, too. That was her other lovely prediction. She always worries I'm going to get hurt in the line of duty."

He smiled slightly. "My mom says that, too. She acts like it's a curse that I'm a cop and Calvin's a firefighter."

He watched Nicole's eyes. She wouldn't look at him, and he could tell she was uncomfortable with this topic, which only made him want to press her on it.

"So . . . explain it to me. How is your job a liability? I mean, besides the hours."

She took a deep breath and blew it out. "Men either think I'm gay or that I'm into some weird sex kink."

"Men do not think you're gay."

She gave him a look as though he didn't know what he was talking about.

"Trust me, Nicole. They do not think that."

"Whatever."

"Fine, believe what you want."

"Well, they definitely think the sex thing. I get all these weirdos. They either want—" She glanced at him and stopped. "You know what? I don't want to talk about this."

He guzzled some water to cool his throat.

"What about Travis Bowman," he said. "You guys dated for a while, and he seems pretty normal."

"No, you're right—he's normal. And also a cheater."

He frowned. "Bowman?"

"He went to his brother's bachelor party in New Orleans and met some girl. And then he told me it didn't count because it was a bachelor party, and I was overreacting."

Emmet looked at her. "He 'met' some girl? You're saying he slept with her?"

"Yes."

"You're not overreacting."

"I *know that*. God. Can we talk about something else?"

He set his plate on the table and studied her expression. Her cheeks were pink, and he could tell she was embarrassed to talk about this with him.

"Sorry."

She laughed. "Why? *You* didn't fuck some random woman in New Orleans."

"Yeah, I mean just, you know, sorry in general. That guys can be dicks."

A knock sounded at the door, and they both glanced over the back of the couch.

"One sec." He got up to answer it, pretty sure it was Calvin coming to catch the end of the game.

It was.

"Hey, you watching the game?" Calvin asked.

"Yeah, it's about to go into overtime."

His brother looked past him. "Who is that?"

"Nicole."

Calvin's eyebrows arched with surprise.

"Hey, Calvin," she called from the couch.

"Hey, Nicole. Sorry to interrupt. I knew Emmet would have the game on."

"No worries. I was just leaving."

Nicole walked over with her jacket folded over her arm.

"So, what's up?" Calvin asked her.

"Nothing. We were just talking shop." She looked at

Emmet, and he had no trouble reading her expression. *Don't share any of that with your brother.*

But Calvin was already making a beeline for the pizza.

"See you later," she said as Calvin helped himself to two slices.

"Later."

Emmet followed Nicole out, pulling the door shut behind him.

"Thanks for the update," he said.

"Thanks for the food."

He stared down at her in the yellow glow of the porch light. A wind gusted up, and she rubbed her arms.

He nodded at her jacket. "You should put that on."

"I will."

But she didn't move. His gaze dropped to her mouth, and for a moment he was back inside her warm truck, trying to remember all the reasons kissing her would be a terrible idea. It was a long list, and one of the reasons was sitting on his couch right now.

Emmet stepped closer, tucking his hands into his pockets so he wouldn't be tempted to touch her.

"We didn't finish our conversation," he said.

"That's all right. Not my favorite topic."

He eased closer, wishing he could read the look in her eyes right now. A minute ago, she'd seemed embarrassed. But now he felt like she was thinking about something else. She gazed up at him with those bottomless brown eyes, and he wanted to just say to hell with everything and kiss her finally. What was the worst that could happen? Besides him making things eternally awkward with one of his best friends?

She could laugh at him—that would suck. Or she could remind him that she had a boyfriend. Or she could give him a hard shove. Nicole was very physical. They'd been sparring partners in a training exercise once, and he'd been turned on by the memory for weeks afterward.

Her eyes narrowed. "What?"

"Nothing."

"Get some sleep, Emmet." She turned away. "I'll see you tomorrow."

CHAPTER

THIRTEEN

CASSANDRA PICKED UP her order and glanced around the café. The Island Beanery was packed today. She was about to take her food to her car when a woman with a stroller got up from a table near the window.

Cassandra swooped in. "Is this free?"

"Yep. Just leaving." The woman frowned down at the crumbs all over the table. "We made kind of a mess, though."

"No worries. It's fine."

Cassandra set her plate down and then grabbed some napkins from the condiment bar as the woman navigated her stroller through the café. Cassandra wiped up the crumbs and then settled into the chair facing the window with her back to everything else.

She took out her phone and checked her messages. Nothing new from Reese. Late last night Paula had sent a text informing the staff that classes were canceled for the remainder of the week. Both the yoga studio and the martial arts academy were closed in the wake of Danielle's death.

Cassandra's stomach knotted as she reread Paula's message. Then she reread her back-and-forth with one of the other tae kwon do teachers who said that Danielle had had a seizure while driving and crashed her car into a utility pole.

Cassandra was still trying to absorb it. She couldn't. Beautiful, bright-eyed Danielle, the vision of health, was suddenly gone.

"Hi."

She jumped.

"Whoa." Alex Breda smiled down at her. "Didn't mean to startle you."

"You didn't. I was just . . . reading."

"Are you alone?"

"What?"

He gestured to the three empty chairs. "They're crowded today. Mind if I . . . ?"

She blinked up at him, at a loss for words. He wore a dress shirt and slacks, and a computer bag was slung over his shoulder. On the plate in his hand was a ridiculously large muffin.

"If you're meeting someone—"

"No. It's fine." She slipped her phone into her purse and gestured to the empty chair across from her. "Please sit."

He set down his plate and pulled out the little café chair. He was too big for it, and he turned sideways to make room for his long legs.

He smiled at her. "So, you've figured out the secret, huh?"

She just looked at him.

"It's eight," he said. "By nine, they've usually got a line out the door."

"Oh. Yes."

She glanced down at her untouched croissant and tore it in half.

"Double shot cappuccino with extra foam."

She turned around as Leyla Breda reached over her and placed a cup of coffee in the center of the table. Then she set a pastry bag beside it.

"And two of our fresh-baked oatmeal cookies, on the house." Leyla winked at Cassandra. "Y'all can share. It's good to see you again, Cassandra."

"You, too."

"Thanks, Ley," Alex said.

She smiled and sauntered off.

"That was nice of her," Cassandra said.

"Yes." He sighed. "She's matchmaking, too, in case you didn't pick up on that. Sorry."

Cassandra glanced over her shoulder as Leyla walked behind the coffee bar and disappeared into the back.

"I didn't realize your sister worked here."

"This is her shop." Alex picked up his coffee and took a sip. "This and the Java Place over at the Windjammer Hotel. You been there?"

"No."

She looked down at her croissant and pinched off the crusty corner, hoping to cover her nerves. She hadn't expected to see Alex right now. She had needed to get out of her apartment, where she couldn't shake the feeling that someone was watching her. Between the anonymous card on her doorstep and the phone call, she'd been so unnerved she couldn't sleep last night. Was this just her paranoia rearing its head again? Or did she have a legit reason for freaking out right now? She was so confused, she didn't know anymore. So she'd needed a break from her apartment, but she hadn't counted on bumping into anyone she knew and having to make conversation.

"Everything okay?" Alex asked.

"What?"

"Your food." He nodded at it, and she realized she had pulverized the bite of croissant into tiny little flakes. "Yes. Fine." She tore off a bigger piece and put it in her mouth.

He looked her over as he set down his coffee cup.

"So, I'm glad I ran into you," he said. "I was going to call you today, see if you wanted to meet."

"Oh?"

Something about his expression put her on guard.

"Have you made headway on the will?" she asked.

He nodded. "Yes. Some." His brow furrowed. "But that's not really what I wanted to talk about."

She just looked at him.

He took another sip of coffee and then slid the cup away.

"Cassandra . . ." His voice was lower now. "Is there anything you want to tell me?"

"What do you mean?"

He looked at her, as though waiting for her to answer her own question. His blue eyes were steady and patient, and she suddenly remembered her grandfather giving her that same look when she was a child and she'd accidentally broken the model sailboat in his office.

She stared at him, determined to wait him out.

"So, I ran a quick background check," he said casually.

"Why?"

"Habit." He shrugged. "I've represented a pretty broad spectrum of people over the years." He paused. "Some of my clients don't always fill me in on relevant data."

She stared at him, not blinking. He didn't blink either.

"What's your point?" she asked.

"Well. I wanted to get some more info."

"About?"

He watched her for a moment. "For instance . . . your driver's license is outdated."

The knot in her stomach was back again.

"And Cassandra Miller isn't really your name."

She bristled. "Yes, it is. It's my maiden name."

"*Catherine* Cassandra Miller is your maiden name."

She bit her tongue as she formulated a response. "I've been going by my middle name since I filed for divorce," she said with a shrug. "I needed a change."

He nodded. "I get that."

"Good."

Nerves started to dance around in her stomach. A *background check*. What did that mean, exactly? How deep would he dig?

"Look." He leaned closer and pinned her with those eyes. "I don't want to put you on the spot here. I just want you to know—you asked about attorney-client privilege the other day, and I want to make sure you know that you can talk to me. I'm a problem-solver. That's what I do."

She stared at him, pulse thrumming as she tried to imagine really *talking* to him, spilling her guts. Part of her was tempted. And part of her wanted to run out of here and never speak to him again—forget about her updated will and everything else.

"I'm your attorney, Cassandra."

She nodded. "I know."

He eased back, looking her over with a mixture of curiosity and concern.

She glanced at her watch. "I need to get going."

"Okay. That's fine." He paused. "Maybe we can talk more later? You can come by the office?"

"Maybe."

"And you've got my number."

"Yes." She grabbed her purse.

He slid the pastry bag across the table. "Don't forget these."

"Oh. Thanks, but I'm trying to avoid sweets."

He gave her that charming smile again. "They're oatmeal. Practically health food."

She laughed, and immediately felt a rush of guilt. How could she laugh today?

"You have them." She stood up. "Thanks, anyway."

NICOLE STEPPED OUT of the San Antonio FBI field office and took out her phone as she headed to her car.

"What's the word?" Brady asked the instant he picked up.

"I just dropped off the thumb drive," Nicole told him.

Ostensibly, the purpose of her trip was to hand-deliver the memory stick containing the surveillance footage Emmet had collected from the convenience store near Aubrey Lambert's apartment. The footage showed a man in a dark hoodie and sunglasses walking down the street toward the back gate to Aubrey's apartment complex.

But the real reason for her visit was to remind Brady's FBI contact of the video evidence they had already dropped off.

"And? Did they take a look?"

"No," she said. "Agent Driscoll was in the middle of something. But he said he'd take a look later today."

Nicole already knew what the special agent was going to say when he opened up the file. The black-and-white footage was grainy at best, and the view of the man in the dark hoodie was from a distance—at least a hundred feet. But who knew? Maybe the FBI's tech wizards would be able to enhance it into something usable. Nicole was more hopeful about the first video they had submitted because the shot was closer, and it actually showed someone *behind the wheel* of Aubrey's car.

"And what about the other thing? The video of the Subaru driving out of the gate?" Brady asked. "They've had that for days now."

Nicole slid behind the wheel of her unmarked police unit. Emmet had beaten her to the new car this morning, and this older one definitely smelled like vomit.

"Yeah, he told me that's next on their list," Nicole said. She turned on the heater, and a blast of cold air shot out.

"You mean they haven't *started* yet? What the hell have they been doing up there?"

"I think they're pretty swamped," Nicole said, trying to shake off the image of the video she'd seen on the agent's screen when she stepped up to his cubicle. Driscoll told her he'd been at his desk since seven this morning combing through videos. "Agent Driscoll's got a child-trafficking case brewing, and it seems to be demanding his whole team's attention."

Brady made a frustrated sound.

"But he promised they'd get to us." She passed through a gate and waved at the guard who'd checked her ID on the way in. "He said he hoped to have something for us by Friday."

"Friday."

She could tell by the chief's tone that he wasn't happy. Neither was she. But Brady's contact was inundated with child porn, and the man had been downing antacids and coffee throughout their brief meeting. She was lucky he'd even agreed to see her, much less do a favor for Brady.

"Chief?"

"Yeah, I'm just thinking."

"If it makes you feel any better, he gave me his personal number. He said to call him by Saturday if we hadn't heard anything by then."

Nicole exited the FBI campus, which was set apart from the rest of the city. The San Antonio field office had once been located in the heart of downtown, a stone's throw from the Alamo. But the combination of the Oklahoma City bombing and 9/11 had resulted in many federal offices being relocated.

"Well, thanks for making the trip," Brady said.

"No problem," she told him, even though it had killed half her day.

"As long as you're up there, I'd like you to swing by the county crime lab on your way back here. See if we can rattle some cages there, too—see what's going on with that DNA evidence."

Nicole cursed inwardly. The county crime lab wasn't "on her way" at all—it was an hour detour, minimum.

"I checked in with Miranda yesterday, and she said—"

"Talk to the lab director," Brady cut in. "See what you can get from him."

Right. Because the lab director probably had nothing going on today and was just waiting for surprise drop-ins from impatient detectives. Brady had sent Nicole on this mission before, and she'd ended up cooling her heels in the lobby until she was lucky enough to get five minutes of the man's time.

Brady was a big proponent of rattling cages to get results, and he always said it was better to do it in person. He believed electronic nagging was too easy to ignore. Nicole didn't disagree with him, but she'd burned her morning driving to San Antonio, and now it looked like the afternoon was going to get derailed, too. She was still trying to track down the Sam Pacheco lead.

Not to mention the other interesting item she'd discovered in the victim's phone records. There were numerous calls between Aubrey and Cassandra Miller—more than Nicole would have expected if the women were mere acquaintances, as Cassandra had indicated. It was yet another bit of info about Cassandra that seemed odd. Clearly, she and the murder victim were closer friends than she had let on. The question was, why mislead a detective about her relationship to the victim? Nicole was tired of being lied to, and she needed to get a straight answer. She had planned to pay another visit to Cassandra at home today and pin her down.

But her follow-up with Cassandra, like everything else on her list today, had been torpedoed by this road trip.

"Lawson? You there?"

"Yes, sir. I was just thinking, we're really swamped today, and I'm wondering if driving out to the lab is the best use of time when—"

"I want you networking," he interrupted. "You need to build relationships with key contacts. That's how things get done around here."

She sat there, at a loss for words. Was Brady mentoring her? Was that the reason he'd sent her driving all over the state to meet with people face-to-face? She'd thought he'd just been wasting her time because he was old-school when it came to phones.

"All right. I'm happy to go by there," she said. "But I had also hoped to make some headway on tracking down the address of the victim's ex, Sam Pacheco—"

"Don't worry about that. Emmet said he'd follow up."

"He did?"

"Yeah, he was in here a minute ago, said he had a new lead."

What new lead? And why the hell hadn't Emmet called her?

"What's your ETA?" Brady asked.

"Probably four o'clock," she said, reshuffling her afternoon. "Five if I hit traffic."

"Okay, call me from the road, let me know what you get."

"Yes, sir."

"And Lawson?"

"Yes?"

"Hang in there. We're bound to catch a break soon."

T HE VISITORS' LOUNGE at the Crossroads Recovery Center had beige walls, beige carpet, and oversize furniture in every shade of beige. The color scheme was probably intended to be soothing, but Samuel Pacheco looked anything but calm as he reached for the empty pocket of his beige jumpsuit for the third time.

Emmet glanced at Adam. "Why don't we move this conversation outside? I need some air."

Adam blinked at him for a moment. "Sure. Yeah."

Emmet got up and led the way through the double doors. The courtyard outside was landscaped with native Texas plants, and wooden benches were scattered along the paths.

Emmet led them to the farthest corner of the yard to a pair of benches under a mesquite tree with a little sign posted beside it: **Prosopis Glandulosa.**

"Have a seat," Emmet said.

Pacheco sat down and stretched his legs out, then crossed his arms over his chest. Adam took the other bench.

Emmet propped his foot beside Adam and pulled a pack of cigarettes from the pocket of his jacket.

Pacheco's eyes locked on the pack.

"Want one?"

"Yeah."

Emmet lit his own cigarette before handing Pacheco one and lighting it for him.

"So, you were saying?" Emmet studied Aubrey's ex-boyfriend through a stream of smoke. "How you found out from Caitlyn?"

Pacheco closed his eyes as he took a deep drag. "Yeah."

"And this was what day?" Emmet glanced at Adam, who was taking notes on their conversation on his little spiral notepad.

"Monday night. We get, like, thirty minutes on the phone. I called her up, and she told me about Aubrey."

"And you're *sure* that was the first you heard about it?"

"Yeah, man." Pacheco tapped an ash near his plastic shower shoes. Shoelaces—like belts and cell phones—were prohibited here. Smoking probably was, too, but Emmet was on a mission to connect with this guy, so he'd brought a pack of cigarettes with him.

"And, so you'd been here, what? Two days, by this point?" Emmet asked.

"Three, man. I told you, I checked in Saturday." He nodded at Adam's notepad. "Be sure you get that right."

Adam looked at Emmet.

"All right, and you said before that you were staying at your folks' place in Austin?"

"Yeah." He took another drag.

"How long was that?" Emmet watched him, trying to get a read on his gaunt features as he walked through the series of events for the third time.

"So, I wrecked my car two weeks ago." Pacheco ran a hand through his longish brown hair. "February second."

Emmet nodded. He'd already jotted down the details about Pacheco's car accident in Corpus Christi.

"My dad drove down to pick me up, and he was like, hey, this is it. You're going to rehab, or your mom and I are done." He flicked his cigarette. "So, they set all this up, and as soon as a bed here opened up, we drove down. That was Saturday morning."

Emmet had already confirmed his check-in date. But he still wanted to nail down some details—namely, what had he been doing since his accident and where had he spent Friday night? Aubrey's whereabouts the night before her murder were still unknown.

"And you were at your parents' place that whole time?" Emmet asked.

"Yeah."

"You didn't go back to Lost Beach? Pick up any stuff? Maybe connect with any friends?"

"My dad went and picked up my stuff at the place where I was staying."

Emmet would bet money Pacheco had at least tried to get in touch with his dealer, if not driven back to Lost Beach to try to see him. And if he'd been in town, had he reached out to Aubrey?

"Did you go with him to help?"

"No, man, I told you. I was at my parents' house in Austin. My fucking car's totaled. I was stranded."

Emmet let his cigarette burn down as he stared at the guy, gauging his credibility. His story was consistent— Emmet would give him that. He'd answered three different versions of the same questions over the past half hour as Adam took notes. But Emmet still felt like he was missing something, like this guy knew something about Aubrey that he wasn't saying.

Emmet stubbed out his cigarette as Pacheco savored his last few puffs.

"So, let me ask you this," Emmet said. "If you had to *guess* where Aubrey was Friday night, what would you say?"

"I told you, she wasn't with me. I was in Austin."

"No, I got that. I'm saying, if you had to guess."

"I don't know." He tossed his butt on the ground and flattened it with his plastic shoe, and Emmet shot Adam a look. "Did you try Lauren, her roommate?"

"She told us Aubrey didn't come home," Emmet said.

"Yeah, but I mean did you ask her about who Aubrey was *with*?"

"Was she seeing someone?"

"Yeah, I mean, she was talking to other people online. We both were. That's how we met in the first place."

"You mean the dating app?"

"Yeah. I think she'd met someone."

"You know a name?" Adam asked.

Pacheco sighed and looked at his feet. "Gimme a sec. I feel like she mentioned it."

Emmet waited, gazing down at Aubrey's ex.

Adam looked at Emmet with a raised eyebrow, then shot a pointed look at the cigarette butt. Emmet nodded.

"Think, Sam," Emmet told him. "Who was she seeing?"

He rubbed his chin, still staring at his feet. "It was like, Brian or Brandon?" His gaze jerked up. "Brenden. That was it. Some guy named Brenden."

"Last name?"

"No idea."

Emmet studied the man's face. The guy had been credible until now, but Emmet's gut told him that this part of his story was bullshit. Witnesses lied all the time, and the real question was *why*. Was this guy lying because he was guilty of something? Or because he wanted to get the police out of his face?

Emmet asked a few more questions that didn't go anywhere and wrapped up the interview. Then he stopped by the director's office for a minute before returning to the parking lot.

Adam was waiting by the unmarked police car.

"You get the cigarette?" Emmet asked.

"Yeah." He held up a small brown evidence envelope. "You think we'll need this?"

"You never know."

They slid into the car.

"His alibi check out?" Adam asked as Emmet started the engine.

"He was admitted here on Saturday, like he said." He glanced at Adam. "Nine a.m."

"Shit."

"I know."

"So, now what? He was our only suspect."

Emmet gritted his teeth and didn't answer. They crossed the parking lot and exited through the electronic gate.

"Could be it's this Brenden guy," Adam continued. "Or maybe he just threw out a name so we'd shut up and go away. That sounded kind of made up to me. What do you think?"

Emmet looked at him. "I think you're getting the hang of this."

N ICOLE TURNED INTO the gas station on fumes and pulled up to a pump.

OUT OF ORDER, read the hand-printed sign.

Cursing, she checked her watch, then circled around and pulled up to wait behind a pickup truck. A text message from Owen landed on her phone.

DNA update?

She grabbed her phone from the cup holder and texted him the same message she'd texted Brady as she was leaving the crime lab.

Nothing new. DNA results Friday at the earliest.
Also I just went by Cassandra's to ask her abt vic's
number on her phone, but she wasn't there.

Owen had agreed that Aubrey's phone records showed
an unusual number of calls to Cassandra if their relationship was limited to student and teacher. And if there was
more to it, why hadn't Cassandra said so from the beginning?

Why don't u call her? Owen responded.

I want to ask her in person.

Face-to-face interviews worked better in terms of deter-
mining people's credibility. Chris Wakefield was a case in
point.

Nicole tossed her phone on the seat and checked the
time again. It was after six, and she still had to go home to
get ready for her date with David. She'd be lucky if she had
time to shower, much less put on makeup or do anything
with her hair.

On the other hand, why stress when there was a strong
chance he was going to cancel anyway?

Then she remembered the look in his eyes when he'd
apologized to her back at the lab on Sunday, which was the
last time she'd seen him. He had seemed so sincere. And
same for last night on the phone. And he had teed up Angelo's, which was known for its wine list and romantic
ambience.

Maybe Siena was right, and she needed to think positive.

Suddenly, she pictured Emmet by his front door with
that heated look in his eyes. He'd seemed like he'd wanted
to kiss her, which was crazy. She couldn't go there with

him. Besides the important fact that she was *dating some-one else right now*, anything with Emmet was guaranteed to blow up in her face. Word would get around at work, as everything always did, and she'd end up being the subject of a bunch of locker room gossip.

Shuddering at the thought, Nicole glanced at the truck in front of her. The driver wasn't nearby, so he was probably in the store buying something. She checked her watch again, then looked at the store.

Nicole glanced at the truck again, and her pulse quickened as she studied the dented bumper and dusty license plate. She'd seen this same pickup on Monday over in Sunset Shores.

The door to the store swung open, and a man emerged. He handed something to a red-haired little boy.

"No freaking way," she muttered, watching them walk together. This was the landscaping guy she had interviewed Monday.

She jumped out of her car just as the man pulled open the passenger's side door.

"Excuse me!"

The kid climbed into the truck cab. The man closed the door and then walked around the front and reached for the gas nozzle.

"Hey!"

He glanced up. A look of dread came over his face, and she felt a spurt of outrage.

"We spoke Monday afternoon?" She pulled her wind-breaker back to show him the badge clipped at her hip. "I'm Detective Lawson?"

He stared at her, nozzle in hand, as she walked up to him. She eyed the side of his truck. **Islandscapes**, it said. Then she glanced into the truck cab at the boy sitting in the passenger seat with a bag of Skittles.

"What's the problem, Officer?"

She smiled. "It's Detective." She nodded at the gas pump. "You mind putting that down, please?"

He replaced the nozzle and turned to face her, hooking his thumbs into his belt loops with the *What could you possibly want with me?* look that she had seen a thousand times.

"I talked to you Monday over in Sunset Shores."

He darted a glance at his pickup. "Do we have to do this now? I've got my kid with me."

"Yes, we do." She dipped her head down and looked into the truck again. "And he looks pretty happy with his Skittles." She eased closer, sizing the guy up. He wore a dark green golf shirt, faded jeans, and mud-caked boots. He had a slight paunch and a resigned look in his pale blue eyes.

"Monday you told me you were not on the beach near Lighthouse Point last Saturday."

His eyebrows arched but he didn't respond.

"Yet a man who fits *your* description was seen at that location in a green truck." She paused. "This witness also described seeing a black dog and a little boy with red hair." She tipped her head toward the truck. "You want to offer an explanation for that?"

He shook his head slightly. "Look, Officer—"

"Detective."

"I'm trying to run a business here. My whole crew is day laborers."

"And? So?"

"So, people at the jobsite see me talking to cops, my guys will up and disappear on me."

She took a deep breath, trying to tamp down her temper. A horn beeped behind her, and she ignored it.

"It's Shaunessy, right?" she asked.

He nodded.

"What is your first name, Mr. Shaunessy?"

He sighed. "Liam."

"Step over here for a moment."

A horn beeped again, and she glanced back at the black SUV waiting behind her. She wanted to flip them off, but instead she turned back to the witness.

"Mr. Shaunessy, like I said Monday, I'm conducting an investigation. In fact, it's a homicide investigation. That means it doesn't matter what you do or don't feel like talking about at your jobsite. I need you to answer my questions truthfully. Do you understand, sir?"

He nodded.

"Were you at the beach near the lighthouse on Saturday evening?"

"I was there with my son."

"And you were flying a remote-control airplane, correct?"

He frowned at this bit of information, then gave a stiff nod. "Yes."

"And your dog was with you as well, correct?"

Another nod.

"While you were on the beach there, can you tell me if you saw anyone else, either on foot or in a vehicle?"

He heaved a sigh. Then he pulled his cap off his head and wiped his forehead with the back of his hand.

"There were some joggers, I think." He snugged the cap back on his head.

"Male? Female?"

"I remember one. A woman."

"All right. What about vehicles?"

He looked down and pursed his lips. "I think there was a blue car parked a ways down from us. I don't remember any people."

"Are you sure? Think back."

He shook his head. "I didn't see anyone. It was just a car parked there between the dunes."

She watched him, trying to tell whether he was being straight with her finally. She was so tired of BS that she wanted to scream.

She took a deep breath. "This remote-control aircraft you were flying—is that like a drone or—"

"It's a stunt plane," he said. "My son got it for Christmas and wanted to try it out."

"And does it have a camera on it?"

His eyebrows tipped up. "A camera?"

"Yes, like a drone cam? Does it have a camera attachment that records video?"

"No."

She felt a jab of disappointment. It had been a long shot, but she'd been hopeful about a possible camera. It was the reason she'd been so intent on locating this witness.

"I got some video on my phone, though," he said.

"You did?"

"My dad gave my son the plane, so I took a video for him on the beach there." He pulled his phone from his pocket and started scrolling through. "Don't know what all's on it, but you're welcome to have a look."

CHAPTER

FOURTEEN

NICOLE TRIED TO apply lipstick while simultaneously searching for a parking space. Seeing nothing, she circled the block again.

"Pick up, Emmet," she muttered at her phone.

It went to voicemail again.

"*Damn* it."

She zipped the lipstick into her purse and grabbed her phone from the cup holder. This time she called Adam.

"Hello?"

Someone pulled out of a parking space, and she slammed on the brakes.

"*Yes!*" she said, switching on her blinker.

"Nicole?"

"Yeah, sorry, I'm talking to myself." She drove past the space and shifted into reverse. "Hey, Adam, you happen to know where Emmet is? I've called him twice, but he's not answering his phone."

"Yeah."

She whipped into the space and parked. It was ten after seven. She was already late.

"Adam? Is he with you or—"

"Yeah, we're here at the station. He's in the chief's office. Wait, no. He just walked into the conference room."

She waited for a car to pass and then shoved open the door. "Great. Could you put him on for me? I'm on my way to dinner and I need to talk to him real quick."

"One sec."

She grabbed her little black purse and got out. It was the same purse as last time, but tonight instead of wearing her sister's dress, she was in her own clothes—a black miniskirt and black cashmere sweater, plus suede ankle boots that made her legs look longer. Not quite as eye-popping an outfit as last time, but at least she wouldn't freeze her butt off walking to and from the restaurant.

"Hey, what's up?" Emmet said, sounding distracted.

"I've been calling your phone." She stepped onto the sidewalk, and the skinny heel of her boot snagged on a crack in the pavement. She pulled it free and then hurried down the sidewalk. "Emmet? You there?"

"Yeah, what is it?"

"You'll never guess who I bumped into *again*."

"Hang on."

She heard muffled voices, followed by quiet.

Nicole glanced across the street at the restaurant on the corner. She looked up and down the block, just in case David was arriving late, too. She didn't want to look like a maniac racing to the restaurant to meet him.

"Okay, what's this?"

"Emmet, listen, I can't talk long but I had to tell you, I just interviewed Liam Shaunessy again."

"Who's—"

"The guy from the beach with the teal green truck. And

the dog and the kid and the toy airplane. And get this, he has video."

"What?"

"*Video*. This guy was with his kid flying a remote-control plane they got for Christmas, and he took a video, and in the background you can see Aubrey's car."

"You're joking."

"No! It's right there on video. And not only that—" She stopped at the corner and jabbed the crosswalk button. She wanted to sprint across, but there was too much traffic.

"Nicole?"

"You won't believe this, but you can actually *see* a man getting out of Aubrey's car. He gets out of the driver's seat. I'm thinking maybe he had her in the front with him already. Maybe he took her somewhere private and had started staging the scene? And then he drove to the beach and repositioned the body and—"

"Wait, wait, wait. You're saying it's the perp?"

"*Yes*. It's right there on video! It's Aubrey's *car*. I mean, the footage is from a distance, but you can see—"

"Where is it?"

"On the beach. Where we recovered the vehicle."

"No, I mean, where is this footage?"

"I emailed the clip to you and to Brady. Check your in-box. And I got the witness's info. He's coming in first thing tomorrow morning to give us a sworn statement."

"Hang on. Let me pull up my email."

"Emmet, it's from a distance, but this is *huge*. We can place this guy at the car as he's dumping the body—"

"Okay, I got it. One sec, let me open it."

The walk sign turned green, and Nicole jogged across.

Brakes squealed. Horns blared. Nicole whirled around to see a silver truck grille coming straight at her.

Her heart skittered.

"Watch out!" someone yelled.

Nicole lunged for the sidewalk. The truck swerved. Screaming, she dove for the hood of a car.

T HE SCREAM TURNED Emmet's blood cold.

"Nicole?"

Car horns, yelling. Then a distant, "*Someone call 911!*"

Emmet jumped up from his chair. "*Nicole?*"

The call went dead.

He dialed her back, heart thundering. Straight to voicemail.

"Fuck!"

"What's wrong?"

He glanced up to see Adam standing in the doorway to the conference room. "Where's Nicole?" Emmet demanded.

Adam just stared at him, confused.

"Where was she *calling you from*?"

Adam shook his head. "I don't know. I think she was in her car."

Emmet dialed her again. Voicemail.

"God*damn* it." He gripped his hair.

"What is it?"

"Did she say what she was doing?"

"She said . . . I think she was on her way to dinner?"

Dinner. She was going to Angelo's.

"Here." Emmet tossed Adam's phone at him and rushed out of the conference room. He crossed the bullpen, snatched his keys and phone off his desk, and spied a couple of uniforms standing by the radio.

They started to move for the door.

"Neil, wait!" Emmet jogged to catch up with them. "Where are you going?"

"Accident downtown," Neil said. "Someone just called in."

"What—"

"Sounds like car versus pedestrian."

CHAPTER

FIFTEEN

EVERYTHING HURT.

The epicenter was her ankle, with waves of pain pulsing up her leg. Her hip felt like one massive, throbbing bruise. And then there was her elbow, which was currently on fire.

Nicole distracted herself by watching people stream back and forth in the hallway as she tried not to puke. The ER was a zoo tonight. Three car accidents, one drug OD, and a man next to her who, from the sound of it, was passing a kidney stone.

"This might sting." The nurse shot Nicole an apologetic look as he prepared to clean the gash on her arm. "I have to get the gravel out."

"It's fine," she said, looking away.

Shit shit shit.

Tears stung her eyes, but she refused to watch as he flushed out the cut.

"You okay?"

She glanced up to see David standing by the curtain.

"Yeah," she said, but the next searing pain stole the breath from her as the nurse lifted a little flap of skin.

David stepped over, his brow furrowing as he glanced at the end of the bed, where her bare foot was propped on a pillow beneath an ice pack. After diving out of the path of a speeding truck, Nicole had scrambled to her feet and turned her left ankle, and now it was swollen to the size of a rump roast.

"How's it feel?" David asked.

She took a deep breath. "Have you seen *Misery*?"

He frowned. "Damn. Really?"

She nodded.

"I'll have them get you something for the pain." He glanced at her foot again. Then he looked at her, and Nicole's stomach clenched because she could tell he had bad news.

"What is it?" she asked.

"I talked to the attending physician, Dr. Chan."

"And?"

"It's a lateral malleolus fracture."

"So, it's broken? Does that mean a cast?"

"You'll need a boot and crutches."

Her stomach sank. "How long?"

"Depends," he said. "Probably five weeks."

Fire tore up her elbow, and she yelped.

The nurse froze. "Sorry. Let me just finish sterilizing this."

Nicole looked at David again, trying to focus on his words and not the sensation of having her skin peeled off.

He moved closer, his forehead wrinkled with worry. He wore charcoal slacks and a blue dress shirt that matched his eyes. He smelled like cologne, too, which reminded her that they were supposed to be on a date right now, not stuck in the ER.

Nicole's mind was still reeling. Everything had been so chaotic with police cars and paramedics and people stopping to gawk as she lay sprawled on the sidewalk. Luckily, no one else had been hurt, but the guy who'd run the light had raced off without stopping.

"He'll be in in a minute to explain," David said.

"Dr. Chan?"

"Yeah."

She took a deep breath. "Can I use your phone? I lost mine back at the accident scene."

"Sure. You want to call your parents?"

"No."

His eyebrows tipped up.

"I mean . . . this would definitely freak them out." She shifted on the gurney. Pain shot up her ankle, and she tried not to wince. "I'd like to call my sister, though."

He entered the passcode and handed the phone over.

"Take your time," David said. "I'll go see about those pain meds."

"Thanks."

She looked down at his phone, disoriented by the unfamiliar screen. The nurse continued to work on her elbow, inflicting agony with his cotton swabs. Gritting her teeth against the pain, Nicole tried to pull her thoughts together. Kate was supposed to be having dinner with their parents tonight. The very last thing Nicole wanted to do was tell them she'd been *hit by a car* and send everyone into a panic. And anyway she hadn't been hit. But the near miss had left her banged up and shaken to her core.

Taking a deep breath, she dialed. Kate didn't answer—probably because she didn't recognize the number—and it went to voicemail.

"Hey, it's me." She tried to sound, if not normal, then at least functional. "I've been in an accident. I was on my way to dinner with David and I tripped and broke my ankle so . . . Anyway, I'm at the ER now. Everything's under control."

Her elbow burned, and she darted a look at the nurse as he dabbed ointment on her cut.

"They're getting me fitted with one of those boots and then David is going to drive me home." A call came in, and Nicole hurried to wrap up. "Anyway, *don't* worry and don't let Mom and Dad freak out either. Everything's fine. I'll call you later, okay? Bye."

She hung up just as David returned.

"You get her?"

"I left her a message. Thank you." She handed back the phone. "You missed a call from someone."

"Thanks. So, Chan's on his way in. He's going to get you taken care of." David glanced at the nurse. "How's the elbow coming?"

"Almost done here," the nurse said, wrapping the gauze. "Don't get it wet for forty-eight hours. And you'll need to change this dressing out twice a day."

The nurse finished taping and then smiled and ducked out, leaving Nicole and David alone in the little curtained-off area. Well, alone except for the kidney-stone guy groaning next door.

"I'm sorry this happened to you," David said.

"Me, too."

"The officer at the scene told me they're trying to get a license plate."

"I know."

He pulled his phone from his pocket and read a text message. His face tensed, and Nicole recognized the look.

"You have a callout?"

He glanced up, and she knew the answer.

"Let me just—"

"It's okay if you have to go," she said.

"I might not. Let me just take this."

He stepped into the busy hallway, and she stared at the empty doorway. Was he really going to leave her here and rush off to work? She knew from the look on his face that he was. He was just nailing down his excuse.

Glancing around the room, she found herself alone for the first time in what felt like hours, although she had no clue what time it was. Her head was whirling, and her entire body felt off-kilter.

She looked at her swollen foot, and suddenly reality crashed over her like a wave.

"Shit." She clutched her stomach.

Five *weeks*? Tears burned her eyes. How was she going to work? Everyone in their department was already under intense pressure, and now she was going to be struggling even more to keep up.

"Hey."

She glanced up to see Emmet, and her heart flipped over. She hadn't seen him since back at the accident scene. He and Adam had been interviewing bystanders as Nicole argued with David about whether she needed an ambulance to take her to the hospital. David had won.

"Excuse me, sir."

Emmet moved out of the way as a nurse rushed through the door and into the neighboring curtain.

Emmet stepped over to Nicole's gurney. "Hi."

"Hi." She wiped her wet cheeks, and he pretended not to notice she was crying.

"Stitches?" He nodded at her arm.

"Just a bandage."

"And the ankle?"

She took a deep breath. "It's broken." The words put a cramp in her stomach. "I'm going to be on crutches awhile."

His stared down at her for a long moment. Then he reached into his pocket and pulled out her phone. The screen was shattered, but just the sight of it made her smile.

"Oh my God. *Thank* you," she said, taking it.

"It was under a car near the intersection."

She examined the phone, then set it on the sheet beside her. She should really call Kate again, but she didn't want her parents racing over here.

She glanced up and caught Emmet's dark expression.

"You look pissed about something."

He scoffed. "Yeah."

"Is it the hit-and-run?"

His jaw tensed. "We can talk about it later."

"Miss Lawson?" Dr. Chan walked into the room and glanced up from his clipboard.

Emmet stepped aside.

"Wait." She reached for his arm. "Would you do me a favor?"

He nodded.

"I think I need a ride home."

Emmet's anger felt like a hot coal in the center of his chest. Nicole hadn't said a word the whole drive, and the pinched look on her face made it clear she was in pain.

He needed to talk to her about what happened. Not just talk—he needed to interrogate her and have her take him through every step of it, from the moment she'd crossed the intersection on a green light, according to witnesses, to the moment she'd ended up flat on her butt and bleeding all over the sidewalk—which was how she'd been when Emmet pulled up to the scene.

She rode beside him in his truck now, the seat racked back to make room for the big boot that went up to her knee.

Emmet pulled into the parking lot of her apartment building. The front-row spaces were full, so he created one on the end.

He looked at her. "Is the elevator here working?"

"Yes." She wrinkled her nose. "It smells like dead fish, but I *think* it's working."

"Sit tight."

She sighed. "No problem."

He went around and opened the passenger door. She tensed as he reached across her to unclip her seat belt.

"I can do that."

"I got it," he said, reaching over the console for the crutches stashed in back.

She eyed them warily. "Would you mind giving me a hand with those?"

"Probably easier if I carry you up."

"Uh, no. Definitely not easier." She took one of the crutches from him. "Here. I need to get the hang of this."

Tamping down his annoyance that she wouldn't take his help, he stood inside the door, close enough to catch her if she lost her balance. Her uninjured foot was covered with a blue hospital sock, and he had no idea where her shoes had gone. She pivoted in the seat and positioned the first crutch under her arm. Her sweater rode up, and he ignored the flash of skin as he helped her get the second crutch under her arm.

"Got it?" He looked up, and her expression was tight but determined.

"Got it. Can you grab my stuff?"

He collected her purse and the bottle of pain meds off the floor. Then he eased back, and she crutched awkwardly toward the building with him beside her. She moved up the cement incline and crossed the sidewalk to the elevator bank near the storage closets.

Emmet jabbed the call button, and the silver doors rattled open.

She moved inside the elevator, and he stepped in after her, hitting the two button. She hadn't been kidding about the odor. It smelled like a bait shop.

Nicole stared up at the ceiling and seemed to be holding her breath. To block out the stink? The pain? The elevator whined and groaned as it made its way up, then shuddered to a stop.

The doors parted, and he held them open. "Go ahead."

She crutched out, then stopped and stared down the long outdoor hallway. Her apartment was near the end.

"I can carry you."

"No."

He knew it was pointless to argue with her. A lock of auburn hair hung over her eyes, and he tucked it behind her ear. Taking a deep breath, she started moving forward. He watched her, his fury building with every awkward step, until finally she neared the door. He took out her keys and unlocked it.

"Thanks."

Emmet followed her inside, switching on the light. She made a little yelp, and he looked down to see her skinny black cat rubbing against her.

"Hey, Lucy baby," she murmured.

The cat sniffed the boot, then rubbed her head against Nicole's bare calf.

"Don't let her trip you," he said.

"She won't."

He locked the door and then scooted around her to move a pair of running shoes out of her path. He dropped them into a corner.

Nicole stood in the middle of the living room, wide-eyed, looking around her apartment like it belonged to someone else. He could see her wheels turning as she tried to envision life on crutches for the next five weeks.

He set her stuff on the counter.

"You want a drink?" he asked.

"God, yes." She crutched over to the breakfast bar. "But I don't think alcohol mixes with my pain meds. He said they're pretty strong."

She looked up at him. Her makeup was smudged, her

hair was a mess, and the perspiration on her forehead told him the brief trip up here had taken a toll.

"You want to call your family?" he asked.

"I will."

Lucy jumped up onto the counter, and Nicole stroked her fur. "Aw. She knows something's wrong."

"We need to talk, Nicole."

She didn't look at him. "I know."

"I interviewed a bunch of witnesses."

She leaned her crutches against the counter and pulled out a bar stool. Slowly, she lowered herself onto it.

He watched her face, hating that they had to have this conversation right now when she was in pain. But they needed to talk while this was fresh in her mind, and once her meds kicked in, he figured she'd be out.

"Four separate people told me that SUV didn't just run the light." He watched her, searching her face for clues. "He veered *toward* you when you lunged out of the way."

She closed her eyes and bit her lip, and he got the feeling this wasn't a surprise.

"Nicole?"

She looked at him.

"Is that how *you* remember it?"

"It's kind of fuzzy but . . . yeah."

"Did you see the driver?"

She shook her head.

No one had caught the license plate, so all they had to go on at this point was a description of the vehicle, a black Chevy Tahoe with silver rims.

"What do you think that's about?" he asked.

"What do *I think*?" She shook her head. "No idea. Maybe someone drunk or high. Maybe someone I arrested who saw me and just, I don't know, snapped?" She shrugged. "I really have no clue."

He stared at her, frustration churning inside him. Why was she shrugging this off? She could have easily been killed.

Nicole closed her eyes. "Oh, damn."

"What?"

"I'm supposed to interview that witness in the morning. Liam Shaunessy."

"What time?"

She pinched the bridge of her nose. "He's coming in at eight a.m. to give us a sworn statement."

"I'll handle it."

"But I told him—"

"Don't argue," he said. "You've got enough to deal with right now."

She shifted on the bar stool and winced.

"Is your pill working?"

"A little," she said, obviously lying. "I'm supposed to elevate my leg." She glanced at the living room, then looked at the hallway to her bedroom.

"I can get you set up," he said.

"I need to rinse off first."

"Aren't you supposed to keep your cut dry?"

"Yes. But I've got iodine all over me. And dirt. And this disgusting street grime." She glanced down and seemed to notice all the little scrapes on her legs. She grabbed her crutches and moved toward the hallway. "I at least need to wash up."

"Wait," he said.

The bathroom door was ajar. He opened it wider and stepped inside.

It looked like a makeup piñata had exploded. Pencils, tubes, and brushes covered the counter. Little foam pads were scattered around the sink. The room smelled like coconuts—probably the shampoo she used that always made him think of sex on the beach.

"It's a mess," she said from the doorway.

He picked up the hair dryer in the sink, shaking his head as he unplugged it. He opened the vanity drawer and swept all the makeup shit into it. Then he pulled back the shower curtain. He grabbed a bar of soap and set it on the side of the sink, then pulled a hand towel from the rack and put it by the soap.

He looked at her. "You really need to do this?"

She nodded. Her eyes looked a little glassy now, so maybe the medicine was starting to kick in, finally.

"You want help?" he asked.

She shook her head.

He scooted past her, careful not to bump her boot.

"Yell if you need anything."

She hobbled into the bathroom. "I will. Oh, I need some clothes. Do you mind?" She turned to him. "Just a T-shirt or whatever to sleep in. They're in my second drawer."

"Sure." He started to pull the door shut.

"Emmet?"

He looked back.

She bit her lip. "Thank you."

"No problem."

Nicole sat on the side of the tub, closing her eyes and listening to the water run as she fought the wave of nausea. Maybe it was the pain meds on her empty stomach. Or maybe it was the lie she'd just told her sister.

She looked down at her cracked phone, which had somehow ended up *underneath a car*. Everything after seeing that big silver grille zooming toward her had been a blur. And then she'd been on the sidewalk bleeding, and David was there yelling at people to move back, give her space.

And then there were sirens, and EMTs, and a terrible shooting pain.

He veered toward you when you lunged out of the way.

She closed her eyes, thinking of Emmet's words as the memory emerged from the shadows. It had been there for hours, lurking, but she hadn't let herself really look at it until now.

She set her phone on the counter beside the folded T-shirt Emmet had put there while she'd been on with Kate. She hated lying to her sister. Well, she hadn't exactly lied—she'd told Kate what had happened, but she'd downplayed the hell out of it so her family wouldn't come rushing over here. Her mom would freak out, and Nicole couldn't deal with it right now. The meds were taking effect, and she was starting to feel out of it.

She finished washing her arms and legs and draped the damp towel over the side of the tub. Then she turned off the faucet. She reached for her crutches, and they clattered to the floor.

"Nicole?"

Emmet was just outside the door.

"I'm fine, just—" She leaned forward, and pain shot up her leg. "*Shit!*"

The door cracked open. "You okay?"

"Don't come in! I'm changing."

"Are you all right?"

"Fine," she said through clenched teeth.

"Damn, what are you doing?" He stepped into the little bathroom and picked up the crutches. She pulled the bath towel up against her bra as he frowned down at her. He'd taken off his jacket and holster, and now just wore jeans and a black long-sleeved T-shirt.

"Why didn't you call me to help you?" he asked, eyeing the heap of torn clothes on the floor.

"Because. I'm fine," she said, even though getting the stretchy black miniskirt over the boot had been agonizing.

She held the bath towel to her chest. "Can you help me stand up?"

He reached down and gently slid his hands under her upper arms to lift her to her feet. She felt a rush of dizziness. His arm came around her waist, and she leaned against him.

"Thanks," she mumbled, reaching for the T-shirt on the counter.

"Here. Lift your arms."

The towel fell away as he helped her pull the shirt over her head.

"I can do this," she said.

"Fine. Do it."

He eased back, watching her as she tugged the shirt around her thighs and reached for the crutches. She tucked them under her arms.

"*No* comments," she said.

"About what?"

"I'd better not hear you telling everyone at work how you saw me naked."

He rolled his eyes. "You're not naked."

"Close enough."

He stepped into the hallway, and she took a moment to shake off the wooziness before crutching past him.

"I think the pill's kicking in," she said.

"I can tell."

She stopped in the hallway. "Kate said she'd pick up my car tomorrow."

"I can do it."

"You've done enough." She glanced at the living room and then at her bedroom down the hallway.

"I got your room ready," he said.

"You did?" She crutched the short distance and stopped in the doorway. The comforter was pulled back and a big throw pillow was positioned at the foot of the bed. The TV on the dresser was on, and a rerun of *Friends* played on mute.

Her heart made a weird little hiccup.

"Thanks," she said.

She moved over to the bed, and he put his arm around her waist to steady her as she handed him the crutches. She sat down and slowly lifted her leg to rest it on the pillow.

"Too high?" he asked.

"No."

She eased back against the stack of pillows.

"You've got your meds here and some ice water. When's your next pill?"

It took her a moment to think. "Four a.m. I need to set an alarm."

He took her phone from his pocket and set it beside the water glass. Once again, he was one step ahead of her sluggish brain.

"Thank you."

He gazed down at her, and there was that concerned look again, the one from the hospital. It put an ache in the pit of her stomach.

She shifted her foot and flinched as pain reverberated up her leg.

"You okay?"

"Yeah, just—" She closed her eyes and sighed deeply. "Fine."

"You should rest." He stepped back, and the ache intensified. "We can talk more about everything tomorrow."

She gazed up at him, heart thudding. He picked up her hand and squeezed it, and a pang of yearning went through her.

"Call me if you need anything," he said.

"I will."

He leaned down and kissed her forehead.

She reached up, resting her hand against his face.

"Thank you," she whispered.

He gazed down at her, not moving. She shifted her thumb, stroking the stubble along his jaw. Heat flared in his eyes as the back-and-forth motion of her thumb set off sparks.

"Nicole—"

She reached up and kissed him, settling her mouth against his. His lips were warm and firm, and she licked against them. He made a sound deep in his chest and took control of the kiss, easing her back against the pillow as he leaned over her.

She was kissing Emmet. *Emmet.* She'd thought of this hundreds of times. Thousands, probably. But the reality was more intoxicating than she'd ever imagined. His fingers combed into her hair as his tongue moved against hers, exploring her mouth. The taste of him was new but somehow familiar, like the smell of him that she loved so much, and she pulled him closer, wanting more of it as she moaned against his mouth.

He jerked away and glanced at her foot. "Are you—"

"I'm fine," she said, pulling him back.

The mattress sank as he sat beside her, and his warm hand settling on her thigh sent a rush of heat through her. His fingers slid to the T-shirt hem, and she knew he was thinking of the black lace underwear she had on.

That she had put on for her date with David.

Guilt swirled into her mind but then swirled right out

again. Emmet's tongue was in her mouth, and he tasted so good it was making her drunk. She moved her hand over his knee, squeezing his muscular thigh through the denim.

He tipped her head back. "Nicole. What the fuck?" He kissed his way down her neck, leaving a trail of fire along her skin as his hand glided under her T-shirt to cup her breast. His thumb found her nipple through her lacy bra, and she arched against him.

He pulled back, lust and confusion warring in his eyes.

She kissed him again, wanting to block all that out. His other hand slid up her thigh, and she kissed him deeper, willing him to touch her exactly where she wanted. His fingers grazed her underwear, electrifying every nerve ending, and then his mouth closed over her nipple, and the heat of it through the fabric made her nearly lose her mind.

He pulled back, and something in his expression made her go still.

"What?" she whispered.

He closed his eyes.

"What's wrong?"

He reached up and unhooked her fingers from his neck. He clasped her hand and rested it on the bed beside him, then glanced back at her boot propped on the pillow.

"This can't happen," he said.

She stared at him.

He looked at her foot again and closed his eyes. "Fuck. I'm sorry."

"For what? I kissed *you*."

He squeezed her hand. "That's the pain meds."

The fog in her brain cleared—at least some of it—and she felt her cheeks flush. What had she just done?

"Hey." He leaned forward, resting his palm beside her. "Don't look like that."

"But I thought you—"

"No, you're right." He stared down at her, and she tried to piece together what he meant. So he *was* turned on? Or he wasn't? Or he *was* but he didn't want to be?

Her head was swimming. She felt drunk and disoriented, and the one clear thought was that she didn't want him to leave yet. If he left now, she wouldn't be able to look at him tomorrow.

"Will you stay?" she asked.

He leaned back. "Nicole—"

"Just for a little while. We can watch a show."

He gazed down at her, the muscle in his jaw twitching. Then he glanced at the TV.

He bent over and started unlacing his boots, and her heart did a joyful skip. He set his shoes by her crutches and walked around to the other side of the bed. He propped the pillow against the headboard, and the mattress sank as he leaned back, stretching out his long legs and crossing them at the ankles. He picked up the remote in the middle of the bed and unmuted the television.

He darted a look at her. "What do you want to watch?"

"Anything."

"Basketball?"

"Whatever you want."

She closed her eyes, and a feeling of warm contentment washed over her. The kiss was over. The weird, wonderful kiss that had left her mind swirling. Her pulse was calming now, and the blood in her veins seemed to be turning thick and sticky, like maple syrup.

She turned her head on the pillow, facing him without opening her eyes. The glow of the TV flickered, and a low sound drifted over her. Her head was spinning, spinning . . .

"Emmet," she murmured.

His big hand closed around hers like a hug.

CHAPTER

SEVENTEEN

EMMET WOKE UP on alert. Something was off. He blinked into the gloom and saw a pair of eyes staring down at him.

"*Shit!*" he croaked, bolted upright.

The cat hissed from the nightstand.

Beside him in the bed, Nicole stirred. She was on her back, a blanket draped over her, oblivious to the warmth of the overheated room.

Emmet sat forward and raked his hand through his hair. Gray bands of light seeped through the mini-blinds. He grabbed his phone off the nightstand and checked the time. It was 6:52. He'd planned to leave after giving Nicole her four a.m. pill, but instead he'd drifted off again.

Shit.

He had to get home.

And shower and check his messages and get to work. The empty hole in his stomach reminded him that he'd skipped dinner last night, so he had to eat something, too.

Emmet got up, eyeing the floor to make sure he didn't trip over the cat. Nicole's body was a shapeless lump beneath the blanket, but it looked like she'd made it through the night with her boot propped on the pillow, so that was good.

He stepped closer to the bed and gazed down at her in the dimness. She was out cold. Gone was the fire in her eyes and the stubborn set of her jaw. She looked . . . soft. He stared down at her, drinking in the sight.

Thwack thwack thwack.

Across the room, the cat pawed at the mini-blinds.

"Damn it, Lucifer." Emmet grabbed his boots off the floor, then stepped to the window. "Out. Let's go." He corralled the cat out the door, and it raced into the kitchen, probably eager for breakfast.

Emmet stopped to adjust the thermostat, then made his way down the dim hallway, his mind filling with all the shit he'd planned to do last night before he'd ended up here.

In Nicole's apartment.

In Nicole's *bed*.

He sank onto the sofa and dropped his boots on the floor.

Fuck.

He scrubbed his hands over his face and tried to think about work. But all he could think of was Nicole's smooth skin and the sound she'd made when he'd kissed her nipple.

A noise at the door had him glancing up. *Shit*. Did David have a key? Emmet hadn't even thought of it.

The door swung open, and Nicole's sister stepped inside. She turned and switched on the light.

"Hey, Kate."

"Good morning, Emmet. I *thought* that was your truck down there." She closed the door behind her and strode into the kitchen, setting down a pair of shopping bags. She looked dressed for work and not at all surprised to see him here.

Emmet shoved his feet into his boots, and she started unloading the bags.

"You want coffee?" she asked.

His stomach growled in response.

"I'm good, thanks."

She lifted an eyebrow skeptically and turned to put a pod into the Keurig. She took a mug down from the cabinet and eyed his wallet and holster on the breakfast bar.

"How is she?" Kate asked.

He stepped over to the kitchen. "Groggy from the meds. And pretty out of it."

Out of it enough to kiss him.

That had been the pain meds, definitely. Those pills made her loopy.

The coffee machine groaned and gurgled, and Kate leaned back against the counter, watching him. She wore a black skirt and pale blue blouse, and he tried to remember what she did for a living. Something in real estate? Damned if he could remember.

The coffee finished, and she unpacked a carton of creamer from one of the grocery bags.

"You've been to the store already?" he asked.

"This is from my place. I wanted to save her any errands today." She poured creamer into her mug and then put the carton in the fridge.

"So." She leaned against the counter again. "What the hell happened, exactly? And don't give me the same bull Nicole did."

Emmet had overheard their phone call last night, and Nicole had downplayed everything, probably to keep her family from worrying.

"We don't know for sure," he said, because he wasn't on

board with Nicole's push to sugarcoat everything. "But what *didn't* happen was some guy didn't accidentally run a red light."

Kate's eyebrows shot up. "It wasn't an accident?"

"No."

"I knew it." She shook her head. "I told her it was just a little *too weird* that someone nearly ran her down after she's been so paranoid lately."

"Paranoid?"

She eyed him over the coffee cup. "She didn't tell you?"

His stomach clenched. "No. What?"

She took a sip, then set the mug aside.

"Nicole told me she thought someone was maybe following her home," Kate said.

Emmet's blood ran cold. "Who?"

"She didn't know. She just said she felt like someone was tailing her around the last few days. I told her it was probably some sleazebag she once busted trying to mess with her head."

Emmet gritted his teeth. Every word of this was news to him. Why hadn't Nicole told him?

"So, did anyone get a license plate or anything at the scene last night?" Kate asked.

"No."

"Well, did you at least have a description? Do you know who it is?"

"We're investigating." He picked up his holster. "We should know more later today."

Kate frowned at him, suddenly resembling her sister. "That's *concerning*, to say the least."

Emmet buckled his belt and grabbed his wallet off the counter.

"Well." Kate folded her arms, watching him. "Thank you for staying with her."

He nodded.

"She doesn't like asking for help." She tipped her head to the side. "But you know that already."

She was baiting him, but he wasn't biting. He grabbed his leather jacket off the back of the chair and shrugged into it.

"Tell Nicole I'll check in with her later."

"Sure. Good luck with the investigation. I really hope you find the guy."

"We will."

"And hey, Emmet, if she stonewalls me again, I'm coming to you."

S HOOTING PAIN PENETRATED her dreams about bacon. Nicole sat up in bed. The space beside her was empty. She blinked at it a moment, wondering if she'd imagined Emmet stretched out there last night in the flicker of the television.

But the nervous flutter in her stomach told her it was real. And the memory of his mouth and his taste and the feel of his stubble under her fingertips was much too vivid to be a dream.

Throbbing pain pulled her attention back to the present. She grabbed the crutches propped by her nightstand and, after two attempts, managed to stand.

"You're awake!"

She glanced up to see Kate in the doorway smiling.

"I was about to come pinch you to make sure you're still alive."

Nicole squinted at her. "Why are you so cheerful?"

"Uh-oh. Sounds like someone needs a pill."

Nicole glanced at the clock and sighed. "Thirty minutes. I can't take one until ten." Nicole hauled herself to the doorway. Every limb ached, even the nonbroken ones.

She stopped at the door and looked Kate over. She was all dressed up, which meant she probably had a closing today. "How are you here right now?"

Kate smiled. "I'm working from home this morning. *Your* home. But I've got a meeting at noon, so you'd better make use of me while you can." She nodded at Nicole's boot. "How's the ankle?"

"All right."

"Liar." She stepped back to make room as Nicole crutched past her to the bathroom. "There's breakfast on the stove."

"Sounds good. I'll be right out."

Nicole tried to avoid her reflection as she went about her morning routine. Then she crutched into the kitchen, where Kate had her laptop open on the bar and Nicole's favorite Snoopy mug beside her.

"I fixed you some coffee," Kate said.

"I'm dying for some." She stopped in the middle of the kitchen. "You made pancakes?"

"Ha. Not a chance. Those are from Mom."

Nicole reached over and lifted a paper towel off a plate and found six crispy strips of bacon.

"I thought I was dreaming." She turned around. "Why didn't Mom wake me up?"

"You were completely zonked, and she wanted you to sleep." Kate eyed her over the rim of her coffee cup. "Those pills must have really knocked you out."

"Yeah." She checked the clock again. She was due for another one in twenty minutes.

She glanced at Kate, and the expression on her sister's face set off a little warning bell.

"What's that look?" Nicole reached for a piece of bacon and winced when a jolt of fire shot up from her hip. She didn't even want to look at the bruise today.

"I'm here to get the straight story," Kate said. "No more dodging me."

Nicole nibbled the crispy bacon, and the salty goodness melted on her tongue.

"I want to know what *really* happened yesterday. Emmet said it wasn't an accident."

Hearing his name put a flutter in Nicole's stomach. She grabbed another piece of bacon and maneuvered over to the counter, where a mug of coffee sat waiting for her.

"I honestly don't know," Nicole said. "Some psycho tried to barrel into me." The memory of that big silver grille flashed through her brain, and a chill went down her spine.

She glanced at Kate, and her sister was watching her with a worried frown.

"Don't worry, though. We'll figure it out."

Kate's eyebrows shot up. "That's it? That's all you have to say?"

"What else do you want me to say?"

"How can you be so calm? You were almost killed yesterday!"

"No, I wasn't."

"You're *severely injured*!"

"That's because I leaped over a car hood and then tripped over my own feet getting up."

"Nicole! You could have been hit."

"It wasn't really that big a thing."

"That's not what Emmet said."

Again, his name made her stomach flutter. She remembered his face during the drive home from the hospital. He'd looked like a thundercloud.

"What all did he tell you?" Nicole asked.

"That someone *intentionally* tried to run you down. He seemed very concerned about it."

Nicole nodded. "Well, we're investigating. We'll figure

out what happened," she said, hoping to project more confidence than she felt. She wasn't up for a debate with her sister right now, not when every inch of her body ached. "I'll update you when we know more. But can you please not freak out about this? I don't want all this getting back to Mom and Dad and having to deal with Mom's hysterics."

Kate sighed. When it came to their mom, Nicole and Kate had each other's backs. Renee Lawson was constantly worrying about her daughters' safety. With Nicole's job, it was understandable. But Kate was a real estate agent, and even she was constantly getting pelted with news articles about people who had been attacked in vacant houses by perverts pretending to be home buyers. Only their brother, Kevin, was spared her constant fretting.

"Okay, fine," Kate said. "But don't hide shit from me, all right?"

"I won't."

She closed her laptop. "Now, I want to hear about the other thing. Spill it."

"Spill what?" Nicole turned and grabbed a fluffy yellow pancake from the plate on the counter. When she turned around, Kate was staring at her expectantly. If it had been anyone else it might have worked, but her sister knew her too well.

Nicole nibbled the pancake. "Emmet spent the night."

Kate rolled her eyes. "No kidding. I bumped into him this morning. Tell me *what happened*."

Nicole bit her lip.

"Oh my God. Did you have sex?"

A chunk of pancake lodged in Nicole's throat, and she swallowed it down. "We kissed."

Kate tipped her head back. "Finally! God. It only took you, what, ten years?"

"What's that supposed to mean?"

"Or fifteen, really, if you count the crush you had on him in high school."

Nicole turned around and put her coffee in the microwave to give herself something to do.

"Well? How did it happen?" Kate demanded. "I want details."

"I don't remember, exactly."

"How can you not remember? It was just last night."

"I was pretty spacey." Nicole rubbed the back of her neck. "He was leaving, and I think I just . . . kissed him."

"And?"

"And that's it." She thought of his hands sliding under her shirt and his mouth on her nipple. "That's what happened."

Kate squinted. "You are so full of shit."

"What?" She turned and got her coffee out. She didn't want to talk about this anymore—not with Kate or anyone. She hadn't even had time to think about it herself, and she wasn't ready to piece it apart yet. Emmet had been so many things last night. He'd been kind, and frustrated, and thoughtful, and infuriating.

And *sweet*. It wasn't a word she'd ever associated with him before. But he'd turned down her bed and put a glass of water out for her.

And the tender look on his face when he'd leaned over and kissed her forehead . . . A little zing went through her as the memory popped into her brain. *That* was what prompted her to throw ten years of restraint out the window—that and the pain meds. He'd kissed her first.

Only his kiss had been short and platonic. She'd been the one to drag him into bed with her and practically beg him to stay.

"Nicole."

"What?"

"You've got this look on your face. What are you leaving out?"

"Nothing." She took a sip of coffee, and it scalded her throat.

Kate sighed. Then she checked her phone and stood up.

"Well, that's obviously crap, but I don't have time to drag it out of you, so you're off the hook. For now."

A knock on the door had them both turning around.

Kate shot Nicole a look and then strode across the living room. She checked the peephole and glanced over her shoulder.

"Oh my God."

"Who is it?" Nicole asked.

Her sister opened the door, but Nicole couldn't see who was there because the entire doorway was taken up by a ginormous flower arrangement.

"How pretty! Thank you so much!" Kate accepted the delivery and used her hip to close the door. "Okay, these are gorgeous." The towering bouquet blocked Kate's face as she returned to the kitchen and set the vase on the counter.

"What?" Kate glanced up. "Why do you look like it's a ticking bomb?" She plucked the little white envelope from the arrangement and held it out. "Open it."

Nicole took the envelope and stared down at it for a moment. This felt like a David gesture. Her mother loved flowers, but she would have bought them at the grocery store. And there wasn't a single other person in Nicole's life who would even think of such a thing.

She tore open the envelope.

HOPE YOU FEEL BETTER SOON.—D

"David?" Kate asked.

Nicole nodded. She tucked the card back into the envelope as guilt washed over her. "Shit," she muttered.

"What? They're stunning!"

"They look really expensive."

Kate waved her off. "So what? He can afford it. Anyway, he left you *stranded* at the ER. What a jerk move! Not to mention that's the second time he's bailed on you for work."

The third. But who was counting?

"He can't help it if he got a callout," Nicole said.

"What? Why are you defending him?"

"I'm not. But I feel so guilty. I don't know what got into me."

Kate smiled. "Besides the narcotics?"

"That's no excuse."

She rolled her eyes. "Calm down. It's not like you *slept* with someone . . . right?"

"We kissed. I told you."

"Well, then chalk it up to the meds and give yourself a break. You'd just been through a trauma."

Nicole stared at the multicolored mix of roses, tulips, and hydrangeas. If only it had been a wilty-looking bunch of pink carnations left over from Valentine's.

"I need to talk to him," Nicole said. "This thing isn't working. Obviously."

Kate sighed. "You're a mess, Nik. I swear. Your love life is just . . ."

She bristled. "What?"

"Interesting. That's the word I was looking for."

Nicole combed her hand through her messy hair. She probably looked as terrible as she felt this morning.

"You okay?" Kate asked.

"Yeah."

Kate lifted an eyebrow at yet another lie. "I really wish I could stay, but I'm running late." She gathered up her laptop and slid it into her computer bag.

"Thanks for coming over. And for running interference with Mom and Dad."

"No problem." She stepped over and gave Nicole a quick hug. "Keep me posted. And be sure to stay on top of your pain meds."

As if she could forget.

EIGHTEEN

CASSANDRA DROVE DOWN Main Street, scanning the sidewalks and trying to get her nerves under control. Malcom wasn't here. He couldn't be. Just last night, he'd posted on social media from an Avalanche game.

But somehow, Malcom always managed to make his presence felt.

No parking spaces available, so she circled the block once more. Regret needled her as she passed the familiar cafés and T-shirt shops. She passed her favorite art gallery that had all the watercolors of boats that she could never afford. Then she passed the old-fashioned candy shop where they made saltwater taffy in a rainbow of flavors. Tears welled in her eyes as she turned the corner. The spark of hope she'd had when she'd first come to the island had dimmed, day by day, until this morning when it had been snuffed out completely.

A driver pulled out of a space on the corner, and Cassandra wedged her little white Mustang into the tight opening.

She jumped out and surveyed her parking job. Not great, but not terrible enough to attract attention. For months, Cassandra had avoided driving her car unless absolutely necessary because her registration was expired and she hadn't wanted to get pulled over and get a ticket, which would create a record of her name and location. But traffic tickets were the least of her worries now.

She waited for a break in cars and darted across the street. She passed the real estate office where they put out water bowls for dogs and posted local listings in the window. Cassandra used to dream about those listings and about one day having enough money to plunk down a deposit on some dilapidated beach cottage that she could gradually fix up. Those dreams seemed absurd now, along with everything else she'd been steadfastly working toward for months.

Nearing the law office, her stomach sank as she spied the sign in the window: **Back soon!** it said over a little clock. The clock hands were set to four p.m., the same as they had been yesterday when she'd come by here.

"Hey there."

Cassandra whirled around. Leyla Breda strode up the sidewalk, her arms loaded with brown packages.

"I thought that was you," Leyla said with a smile. Today she wore a baseball cap and paint-spattered jeans. "You looking for Alex?"

"Uh, yeah."

Crap. Cassandra had no desire to chitchat with Alex's sister, but what choice did she have?

"He's out, I'm afraid." Leyla stopped at the door and pulled a key from her pocket. The top package fell off the stack.

Cassandra stooped to pick it up. "Do you know when he'll be back?"

Leyla opened the door and stepped into the office. Setting the boxes by the door, she turned around. "Sorry." She huffed out a breath. "What's that?"

Cassandra handed her the package. "Will he be in today or—"

"Tomorrow. He's in Houston taking care of some business." Leyla added the box to the pile of packages from Amazon, IKEA, Pottery Barn. "Geez, look at all this. And there's more at my apartment. I get to be his post office until his lease starts next month."

Leyla looked up, and her smile faded as she studied Cassandra's face. "Everything okay?"

"Fine. I was just, you know, hoping to talk to him today."

"Did you try calling him?"

"I left him a voicemail this morning."

"Oh. Well . . ." She put her hand on her hip. "He's probably in a meeting or something. I'm sure he'll get back to you."

Cassandra was pretty sure he would, too. But by the time he did, it might not even matter.

Leyla's brow furrowed as she looked her over.

"Are you sure you're all right?"

Tears burned her eyes, but she blinked them away.

"If it's something urgent," Leyla said, "I can text him for you."

"No."

Leyla's eyebrows arched.

"I mean"—Cassandra took a deep breath—"it's nothing urgent. Nothing like that." She fixed a smiled on her face. "There's no need to bother him. I can talk to him tomorrow."

She rushed away before Leyla could ask any more questions and got back in her car.

Shit.

Shit shit shit.

She'd been counting on Alex, and she couldn't do what she needed to do without him.

Cassandra wiped the tears from her cheeks and started her car. She pulled out of the space and headed . . . where? She didn't know what to do now. Her entire plan—like all of her plans—was falling apart.

She turned off Main Street and drove past the yoga studio. Her heart squeezed as she saw the pile of flowers and cards left at the door. The pile had doubled since yesterday as word spread about Danielle's death. The funeral was scheduled for Saturday, and Reese had already asked her to go.

Cassandra gripped the steering wheel. Her breath started to come in short, shallow gasps, and her heart started pounding. Sweat broke out on the back of her neck.

Not again.

She pulled into a parking lot and shoved her car into park. She clutched the wheel and bent her head forward.

Breathe.

In . . . and out. In . . . and out.

She wasn't trapped.

Her plan was shot to hell, yes. But she could make a different plan that didn't involve Alex Breda or talking to police.

She had options.

Breathe through it.

She leaned back and stared through the windshield at the brick side of a building and the sign painted there: **Rosita's Mexican Café**. Flipping the visor down, Cassandra checked her face in the mirror. Her hair was oily, her skin looked pale, and the puffy bags under her eyes hinted that she'd been crying. No wonder Leyla Breda had seemed worried.

And maybe it was good that Alex was out of town. Cassandra looked like a basket case. She was in no condition to talk to him or anyone else right now.

She flipped the visor up and took a deep breath. The moment was over. Her pulse began to return to normal, and as she stared at the brick wall, a plan started to take shape. *Mexico.*

It was a new plan. A better one.

The only plan, really, that stood a chance of succeeding, and probably the one she should have had all along.

N ICOLE CRUTCHED PAST Cynthia's empty desk, relieved not to be waylaid with questions about her injury. David's office door was closed, and she stopped in front of it, listening in case he was on the phone.

No sounds from the room. But she hesitated anyway, debating what to say.

"Hey."

She glanced over her shoulder as David stepped out of the autopsy suite. He wore blue scrubs, and the surgical mask hanging around his neck told her he'd just finished a procedure.

He walked over, his brow furrowed with concern. It was the reaction she'd been getting from everyone today.

"Why aren't you in bed?" he asked.

She drew back. "It's two in the afternoon."

"I thought you'd take a few days off."

Irritation needled her. "Why would you think that?"

"Because." He reached around her and opened the door. "You need to rest and recover."

"Right. Yeah." She crutched into his office. She didn't feel like making the effort to sit, so she turned to face him. "The thing is, I'm in the middle of this thing called a murder investigation? My whole department is slightly swamped right now?"

He lifted an eyebrow. "I'm guessing by your mood that you didn't sleep well."

She took a deep breath. Okay, so maybe she was being a bitch. But his assumption that she would take a few days off irked her.

"You're right, sorry," she said. "I'm a little edgy today."

"Have a seat. Please." He walked around her and sat down behind his desk. "How's the ankle?"

She glanced around, then lowered herself into the guest chair and propped her crutches against his desk. He looked her over, probably shocked to see her in a denim miniskirt today instead of her usual unisex field uniform. She didn't have a lot of clothes that fit over her boot.

"It's okay," she told him. "Better than last night."

"You're not supposed to drive, you know."

"Actually, Chan said I was fine to drive. It's my *left* ankle, so—"

"No, I mean the pain medication. Don't operate heavy machinery, and all that."

"Oh. Owen—one of my colleagues—drove me here. We came to see Miranda about something, but I wanted to stop by first and talk to you." She took a deep breath. This conversation was off to a bumpy start. "I wanted to thank you for the flowers. They're really beautiful."

He nodded. "I'm glad."

"Especially the roses." Her stomach started jumping around. "My apartment smells amazing."

"Nicole." He leaned forward. "Why do I get the feeling you didn't come here to talk about flowers?"

She took a deep breath. "No, you're right. The thing is—"

Someone tapped at the door and then opened it.

"David, you've got—" Cynthia stopped when she saw Nicole sitting there. "Hello. I didn't see you come in."

Nicole smiled. "Hi."

"What's up, Cynthia?"

"You've got a message from Dr. Schuler in Dallas. He needs you to call him."

"I will. Thanks."

She closed the door, and they were alone again.

David looked at her.

"So. I wanted to thank you for the arrangement," Nicole said. "And I also wanted to tell you I've been thinking a lot about how things have been going. And I don't think this is working out."

"'This' meaning us."

She nodded.

He leaned back in his chair and looked at her for a long moment as she tried to read his expression.

"It's that detective, right?"

She blinked at him. "What?"

"The one at the hospital last night. Emmet."

"He's not the issue."

"No?"

"No." Guilt needled her. "Well, maybe he's part of the issue. But the real problem is us. Remember our first date? You told me all about how your life is dominated by work, and you feel like there's no room for anything else."

He nodded. "I really want to change that."

"See, that's the thing. I don't think you do."

"Nicole." He sounded irritated. "I can't help it if I have a demanding job."

"Look, I get it," she said. "Believe me, I know how hectic it gets around here."

"Then why are you piling on with criticism?"

She sighed. "David, let me ask you something. How many miles did you log last week?"

"What, you mean running?"

"Yes."

He frowned. "I don't know. Maybe forty."

"You ran *forty* miles last week?"

"I've got a race next month."

"Well, okay. Wow. That goes to my point."

"What? That you don't want me to train?"

"No! Train," she said. "Do what makes you happy. My *point* is that between your job and your training regimen, there's not much room in your life for a relationship."

He shook his head. "I disagree. I think I can juggle more than one thing if I put my mind to it."

His words stung, even though she doubted he meant them to. She didn't want to be something he had to *put his mind to*. She didn't want to be an item on his to-do list.

"David, I don't think we should keep pretending this is working when it's not."

There. She'd said it. She watched his face, but his expression didn't change.

She bit her lip. "What?"

"So, you think it's not working," he stated.

"I don't, no."

He sighed. "Okay. Fine, then. Let's both stop pretending."

He stared at her, and something in his look made her squirm in her chair.

Her phone vibrated with a text message, and she pulled it from her pocket. "That's Miranda. They're waiting for me in the lab."

David pushed his chair back and stood up. He came around the desk as she collected her crutches. "You need a hand?"

"Thanks. I've got it." She managed to get to her feet and glanced up at him.

He looked peeved, which wasn't what she'd expected. She'd thought he'd be disappointed, maybe even hurt.

The phone on his desk rang, and he glanced at it but didn't move to pick it up. He checked his watch.

"I've got a procedure starting."

She moved for the door. "I'll get out of your way."

He reached around her and opened the door. "So, I assume you're here for the Danielle Ward case?"

She stopped in the doorway. "I thought it was the Aubrey Lambert case. The other thing was a seizure, right?"

"Did you get my report?" he asked. "I sent it over this morning."

"I haven't seen it yet. Why? What happened?"

"No evidence of seizure, heart attack, stroke, or anything else that would have caused her to lose consciousness."

"Wait." Nicole stared up at him. "Are you telling me Danielle Ward wasn't an accidental death?"

"I'm telling you I wasn't able to find an underlying cause for her to lose control of her car and crash into a utility pole. That's why I flagged it for the crime lab, so they could take a closer look at the vehicle."

A ball of dread formed in Nicole's stomach as his words started to sink in. "But . . . if she didn't have a seizure or something, then what caused her accident?"

"You're assuming it was an accident."

"You're saying it wasn't?"

"I'm *saying*, go talk to the crime lab."

CHAPTER

NINETEEN

"HERE YOU ARE."

Emmet glanced up to see Adam in the doorway of the conference room. "Hey, Adam, what's up?" he asked, flipping through the police report from Nicole's incident.

"I got a lead."

"What's that?"

"A lead. With the Lambert case."

Emmet shoved the report aside and grabbed his notepad from the witness interviews. All four witnesses agreed the vehicle involved was a black SUV with tinted windows and silver hubcaps. But accounts differed on the model of the vehicle. The three Emmet had talked to said it was a black Chevy Tahoe, while the witness Adam had interviewed said it was a black Suburban.

"Don't you want to hear this?"

He glanced up, and the excited look in Adam's eyes pulled his attention away from the report.

"I do, yeah."

"So, yesterday you said you thought that name Sam Pacheco gave us was bullshit."

Emmet leaned back in his chair. "Brenden. What about it?"

"Well, I wanted to follow up. I think it's important that we nail down who Aubrey Lambert spent the night with right before she was murdered."

"You're right, we should."

"And I figured it out. I went to her AA group that meets over at the Methodist church and interviewed a couple people who knew her. Turns out, she's got a boyfriend there in the group."

"Her AA group," Emmet said.

"Yeah."

Emmet stared at him, impressed. "Who is this boyfriend?"

Adam pulled a spiral notebook from his pocket. He was in his field uniform today—a navy golf shirt and brown tactical pants—and Emmet tried to picture him crashing some AA meeting. He needed to learn how to look less conspicuous.

"Scott Kinney," Adam said. "He's thirty-six."

"Yeah? Interesting. And he admits to being Aubrey's boyfriend?"

"Well, I don't know if 'boyfriend' is really the term," Adam said. "Sounds more like friend with benefits. He said they hooked up every now and then. Including last Friday."

"This guy seem legit?"

"Yeah, I mean, he admitted spending the night with her, didn't seem evasive about it or anything."

Emmet laced his hands together behind his head. "What about his demeanor? He seem broken up about her death?"

"Honestly? Not so much. I don't think he really knew her all that well."

"He have an alibi for the time of the murder?"

"I asked that. Indirectly. He said he flew to Dallas on Saturday afternoon for some kind of meeting."

"So, he was in Dallas?"

"That's what he claims."

Emmet watched him, trying to gauge the usefulness of this new lead. Adam was fairly new at detective work, so Emmet wasn't sure he trusted his judgment on whether or not this guy was being straight.

"Nice work."

Adam smiled. "Thanks."

"We'll need to corroborate his story."

"Yeah, I know. I wasn't planning to just take him at his word."

The chief leaned his head into the conference room. "Good, you're here."

"What's up?" Emmet asked, and he could tell from Brady's expression something was wrong.

"Just got a call from the crime lab."

Emmet's attention perked up. "The DNA came back?"

"This is on the other thing," Brady said. "The Danielle Ward case."

Adam looked blank. "Danielle who?"

"The traffic fatality from Tuesday," Emmet said. "The woman who hit the utility pole downtown." He glanced at the chief, and Brady's grim look put Emmet on alert. "What's the problem?"

"Sounds like it wasn't an accident," Brady said. "The crime lab says someone tampered with her brakes."

NEED FOOD."

Nicole glanced at Owen and sighed.

"Aren't you hungry?" he asked. "We skipped lunch."

"I'm good." She was still full from homemade pancakes. "But if you're hungry, we can stop."

Owen was already pulling into the vacant lot beside a construction site on Seaside Boulevard. They were putting up another condominium complex, and several food trucks had set up shop.

Owen shoved the car into park. "Want anything? My treat."

"I'm good."

"Be right back."

He slid out and got in line with a handful of construction workers in yellow hard hats.

Nicole checked her phone, anxious for reasons she couldn't quite pinpoint. She had messages from Siena and her brother, along with several from her mom, who wanted to know if she was getting any rest this afternoon. Clearly, her mother assumed she was off today, and Nicole didn't tell her otherwise.

Nothing from Emmet since 10:20 a.m. when he'd responded to her Thanks for your help last night message with a thumbs-up emoji.

An emoji.

No words. No acknowledgment that he'd spent the night in her bed or that he'd woken her up to give her her pill in the middle of the night. If it hadn't been for the empty beer bottle in her recycling bin this morning, Nicole might have thought she imagined the whole thing, including their earth-tilting kiss.

Another wave of guilt hit her at the thought of David. She tried to shake it off. He hadn't even seemed all that upset by their conversation. Instead, he'd been . . . mildly annoyed—which just reinforced her ongoing impression that his heart hadn't been in it. And if she was honest, hers hadn't been either.

Owen slid back in the car with a pair of foil-wrapped tacos, and their unmarked police unit instantly smelled like grilled onions.

"Sure you don't want one?" he asked.

"I'm fine."

He unwrapped a taco and tore open a salsa packet.

"Brady just pinged me," Owen said. "He wants me to lead up the new homicide case."

Irritation needled her.

"Why not Emmet?" she asked.

"I don't know."

"Doesn't he think they're linked?"

Owen chomped into his taco. "I don't know what he thinks. All I got was a text message." He chewed his food, watching her. "You think the cases are connected?"

"Uh, *yeah*. Don't you?"

"I don't know." He took another bite of taco and watched her as he chewed.

"Owen, come on. We get, like, three to four homicide cases a year. And now we've got two in one week, and both were staged to look like accidents?"

He grabbed his water bottle from the cup holder and took a long sip.

"What's that look?" she asked.

"I don't know. Sure, the timing's weird, but that doesn't necessarily mean they're connected."

"It's not just the timing."

"What else?"

She sighed.

"Why are you all ticked off?" he asked.

"I'm not." Did she really have to spell out the obvious? Well, it was obvious to her anyway.

But maybe she was just cranky because of everything else going on. Her ankle was killing her, for one. And she didn't want to take any more pain meds because they made her feel spacey. Not to mention, they led her to make stupid decisions.

"Lay it out for me," Owen said, finishing off his first taco. "Why do you think the cases are connected?"

"Couple things," she said. At least he wanted her take, which she appreciated. "First off, Danielle co-owns the Banyan Tree downtown."

"And?"

"*And* that's where Aubrey Lambert took yoga."

"Okay. True. But they have a lot of classes there. Macey's been there, too. They probably have hundreds of students. More if you count the martial arts place next door."

"Okay, well, don't forget Cassandra Miller."

Owen unwrapped his second taco. "What about her?"

"The woman who found the first victim just *happens* to teach yoga at that same location." She stared at him, but he didn't react. "Don't you think that's odd?"

"Maybe." He took a big bite.

"Owen, come on."

"Could be a coincidence," he said around a mouthful of food.

"Two murder victims and a person who discovered one of the bodies, all randomly connected to the same yoga studio? That's not a coincidence, that's a pattern."

"Okay, well, assuming you're right, then what does it mean?"

She shook her head.

"I'll admit it's odd," he said. "But what are you saying? Someone's got it in for this yoga place?"

"I don't know."

"Or are you saying they're connected through this Cassandra woman, who happens to work there?"

"Maybe."

"Maybe what?" Owen sounded frustrated, and she didn't blame him. She was frustrated, too. With every clue they unearthed, it seemed things got more complicated instead of less.

She looked out the window, wishing she could put into words this feeling that something was off about Cassandra Miller. Nicole knew it in her bones, but she couldn't articulate what it was, exactly. Weirdly, Cassandra even *looked* like one of the victims, Danielle Ward. Nicole had mistaken Danielle for Cassandra the morning after the murder when she and Emmet had gone by the studio to interview her about finding Aubrey's body. Did the resemblance mean anything, or was it just another oddity about the two cases? Nicole felt sure there had to be a link between these deaths. She'd gone over to Cassandra's place yesterday afternoon for a follow-up, but Cassandra hadn't been home and then everything got derailed when Nicole ended up in the emergency room.

"Look, maybe you're right," Owen said. "I don't know." He finished off the second taco and balled up the foil. "I'm just telling you, if you plan to go to Brady with this, you better have at least a theory about what it means."

"Honestly," she said, "I have no idea what it means. But I'm certain it means something."

EMMET MOUNTED THE steps and looked out over the beach. The sun had broken through the clouds and people were out jogging again, despite the near-frigid temperature. He turned away from the view and rang the doorbell. When he heard footsteps on the other side, he held his badge up to the peephole.

The door swung open.

Scott Kinney had lost weight since his driver's license

photo four years ago. His skin was tan, and he had the sinewy look of a long-distance runner.

He nodded. "Detective."

"Mr. Kinney. Thanks for making the time."

"No problem. Come on in."

Emmet wiped his feet on the monogrammed welcome mat before stepping into a house that looked like something from *Architectural Digest*. Bleached wood floors, soaring ceilings, huge picture windows looking out over the beach.

"I just got off a conference call," Kinney said, leading him through the room. He wore faded jeans and an untucked white dress shirt. No shoes.

He glanced at Emmet as he passed a huge round table consisting of a piece of glass atop a driftwood pedestal. On it was an open laptop computer. "Want coffee or anything?" he asked.

"No, thanks."

The kitchen looked like one of those showrooms where all the appliances cost as much as a car. Kinney opened a Sub-Zero refrigerator and grabbed a bottle of water. He leaned back against the immaculate white countertop and twisted off the cap.

"How is the investigation coming?" Kinney asked, like they were talking about the weather.

"Fine."

He shook his head. "It's terrible about Aubrey. I don't think it's really hit yet."

Emmet glanced around, looking for any sign of anyone else living here. He saw no purse, or car keys, or stray pairs of shoes kicking around. No kids' toys or evidence of a pet.

He looked at Aubrey's boyfriend, who was twelve years her senior.

"How did you hear about Aubrey's death?" Emmet asked.

"Everyone was talking about it at the meeting yesterday." He set the water down without taking a sip. "I didn't believe it at first." He shook his head. "Still seems unreal."

"The AA meeting?"

"That's right."

"How often do you go?"

He made a face. "Less than I probably should. I try to make it when I'm in town. But I'm in Dallas a lot for work, and it's harder to get to one."

"What do you do?" Emmet asked.

"I'm in software sales."

"And your job's based in Dallas?"

"All over." He gave a shrug. "But I've been living here ever since my wife and I split."

"And how long has that been?"

He sighed heavily. "A year and a half. At first I was staying here at the beach house until I could get my own place set up. But so much of my work is remote, I just decided to base here. I like it better than Dallas."

Emmet glanced at the wall of windows overlooking the water. "I can see why."

Kinney watched him, his expression guarded. "So, have you guys determined what happened? I heard a rumor she was strangled?"

"We can't get into details at this time," Emmet said. Strangled? Had he just thrown that detail out as a distraction or had he really heard that? Emmet studied the guy's face until he crossed his arms over his chest and seemed to get uncomfortable.

"So, like I told the officer yesterday," Kinney said, "I flew to Dallas Saturday afternoon. My flight was at two fifteen. I can pull up my ticket if you want to verify it with the airline."

"We already did."

His eyebrows shot up. "You did?"

"I'd like to know more about Aubrey's state of mind on Friday. You spent the night with her, correct?"

"Right. We went to a meeting and then decided to grab dinner."

"Where'd you go?" Emmet asked.

"The Shrimp Hut. They were pretty busy, so we got our food to go and came here."

"And when did Aubrey leave?"

He looked at his feet and rubbed the back of his neck. "I don't know. Probably around ten thirty? I took her back by the church to pick up her car. She said she had a bunch of errands to do that day."

Emmet watched him closely. So far, everything he was saying fit with what he'd told Adam. And it also fit with the facts they had already gathered.

"What about her demeanor?" Emmet asked.

"Demeanor?"

"Yeah, did she seem upset to you? Distracted? Stressed out about anything?"

"Well, no. I mean, we'd just come from an AA meeting, so there was the usual baggage."

"Such as?"

"Ah, God. How much do you want to know? I mean, she had shit with her parents, like everyone. Also, she lost her brother to drugs a few years back, so she'd been through some depression."

"What about problems with an ex-boyfriend?" Emmet asked. "She mention anything to you or maybe in the meeting?"

"No."

"Anything at all?"

He shook his head.

"What about financial problems?" Given the timing of

her asking for a raise at work, Emmet was wondering if Aubrey owed someone money.

"She never said anything. I mean, I paid for everything whenever we were together, and she seemed cool with that. She had a crap job, so . . ." He shrugged.

"So . . . no money issues, that you know of? No guy problems?"

"Well, no *boyfriend* problems. She might have had some guy stuff."

Emmet's attention perked up. "How do you mean?"

"Well, she sometimes complained about men hassling her at the bar. You know, the customers grabbing her ass and all that. It was one thing she hated about her job. The 'creepers at work' she called them. Sometimes they would wait around after her shift." He frowned. "One guy even followed her home a couple nights ago. She told me she wanted me to drive to dinner, just in case he'd followed her to the meeting."

"This was on Friday?"

"Yeah. Sorry. I forgot about this until just now. She mentioned it when we were headed to dinner, so we took my car."

"What about hers?"

"She left it there at the church where the meeting was. Then I dropped her off the next morning to pick it up."

Emmet's pulse was thrumming now. "So, you're saying on *Friday night* she was worried some guy might be following her?"

"Yeah." He swallowed, looking guilty as if he was just now absorbing the potential importance of what he was saying.

"Did Aubrey know this guy's name?" Emmet asked.

"No. Just that he drove a black SUV."

"A black SUV?"

"Yeah, she said it was a black Tahoe."

* * *

NICOLE HOOKED HER purse over her shoulder and grabbed her crutches.

"Sure you don't mind?" she asked Adam.

"Not at all. It's on my way."

He looked worried as he watched her get to her feet. She crutched across the bullpen, navigating her way through the cubicles. As she neared the door, Brady stepped out of his office and frowned at her.

"You have a minute?" he asked.

"Um, sure." She glanced back at Adam.

"I'll wait outside," Adam said.

"Thanks."

She followed Brady into his office and was startled when he closed the door.

"How's the ankle?" he asked.

"All right," she said, deciding to stand since he was standing, too.

"I'm putting Owen in charge of the Danielle Ward case."

She nodded. "He mentioned that. I have to say, I was a little surprised."

"You've got enough to deal with with your injury."

"Yeah, no. It's not that I wanted to lead the case," she said. "I just assumed Emmet would lead it. Since it's most likely connected to the Aubrey Lambert thing."

Brady folded his arms over his chest. "How?"

"Well . . . the yoga studio. Both victims were affiliated with the Banyan Tree. One was a teacher, one was a student."

Brady sank into his desk chair and looked up at her. "Danielle taught at the martial arts academy, I thought."

"She taught at both, actually. And it's all one place. Danielle and her partner own it together. And then there's

Cassandra Miller, who *works* at the Banyan Tree and also happened to find the first victim dead in her car."

Brady watched her, and she couldn't tell whether he'd connected these dots previously or not.

"What's your theory?" he asked.

"*My* theory?"

"You think these murders are linked. How? Are you saying the killer knows all these women?"

Nerves filled Nicole's stomach as she watched the chief's expression. He looked skeptical. Brady always looked skeptical, but right now even more so than usual.

She cleared her throat. "That's a possibility, yes. That the killer knows all of them. Or maybe he has some connection to the studio. Or maybe he's targeting women from there, for some reason."

"So, a serial killer, then."

"Well, no." It sounded far-fetched when he said it out loud. "Technically, a serial killer is a minimum of three deaths. And I'm not saying that's what we're dealing with. For one thing, these aren't sex crimes, in the traditional sense."

"No rape," he said.

"Right."

His frown deepened. "You know what I always say about motive."

"Sex, money, exposure."

The three most likely motives for crimes—a mantra that Brady came back to again and again. And although he had decades longer than she did on the job, Nicole had also found his mantra to be true.

"So, which do you think it is here?" he asked.

Her nerves started up again. "I don't know yet. I'm still working that out. But you can't deny the connection."

"Could be a coincidence."

She wanted to argue with him, but she clamped her mouth shut.

He shook his head. "You know, my first ten years on this job we had *one* homicide. Guy who got drunk and went after his wife's boyfriend with a shotgun. *One* murder in the first ten years." He sighed. "Now, our population's tripled. We've got a steady stream of drug traffic, shootings, sexual assaults." He shook his head. "We're on our second murder this year, and we're not even out of February."

Nicole just looked at him. He sounded . . . *sad*, almost. And nostalgic for a better time. And she didn't know Brady did nostalgia. He'd always been so straightforward, so no-nonsense. Get out there and get shit done, no excuses.

He stood up. "Go home, Nicole. Take care of that ankle."

"I will."

"I want you to take some time off."

"Sir?"

He rested his hand on her shoulder. "Take a few days. Come back Monday."

"But . . . what about the Aubrey Lambert case? And Danielle Ward?"

"We'll cover them. You need to take care of your health. You can't take it for granted."

Her stomach clenched. "Sir, I'm fine. Seriously. My ankle's healing, and I've got work to do. Emmet needs my help with the investigation and—"

"This is Emmet's call."

She drew back. "Excuse me?"

"Emmet's the lead and this is his call. He thinks you need to take some time to rest, and I agree with him."

"But . . . I can't just—"

"You can, Nicole, and you will." He stepped around her and opened the door. "Take the weekend off. We'll handle things here."

* * *

EMMET'S PHONE BUZZED as he was getting in the shower. It couldn't be his food delivery—he'd just placed the order. He dunked his head under the hot spray and let the water sluice down his back. He'd hit the gym after work in an effort to blow off some steam, but it hadn't helped, and the ball of tension that had been sitting in the pit of his stomach for days now was still there.

Six days in.

And he still didn't have a suspect. With every hour that ticked by, everything got more complicated. And no matter what he did, he couldn't get rid of the ice-cold certainty that he was missing something critical, and until he figured out what it was, nothing he did was going to bring this case into focus.

Another call came in, and he leaned out of the shower. His phone was on the edge of the sink, and he saw the number lighting up the screen.

He yanked a towel off the rack and stepped out to grab it. "Hello?"

"Why aren't you answering?" Nicole demanded.

"I was in the damn shower. What's wrong?"

"What's *wrong*? What's wrong is Brady just sent me home and told me to take the weekend off."

Emmet ran the towel over his head. "Yeah?"

"He also told me you want me off the case."

"I do."

"What the hell, Emmet?"

"Hang on." He set the phone down and wrapped the towel around his waist. "There have been some new developments. I talked to Scott Kinney. Do you know who that is?"

"Yeah, Aubrey's boyfriend. Adam told me about him."

"He's the man Aubrey spent Friday night with." Emmet

leaned back against the sink. "I went over to his house to interview him, and he said Aubrey mentioned that some guy had been tailing her around, following her home from work, stuff like that, and that he drove a black Chevy Tahoe."

Silence on the other end.

"Nicole?"

"Okay. So Aubrey was being followed?"

"Possibly."

"What does that have to do with you kicking me off the case?"

"Nicole."

"What?"

"The person who almost hit you last night was in a black Tahoe."

"Emmet, are you serious right now? *That's* the problem?"

"Yes. It's a major problem."

"Why?"

He laughed. Was *she* serious right now? How was it that he was hyperaware of the potential danger she was in and she was ready just to shrug it off?

"Because there could be a connection between Aubrey Lambert's murder and you nearly getting run down last night," he said. "We don't fully know what's going on, and until we get to the bottom of it, you need to take a step back from the case."

More silence on the other end.

He could practically feel her hostility coming through the phone.

"Anyway, you're injured," he said. "You need a chance to recoup, so the timing works out."

She muttered something he couldn't hear, but he caught her tone.

"I understand you're annoyed," he said.

"*Annoyed? Try furious!*"

"Nicole—"

"Are you out of your freaking mind, Emmet? We have *two* homicide cases in our laps now. And every one of us is stretched paper thin. You're slammed, me and Owen are up to our eyeballs, and Adam isn't even officially a detective yet. This is no time for *any one of us* to be taking a vacation!"

Emmet gritted his teeth. He'd known she wouldn't be happy, but she was just going to have to deal with it. He wasn't going to budge on this.

"Listen, it's not that big a—"

"No, you listen," she said. "I don't appreciate you going around me and talking to Brady about my work behind my back. Just because you're the lead on this case doesn't make you my boss. And anyway, this is a boneheaded plan! We're almost a week in and we don't even have a suspect yet, which means we need more help, not less."

Frustration filled his chest, and he stalked into his bedroom. "Yeah, well, it's been decided, so deal."

"'Deal'? That's it? That's all you can say?"

"Yeah. It's my case, so it's my call."

Silence again, but this one sounded different from the rest. Had she really just hung up on him? He looked at his phone. She had.

"*Fuck.*"

CHAPTER
TWENTY

"I'M SURPRISED YOU'RE not happy," Kate said over the phone.

"Why would I be happy about being sidelined in the middle of a major case?"

Nicole sank onto her bed and leaned her crutches against the nightstand.

"Well, you're always talking about getting called out on weekends and having no social life. Maybe you can actually relax for a few days."

Relax. Right. Nicole reached for her shorts on the floor and yelped when a bolt of pain shot up her leg.

"You okay?"

"Yes." She squeezed her eyes closed. "I just tweaked something."

"See? Brady's right. You need a break right now."

"I'm fine."

"Nik, you're not *fine*. Come on. You've been through an ordeal. I'm surprised you're not freaking out like Emmet, and the fact that you're not tells me maybe you're just a little too immersed in your work. I mean, *hello?* You could have easily been killed yesterday."

"Well, I wasn't."

Her sister sighed. This conversation was going in circles, and it was time to jump off.

"Kate, let me let you go, okay? I just got home, and I'm trying to change clothes."

"Sure. Call me if you need anything."

"I will."

"I mean it. It's okay to ask for help, you know. You don't have to do everything by yourself."

It sounded so much like what Emmet had said to her just the other night, only he'd been talking about work. Nicole didn't like relying on other people. She'd always strived to be self-sufficient—which made it all the more exasperating that she had this injury to deal with.

After hanging up with Kate, she set her phone on the nightstand. Carefully this time, she leaned forward and grabbed her favorite shorts off the floor—the loose cotton ones with sunflowers all over them. They were the easiest thing she had to pull on and off over her big boot. She wiggled into the shorts and then flopped back on the bed and stared up at the ceiling.

Frustration churned around inside her. She knew Kate was right—to an extent. Last night *had* scared the hell out of her, and every time she thought about it, she got this panicky feeling like someone was reaching inside her and squeezing her lungs in a big fist. So, yeah, she'd been on edge today, maybe a little snappy. Even David had commented on it.

But work was her comfort zone. She was good at it. And whenever she felt unsettled with some aspect of her life, she dove headlong into her job to distract herself. Now, though,

Emmet and Brady had yanked that option away. What the hell was she going to do for three whole days?

"Screw it."

She grabbed her crutches and pulled herself up. What she *wasn't* going to do was sit around and mope. The case needed her. Both cases did. And if she couldn't show her face at the police station, then she'd work remotely. She could start by catching up on the reports she hadn't had time to read because she'd been too busy interviewing witnesses and driving back and forth to the crime lab. Maybe she'd find some key nugget of information that everyone else had overlooked. She had no idea what it might be, but she knew—she *knew*—that these two homicides were connected in some way, and she was determined to figure out the link.

Nicole grabbed her computer bag off the sofa. Hitching it onto her shoulder, she crutched over to the bar. She slid David's flower arrangement aside and took out her laptop.

A knock sounded at the door, and Nicole turned to look at it.

Damn.

She took a deep breath and crossed the living room. Peering through the peephole, she confirmed what she'd suspected. She opened the door, and Emmet strode inside.

"What are you doing here?" she asked.

"I'm here to finish the conversation we were having when you hung up on me." He stared down at her, hands on hips. He wore a faded gray T-shirt and jeans, and he hadn't even bothered to put on a jacket.

"I have nothing more to say." She closed the door and crutched over to the sofa. The basketball game was playing at low volume. She propped her crutches against the armchair and lowered herself onto the couch.

"Nicole."

"What?"

He sat down on the arm of the sofa. "What is *with* you?"

"Nothing."

"Look at me."

She glared up at him. His hair was still damp from his shower as if he'd rushed straight over here.

"You hung up on me," he said.

"Yes."

"Don't you think you're being a little immature?"

She reached for the remote and turned up the volume.

He rolled his eyes.

She gazed at the television, fuming. Had he come all the way over here just to rub her nose in this? She stared at the game, pretending to watch as she ignored the smell of his bodywash.

He propped his ratty sneaker on her coffee table and bent his head down, forcing her to make eye contact.

"What?"

"The thing is, *I'm* the lead here," he said. "And I have to think about the safety of you and everyone else on this team."

"I appreciate the thought," she said, matching his calm, reasonable tone. "But, unfortunately, we don't have that luxury right now given that we have two active murder investigations and no suspects."

His jaw twitched, and she could tell she'd hit a nerve.

"And anyway, I'm capable of assessing my own risks," she said. "I don't need you to do it for me."

"Maybe you do."

Anger swelled inside her. "No. I don't. That's part of what I signed up for when I became a cop. And as I already *told you*, I really don't appreciate you treating me different than Owen or Adam or any other man I work with."

"Well, I don't appreciate you keeping shit from me," he

said. "Like the fact that you noticed some guy tailing you around town. Kate told me about that."

"So?"

"So, don't you think that might be something you want to let me know? We're in the middle of a homicide investigation. *Two* homicide investigations. Why did I have to learn that from your sister?"

She shook her head. "You still don't get it."

His eyebrows shot up. "Don't get what?"

"Emmet. We work in a small town. Running into guys I've arrested comes with the territory. It happens to me all the time. Same for people I'm investigating, or people who don't like me, or people who don't like cops for whatever reason."

"Nicole, a black SUV—most likely a Tahoe—tried to run you down last night. And we have reason to think one of our murder victims was being tailed by a black Tahoe."

"That has nothing to do with this."

"How the hell can you say that?"

"Because. The person I saw following me was in a silver *car*. Last night's incident was a sport utility vehicle. And anyway, black SUVs are everywhere. You have no proof that those incidents are related. It could have just been one of the many local dirtbags who has a beef with me."

His mouth tightened. "Well, I'm going with worst-case scenario because that's how I am."

She shook her head and looked at the TV. She reached for her plastic cup of water, but it was empty.

"When's your next pill?" he asked.

"Never." She glanced at him, and his brow furrowed with concern. "They make my head fuzzy, so I quit taking them."

He watched her for a long moment.

Then he got up and went into the kitchen, and she saw

him look at the flower arrangement. Her stomach tightened as he stared at the little white envelope by the vase.

Nicole looked at the television, emotions pinging around inside her as she listened to him moving around in her kitchen. He returned with a pair of cold Coronas.

"Here."

He handed her a beer and sat down on the sofa beside her.

She took a sip, then set the bottle on the coffee table and stared at the game.

"I know you're pissed off at me," he said.

"You're very perceptive. Maybe you should be a detective."

He sighed.

Okay, so she was being immature. She knew that. But this whole situation infuriated her. She didn't like being told what to do by anyone, but she could handle it coming from her boss. She *couldn't* handle it coming from Emmet. They were equals, and he was using his position as lead detective to manipulate Brady into sidelining her.

"Nicole, look at me."

"What?"

"Would you look at me, damn it."

She did, and the intensity in his eyes made her stomach fill with nerves.

"Last night on the phone when I heard you scream"—he shook his head—"my heart fucking stopped."

Her throat tightened. She watched his face, trying to read everything there. She'd thought he was frustrated with her, but it was more than that.

He picked up her hand and pressed her palm against his sternum. "I couldn't breathe, Nicole."

She stared at him, absorbing the solid heat of him through his T-shirt.

"Do you understand what I'm saying?"

She couldn't speak.

He leaned forward, and her pulse skittered as his attention dropped to her mouth. And then he kissed her, settling his lips on hers.

Nicole's mind reeled as his tongue slid against hers. Emmet was kissing her. And she wasn't drunk or dreaming or high on pain meds. His mouth was warm and avid, and she tasted her beer on his tongue. He eased her back against the cushion, and she made a soft noise that was part surprise and part immense relief.

His palm settled on her thigh, and she felt the heat of it everywhere.

"Nicole. God."

He kissed her harder, and she ran her fingers into his thick hair that was still damp and cool from the air outside. He slid his hand up her leg, and a warm shudder moved through her. She tucked her fingers into the waist of his jeans to pull him closer. He tasted so good again and he smelled amazing, and she wanted to inhale him, even though two minutes ago he'd made her want to smack him. How did he do this to her? She wanted to push him away and also consume him—both at the same time.

She pulled back to look at him, and the intensity in his eyes sent a jolt of yearning through her.

"You okay?" He glanced at her boot.

She shook her head.

"No?" His face fell.

"Could you just—" She leaned forward. "I need to prop it up."

He scooted over, and she lifted her boot onto the sofa and settled back against the cushion. "Better."

He waited a moment, and she could see him trying to figure out how to best position himself. He shifted closer and leaned over her, gazing down at her as he stroked a finger over her cheek.

And then he kissed her again, and it was gentle and sweet, and once again she felt a flood of emotions. She reached up, curling her fingers into his hair as his hand glided under her sweatshirt and grazed her ribs on the way to her breast. No lace this time, but he stroked her through her bra, making a little circle with his thumb, and she whimpered at the sensation. He undid the clasp and pushed her sweatshirt up, and cool air wafted over her. She'd always been self-conscious about her smallish boobs, but the hungry way he was looking at them gave her a burst of confidence, and she tugged the bra and sweatshirt over her head and tossed them on the floor.

He closed his eyes briefly, and then he was leaning over her again, kissing her lips before making a line down her neck and over her collarbone. He wrapped her breast in his palm and his hot mouth closed over her nipple.

Desire seared through her, and she made a little moan as she pressed against him. It was like last night, but even better because it was bare skin, and God, he knew just how to use his tongue and his hands to turn her on. She closed her eyes and tipped her head back.

"Nicole?"

"Hmm?"

"Is David coming over?"

Her eyes flew open, and it was like being doused with cold water. "No."

He pushed up on his hands. "You sure?"

She propped herself on her uninjured elbow, and his gaze darted to her bare breasts.

"We broke up."

He stared down at her, and something flickered in his eyes.

"What's wrong?" she asked.

He bent down and gave her a quick kiss. "Hold on to me."

"What?"

He took her hand and curled it around the back of his neck. Then he scooped her up off the sofa with one swift motion.

"Oh my God." Her heart made a little lurch, and she gripped his shirt as he carried her through the living room. "Watch my—"

"I know." He stepped sideways through the doorway, taking care not to bump her boot as he carried her down the hall and into her bedroom. It was messy and dark, and the light from the closet spilled out over all her discarded clothes on the floor. He set her down in the middle of the unmade bed and then reached over and grabbed a pillow for her boot. He propped it under her foot, then gazed down at her with a simmering look.

A lock of hair fell over his face as he leaned over her. "Want to watch TV?"

She blinked up at him. "What?"

He smiled. "Kidding." He traced his thumb over her chin and his smile faded. "But seriously . . . we don't have to do this now." He glanced at her ankle. "I don't want to hurt you."

"You won't."

His eyebrows arched. "You sure?"

"I'm sure."

CHAPTER

TWENTY-ONE

EMMET STARED AT her, and she realized the absurdity of her words. She was fairly sure he *would* hurt her. Badly. This whole thing was emotional suicide, which was why she'd resisted it for so long. She was about to end ten years of joking, and banter, and healthy competition—all things that had helped them both excel at their jobs. They'd established a professional equilibrium that was tried and true— and she was about throw it all away, forever.

But she didn't care. All she cared about was that he was back in her room again, and she wanted him to stay. She pulled him down, and he was kissing her with so much pent-up need, and she refused to think about the repercussions. She'd spent years ignoring her attraction to him and keeping her feelings locked tightly away. *Ten whole years*, but now she didn't think she could wait another minute to know what it would be like with him.

She tugged at the hem of his shirt, and he yanked it over his head. Then he turned and took off his boots, and her pulse kicked up another notch as she heard the dull *thud* of them hitting the floor. He took off his jeans and stretched out beside her on the bed in only his black boxer briefs, and she felt a flood of anticipation.

Emmet was in her bed.

He scooted closer, close enough for her to feel the heat coming off his skin, and she ran her fingers over the muscles of his shoulders and chest. She'd seen him with his shirt off over the years—of course she had—and she'd even seen him change clothes a few times at some rain-soaked, backwater crime scene. But being alone with him and having a chance to actually touch his body was a whole new level of temptation. She grazed her fingers over his chest, feeling the hair there, and he tensed as she traced a path to his navel and lower. She rested her hand on the hard ridge of his erection, and his eyes went dark.

"Is this a bad idea?" she whispered.

He cupped her breast and toyed with her nipple. "You want us to stop?"

"No."

He kissed her, hard, and relief surged through her as she felt all that energy that told her he wanted this—at least in this moment—just as much as she did. He eased over her, nudging her good leg open with his and settled his weight on her, and she moaned at the heavy heat of him. She ran her hands down his muscular back. He felt so good, every part of him, and she wished she could get on her knees and run her hands over his entire body.

He kissed his way down, pausing to give attention to her breasts—which he seemed to really *like*, if his approving groan was any indication—before sliding lower. She felt her sunflower shorts gliding down her legs, along with her underwear, and she sat up to watch as he carefully slid them over her boot with a look of intense concentration.

She laughed.

"What?" he asked, dropping her clothes to the floor.

"Just—nothing. You looked so serious."

His gaze moved over her, and all humor evaporated as the reality of what they were doing crashed over her. She was naked. With Emmet. He was drinking in the sight of her like he wanted to memorize everything.

He crawled over her and planted his elbows above her shoulders.

"You are so hot." He kissed her mouth, then her chin, then her neck, and butterflies swarmed in her stomach as he made his way down her body.

"Emmet."

He kept going, and she touched his shoulder.

"Emmet."

But he wasn't listening, and then she felt his hot mouth and nearly shot off the bed.

"Oh my God." She gripped his shoulders. "Emmet."

"Shh," he said, but it was more like a breath of air on her thigh, and then his mouth was back, making her crazy.

She needed him to stop. Soon. She wanted him with her when she came. But he was so intent on what he was doing, and so good at it, that she couldn't form words. The tension started to build inside her, and she felt a twinge of panic that this was going to be over much too fast, and she squeezed his shoulder.

"Emmet, *please*. Wait."

He kissed his way back up her body. "You want me to stop?"

"No, just—I want you with me."

He gazed down at her. "Got it."

He sat up and reached for his jeans on the floor, and she heard him ripping open a condom. He didn't need it really, but she kept her mouth shut as he got rid of his boxers.

And then the mattress shifted as he moved between her legs again.

"I don't want to hurt your ankle."

"You won't. Come here." She rested her hands on his waist and eased him toward her, and his gaze locked on hers as he adjusted her leg and pushed himself inside her. *Oh my God.* Sensation flooded every nerve ending as he pressed deeper than she'd ever thought possible.

"Nicole?" His voice was strained.

She made a little squeak that didn't even sound like her, and he started to pull away.

"No." She hooked her good leg around his hip and pulled him closer. "I like it."

Heat flared in his eyes, and then he was moving over her, watching her intently with those hazel eyes, as though he needed to see her reaction to everything. She ran her hands over his back, loving his warm skin and the flexing of his muscles under her fingers.

"Oh . . ."

"You like that?" His breath was hot against her ear.

She tried to respond, but her ability to form words was rapidly disappearing. She pulled him closer with every surge as the need inside her built and built until her vision started to blur. This was Emmet. *Emmet*, whose body she'd known so well for so long, but she'd never known him like this. Being fused together with him felt both strange and totally natural at the same time. Everything he did felt *so amazingly good*, and the hazy look in his eyes told her he felt it, too.

He leaned down and took her nipple into his mouth and suddenly it was too much, and she cried out and came apart. He gripped her hips and kept going through wave after wave, and then he made a final, shuddering push and collapsed.

For a moment she just lay beneath him, absorbing the solid weight of his body. Then he pushed himself up.

"You okay?"

She closed her eyes and made a little rasp.

He pulled out and rolled onto his back, dropping his arm over his eyes. "Fuck."

Nicole melted into the bed—a puddle of relief and pleasure. She wasn't sure she could speak. The aftershocks pulsed through her, but she still couldn't quite believe it had happened.

She turned to look over at him. He stared up at her ceiling, arms at his sides now, and she studied his profile.

He looked at her. An endless beat passed as she tried to think of what to say.

Then he smiled slightly. He sat up and got out of bed, and she watched him, overcome with awe as he crossed her bedroom in the dark. He disappeared down the hallway, and when he came back a few minutes later, he had her crutches. He propped them against the nightstand.

"You need anything?" he asked, reaching for his jeans.

He was leaving.

A cold feeling swept over her, and she realized she was utterly unprepared for how shitty this would feel. She sat up and reached for the sheet.

"I'm good," she said, tucking it under her arms.

He dug his wallet out of his pocket and put it on the nightstand.

Oh. So . . . maybe he wasn't leaving? Maybe he was just putting the condoms by the bed?

He lifted the sheet and slid in beside her, and the pang of hurt from three seconds ago dissolved completely.

God, she was a mess already.

She sat up on her elbow, her head still spinning as she stared at him in the dimness. How had this happened tonight, of all nights? When he'd showed up at her door, she'd been spitting mad. Now her body felt charged, and every nerve ending seemed to be singing with glee.

Of course Emmet would be good at sex. Why was she surprised? He was a natural athlete, and he was good at reading people. What she hadn't expected was the way he watched her so closely the whole time, every move, as though her response truly mattered to him.

He lifted an eyebrow. "What's that look?"

She bit her lip. Then she traced her finger down his front. "Again."

He laughed. "Right now?"

She nodded.

"You have to give me a minute."

He pulled her down and settled her beside him, tucking her head against his chest in a way that put a little ache inside her. His skin was damp from exertion, and she closed her eyes and reveled in it.

"You need a pain pill?" he asked.

"I'm not taking them." She stroked her finger down his chest, over his six-pack abs, then back up again. "They make my brain muddled." She looked up at him. "I don't want to make impulsive and ill-advised decisions."

He picked up her hand and kissed it. "Too late."

His tone was joking, but there was some truth in the words.

She shifted on the bed and tweaked her ankle. "Ouch."

"Nicole. Take a damn pill."

"I'm fine."

She closed her eyes and counted to ten, and the flash of pain faded to a dull throb. Emmet lay beside her in the dark and she listened to the steady thrum of his heart.

She sat up on her elbow again and looked at him.

"What?" he asked.

"Do you think this is a mistake?"

He groaned and closed his eyes. "Do we have to talk about this now?"

She just watched him, waiting for an answer.

He sighed and looked at her. "Maybe."

Her stomach knotted. It wasn't the answer she wanted to hear. But at least it was honest. Their relationship was fraught with complications, and always had been. The attraction was there, and the friendship, but everything else about this made their situation thorny.

At least he was being straightforward and not giving her some line so he could stay in her bed awhile longer.

She rested her hand on his stomach. "Will you promise me one thing?"

His eyebrows tipped up.

"Don't tell everyone."

His brow furrowed. "I won't."

"I mean it." She wanted him to understand how important this was to her. "If people find out, you look like a hero, but for me it's a career wrecker. I have enough problems getting the guys at work to take me seriously."

"Wow. You must think I'm a real asshole."

She could tell by his voice, he was pissed.

"No. I don't. But I know how things are."

He sighed. Then he turned and got out of bed.

Now was he leaving? She watched him with a hollow feeling in her stomach as he walked out of the room. She heard shuffling in the kitchen, and he came back with a glass of water and her medicine. He set the glass down, then twisted the cap off the pill bottle and shook one out.

She sat forward, and the sheet fell around her waist as she reached for the pill. She swallowed it and he handed her the water. It felt cool on her parched throat, and she tipped the glass back, draining it.

Emmet watched her, and the intense look in his eyes

sent a warm shiver through her. She knew what that look meant.

"Now?" she asked.

He nodded.

He rested his knee on the bed and leaned over her. He took the glass and set it on the nightstand.

Nicole slid down flat and gazed up at him in the dimness. She knew the answer to her question. She'd known it before she even asked. This *was* a mistake. But right now, she didn't care—she only wanted to feel him again.

"Come here," she said, and pulled him down for a kiss.

CASSANDRA TURNED INTO her parking lot, darting her gaze at all the shadows. The spaces near the front were taken, so she parked in a dark spot at the edge of the lot.

She gathered up her grocery bags, then looked around again before opening the door.

A man watched from the shadow of an oak tree. Tall, heavyset. A cigarette glowed in his hand. Cassandra didn't know his name, but he'd been coming around for months, and she was pretty sure he'd moved in with the lady in the unit behind her. The woman didn't let him smoke, apparently, and he was constantly skulking around outside, watching people coming and going and giving Cassandra the creeps.

Ignoring his stare, she trained her gaze on her door and strode up the sidewalk with her bags. After letting herself into her apartment, she locked the door and slumped back against it.

She could do this.

She had a plan.

She dumped her bags on the kitchen counter and went straight into the bathroom. After splashing water on her face, she went to her bedroom closet and flipped on the light. Rows and rows of empty shelves stared back at her. She grabbed her backpack off the floor and tossed it onto the bed. Turning back toward the closet, she paused in the doorway as a familiar scent wafted over her.

No.

Her heart skipped a beat as she identified the smell: Gucci Pour Homme.

She darted a look at the bed. The cheap comforter barely covered the mattress. She dropped into a crouch to look underneath. Nothing.

Get a grip. You have to get a grip!

She reached under the bed and dragged out the gym bag she'd stashed there. She dropped it onto the bed beside the backpack, then unzipped the main compartment and surveyed the contents.

Jeans. Socks. Wool sweaters that she hadn't worn in more than a year.

She rummaged through the clothes, and her hand closed around something smooth and hard. She pulled out the pistol and studied it. It felt heavy and awkward in her hand—not surprising, really. It wasn't hers, and she had never even fired it. It had been a gift from Jess before she'd left.

Just in case, Jess had said.

Cassandra had taken it reluctantly, more worried about having a gun in her possession than actually needing to use it. But then everything went sideways, and she'd realized Jess was right.

A loud knock at the door made her jump and turn around.

Dear God, who would show up here at ten p.m.? She shoved the pistol back under the pile of sweaters. But then she changed her mind.

She crept down the hall, gripping the gun in her hand as she eyed the front door. Maybe it was that detective again. Or maybe it was Reese, wanting to know the plan for Danielle's funeral. Cassandra had been dodging phone calls all day.

Keeping her body near the wall, she leaned to check the peephole.

Alex Breda. She breathed a sigh of relief.

But her relief disappeared as she realized what this meant. Alex wasn't a part of her new plan. In fact, he could have nothing to do with it.

He looked straight at the peephole, clearly aware that she was standing on the other side of the door.

She glanced around frantically. She wanted to stash the gun back in her bedroom, but part of her wanted it close.

She stepped over to the counter where she'd dumped her grocery bags and grabbed the box of tampons she'd just bought. She opened the box and tucked the pistol inside, then stashed everything in the bag and slid all the groceries to the back of the counter near the microwave. There. Out of sight but accessible.

She returned to the door and took a deep breath before pulling it open.

Instead of the surfer-boy clothes she'd seen before, to-night Alex wore a dark suit and a dress shirt with the top button open. His charming smile was nowhere.

"Hi," she said, feigning confused surprise. "What brings you here?"

"I got your message."

He stood there staring at her, and nerves filled her stomach because she hadn't expected this now, and she wasn't prepared. For a tense moment she considered making something up.

He sighed. "Cassandra, I've been up since four a.m., I skipped dinner, and I just spent five hours in my car. You want to let me in, please?"

She pulled the door back, and he stepped inside.

TWENTY-TWO

A LEX TOOK A long look around her living room, no doubt picking up every strange detail, and she realized she'd never had a man in her home.

Not this home, at least.

"Do you . . . want something to drink?" she asked, mainly to distract his attention from his survey of her apartment.

"No."

"Are you sure?" She walked around him to the kitchen. "You said you skipped dinner."

"I'll get something later." He glanced at his Rolex, then ran a hand through his thick hair.

She stood beside the bar that separated the kitchen from her nearly empty living room, not sure of what to do or say. But she had to say something, and fast.

"Well, I'm really anxious for an update." She leaned back against the counter. "You know, about the will? It's been almost a week now, and I thought maybe you'd have something."

He leaned his hip against the counter and watched her, those blue eyes taking in everything.

"Bullshit."

"Excuse me?"

"Cassandra, I've been practicing law for ten years. I deal with liars all day long. And—no offense—you're not very good at it."

Her chest tightened. She forced herself to hold his gaze, and not to fidget, as she tried to come up with another story.

"Is this about Aubrey Lambert?" he asked.

Her stomach dropped. What did he know about Aubrey? She stared at him wordlessly for a moment, and then made herself respond.

"Why do you say that?"

"My brother mentioned you were involved in the case," he said.

"Your brother?"

"Owen Breda. He's a detective with Lost Beach PD."

His *brother* was a police detective. Of all the lawyers she could have picked . . .

Cassandra's chest constricted and the room seemed to tilt.

"Whoa." Alex reached for her arm as she swayed on her feet. He grabbed her elbow and steered her into the living room. "You need to sit down." Her body hit the futon with a graceless *squish*. "You okay?"

She nodded, leaning her head into her hand.

Alex walked into the kitchen, and she squeezed her eyes shut, trying to pull herself together. How did this keep getting worse? With every day that went by, another anvil fell out of the sky.

"Here." He stood over her now with a glass of water.

She took it.

He sat down beside her on the futon. "Drink," he said.

She drank.

Then she put the glass on the floor beside her foot because she didn't have a coffee table or any other furniture in here.

"Cassandra."

She looked at him. Her pulse was racing now, and she knew her panic must be written all over her face.

"Whatever trouble you're in, I can help."

He sounded so calm. And capable. She wanted desperately to believe him. And then the side of his mouth ticked up.

"I told you, I'm a problem-solver. That's what I do."

She looked away—she had to. She couldn't look at his handsome face while she was trying to make rational decisions.

"Talk to me."

She took a deep breath. Held it in for three seconds. Exhaled.

"I don't know where to start," she said.

He nodded. "Start at the beginning."

She stared at him, studying his clear blue eyes. He looked intelligent. He had to be if he was a lawyer, right? Cassandra hadn't even gone to college. Maybe if she had, maybe if she'd had an education to rely on instead of her looks, she wouldn't have gotten herself into this mess.

She cleared her throat. "The first time we met . . . I asked you about attorney-client privilege."

He nodded.

"That applies to whatever I tell you, correct?"

"Mostly."

"Mostly?"

"Well, for example, I can't help you rob a bank." His tone was joking, but his expression turned serious when she didn't laugh.

She swallowed. "I think I may be guilty of a crime."

Her heart skittered as soon as the words were out. God, she was really doing this? Was she really confiding in him? Once she did, there was no going back.

She studied his face, but he didn't seem to react.

"You don't look surprised," she said.

He tipped his head to the side. "I actually hear that a lot."

"Oh."

She looked down at her Reebok sneakers. She didn't have class this week, but she'd been walking around in workout clothes anyway, mainly out of habit. The whole week had been like a waking nightmare.

"You were starting at the beginning?" he prompted.

"Right. So . . . I told you about my name and how I switched to my maiden name after I filed for a divorce."

"Because you needed a change."

"I did. But that was only part of the reason." She paused, watching his face carefully. "My husband is Malcom McVoy."

His face showed no reaction.

Alex shook his head. "Never heard of him."

"He's been in the news some. At least, his company has, McVoy Systems. Anyway, after my lawyer served Malcom with divorce papers, I decided to drop off the radar."

"You went into hiding?"

"I basically left town and did everything I could to cover my tracks and not leave a trail. I had to go somewhere where he couldn't find me. The divorce blindsided him, and I couldn't be there for the fallout."

Alex watched her, as though he was trying to read between the lines. "Was he abusive?"

"Not physically. But in other ways."

"He was controlling?"

She laughed. She didn't know why—it was just such an *understatement*.

"Controlling in the extreme," she said. "He controlled all the money, the credit cards. He tracked my every move and was constantly spying on me—"

"Spying?"

She bit her lip. Interesting that he'd zeroed in on that one particular word.

"He has a thing for spyware," she said. "And he uses it to . . . let's just say *influence* the people around him."

Alex's brow furrowed. "So, am I to assume you've been keeping up with him through your divorce lawyer? When did you file?"

"Six months, three weeks, and five days ago."

His eyebrow arched.

"And, yes, I have been communicating through my attorney, who swore that he would keep my whereabouts secret from Malcom. Attorney-client privilege and all that. But I've come to the conclusion that he sold me out."

Alex leaned forward. "Your *lawyer* did?"

"That's the only way I can figure that Malcom could have found me down here. I left my phone and credit cards behind. I stopped using my email and social media. I removed the tracking device from my car."

"A tracking device?"

"I told you, spying is *his thing*."

Alex frowned. "Is there a chance he found you through one of your friends, maybe?"

She scoffed. "Friends? I don't have any." She had one, but she wouldn't tell anyone about Jess, not even this new lawyer, who by all appearances seemed trustworthy. "When I say he's controlling, I mean *every* aspect of my life." She paused. "Being a man, you probably can't imagine. Just trust me on this."

"Okay." He paused. "And what, exactly, made you need to drop off the radar?"

She picked up the glass and took a long sip. This was where things got sticky. She needed to choose her words carefully, even with someone who claimed to be on her side. Trusting an attractive man was what had gotten her into this in the first place.

"My husband has a very lucrative business," she said. "Some of it also happens to be illegal. I found out about it, and that's when I decided I had to get out."

"How did you find out?"

"His accountant. She'd been doing our taxes for years, and she came to our house one day and told me she'd discovered Malcom was running two sets of books to conceal his operation. She was thinking of turning him in and wanted my help. I think she thought if we reported his operation together, we could make a stronger case and ensure ourselves immunity."

"His operation?"

"The illegal one." Cassandra didn't elaborate, and she didn't plan to. She felt like she was risking her neck enough just talking about this at all, much less providing key details.

"What did you do when you found out?" he asked.

Cassandra thought back to the screaming fight they'd had in the middle of her kitchen. It was nine at night. Malcom was away on business and the maid was gone, and Cassandra had been about to get into the tub with a book and a glass of wine when Isabel showed up at her door to drop a grenade in her lap.

"I basically called her a lying bitch and told her to go to hell."

Alex's eyebrows tipped up.

"I knew she was sleeping with my husband."

"Your accountant was?"

"Yes. So when she showed up, I didn't want to hear anything she had to say, and it wasn't until four days later that I realized Isabel was telling the truth and I had to get out of the marriage."

"What happened four days later?"

Cassandra looked at her feet. The words seemed to get stuck in her throat.

Alex leaned closer. "Cassandra?"

"Four days later . . . she was murdered."

Alex stared at her. He rubbed his jaw.

"Malcom killed her," she added.

Cassandra had never said the words out loud, and they sounded strange. Dangerous, even.

"It was a hit-and-run, meant to look like an accident. I don't know who was behind the wheel, but whoever it was, it was Malcom's doing."

"You know this for a fact?" he asked.

"I know because I know. And I'm worried that makes me an accomplice."

Alex blew out a breath and looked at his expensive leather shoes. Bruno Maglis, six hundred dollars. Cassandra had bought Malcom a pair for Christmas two years ago.

She got up and went into the kitchen to refill her glass.

"Do you want something to drink? I have alcohol."

"No."

Alex joined her in the kitchen, watching her and looking pensive. She knew what he was going to say before he opened his mouth.

"What does any of this have to do with Aubrey Lambert?"

Tears stung her eyes at the mention of Aubrey. She glanced at the dream catcher in the kitchen window. It had been a birthday present.

Aubrey was Cassandra getting careless. Aubrey was

Cassandra making the mistake of thinking she could come down here, more than a thousand miles from her old life, and make a new start. Make a new life.

Make a friend.

Cassandra leaned back against the counter. "I believe he killed Aubrey, too. Or *had* her killed." She folded her arms. "Malcom doesn't like wet work."

"Wet work?"

"Anything with blood. He has people for that. Now, if it were *me* . . . maybe he would take a personal interest."

Alex just stared at her, probably wondering what on earth her husband's business was. He probably thought Malcom was in the mafia or something.

"Anyway, Malcom was in Denver the day Aubrey was killed. I saw his post on social media. So I think he sent one of his people down here on a mission for him."

She reached beneath the stack of junk mail sitting on the counter and pulled out the thick white envelope with her name printed across the front. She handed it to him.

"He sent me that."

"What is it?" Alex asked, opening the envelope.

"It's a sympathy card. It landed on my doorstep two days after I discovered Aubrey's body on a deserted beach during my evening run. *I* was the one to find her. And when I got this card, I knew all my worst, most paranoid, most irrational fears were happening."

"What fears?"

She watched him and knew he still wasn't really getting it.

"It's a warning murder. He killed her to send me a message."

Alex blinked down at the card. Then he placed it on the counter.

"If he viewed you as a danger to him—you could expose his criminality and land him in prison, correct?"

She nodded.

"If he viewed you as a danger, why not threaten you directly? Why come down here and go after your friend?"

"I think he knows it would raise suspicion if both his *mistress*—who also conveniently happened to be his accountant—and his *wife* suddenly turned up dead within a six-month period."

"Do investigators know about their affair?"

"Yes. He was questioned about their relationship when everything happened. I think something about her 'accident' raised some suspicion. That was when I went to see my first lawyer, and the advice he gave me is how I ended up here." She shook her head. "But now my divorce is stalled, my legal bills are piling up, and the person who was supposed to get me out of this whole thing just got me in deeper. I don't know what to do."

Alex ran his hand through his hair. He was watching her with that skeptical look she'd seen before—when she went to see that first lawyer, in fact. Very few people truly comprehended what Malcom was capable of.

A few men who worked for him knew.

And Cassandra.

And possibly Isabel. Although Cassandra didn't really believe Isabel had known. If she had, she never would have dreamed she could expose Malcom and get away with it. He had eyes everywhere, both human and digital.

Cassandra watched Alex's expression. Something flickered there—just for a moment—but she recognized it.

Doubt.

"You don't believe me," she said flatly.

"No, I do. I just—" He rested his hands on his hips. "Help me understand. You're saying he killed your friend as a veiled threat to you."

"Friends."

"Come again?"

"Aubrey." Her stomach clenched. "And . . . I think maybe Danielle, too? My boss. I don't have proof, though. Right now, it's just a hunch."

A depraved, paranoid hunch. Like everything else that had so far turned out to be true.

"A hunch based on . . . ?"

She swallowed. "Well, we're friends, for one thing. And we look alike. People are always mistaking us for each other, saying we could be sisters. I think he could be trying to make a point to me."

"You think he murdered two people to make a point to you?"

"I think it's possible."

Alex shook his head. "If you're right—"

If. He didn't really believe her.

"—what is the message he's sending?"

"It comes back to control," she told him. "He's saying, 'I can get to you *anywhere*. And there's no way you're getting out of this marriage alive.'"

Alex stared at her, and she thought that maybe, just maybe, her words were starting to sink in.

"It's a warning, Alex. He's telling me exactly what will happen if I insist on following through with the divorce. I'll have some kind of 'accident.'"

He tipped his head back and looked at the ceiling.

"What about Lucas?"

The question startled her. "My brother? What about him?"

"Was that real, or did you just want to get me to agree to work for you for cheap?"

"No."

"No?"

"No, I mean, *yes*, my brother is real. And he lives in a

group home in Arizona. He's one reason I can't just walk away from my marriage and never look back. I need money."

Alex stared down at her, and she could tell there was a debate going on in his mind. He prided himself on being a problem-solver, and she could tell he wanted to solve hers. But she also suspected he was regretting the day he invited her back to his office and agreed to let her drag him into the dumpster fire that was her life.

And for a discounted rate, even.

He was probably standing there right now, thinking of how he could get himself out of this. She couldn't really blame him.

"Here's the thing, Cassandra."

Her shoulders tensed. Here it came.

"You should have come to me earlier," he said.

Guilt gnawed at her. He was right. If she'd come to him sooner, and told him the truth, and asked him to help her go to the police, maybe Danielle would be alive right now.

Alex eased closer, pinning her with a stern look. "No more lies. I mean none, or I'm out."

She gazed up at him, letting the words sink in. *No more lies.* Not even lies by omission? That wasn't possible—she'd omitted a ton already. But she bit her tongue and nodded.

"I can't help you with your problem unless you're honest with me. Information is king in my business. You understand?"

"I understand."

"Okay." He nodded. "Here's what we're going to do."

TWENTY-THREE

NICOLE CAME AWAKE slowly. She registered the throb in her ankle. The patter of rain on the windowsill. Then warm weight lodged against her side.

Slowly, she sat up and blinked into the dimness. Judging by the light, it was early. But maybe it only looked that way because of the rain. Lucy slept soundly beside her.

Nicole reached for the phone on the nightstand and flipped it over. Eight forty-two.

She flopped back against the pillow and stared up at the ceiling as the night came back to her in cinematic flashes. Emmet sliding off her clothes. Hovering over her. Kissing his way down her body.

Emmet leaning over her and whispering goodbye before slipping out in the dark.

Another throb started up, deep inside her. What time was that? Had it been in the wee hours of the morning, after she'd drifted away in an orgasm-and-drug-induced haze? Or had he spent the night? And what had he said to her before leaving? She wished she could remember his parting words.

That was it, no more pills. She hated that her brain felt fuzzy, and hated even more that the details of her night with him were probably lost to her forever.

Sitting up again, she looked around her messy room. She grabbed a T-shirt off the floor and pulled it on, then collected her crutches from the nightstand and positioned them carefully before pulling herself up. Lucy got to her feet and stretched her spine before jumping off the bed and racing to the kitchen.

Three full days of no work. What was she going to do with herself? She stopped in the bathroom for a minute and then made her way into the kitchen, where the cloying smell of roses seemed to taunt her.

Her open laptop reminded her of what she'd been doing when Emmet showed up at her door and dragged her into an argument.

She glanced at the beer bottles sitting on the coffee table, and a cold feeling of dread settled over her.

Is this a mistake?

She remembered his face in the dimness.

Maybe.

It couldn't happen again. That was a given. There was no way she could maintain any kind of professional facade at work if she was secretly sleeping with Emmet. And there was no way for them to have a relationship openly while working for the same tiny police department. It wasn't only distracting, it was flat-out dangerous, and Brady would never stand for it. One of them would have to leave, and that definitely *wasn't* happening. Both of them lived for their job.

A sour ball formed in her stomach as reality sank in. She had become what she'd never wanted to be, one of Emmet's hookups.

Her phone chimed from the bedroom, and she looked back over her shoulder. She really needed coffee, but what if it was Brady calling to say he had reconsidered and he wanted her back at work?

Yeah, sure. Because the chief was so wishy-washy once he'd made a decision.

She crutched back to the bedroom and grabbed the phone off the nightstand.

Kate.

She connected the call. "Hey."

"Is he still there?" Kate whispered.

"Is who still here?"

"Nicole."

"What?"

"I swung by your place last night and saw his truck."

Nicole sighed. "He left this morning."

A squeal pierced her ear.

"Oh my God! *Yes!*"

"Calm down," Nicole said.

"Are you kidding me? You *slept* with Emmet, and you want me to calm down? You did sleep with him, right?"

She hesitated. But there was no getting out of it. "Yes."

"Well? How did it happen?"

Nicole put the phone on speaker and carefully balanced it in her hand as she took small steps toward the kitchen. She needed caffeine for this.

"We got in a fight," Nicole said.

"What?"

"We had this whole argument about—I don't know— work, I guess."

My heart fucking stopped.

Heat rippled through her as she remembered the look on his face when he told her that.

"Well, how *was* it?"

Nicole's throat felt tight. "Good," she said softly. "Really, really good. But then he left, so . . . I honestly don't know."

Silence on the other end.

"Hello?"

"Well. That's to be expected," Kate said. "It's a workday. I mean, you're not saying he sprinted out of there right after?"

"No, he stayed for a while."

Actually, Nicole had no idea. It could have been right after. But she was embarrassed to tell even her own sister that the man she'd been fixated on for an entire decade had had sex with her and fled.

Nicole wouldn't be able to look at him again. And yet she'd have to work with him *every day*. Side by side in cars. In meetings. In stuffy conference rooms surrounded by co-workers. Detectives, no less—people trained to pick up on cues and body language.

Who was she kidding? Even if Emmet kept his promise and stayed quiet, it was only a matter of time before everyone knew.

"Anyway, it was a one-off," she told Kate.

"What? Why?"

"Because we work together. This can't go anywhere."

"It already *is* going somewhere."

"No, it's not."

Kate sighed. "Nicole . . ."

"What?"

"Have you ever noticed that when bad things happen to you, Emmet is the first one to show up? Like when you were assaulted at that crime scene, or when you got rear-ended, or when you landed in the emergency room with a broken ankle?"

Nicole crutched across the kitchen, careful not to trip over Lucy, who was circling and making pitiful mewing noises. "That's because we work together and he's in the loop on my day-to-day."

"Yes. That's my point. He's in the loop and he's always looking out for you."

"We're cops. That's part of the job."

Another sigh. "Okay, whatever. Anyway, let's talk soon. I really want to catch up. Are you free tonight? We could get together for drinks. Or are you seeing Emmet?"

"I'm not seeing anybody. I'm in the middle of a big case." Her phone dinged with an incoming call. "Just a sec. That's the crime lab. I need to call you back."

"*Don't* forget," Kate said.

"I won't." She hung up and clicked over. "Hey, Miranda."

"Hi." She paused. "Did you get my text?"

Nicole looked down at her phone. She'd missed a slew of messages while she'd been sleeping in. *Damn pills.*

"I missed it. Sorry. What's up?" Nicole leaned her crutch against the counter and reached for the cabinet where she kept the cat food.

"We got the labs back," Miranda said. "They just came in."

Lucy jumped onto the counter. Nicole had moved her bowls higher so she wouldn't have to crouch down to feed her. She scooped food, and Lucy knocked her hand out of the way in her rush to the bowl.

"Which labs?" she asked Miranda.

"All of them."

Nicole's gaze landed on her coffee machine. The little green light was on, meaning someone had used it in the past two hours, before the automatic shutoff.

A spark of hope ignited inside her. He *had* stayed the night with her.

"Nicole? You there?"

"Yeah. Sorry."

"Well, you remember I swabbed the mirror, too, right? On the chance that even *if* he was wearing gloves, he might have touched his face or something, and deposited DNA on the mirror when he adjusted it."

"Yes?"

"Well, today is your lucky day," Miranda said. "We got a hit. This guy is in the system."

CASSANDRA PULLED THE wool sweater over her head and tossed it on the bed. It was too heavy. And itchy. She would be sweating bullets in the meeting, which would make her look guilty as hell.

She returned to the closet and surveyed her other choices. What little clothing budget she had had been spent on yoga clothes for work. But she couldn't show up for a meeting with the police in a hot-pink sport bra. Besides a wool sweater, her next best option was a long-sleeved workout shirt in a somber gray. She pulled it on and tucked it into her jeans, then stepped into the bathroom to check her reflection.

Her outfit was okay, but her face looked terrible. Her eyelids were puffy, and she was already getting that eye tic that happened when her nerves were frayed.

She stared at her reflection, and sure enough, there it was.

She squeezed her eyes shut. *How* was she going to do this? Alex's plan was crazy. And she couldn't believe she'd agreed to it. What had sounded so reasonable at eleven last night seemed ludicrous in the light of day. Alex Breda, with his deep voice and his *trust me* eyes, had persuaded her to scrap her plan and follow his instead. Using all his fancy legal terms, he'd convinced her that his plan had a chance of succeeding.

Not just a chance, a high probability.

But Cassandra didn't see it—she was a pessimist. Maybe because she knew a few things that Alex didn't.

Such as that her husband had no limits. There was nothing Malcom wouldn't do to maintain control. He needed control over his money, control over his image, and—since Cassandra impacted both of those things—control over his wife. This was a man who took the underwear from her laundry hamper and had it tested for DNA because he believed—wrongly—that she was having an affair. This was a man who got his own brother fired from his job after he'd said something embarrassing about Malcom's "humble roots" to a reporter. This was a man who had his accountant *hit by a truck* when he found out she planned to report his business to the feds.

Malcom's response to any problem that threatened his ego or his bank account was to lash out, to clamp down, to exert control and exact punishment. And his wife leaving him was the mother of all problems because it threatened everything.

Cassandra had understood that divorcing him wouldn't be easy, but she'd set this process in motion because she knew that the longer she waited, the more entangled they would become until she was neck-deep in his criminality and trapped in the marriage forever. She couldn't live like that, beholden to a man who had that sort of leverage over her and who spied on her every move.

She went into the kitchen and grabbed some ice from the freezer. Tucking the cubes into a napkin, she made a pack and pressed it over her eyelids.

She sucked in a breath and held it in. Then blew it out. She repeated the process over and over while reviewing the day's schedule in her head, envisioning every part of it going to plan. Maybe if she visualized success she could make it happen.

Her phone chimed from the bar, and she pulled the ice pack away.

Reese again.

Cassandra had told her she'd ride with her to the funeral tomorrow. They'd even agreed to go shopping together today for something to wear—which obviously wasn't happening now.

Cassandra dropped the ice into the sink and grabbed the phone. "Hi. Sorry I didn't call you back. I—"

"Cassie, did you hear?"

Her gut clenched. "No. What?"

"I just talked to Jeremy," Reese said with a wet sniffle. "He said he'd call you."

Jeremy taught tae kwon do with Paula, and Cassandra braced herself for more bad news.

"What happened?"

"I'm not sure, but . . . some detective just showed up at his door. He's interviewing everyone on staff, apparently. You and I are probably next on his list."

Cassandra swallowed. "Interviewing everyone about what?"

"There's a rumor going around that Danielle's car accident wasn't an accident at all. They're saying her brakes were tampered with."

Cassandra's throat went dry. "Her brakes . . . what?"

"Cassie, people are saying she was murdered."

E MMET SWERVED AROUND a truck and sped through the yellow light. He was late for the meeting, which wasn't a good look when he was supposed to be leading it.

His phone buzzed and he dug it from his pocket. Nicole.

"Hey, you're up," he said.

"I've been up."

The knot in his chest loosened. He'd been worried things might be weird with her today, but she was prickly as ever.

"How do you feel?" he asked.

"Fine. Where are you?"

"Heading into the team meeting. I'm late, actually."

"Well, I'm glad I caught you. Wait up, okay?"

"What?"

"I just pulled in."

Emmet turned into the parking lot of the police station and spied Nicole's pickup on the other side of the lot. Cursing, he parked on the end of the row as Nicole slid from the driver's seat and tucked her crutches under her arms.

She glanced up as he strode over.

"What are you doing here? You're supposed to be home," he said.

"I was. But the labs came in."

He squeezed between her pickup and the neighboring car and took a moment to look her over. Her hair was damp, as though she'd just gotten out of the shower, and she wore her denim miniskirt again with a thick blue sweatshirt.

"I talked to Miranda," she told him.

Her cheeks were flushed pink, and he had the sudden urge to kiss her—right in front of the police station, which she definitely wouldn't appreciate since she'd made him promise to keep everything top secret.

"What's wrong?" she asked.

"Nothing." He settled for tucking a coppery lock of hair behind her ear. "What did Miranda have?"

"We got a DNA hit," she said excitedly. "Remember the mirror in Aubrey's car? How it had been adjusted for someone taller?"

"Yeah?"

"Miranda took a swab and got touch DNA off the glass.

This guy is in the system." She reached across the seat and grabbed a file folder. "I printed him out."

"Who is it?"

"John Krueger." She handed him the file. "He's got a rap sheet in Colorado. That's *Boulder*, Colorado. He's thirty-two, ex-military. He got arrested for aggravated assault after getting into a bar fight six years ago and putting two guys in the hospital."

Emmet opened the file and scanned the arrest record, which included a mug shot. Krueger was white, heavyset, and had shaggy brown hair. He could have easily been the guy in the surveillance footage from Aubrey's apartment. Or he could have just as easily not have been. Impossible to tell.

"And that's not our only link to Boulder," Nicole went on. "You know that, right? Cassandra Miller happens to be from Boulder, too. Don't you think that's interesting?"

He glanced up from the paper. Nicole's eyes danced the way they did when she landed a big lead.

"Cassandra Miller, the yoga teacher," he stated. She was still hung up on this woman?

"Yes. But that's not her real name. Or not her full name, I should say. It's *Catherine* Cassandra Miller, married name McVoy. Her husband is Malcom McVoy, and he owns this multimillion-dollar tech company. They make surveillance drones for the Defense Department. The guy's loaded, it turns out. Which makes it weird that his wife is down in some Texas beach town teaching yoga."

Emmet closed the file.

"How's *that* for a coincidence?" she asked. "We need to tell Brady."

"I will. But you're not even supposed to be here. You're off, remember?"

"But—"

"You can have all the credit," he said, "but you'd better not show up to the team meeting."

She thrust her chin out.

"I'm serious, Nicole. Brady will be pissed. He wants you on leave."

"Fine." She reached in and grabbed another file folder from the passenger seat. "There's what I found on Cassandra Miller. No arrest record, but you need to look at her, too. I'm telling you, *she's involved* in this somehow. She's using a fake name, and the Boulder connection is too weird to be a coincidence."

Nicole turned back to her truck, and he watched with suspicion as she stashed her crutches inside.

"Where are you going now?" he asked.

She hitched herself into the driver's seat, and he held her elbow to steady her as she swung her boot inside.

"You said I'm not welcome at the team meeting. So fine. Go have your meeting. Just fill me in on any updates. The DNA is in, and they're expecting to hear back from the FBI today, too. Brady's contact was going to get those video clips analyzed, remember? Liam Shaunessy's clip could be critical."

Without further argument, she pulled on her seat belt.

Emmet rested his hand on the top of the door. "You're going home now, right?"

"Sure." She shrugged. "Brady's orders."

She definitely was *not* going home.

"Nicole—"

"You're late for your meeting." She reached for the door, and he stepped back. "Let me know how it goes."

TWENTY-FOUR

EMMET SLIPPED IN late and took the empty seat next to Adam.

"Glad you could make it." Brady checked his watch and tapped his pencil on the legal pad in front of him. "Where's Owen? He was supposed to be here ten minutes ago with his brother."

Emmet frowned. "Joel is coming?"

Joel was busy with the multiagency task force that worked out of the sheriff's office. Technically, he was still part of Lost Beach PD, but he hadn't been to a team meeting since Operation Red Highway.

"Not Joel. Alex," the chief said.

"Alex the attorney?"

"He wants to meet with us. Apparently, his client thinks she might know something relevant to our investigation."

Emmet stared at Brady, then glanced at Adam, who looked as confused as Emmet felt.

The conference room door opened, and Owen walked in with his brother close behind him.

"Sorry." Owen nodded at the chief. "Small delay."

Owen gestured to a chair at the end of the table, and Alex Breda pulled it out as he glanced around the room. In a dress shirt and tie, Alex looked like a Brooks Brothers version of his older brother.

"Thank you for meeting," Alex said, as though this whole thing had been set up for him.

And maybe it had been. Emmet had thought this was their regularly scheduled team meeting to catch up on the case, but what the hell did he know? Not like he was the lead detective or anything.

Emmet shot a glare at Owen, but Owen was staring at his brother with a look that Emmet couldn't read.

"So? Where is she?" Brady asked.

"Slight problem," Owen said tersely.

Brady shifted his attention to Alex.

"I'm afraid my client—"

"You mean Cassandra Miller, correct?" Brady interrupted.

"Yes. I'm afraid Ms. Miller is . . . unavailable to meet this morning."

"How come?" Brady demanded. "Wasn't this your idea?"

"Yes, actually. But—"

"She was supposed to meet us at the office," Owen said, cutting off his brother. "But she never showed."

Brady frowned. "Whose office?"

"Mine," Alex said.

"Did you try calling her?"

"She's not answering her phone or her door," Alex said. "And her car isn't there, so—"

"Wait." Emmet leaned forward. "Back up. *What* exactly is it that you think she knows?"

Owen looked at his brother, and some sort of silent communication passed between them.

Brady tossed his pencil on the table. "Do I need to remind everyone that this is a homicide investigation? What does this woman know about this case?"

"And are we talking about Aubrey Lambert's case or Danielle Ward?" Emmet asked.

Owen glanced at his brother before looking at Emmet. "Both."

Emmet slumped back in his chair. So Nicole was right.

"Somebody better tell me what's going on." Brady folded his arms over his chest.

Alex cleared his throat and scooted his chair forward. "Our intent was for Ms. Miller to give you a statement."

"About what?"

"In her absence, I can't get into much detail," Alex said. "But I *can* tell you she believes that both crimes may somehow be connected to her estranged husband."

"Malcom McVoy," Emmet said.

Brady looked at him. "Who?"

"Cassandra's husband." Emmet shook his head. "I can't believe it. Nicole totally called it."

"What does Nicole have to do with this?" Owen asked. "I thought she was on leave?"

"She is."

"Wait," the chief said, clearly losing patience. "We're talking about the yoga instructor, right? You're telling me she's married to someone named McVoy?"

"Malcom McVoy," Emmet said, "whose company in Boulder, Colorado, makes surveillance drones for the Defense Department."

Alex looked surprised. "You're already investigating him?"

"Nicole is. She's onto this whole thing." Emmet looked at Brady. "She connected the dots between Cassandra Miller—who discovered the first victim—and Malcom Mc-Voy. And she thinks he's somehow connected to a guy named Krueger—also from Boulder—whose DNA was found inside Aubrey Lambert's car."

Brady's brow furrowed. "When did we get that?"

"Just this morning," Emmet said. "The DNA results came back from the rearview mirror."

Quiet settled over the room as everyone absorbed this new info. For the first time, different puzzle pieces were starting to fit together. But the person who could probably make sense of the full picture was suddenly missing.

"So, you went by this woman's house? Cassandra Miller?" Brady asked.

"Yes, and she's not there," Owen told him.

"I'll try calling her again," Alex said, pushing his chair back.

He stepped out of the conference room, and Brady looked at Owen.

"Excuse me," Adam piped up. "Does it strike anyone else as weird that this witness who knows all this is suddenly MIA?"

"Yeah, I don't like it," Owen agreed. "Alex talked to her late last night, and she told him she'd meet at his office this morning before coming in to give us a statement."

Brady's gaze swung to Emmet. "Where's Nicole?"

It took him a moment to realize the chief was asking because Emmet had obviously talked to Nicole this morning and not because he'd spent the night at her house.

"Working from home," Emmet said, although he highly doubted it.

"Get her in here," Brady ordered. "She knows the witness better than the rest of us. Maybe she can figure out where to find her."

CASSANDRA PARKED HER car beside the dumpster and glanced up and down the alley before getting out. She hitched her backpack onto her shoulder, then walked to the back of the yoga studio and used her key to unlock the door.

"Hello?" she called, stepping into the dark hallway.

She locked the door behind her and switched on the light. A cart filled with used white towels sat against a wall. Cassandra made her way down the hallway, listening for any sign that she wasn't alone. She wasn't expecting Paula here—Danielle's funeral was tomorrow, and she was no doubt busy with logistics—but Cassandra kept on alert in case another staffer had dropped by. She crept past the laundry cart, listening intently, but the building was silent, and the faint scent of sandalwood incense hung in the air.

She paused at Danielle's office and tried the door. Locked. Then she walked past the restrooms and leaned her head into the changing room. Most of the lockers were open and empty. But the lockers on the end, which were reserved for staffers, were all closed.

Cassandra took a moment to check both restrooms to confirm that she was alone before returning to the changing room. She set her backpack on the wooden bench and quickly tapped in her code. The door to her locker popped open with a *snick*.

Cassandra's pulse thudded as she stared at the orange shoebox that she'd crammed into the space. She'd had to shove it in vertically. She pulled the box out and glanced around one last time before opening the lid.

Inside was a collection of items she'd hoped she would

never need: an envelope of cash, a passport, a pair of hair scissors. She nudged aside the box of Revlon Ultra Light Natural Blonde and found the backup burner phone that she'd purchased in August. She'd memorized the number but had never given it to anyone, not even Jess.

Cassandra tucked the burner phone into the zipper pocket of her backpack. Then she grabbed the passport and cash and dropped them into the main compartment with her clothes and her other cell phone. She started to zip the backpack but stopped, staring down at the hair dye. What the hell? It wouldn't hurt to have it along, just in case. She added it to her pack, then closed the empty shoebox and wedged it back into the locker.

Clink.

Cassandra froze. Her heart thrummed inside her chest as she listened. The noise had come from the lobby, it sounded like. Slowly, silently, Cassandra closed the door to her locker. Her backpack wasn't zipped, but she didn't want to risk making a noise. She picked up the backpack, holding it closed with her hand. She heard keys jangling as she crept toward the hallway.

"Yeah, I'm here now."

Reese.

"Let me call you when I leave. . . . Okay, bye."

Cassandra zipped the backpack and slung it over her shoulder before stepping into the hall.

"Hey."

Reese glanced up from her phone, startled. "Oh, hey. The door was locked. I didn't know anyone was here."

"I parked out back." She nodded down the hall. They rarely used the back door, but she hoped Reese wouldn't make an issue of it.

Cassandra stepped toward her. "You look nice today."

In truth, Reese looked like hell, same as Cassandra did.

She had clearly been crying. But instead of her usual active-wear, she was wearing black jeans, a pale pink sweater, and boots.

"Yeah, well . . ." Reese shook her head. "I'm headed to my parents' house. I just need to be home, you know? This week has been . . ." She trailed off.

"I know." Cassandra sighed. "Did you talk to Paula?"

"Yeah. She knows we're coming to the service tomorrow."

Cassandra felt a pang of guilt.

"Ten fifteen still okay?" Reese asked. "It starts at eleven."

"That's good, yeah."

Reese looked her over, seeming to notice her appearance for the first time. "Where are you off to?"

"Me?"

"Your backpack looks stuffed."

"Oh. Yeah. Just . . . doing some errands. I came by my locker to pick up some clothes I need to wash."

Cassandra's phone chimed, saving her from more questions. "I need to get that. I'll see you tomorrow, okay?"

"Sure."

Cassandra hurried down the hallway as her phone chimed again. *Alex.* Of course. She unzipped the backpack and switched the phone to silent and then pulled out her burner phone and pretended to answer the call in case Reese was watching.

"Hi, how's it going?" Cassandra pressed the phone to her ear as she unlocked the back door and stepped into the alley.

As the door swung shut behind her, she breathed a sigh of relief.

She hated lying to Reese.

She hated lying, period. And as Alex had pointed out last night, she wasn't very good at it.

She stopped to dig her keys out and turned to lock the door. A breeze kicked up, and the smell of garbage wafted over from the dumpster. Along with another smell.

Cassandra went still.

Gucci Pour Homme, Malcom's cologne.

Gravel crunched behind her. An urgent voice in her head screamed *Run!* but somehow her feet stayed cemented in place.

"Hello, Catherine."

The air in her lungs disappeared as something cold and hard pressed against the back of her neck.

Her heart pounded frantically. *He's going to shoot me. Right here by this dumpster.*

She thought of her brother's smiling face, and tears sprang into her eyes.

"Turn around."

She didn't move. Or breathe. Her pulse roared in her ears, and all she could think of was Lucas. *I'm sorry, Lucas. I'm so sorry.*

An arm reached around and plucked the phone from her hand.

Then a voice growled in her ear, "I *said*, turn around."

THE MAN WORE a stained undershirt and board shorts, despite the cold. His feet looked warm, though, in a pair of thick white socks inside his sandals.

"Mr. Gregus, how long have you lived at this address?" Nicole asked him.

He blew out a stream of smoke and squinted. "'Bout three months."

"And have you formally *met* Cassandra Miller?"

"Nope." He flicked his ash on the sidewalk. "But I know who she is. She teaches yoga at that place over by the doughnut shop."

This guy was creepy, and it wasn't just the way he slouched against the side of the building, watching people come and go as Nicole conducted the interview. He knew a hell of a lot about Cassandra's daily routine for a casual observer.

"And are you *sure* it was nine fifty when you last saw her?" Nicole asked.

He nodded.

"You're certain of this?"

"Yeah." He sighed. "She was getting in her car. The lady in 110 was out here, too, with her dachshund. You can ask her."

Nicole glanced back at the parking lot. According to this neighbor, Cassandra had a white Mustang that she typically kept parked at the corner of the lot, under the shade of a tree. She almost never drove it, he said, but she'd been getting into it this morning.

"Is that all?" He tossed his cigarette on the ground, and she gave him a pointed look.

Nicole's phone chimed, and she pulled it from her pocket. Emmet.

"One moment," she told the guy.

She crutched to the end of the sidewalk to answer the call.

"Hey, what's up?" she said.

"We've got a problem."

Her stomach tensed.

"Cassandra and Alex were supposed to come in so she could give us a statement," Emmet said. "She didn't show."

"Cassandra . . . and Alex Breda?"

"Yeah."

"A statement about what?"

Muffled noise on the other end of the phone. It sounded like Emmet was in a car with the windows down.

"Emmet?"

"Turns out you were right. Cassandra believes her husband may have something to do with the murders, so she went to Alex for legal advice."

A chill went down Nicole's spine. She moved a few more steps away from Cassandra's nosey neighbor.

"What exactly did she say?" Nicole asked.

"Nothing, yet. All this is from Alex. And he's been pretty cagey about it since this woman's not here to tell us herself."

"Well, where is she?"

"We don't know. Alex convinced her to come talk to us, but she never came in for the meeting, and now she's MIA. We're on our way to her place—"

"She's not here."

"What?"

"I came by the apartment to interview her again, and she's not here. Her neighbor says he saw her getting into her car—"

"Fuck."

"That was around nine fifty."

Nicole glanced over as an unmarked police unit pulled into the parking lot. She slid her phone into her pocket as Emmet whipped into a space and got out.

He shot a look at Cassandra's neighbor before walking over to her.

"I thought you went home," he said.

"Gimme a break."

Emmet glanced around the parking lot. "You say she left here around ten? That's an hour ago."

"He's eavesdropping," Nicole said in a low voice. "This guy lives in one of the first-floor units with his girlfriend. He told me he was out here smoking when Cassandra came out and loaded up her car."

Emmet frowned. "She *loaded* it?"

"He says she put a duffel and a couple grocery bags in the trunk, then went back inside for a backpack. Then she left."

"Damn it." Emmet raked his hand through his hair and glanced around. "She was supposed to meet Alex at his office at ten o'clock, but she never came."

"You think she skipped town?"

Emmet shook his head. "No idea." His gaze settled on her.

Nicole stared up at him.

"You were right," he said.

"About?"

"She's key to this whole thing. She thinks her husband has something to do with the murders."

"Why?"

Emmet's phone buzzed and he pulled it from his pocket. "Yeah?" He listened a moment. "Yeah, I'm here with Nicole. No luck. A neighbor saw her packing up her car this morning." He glanced back at the apartment building. "Okay, we'll head over there next."

He hung up the phone. "Come on. I'll drive."

E MMET SPED TOWARD the Banyan Tree as Nicole sat beside him, scrolling through text messages. He'd known she wouldn't go home and sit around waiting for updates—not when everything they'd been working on was finally coming to a head. Even injured, she was physically incapable of staying on the sidelines.

"Owen said he just got there, and the place looks closed," Nicole reported.

Emmet glanced at her in the passenger seat. With that clumsy boot on her foot, he was worried about her involvement right now. He worried about her all the time anyway, but her injury ratcheted things up to a whole new level.

She glanced at him. "What?"

"Nothing."

They had some talking to do, but now definitely was not the time.

He thought about her constantly. The situational awareness

that had been drilled into him throughout his police training applied to her specifically, almost like she was an extension of himself. There was no one else who commanded so much of his attention, and she'd been dead-on when she'd accused him of treating her differently from Owen and Adam and everyone else. He was always aware of her location, her activities, her level of risk. He knew she saw his protectiveness as an annoyance, like a big brother she didn't need, but the irony was that his feelings toward her were anything but brotherly.

Emmet whipped into the parking lot, which was only half-full. Most of the cars looked to be people coming and going from the doughnut store.

"Over there," Nicole said, pointing to the police unit parked beside a white SUV.

Owen and Adam stood on the sidewalk in front of the Banyan Tree talking to a woman with a long blond ponytail.

"Is that Reese?" Nicole asked.

"Looks like." Emmet pulled into a space and glanced at Nicole. "You need a hand?"

"I've got it."

She pushed her door open. Emmet reached into the back for her crutches, and she hauled herself to her feet as he jogged around the car and closed the door for her.

They approached Owen and Adam on the sidewalk, and Emmet could tell from the tone of Reese's voice that something was very wrong.

"Ma'am, are you *sure* she didn't have someone waiting for her?" Owen was asking.

"I don't *know*." Reese sounded stressed. "She told me she was running errands. I figured she was alone."

Nicole crutched over. "Hi, Reese. How's it going?"

She turned around and seemed confused to see two more cops approaching her.

"Sounds like Cassandra stopped by to retrieve some things from her locker," Owen said. "But now she's not here, and her car's parked in back."

"Her car is here, but she isn't?" Nicole asked, clearly alarmed.

"Apparently."

Emmet turned to Reese. "What was she getting from her locker?"

"I'm not sure." Reese shook her head. "She said something about doing laundry?"

"Did you actually see her open the locker?"

"No."

"And she was alone when you saw her here?" Nicole asked.

"Yes." She darted a panicked look at Owen. "And now she's gone, but she left her car. I don't understand. What is this about?"

Emmet ignored her question. "Ma'am, do you know whether there are any security cameras on the premises?"

Her eyes widened and she shook her head.

"No, you don't know, or *no*, there aren't any—"

"I have no idea," she said. "You'd have to ask Paula. She and Danielle are the owners."

"How do we reach Paula?" Owen asked.

Reese took out her phone, and Emmet motioned for Nicole to step aside for a private conversation.

"We need to call Brady," Emmet said.

"Are you thinking what I'm thinking?"

He nodded.

Nicole turned to Reese, who was scrolling through her contacts for Owen. "Do you know which locker is Cassandra's?"

Reese glanced up. "I'm not sure of the number. But it's the top one on the end, all the way down on the left.

Emmet and Nicole moved for the front door of the studio. It was unlocked, but all the classrooms were dark. The only lights on were in the locker room and the main hallway. Emmet stepped into the locker room, checked the ones on the end, and quickly stepped out again.

"Locked, I assume?" she asked.

"Yep."

He strode down the hallway, and the *clack* of Nicole's crutches echoed through the long corridor.

"What do you think she wanted out of her locker?" she asked from behind him.

"My guess? A go bag. Maybe she was keeping cash or supplies or something—whatever she might need to leave town in a hurry."

"I don't see any cameras inside anywhere," Nicole said.

"There weren't any out front either." He pushed open the back door and held it for her as he glanced around. "None back here either. *Shit.*"

His gaze fell on the little white Mustang parked beside the dumpster. He pulled a pair of latex gloves from the pocket of his jacket as he stepped over to check out the car.

"Colorado plates," Nicole observed.

He tried the door. "It's open," he said, glancing at her over the roof.

He reached inside and popped the trunk as Nicole crutched over.

Emmet braced himself for the possibility of a duffel bag with a dead woman inside it.

There was a duffel back there—not nearly big enough for a body—and several grocery bags containing snack foods and toiletries. Beneath the bags was a pallet of bottled waters.

"Looks like provisions," he said. "I think she got cold

feet about coming in to talk to us and decided to hit the road."

"And then what?"

He looked at her. "I think somebody grabbed her."

"Hey."

They glanced up as Owen stepped outside.

"Brady needs all of us back ASAP."

"Why?" Emmet asked.

"The FBI is here."

TWENTY-SIX

Nicole had expected Agent Driscoll from San Antonio, but it wasn't just him. No fewer than *three* federal agents were crowded into the conference room with Brady, Owen, and Adam, and everyone stood huddled around the giant whiteboard where photographs from Aubrey's case had been put on display.

"How can you be sure?" Brady was asking Driscoll as Nicole followed Emmet into the room. "He's wearing shades."

"Doesn't matter," Driscoll said.

"Our program can penetrate disguises," another agent put in.

This guy was young, thin, and wore wire-rimmed glasses. Nicole had never seen him before.

"The program analyzes numerous features—some of which are impossible to cover, even with plastic surgery." The agent pushed his glasses up on the bridge of his nose and then pointed to a photograph taped to the whiteboard.

"For example, the distance between nostrils. The placement of the ears on the side of the head. Features that are nearly impossible to alter. The program comes up with a score—a probability, if you will—and assigns it to the image."

Nicole moved closer to the whiteboard, where someone had taped up several new photographs. She recognized a still image from the video that Liam Shaunessy had recorded on his phone. Technicians had zoomed in on the man getting out of Aubrey's car and enhanced the picture so that the distant image looked remarkably clear.

"And this one is a high probability?" Brady asked, sounding skeptical as usual.

"Very high," a third agent responded.

The third guy was older—probably midforties—and wore a navy windbreaker with FBI printed on the back in yellow block letters.

"We have virtually no doubt that this man is John Krueger," he added.

"Our CSI confirms that," Nicole said.

Everyone turned around to look at her.

"She recovered some DNA from inside the car," she told them. "It comes back to John Krueger of Boulder, Colorado. The hit came in this morning."

"*Previously* of Boulder, Colorado," Driscoll said. "We don't think he's there anymore. We've been trying to locate him for months."

"Why?" Emmet asked.

Driscoll glanced at the other agent, and Nicole could tell they were about to get some kind of evasive answer.

"He's wanted in connection with something we're investigating," the guy in the windbreaker said.

"And you are?" Nicole asked.

"Special Agent Raddick."

"I'm Detective Lawson. Good to meet you. What exactly is it you're investigating?"

"I'm afraid we can't—"

"We think he works for Malcom McVoy," Driscoll said, earning a glare from Raddick. But Driscoll didn't seem to care, and Nicole's opinion of Brady's friend immediately shot up. "Agent Raddick is with our D.C. office. He flew down this morning after John Krueger's name came up through our facial recognition program."

Quiet settled over the room as Nicole and everyone else absorbed the gravity of this development. This federal agent had gotten on a *plane* from Washington? What in the world was this about?

"And what is it McVoy does, precisely?" Brady folded his arms over his chest. "We hear his company works for the Defense Department?"

"We can't get into details." Raddick shot a look at Driscoll. "His work for DoD is highly sensitive."

"Obviously, the concern is that some of his business dealings may be illegal," Driscoll said.

"And his estranged wife knows about it," Nicole stated. "*That's* why she's a target?"

Raddick nodded. "Possibly. We've been trying to locate her, hoping maybe she can tell us what she knows."

"Well, she's missing," Emmet said. "We think someone grabbed her just outside her workplace this morning. Her car is still there, but she isn't."

"When was this?" Raddick asked.

"Twenty minutes ago," Emmet said. "She was last seen by a co-worker inside the building. But now she's gone."

Driscoll cursed. Raddick pulled out his phone and started making a call.

Brady stepped over to Nicole. "You're sure she's gone?"

"She's gone," Owen said. "Alex has been trying to reach

her all morning, and she's not answering. He circled by his law office again, just in case, but no luck."

"I have her phone number," Nicole said. "We should do an emergency ping, see if we can locate her."

"Do we know that she has her phone with her?" Brady asked.

"No," Nicole said. "I mean, if she's been kidnapped, then she probably doesn't. But it can't hurt to try."

E VERYTHING WAS BLACKEST black.
      Even with her eyes open, Cassandra couldn't see a thing, so she kept them closed as she tried to calm her nerves. But her usual deep breathing exercises were difficult with a strip of duct tape covering her mouth.

Don't panic. Think!

She'd been in the back of the trunk for a while now—at least half an hour—which meant he'd definitely driven off the island. With every minute that ticked by, her panic expanded. Her heart drummed frantically, and her skin was slick with sweat.

Would Alex be looking for her by now? What about his brother, the police detective? She hoped they were searching, but even if they were, would their search extend beyond the island?

The car hit a bump, and Cassandra bit her tongue. Her heart rate spiked as she absorbed what was happening.

Malcom was going to kill her.

It was a reality, as real as the metallic taste of blood in her mouth. As soon as they got wherever they were going, it was only a matter of time.

Unless she could somehow come up with a plan.

A plan.

Something she could carry out from the trunk of a car,

with her hands bound with zip ties and a strip of tape over her mouth.

Think.

She swished the blood with her tongue. She couldn't spit it, so she swallowed it down, along with a hot lump of terror lodged inside her throat.

Think, think, think. You don't have much time.

Alex would be looking for her. Calling her. Her backpack was in the front seat of the car with Malcom.

At least she thought it was. Unless he'd ditched it somewhere?

Malcom had grabbed the phone from her hand and tossed it into the dumpster behind the yoga studio. But that was her backup burner phone, the one she had kept in her locker. The phone Alex knew about was in the inside pocket of the backpack. Was the ringer on? Her thoughts were muddled, and she couldn't remember. If it was, Malcom would have heard it by now and probably gotten rid of that phone, too.

She sucked a breath through her nose and could have sworn she smelled his cologne again. She'd smelled it in her apartment, too, but convinced herself it was her overactive imagination. So many times over the past few months, she had thought she felt his presence, and so many times she chalked it up to paranoia. But now she knew at least some of those times she hadn't been paranoid at all—she'd been perceptive. Her subconscious brain had been picking up on danger and trying to warn her, like an animal at a watering hole sensing a predator.

Why hadn't she listened to her instincts?

The vibrations changed pitch, and her pulse spiked again. The car was slowing. She pressed her ear to the scratchy carpet, straining to hear. The road seemed different now. Were they exiting a freeway?

They came to a stop, and she held her breath. Then they rolled forward, and she pictured him moving through an intersection.

Where is he taking me?

Tears burned her eyes, but she willed them away. What would crying do? She had to *think*.

The dark trunk space smelled like warm rubber. From the spare tire, probably. Was there anything else back here that she could use as a weapon? The trunk had been empty when he'd shoved her into it. And anyway, her hands were bound. She strained against the zip ties once again, but the plastic bit into her wrists. She clenched her teeth and kept pulling, tearing her skin. If she was going to die today, at least she could leave some blood behind, something for the police to find.

Oh God oh God oh God. Blood seeped from her wrists, and panic started to overtake her.

Alex was right.

She should have done something sooner. At her first inkling that something was wrong, she should have gone to the police and spilled the entire story about Malcom and his business and the phone calls she'd overheard in the middle of the night.

And her suspicions about Isabel's death.

But she *hadn't* gone to the police. She'd been too afraid. And now it was too late. What was done was done.

I'm sorry, Lucas.

Tears seeped from her eyes as she thought of her brother's face. She thought of his crooked front tooth and warm brown eyes. She hadn't spoken to him in almost seven months now, not even on the phone. It was the longest she'd ever gone, and a slimy ball formed in her stomach as she thought about abandoning him forever, leaving him alone in the world.

No.

She wouldn't do it. She wouldn't give up. She gritted her teeth and strained against the zip ties until tears streamed down her cheeks.

The car slowed and then made a turn. Where were they going? So much time had elapsed. And with every minute that went by, they got farther and farther away from anyone who might be trying to find her.

She should have listened to Alex.

And even before that, she should have listened to her gut.

She should have known that no matter what she did, no matter how far she ran or where she hid, Malcom would find her and bring her back. Because he couldn't let go. He could *never let go.* He was all about control.

The car slowed again and swung a left, and Cassandra's stomach roiled. Bile filled her throat, and she swallowed it down. If she threw up now, she'd probably choke on her own vomit.

Beneath her ear, the sound of the road changed pitch. It was bumpier here, like uneven pavement. Or some crappy dirt road in the middle of nowhere. They jostled along over ruts and ridges.

Where on earth was he taking her?

She pressed her feet against the side of the car. At least she had her feet free. Maybe she could kick him in the face when he opened the trunk. It might be tantamount to suicide if he had a gun pointed at her. But she had to do something.

She needed to move her body so that she was facing out and get her legs in position to kick something. She struggled to roll onto her back, but her knees were crammed against her chest. She bent her legs back awkwardly and managed to roll toward the back of the car.

A faint glow caught her attention.

A fluorescent release pull. If she could get her hands on it, maybe she could open the trunk and jump out at a stop. Or at least get someone's attention.

Suddenly the car turned sharply, then slammed to a halt.

Cassandra held her breath. She listened. Sweat trickled between her breasts as she tried desperately to come up with a plan.

The car shifted as the driver got out. The door slammed.

Heart pounding, Cassandra bit her tongue and waited.

NICOLE EMERGED FROM the restroom to find the bullpen nearly empty.

"Where'd everyone go?" she asked the officer sitting at his computer. "Neil?"

"Huh?"

She crutched over to his cubicle, glancing at the conference room that, minutes ago, had been filled with cops. Now the door was open, and the room was empty.

"Brady and the feds and everyone else," she said. "Where are they?"

"Uh . . ." He glanced over his shoulder. "I think they left? Emmet headed out the back with Owen."

Nicole hurried down the hallway, her stomach sinking with every step. No *way*. They wouldn't dare leave her behind.

Would they?

Fury swelled inside her as she pushed open the door and stared out at the employee parking lot.

A Lost Beach police car was turning out of the lot, followed by an unmarked gray sedan that probably belonged to the feds.

"No freaking way." She pulled her phone from her pocket.

"Nicole!"

She turned, and Emmet was waving her over to a police unit on the corner.

She loped over to join him. He'd waited for her. She felt so grateful she wanted to kiss him.

He rounded the front of the car and opened the door. "Come on, we're late."

"Thanks for waiting."

He shot her a look as she lowered herself inside. "Would you ever speak to me again if I hadn't?"

He stashed her crutches in the back and then jogged around and got behind the wheel.

"So, what the hell happened?" she asked. "Where is everyone going?"

"The FBI pinged her cell phone."

"And?"

"It bounced off a cell tower about forty miles north of here, just east of Highway 77."

"She's in a car with him."

Emmet darted a glance at her as he whipped out of the parking lot. "Or her phone is in a car with him. She could be anywhere."

"Let's just hope she's alive."

THE LIGHT WAS blinding.

Cassandra squinted into the sun as Malcom reached into the trunk.

"Let's go," he said, dragging her out by her bound arms. She stumbled against him as her feet hit the dirt. Then he wrenched her around.

She yelped with pain, but the sound was muffled against the duct tape. Where were they? He'd parked beside a corrugated metal wall topped with razor wire. Piles of old tires lined the base.

Cassandra looked around frantically. They seemed to be in the middle of a barren wasteland. The road nearby was made of dirt, not pavement, and there wasn't a car or a building anywhere—just empty brown fields as far as she could see.

She darted a look at Malcom as he slammed the trunk. She made another sound—*Where are we?*—but it came out like a muted plea.

Ignoring her, he yanked open the back door of the car and dragged out a hard-sided case.

Cassandra's stomach sank. She recognized the dull gray case instantly. Malcom pulled it to the patch of dirt in front of her and laid it on its side at her feet.

He crouched down and glanced at her. "You know what this is?"

She just watched him, heart racing, as he entered a passcode into a digital keypad. The case lid popped open with a quiet *click* that sent a rush of dread through her.

He glanced up at her, and a sinister smile spread slowly across his face.

Cassandra's heart galloped. Her throat felt tight. She stared down into the icy blue eyes that she'd once thought were sexy, seductive, even loving.

But her husband wasn't capable of love.

Well, he was. *Self*-love. It was the only kind he knew.

A gust whipped up, turning her clammy skin to ice, and she stifled a shudder. She couldn't appear weak in front of him. That would only make it worse.

He reached into the case and pulled out a black drone. The quadcopter was surprisingly small, no bigger than a football, and he held it in the palm of his hand.

"Brand-new," he said. "Only the best for my wife."

She made a muffled sound. She needed the tape gone if she was going to have any hope of reasoning with him.

He stood up. His smile widened as he reached over and tugged the corner of the duct tape.

"Don't scream, babe."

He gave the tape a yank, and her face felt like it had been seared off. Tears sprang into her eyes, and she staggered backward.

"You were saying something?" He tossed the tape to the ground.

She tried to move her lips, but they didn't seem to work. She ran her tongue over them and tasted glue.

"This plan . . ." she croaked. "It's never going to work, Malcom."

"Ah, but you don't know the plan." He smiled again, and the giddy look in his eyes chilled her to her core. "And it *will* work because you've already laid the groundwork for me by making arrangements to leave town. Thank you, by the way."

The drone in his hand came to life with a buzz. It lifted into the air, and he tipped his head back to watch.

"Beautiful, isn't she?" He used a remote control to make it do a series of wide circles over their heads.

While he was distracted, she darted her gaze around. Where *were* they? Someplace isolated, obviously. She glanced back at the corrugated metal wall. The winter sun glinted off the coils of razor wire along the top. A few yards away was a rusted gate with one of those electronic keypads mounted on a pole beside it. Over the drone's hum, she heard the faint noise of some sort of heavy machine off in the distance.

"Don't you want to see?"

She turned to Malcom. His state-of-the-art device

hovered over them, but he wasn't admiring it anymore. His attention was on an iPad now.

Swallowing the sour taste in her mouth, she stepped over. On the tablet's screen was a video feed showing an aerial view of the silver car and the tops of their heads.

The drone gained altitude, and she looked up to watch it sail to the other side of the wall. She glanced at the tablet, and her stomach took a nosedive.

The screen showed a hideous labyrinth of . . . junk, apparently. Smashed cars. Rusted appliances. Piles of rebar.

She jerked her gaze to his. "What is this?"

"Watch."

He stepped closer, shoving the tablet in front of her, and the scent of his cologne made her want to retch.

The drone dipped lower, making her dizzy as it zoomed over rows and rows of auto carcasses, old refrigerators, rusted tractor wheels. It came to a clearing in the dirt, and then a yellow backhoe appeared on the screen. Someone in a white hard hat was operating the machine, and her heart gave a lurch. Was this someone who could help her?

"Do you like it?"

She looked up at Malcom. "Like what?"

He nodded at the screen, and the camera dipped lower. She watched the big yellow claw reach down and scoop a mound of dirt.

"What . . . ?" Her voice trailed off as understanding dawned.

"For you, Catherine. Your final resting place."

CHAPTER

TWENTY-SEVEN

THEY SWUNG ONTO the dirt road and followed the cloud of dust. They had caught up to the others, and Nicole was keeping track of updates on Emmet's phone as he drove. She entered their location into her navigation program, and her stomach sank.

"Oh no."

Emmet glanced at her. "What?"

"According to this map, we're nearing a place called Rio Grande Salvage."

"What, like a junkyard?"

"I have no idea." She glanced at him. "But that doesn't sound good."

The cars in front of them sped up. They were a three-vehicle caravan, and someone had determined that they were better off without sirens. Nicole glanced out the window as they traversed what looked like fallow farmland.

"I don't like this," she said.

Emmet's jaw tensed.

"This feels to me like a dumping ground," she added. "Why else would he possibly take her all the way out here?"

He shook his head.

"You think we're too late?"

Emmet didn't reply. But she knew him well, and the grim look on his face was answer enough.

Shuddering, she glanced out the window again.

"*Damn it.*" She pounded her fist on the door.

"It's not your fault, Nicole."

"I should have pushed harder."

"Harder for what?"

"With Cassandra. I *knew* she was lying, and I should have hounded her relentlessly until she told me what was going on."

"It's possible she didn't even know what was going on." Emmet glanced at her. "Have you thought of that? Sounds like her husband is the mastermind here."

"She knew something about all this. I could tell. My radar was up with her from our very first conversation."

Emmet looked at her. "You know who that D.C. guy is, right? Special Agent Raddick?"

Nicole's stomach tightened. "No. What about him?"

"He's in the counterintelligence division. I looked him up."

"Counterintelligence . . . as in espionage?"

Emmet nodded. "Makes you wonder what Malcom Mc-Voy's wife might have learned about her husband's business before she decided to leave him. Maybe he was selling sensitive technology to a foreign government or something."

"Then this whole thing is a matter of national security. No wonder the feds are so intent on talking to her."

Emmet lifted an eyebrow. "If she's still alive."

The cars in front of them slowed, and Emmet tapped the

brakes. One by one, their three vehicles pulled to a stop beside a high wall made of corrugated metal. A solid black security gate barred the entrance.

Emmet's phone buzzed, and he reached for it.

"Davis," he answered, then glanced at Nicole. "Okay, roger that."

She pushed open her door before he could tell her to stay in the car.

"Nicole."

She reached for her crutches in the back.

"You need to stay here," he said.

She planted her crutches and pulled herself to her feet.

"Nikki, come on."

She glanced at him over the roof of the car. "What?"

"You need to stay back. You're not in any shape to participate in a takedown right now."

"Is that what this is?"

Before he could answer, she turned to look at the other two vehicles. All three federal agents were crowded around the trunk of their unmarked unit, dragging out tactical vests and weapons. Owen and Adam were doing the same from the LBPD vehicle.

Nicole watched Emmet pop the trunk of their car and pull out a Kevlar vest. Her throat went dry. She'd seen him gear up before, but it felt different now.

"You can't do this on crutches," he said, strapping the vest on.

He gave her a sharp look as he slammed the trunk shut and walked over to hand her an extra vest. "I repeat, *stay here*. Better yet—stay inside the car."

She took the vest from him.

"Yo, Emmet, come on, man."

They looked over, and Owen was motioning him to

the huddle, where they were obviously putting together a plan.

Emmet dug his phone from his pocket. "Here." He held it out it to her. "Call Brady and give him an update for us."

She took the phone, which was obviously her consolation prize.

"And do it from the car, okay?"

She looked at the huddle again, where everyone was gearing up to either go *over* or *through* that big black gate somehow.

"Nicole."

She looked at Emmet. He reached up and gently touched her cheek, right there in front of Owen and Adam and everyone.

"Please?" he said, and the plea in his eyes made her chest hurt.

"Fine."

His hand dropped. "Thank you."

TWENTY-SIX ACRES," AGENT Raddick was telling everyone. "Looks like it's divided into rectangular sections."

Everyone peered down at the satellite map on the agent's tablet.

"I called the number posted on the gate there."

Emmet turned around as the younger FBI agent rushed over with his phone in his hand. His cheeks were flushed, as though just wearing his vest was putting a strain on him. He seemed to be the tech expert here. Did the guy even have SWAT training? Emmet doubted it. He seemed like he spent more time in front of a computer than conducting tactical operations.

"And?" Driscoll asked him.

"And someone's coming."

"Who?"

"I don't know," the agent said. "The voice was all garbled. But someone definitely picked up."

A low metallic groan had everyone turning toward the entrance. The gate was tall—at least fifteen feet—and it slid open slowly on a rusty wheel.

A stocky man in a white hard hat walked out. He wore mud-streaked jeans and a fluorescent orange vest. He stopped short when he spied the group of cops in tactical gear. His hands shot into the air, and he let loose a stream of Spanish.

"Shit." Raddick looked around. "Anyone speak Spanish?"

Driscoll walked over and started talking to the guy, clearly trying to calm him down. The man kept his hands above his head as Driscoll did a quick pat-down. Then they spoke for a few moments, and Driscoll showed the man something on his phone. The man nodded.

Driscoll pointed to the nearest stack of tires, and the guy cast another wary look at the cops before walking over and taking a seat on the ground.

Driscoll tromped back over, tucking his phone into his pocket. "He's here."

"Who?" Emmet asked.

"McVoy. This guy identified him from a photo. Said he got here about twenty minutes ago and he was alone."

Emmet shot a look at Owen.

"How did he get here?" Owen asked.

"In a silver car."

A silver *car*. Such as the one that had been tailing Nicole this week? Emmet glanced over his shoulder to where she leaned against the squad car, talking on the phone with someone—presumably Brady—while watching him intently. She'd put the Kevlar vest on at least, but she did not look happy to be on the sidelines.

Well, that was too bad. Emmet didn't like her presence here at all, and his concern for her safety was a huge distraction when he needed to be focused on the mission.

"Where is he now?" Owen asked the agent.

"In sector five. *Cinco*, he said. He told me that's the far northwest corner of the property. He drove over there in his car."

"And what's he doing here?" Emmet asked.

Driscoll shook his head. "The guy claims he doesn't know, so that's as far as I got. I think he's scared shitless. I get the impression McVoy paid him off to let him in here in the first place."

"We need to get in there," Emmet said.

"Shouldn't we wait for backup?" the tech guy said.

"No time," Driscoll responded. "She could be alive."

"We're burning time already," Owen added. "And the longer we stand around, the more we risk McVoy figuring out we're here, and then we lose the element of surprise."

"Let's try to keep the temperature down, okay?" Raddick looked around as everyone checked their weapons. "We want him in custody, not dead. We need to question him."

That wasn't Emmet's top priority, but he didn't waste time arguing.

"We need to move *now*," Emmet said. "How far away is sector five? We talking half a mile? What?"

"I didn't ask," Driscoll said. "Let's take the cars. They'll provide cover in case he's armed."

Owen sneered. "This guy makes war toys for the DoD. You bet your ass he's armed."

N ICOLE WATCHED WITH a mix of dread and envy as the vehicles rolled through the gate and disappeared into what looked to be a maze of junk: crushed cars, piles of tires, rows and rows of rusted-out appliances. She waited until they were gone and texted Brady.

Then she crutched toward the still-open gate, nodding at the guy in the hard hat who sat obediently at the base of the wall. Agent Raddick had cuffed the man's hands behind him, probably in case he got any ideas about picking up a phone and tipping someone off about their presence here.

The smell of diesel and rotting vegetation wafted toward her as she entered the salvage yard. It was eerily quiet except for the faint sound of a distant machine—maybe a truck or bulldozer. Just inside the gate was a dilapidated trailer, likely where the groundskeeper worked. Judging from the solar panels and satellite dishes mounted to the roof, he possibly even lived there, too.

Nicole glanced around, looking for any other vehicles. There was an old moped parked near the trailer, but that was it.

A low hum overhead pulled her attention skyward.

A drone.

Dread washed over her as she stared up at the distant dot. Was it one of McVoy's? It was way the hell up there, making a wide loop over the property. She had to tell Emmet.

She reached for the phone in her pocket. But it was *Emmet's* phone.

"Crap!"

She pulled her phone from the other pocket and texted Owen. She had to warn them. Their stealth approach was blown to hell, and their risk level had just increased exponentially.

!!Drone surveillance!! You copy?

She waited, heart pounding, as her stomach filled with acid.

You copy??

She stared down at her cracked screen. No answer.
"Damn it."
Nicole rushed back to the car.

M ALCOM HOPPED DOWN from the backhoe and pointed
the pistol at her face. The front of his black shirt was
streaked with dirt.

"Over there." He gestured to the hole.

"Malcom—"

"Now. Come on." He strode up to her, anger flashing in
his eyes, and Cassandra knew he was on a short fuse. Malcom hadn't been satisfied with the hole the man had dug,
and then he'd gotten angry and embarrassed when he
climbed into the backhoe himself but couldn't get it running at first.

He was at his most dangerous when he was embarrassed.

"*Now!*" He yanked her arm, and she stumbled toward
the mound of dirt.

"Don't do this, Malcom. Please."

She turned to plead with him, and fury in his eyes flared.
He gave her a shove that sent her tripping into the hole,
where she landed on her side, hard. She scrambled to her
feet and screamed—a shrill, panicked sound that echoed
off the high dirt walls.

He stepped to the edge of the hole and aimed the gun
at her.

TWENTY-EIGHT

Emmet moved into position behind the car door, lined up his sights, and took the shot.

Pop!

McVoy whirled around and staggered back, then lurched behind a rusted camper van.

"Is he hit?" asked the FBI agent in the radio hooked to Emmet's ear.

"I don't know," Emmet responded.

"FBI!" someone yelled from the cover of a concrete barricade. "Drop your weapon!"

McVoy darted from the camper van to a yellow backhoe. He wore a black shirt and jeans, but no visible body armor.

"Behind the backhoe!" Emmet yelled.

A bullet pinged off the metal by Emmet's head, and he ducked down behind the car door.

"Shit." He glanced over his shoulder at Owen. "That was fucking close."

"Cover me," Owen said.

"Where are you going?"

"The smashed Camaro just over there. Three . . . two . . . one—"

Owen sprinted for the car and dove behind the rusted-out vehicle as the bullet ricocheted off it.

Okay, this guy was officially crazy. He was outnumbered six to one, and still he wanted to engage in a firefight. This was starting to feel like suicide by cop.

Adrenaline pumped through Emmet's veins as he rested his arms on the door and peered over it, lining up his sights again. Another blur of movement. McVoy darted behind a stack of tractor tires.

"Where is he?" asked one of the feds over the radio.

"Behind the tires," Emmet replied.

Seconds ticked by. Sweat seeped into Emmet's eyes as he watched the scene. Driscoll crept toward the tire tower, weapon clutched and ready. Owen spotted him and gave him the all clear. Driscoll lunged around the tires.

No sound, nothing.

"Where'd he go?" Raddick asked over the radio.

An engine fired to life. Emmet whirled around just in time to see a silver car burst from behind a rusted shipping container. He was getting away!

"In the car, in the car!" voices yelled over the radio.

Emmet jumped out from behind the door. He lunged in front of the car and took aim.

Pop!

The windshield cracked. The car swerved. Emmet leaped out of the way as the car barreled toward him, then careened around a curve.

"Shit!"

He ran after it and heard a deafening shriek of metal.

* * *

T HE AIRBAG SMACKED her, and Nicole dropped her head
back, stunned.

She shook off the daze. A blur of movement caught her
eye—McVoy stumbling away from the silver car, clutching
his shoulder.

Nicole grabbed her weapon from the passenger seat as
gunfire erupted outside. She pushed the door open.

Pop!

Pop! Pop!

Bullets seemed to be flying in all directions. McVoy
crumpled to the ground, clutching his knee now. Emmet
was on him almost instantly. And then Owen and Adam.

Nicole watched in shock as they wrestled the man onto
his stomach and slapped cuffs on him. Then the FBI agents
were there, everyone crowded around trying to help get the
kicking man under control.

Nicole grabbed her crutches. She struggled with the airbag, slapping it out of her way so she could get the crutches
positioned and haul herself from the car. She hurried over
to the heap of bodies.

McVoy was on his stomach in the dirt, cursing and
bleeding. Agent Raddick crouched beside him as everyone
else got to their feet.

She looked at Emmet. "He's disarmed?"

"Yeah." Emmet's chest heaved, and his eyes looked wild
with panic as he glanced from the crashed police car to her.
"Are you okay?"

"Yeah."

He stepped closer. "You sure?"

"I'm okay."

A steady *whump-whump* filled the sky, and Nicole

looked up to see a police helicopter nearing the salvage yard.

"There's our backup," Owen said. "Just in time."

The helicopter swooped low, kicking up dust, and Nicole turned away and shielded her eyes from the grit.

Emmet moved away from the crowd. Nicole's heart lurched as he stumbled toward a pile of tires.

"Emmet?"

He leaned against the tires, and she noticed the blood dripping from his fingertips.

"*Emmet?*" She rushed over.

"Damn, Nicole." He closed his eyes. "He got me."

THE MOBILE COMMAND center was swarming with FBI agents and crime scene techs. Nicole made her way around a scrum of sheriff's deputies and paused at the base of the trailer's portable steps.

"Damn crutches."

The door swung open and Adam stepped out, thank God.

"Hey, is Brady in there?" she asked him.

"He's talking to the Washington guy."

"Get him for me, would you?"

Adam hesitated a moment, then ducked back into the trailer.

Nicole surveyed the scene around her. Every law enforcement agency in the tri-county area was represented here, even the Coast Guard. Evidently, no one wanted to miss out on the action.

Within minutes of McVoy's arrest, Cassandra had been transported to the hospital to get checked out. Her injuries had seemed minor, but she'd been shaking uncontrollably and was practically catatonic from shock. Detectives would need to interview her to understand the details of her abduction. One thing was obvious—if police hadn't arrived the moment they did, Cassandra would likely be dead at the bottom of that pit right now.

Nicole checked her phone for the hundredth time. And for the hundredth time, she felt a stab of fear.

"Lawson."

She glanced up to see Brady leaning out of the trailer. "What is it? I'm in the middle of something."

"I finished that video statement," she said. "They got everything they need from me."

"Good."

"Any word from the hospital?" she asked.

"No."

"The FBI sent someone over there. Can you ask?"

Brady ducked back into the trailer. The feds had sent an agent with Emmet to obtain a statement from him as soon as he was finished getting treated, but that was more than an hour ago. Seventy-two minutes, to be exact.

The chief came back. "No word."

Fear clawed at her.

"I want to head over and get an update," she said.

The chief looked her over with a frown, and seemed to pick up on how anxious she was.

"Fine. Go," he said. "Take the SUV. Let me know what you hear."

"Will do."

She crutched over to the police SUV and luckily found the keys inside. She stashed her crutches in the passenger seat and pulled the door shut.

Quiet, finally.

For a moment she stared at the dashboard in a daze. The past ninety minutes had been pandemonium as dozens of first responders converged on the scene. Nicole hadn't seen

Emmet since he had been loaded into an ambulance and rushed to the hospital amid a wail of sirens.

A flesh wound, he'd said. Right. That's why it had been bleeding so profusely it needed a tourniquet. Tears burned her eyes as she started the car.

Someone pounded on the window, and she jumped, startled. Owen.

She buzzed down the window.

"You going to the hospital?" he asked.

"Yeah."

"I just heard from one of the agents who's there guarding McVoy. Sounds like he just went into surgery for his knee."

Nicole couldn't give a damn about McVoy's injuries.

"He told me Emmet's out."

Her heart clenched. "*Out?* You mean he's—"

"He's out of the hospital," Owen told her. "They stitched him up and sent him home."

CHAPTER

THIRTY

Nicole crutched up to Emmet's front door just as it opened.

Calvin stepped out with his phone pressed to his ear, followed by Kyle. Both firefighters wore chunky rubber boots and had soot on their faces, as though they'd just come from a callout.

"Yeah, I'm sure," Calvin said into the phone. "Really. I *just* talked to him, Mom." He looked at his friend and shook his head. "Yeah, I will. Bye."

He slipped the phone into the pocket of his work pants and turned to Nicole.

"Is he here?" she asked.

"Yeah, he just got home."

She glanced at Kyle. Both he and Calvin reeked of smoke.

"Where are you coming from?" she asked.

"Warehouse fire near the marina," Kyle said. "Owen called us as we were wrapping things up."

Nicole's chest tightened as she glanced at Calvin again. "How is he?"

"Looks okay. But fair warning—he's in a shit mood."

She stepped around him.

"Hey, Nicole."

She looked over her shoulder, and Calvin was watching her with a curious expression, as though suddenly realizing that this was the second time he'd bumped into her at his brother's apartment in less than a week, and there might be something going on.

"Don't let him scare you away," he said.

She nodded and reached for the door.

Clothes littered the darkened foyer—socks, a T-shirt, Emmet's mud-caked boots. She crutched over the threshold and shut the door behind her. Emmet's empty holster sat on the breakfast bar, alongside his backup pistol and a pair of six-round mags.

Nicole's stomach tightened. The empty holster confirmed that he'd discharged his duty weapon today, and it was now evidence in an internal investigation.

"Fuck!"

She glanced at the hallway. A sliver of yellow light spilled from the bathroom. She followed the sound of curses.

"Cal? Can you gimme a hand here?"

She paused in the hall and pushed open the door.

Emmet sat on the side of the tub in a pair of gym shorts, no shirt. The top of his left arm was wrapped in a bandage, and he had his bare foot propped on his knee.

"Fuck." He glanced up and looked surprised. "Hey. I thought you were Calvin."

She moved into the bathroom. "What happened to your leg?"

"Nothing." He stood up. "Just some glass, I think."

He stepped around her and opened a cabinet. She looked

him over as he rummaged through a shoebox filled with first aid supplies.

Muttering a curse, he shoved the box back into the cabinet and stalked out of the room.

She stared at the empty doorway. Then she followed him into the kitchen, where he was opening and closing drawers. He grabbed a pair of tweezers and sat down on a bar stool.

"The scene still active?" He glanced up from his leg, and she noticed the thin cut there.

"What happened?"

"Caught some glass at the junkyard."

"Why didn't they do this at the hospital?"

"I don't know. They were distracted." He bent over the cut, and she watched him dig a sliver of glass from his skin. He deposited it on the counter and looked up.

"How's your arm?" She nodded toward the thick bandage wrapped around his biceps.

"Fine."

"Fine?"

"Yeah."

"You took a freaking bullet. How can it be fine?"

"It barely grazed me. I just needed a few stitches."

He got up and walked around her, and her stomach plummeted as she saw the giant purple bloom on his shoulder blade.

"What is *that*?" But she knew exactly what it was. He'd been shot in the back, close enough to make a bruise through the Kevlar.

"Nothing," he said, opening a cabinet.

"You didn't tell me you were shot in the back."

"I wasn't."

Tears burned her eyes, and she reached for the bruise.

"Ouch!" He whirled around.

She pulled back and bit her lip. Then she looked at his bare chest. His heart was just inches away from where two bullets had hit him, and that was it. Game over. All the terror, and stress, and frustration of the past four hours came pouring forth in one big wave.

"Shit," he said with a sigh.

She buried her face in her hands.

"Don't get upset."

She choked back a sob. "Don't tell me what to *do*!"

"Nicole, come on."

He reached for her hands to pull them away from her face, but she turned away. She couldn't look at him as another sob burst out of her.

"Hey." He wrapped his warm arms around her, crutches and all. "I'm fine, all right? Look at me."

She leaned into him, wiping her cheeks.

"Come on. Don't. There's nothing to cry about."

She let out a strangled noise and pressed her fist into his chest. "Would you *stop* with that shit? You were shot today. Twice! I can cry if I want."

She looked up at him, furiously wiping tears and snot from her face. She hated him seeing her like this. She rarely cried, and when she did, she made sure no one was around to see it. She tried to turn away, but he kept his arms wrapped around her.

"Hey."

She squeezed her eyes shut.

"Nicole."

Her heart hurt. And her stomach. And her brain. Never in her life had she experienced such bone-deep terror as watching him get loaded into that ambulance and whisked away. She'd spent every minute of the past four hours imagining him bleeding out on some gurney because that "flesh wound" had actually been a nicked artery. And it *could have happened*. If not for that Kevlar vest, he would surely be dead right now.

She opened her eyes, and his expression was pleading.

"Please don't cry. Okay? You have no idea what it does to me. And anyway, I'm fine."

She sucked in a breath to steady herself and pulled back. She couldn't tell him how scared she'd been. She wiped her cheeks, then he eased her against his chest and kissed the top of her head.

"I hate that you got shot," she whispered.

"Yeah? Me, too. I'm pissed. And now I'm going to be stuck behind a fucking desk until I'm cleared to work again."

She choked out a laugh. "*That's* why you're mad? Not your gunshot wound?"

"It's just a few stitches. I'll barely have a scar."

She sighed deeply and closed her eyes. Her ear was pressed against his sternum, and she could hear his heartbeat.

"Hey."

She pulled back, and the tender look in his eyes made her insides twist. She wiped her wet nose.

He took her crutches from her and leaned them against the counter.

"What are you doing?"

"Come here," he said, reaching down and carefully lifting her off her feet. He walked her into the living room and deposited her gently on the couch. Then he tossed the cushion to the floor to make room for her boot.

She gazed up at him as he leaned over her, resting his weight on his palm. They were alone again, finally. And it was strangely similar to last night, when they'd been on *her* couch, and one kiss had turned into a mind-blowing sex binge. But last night all she could think about was getting him inside her, and now she was thinking about how close he'd come to death.

He stroked the back of his finger over her wet cheek.

"I promise I'm fine."

She took a deep breath. "You could have died today." She rested her fingers against the stubble along his jaw. "You really scared me."

"Yeah?" His eyebrows arched. "Now you know how I feel every damn day."

"You do not."

"I do. You terrify me, Nicole. You're so stubborn and fearless all the time." He shook his head. "If anything ever happened to you . . ." He shook his head again.

"What?"

He leaned closer, close enough for her to see the flecks of gold in his eyes in the light from the kitchen. The silence stretched out, and something passed between them. She didn't know what it was, really—some sort of understanding or acknowledgment.

This was more than a one-night thing. Much more. They were bound together by a tangly vine of friendship, and loyalty, and intense physical attraction that refused to be ignored, especially now that they knew how next-level hot they were together. There was no way she could ever go back to *not knowing* what it was like to be with him, and— for her at least—sex would never be the same.

She traced her finger over the snowy white bandage on his upper arm.

"So." She took a deep breath. "How many stitches are we talking about?"

He hesitated a beat, and she knew he was thinking of lying. "Six."

She pursed her lips. "That's going to leave a scar."

"Probably."

She met his gaze, and he leaned down and kissed her. It was soft and slow, and she felt him sink into it. She did, too, absorbing his taste and his smell, relieved beyond words to be with him like this. She'd been so worried, frightened out of her mind. And now he was right here, and she could feel him and taste him and assure herself over and over that he was alive and breathing.

He moved from her mouth to her neck.

"Emmet."

"Hmm?"

"We shouldn't do this again."

He stopped and looked up. "Why not?"

"You know why. It's going to be a problem at work. It's *already* a problem. We were in the middle of the op today, and all I could think about was you getting shot. And then you *did* get shot, and I nearly fell apart."

He gazed down at her, and the unguarded look in his eyes put a lump in her throat.

"I don't think we can *not* do this again." He watched her for a beat. "Do you?"

She gazed up at him and bit her lip.

He brushed a lock of hair out of her face. "I've been wanting this for years, Nicole. And now that it's happening, I don't want it to stop."

"Years?"

He nodded.

"Why didn't you tell me?"

"When?" He smiled. "You've been busting my balls all this time and competing with me. I figured a relationship with me was the last thing you wanted. And you've had a thing for my brother."

She squirmed to sit up. "I do *not* have a thing for your brother. I have a thing for *you*."

He smiled slightly. "Yeah, I kinda picked up on that

recently." His smile dropped away. "But then you started going out with David, and I've been losing my mind."

He'd been jealous. Nicole had sensed it, even though he'd never said anything outright—it was based on his foul mood whenever the subject of David came up.

She leaned back on the cushion. "Well, I'm glad you're done being clueless. But none of this addresses the real problem. We work together. Our department is too small to keep secrets, and as soon as Brady gets wind of this, he's going to want to put a stop to it. And with good *reason*. Emotional entanglements cloud people's judgment, and it's not safe. Today was a perfect example. Everything devolved into a shoot-out, and I wasn't thinking about protocol or Adam or Owen or even the armed subject we were trying to arrest—all I could think about was *you*."

He sighed. But he didn't argue because he couldn't. She knew that when everything was going sideways, he'd been thinking about her, too.

"Stop worrying," he said.

"How can I stop worrying?"

He rolled his eyes. "Just . . . stop, all right? We'll figure something out."

"But—"

He kissed her to cut her off. And she let him. He tasted so good, and the heat of his body reminded her of how much she loved the way he touched her.

I've been wanting this for years.

He kissed her deeper, harder, and heat rippled through her as his hand slid up her thigh.

"Have I told you how much I like this skirt?"

His hand glided beneath it, and she arched her hips.

"You haven't, no."

He slipped his hand between her legs.

"I fucking love it."

She tipped her head back, savoring the low groan in his chest as his fingers found her.

"We really shouldn't do this tonight," she said. "Aren't you supposed to . . . rest or—*oh my God*."

His mouth settled on hers as his fingers worked their magic, and she felt him smile against her lips. "Not a chance."

THIRTY-ONE

Six weeks later

CASSANDRA ENTERED THE office and was surprised to
see a young woman seated at the reception desk.

"Can I help you?"

"Um . . ." She stepped over. "I'm here to see Alex Breda?"

"Is Mr. Breda expecting you?"

"No."

"And your name, please?"

"It's Miller." She cleared her throat. "Cassandra Miller."

Alex's office door opened, and a woman stepped out.
She was strikingly beautiful and almost as tall as Alex. She
hitched a Fendi purse onto her shoulder as she preceded
him down the hallway.

"Thanks for your time," she said, looking back at him.
"I really appreciate it."

"Of course." Alex glanced at Cassandra as he ushered
the woman to the door and opened it. "I'll be in touch."

After she was gone, he turned around.

"Hey there." He looked Cassandra up and down, and she

could tell by his expression he knew she was on her way somewhere.

"Sorry to just show up," Cassandra said. "You have a minute? This shouldn't take long."

"Sure." He darted a look at the receptionist, who was watching them curiously. "Hold my calls, Emma, would you?"

"No problem."

He led her down the hall, and this time the floor wasn't lined with moving boxes. There were pictures on the walls now, and Cassandra stopped beside the door, where the framed magazine article he had taken down was now prominently displayed: **Breda & Braxton Take On H-Town**.

So his sister had won the argument.

"Come on in," he said.

Cassandra lingered in front of the article for a moment. She'd read it online, hoping for a few more clues about her semi-famous attorney. But the write-up had offered little in the way of personal gossip.

"So, I've been wondering," she said, stepping into the office and taking the empty visitor's chair. His boxes had been unpacked, and now his credenza was loaded up with binders and law books.

"Yes?" He lifted an eyebrow.

"What made you leave Houston? From everything I've read, your practice there was thriving."

He leaned back in his chair, watching her warily. Today he wore a light blue dress shirt that matched his eyes, and the sleeves were rolled up.

"It was," he said.

"So? What happened? Falling out with your partner?"

He didn't answer at first, and she prepared for a deflection. It was none of her business, really, but given what they'd been through over the past six weeks, she decided, why not just ask?

He leaned forward, resting his forearms on the desk. "Some partnerships are toxic."

Aha. So, she'd guessed right.

"If you know what I mean."

She sighed. "I do, yes." She looked around his office. "Well, I'm glad you're here now. I don't know where I would be without you. Actually, I do. I think I'd be dead."

Alex frowned. But he didn't argue, and they both knew it wasn't an exaggeration.

She pulled an envelope from her purse and set it on the desk.

"That's for you."

He looked at it but didn't touch it.

"I have to say, I feel a bit like a mobster showing up here with a thick stack of cash."

He smiled. "I take all forms of payment."

"Yeah?"

"Yep." He took the envelope and slid it into his top desk drawer. "Thank you."

"Thank *you*."

"So, am I guessing right that you're leaving town?" Alex asked.

"I am, yes." She sighed. "At least for a while. I wanted to get you paid before I go so you wouldn't think I was trying to skip out or anything."

He smiled.

"I'm glad you came by. I've got an update from the prosecutor's office."

Cassandra tensed. Anything to do with Malcom still made her queasy. He was under house arrest awaiting trial, but she still found herself looking over her shoulder all the time. Every now and then she even caught a whiff of his cologne. PTSD, her therapist had told her. But Cassandra couldn't stamp out the fear. She'd discounted her instincts before and she'd been wrong.

She cleared her throat. "What's the update?"

"Well, you heard about how John Krueger was arrested in Brownsville."

She nodded.

Malcom's hired gun had been apprehended trying to sneak across the border in the back of an eighteen-wheeler.

"He's cooperating now," Alex said.

"Cooperating?"

"Not surprising, really, since his DNA was recovered from the crime scene. They have quite a bit of leverage over him."

"So, cooperating as in . . . ?" She gripped her purse strap, waiting for him to finish the sentence.

"He's implicating Malcom in the murder-for-hire scheme. Which—as you know—is a capital offense here."

Cassandra sat back in her chair. A capital offense.

Alex had explained all this weeks ago, but it hadn't seemed real then. She'd been too traumatized to wrap her mind around it.

"And I hear the feds are talking to him about McVoy Systems, too," Alex said. "I don't know the nature of their conversations, but it can't be good for Malcom."

She nodded.

"All this is good for you, though." He watched her with that eagle-eyed gaze, and she knew there was a subtext here. All this was good for her *provided* that she'd told Alex the truth when she'd said she was never involved in her husband's business dealings.

Good thing for her, she had been telling the truth. Her knowledge only extended to a few overheard phone calls to China in the middle of the night. In the days after her abduction, federal agents had debriefed her about those conversations at length. On Alex's advice, she'd revealed to them every detail. From what she had gathered, Malcom had been selling drone technology to U.S. adversaries while simultaneously fulfilling contracts for the Defense Department.

Alex was watching her reaction closely.

"That's good news," she said.

"Is it? You look a little dazed."

"I am." She bit her lip. "He's a monster, yes. And he tried to kill me. But . . ." She looked down at her lap. "I don't know. It's weird. It's strange to think of him on death row." Not so long ago, she'd loved him enough to marry him. She never would have imagined "till death do us part" could turn out this way.

She looked at Alex, and the empathy in his eyes was yet another reminder of why she felt sure that it didn't matter *where* he practiced law. This man could hang up a shingle on a deserted island and probably make a go of it.

"That brings me to the other update," Alex said. "I'm expecting your divorce to be finalized pretty soon. We've got a hearing scheduled—" He turned to his computer and tapped the mouse, opening his email. "Looks like . . . April twenty-fifth. That's a Tuesday." He looked at her. "Can you make it?"

"Wouldn't miss it."

"Good. It's a date."

She smiled. That was her cue to leave. Besides being smart, and handsome, and a bulldog on her behalf with prosecutors, her lawyer also happened to be extremely charming.

And another charming man was the last thing Cassandra needed at this moment in her life.

"Well, thank you." She smiled and stood up. "I mean it."

"Of course." Alex stood, too. "So, what's next for you?"

"A road trip."

"Oh?"

"I'm going to visit my brother in Arizona. Then some traveling. Maybe see the desert, visit a few national parks."

"Sounds nice."

"I think I need some time away from people for a while."

He walked around his desk and opened the door for her. "Be careful, Cassandra."

"I will."

"Really."

"I know. Really." She turned to look at him, touched by his concern.

"And if you get in any trouble, give me a call." He held his hand out to her, and she shook it.

"You know I will."

NICOLE ELBOWED HER way through the crowd. Between the tourist season ramping up and a Sunday-night basketball game, Finn's was packed. She spied Kyle and Calvin at the pool table in back.

But no Emmet.

Her stomach tightened with disappointment. She hadn't heard from him since this afternoon when they'd traded text messages. He'd told her he had some stuff to take care of this evening, but he'd try to call later. She'd thought he meant family stuff, because he'd been vague about it, but now Calvin was here, so she didn't know what to think.

"Nik."

She turned around, and Kate was waving at her from a booth across the bar. Nicole walked over and slid into the seat beside Siena.

"We ordered you a margarita," Kate said.

"Thanks."

Nicole didn't really want a margarita. But she also didn't want to raise a bunch of questions with Kate.

"Where's Emmet?" Siena asked.

"Working, I think," Nicole said.

Kate frowned. "You think?"

Nicole grabbed the plastic menu from the end of the table. "Yeah, today was crazy busy. I haven't really talked to him."

She skimmed the menu, and when she glanced up, Kate and Siena were eyeing her with concern.

"Everything okay?" Kate asked.

"Sure. Why?"

The server walked over, saving Nicole from more questions.

"I'll have your wings, please," she told her.

"Make that two orders," Kate said.

The server jotted it down and walked away.

"Mind if I scoot out to go to the restroom?" Siena said. "No fair gossiping without me."

When she was gone, Kate turned to Nicole. "Okay, what's the deal?"

"What deal?"

"You've been dodging my calls all week, and now you're upset. What's up with Emmet?"

"I told you. He's working."

Kate just stared at her.

And this was why Nicole had been reluctant to come out tonight. It was impossible to be around her sister and fake it.

"He's, I don't know, acting weird lately," Nicole said.

Kate's eyes narrowed. "Weird how?"

"Just . . . evasive, I guess, whenever we're together."

"Evasive. You mean like avoiding sex?"

"No, we're having sex all the time."

Kate's eyebrows tipped up. "Is that a problem?"

"Not at all. It's good. Just . . . that's all we do. He comes over or I go to his place, we have sex, then he's crashed out until morning. And then at work, he's either avoiding me or he's off doing something else and we're completely apart."

"Well . . . isn't that better?" Kate asked. "You said you can't work with him anymore without it being weird and awkward, so—"

"No, I can't. I just—" She shook her head, frustrated. "We're apart at work, and then when we're not at work, it's like he won't communicate with me except physically. And I *know* something's going on."

Kate just stared at her. "Something . . . such as a person, you mean?"

The words were like a dart to her chest.

But Emmet wouldn't do that to her. He was faithful. In her heart, she knew that. But she also knew that he was avoiding conversations with her for some reason, and she felt certain something was wrong.

"Not a person," Nicole said. "But there's something off, I can tell."

Kate gave her a sympathetic look. "You should talk to him."

"I know."

"Or maybe ask Calvin."

Nicole looked at Emmet's brother across the bar. "No. This is between us." Part of her felt guilty even discussing it with Kate. The only person she really wanted to talk to about this was Emmet.

"Well, are you seeing him tonight?" Kate asked.

"Probably."

Nicole was embarrassed to say she didn't really know. This afternoon—like yesterday afternoon—Emmet had been mysteriously absent from work. She'd asked him about it, and all he'd said was that he was following up on something for Brady.

The server returned with a tray of drinks and set them on the table.

Nicole slid her margarita in front of her and poked at it with the straw.

"Sit him down right when you see him," Kate said. "Don't let him distract you."

"Ha. Easier said than done."

"Okay, now you're just gloating." Kate sipped her drink. "And you know I've been in a dry spell."

"I'm not gloating. It's just a fact," Nicole said. "It's how we connect."

And even knowing they should be talking more, whenever Nicole got around him, they couldn't keep their hands off each other, whether they were making dinner, or showering, or watching TV. She had expected things to taper off, but they hadn't at all, and Nicole getting rid of her ankle boot last week had only added gasoline to the fire.

Kate sighed, probably reading Nicole's thoughts.

"You *are* gloating, but I'm happy for you," Kate said. "At least one of us is having sex on a regular basis."

Siena returned and slid into the booth. "Okay, I heard the word 'sex.' What'd I miss?"

"Nothing," Nicole said. "We were just talking about Kate."

Siena looked at her. "What? With who?"

"No one." Kate rolled her eyes. "That's the point."

EMMET AWOKE TO the sound of clanging pans. He glanced at the clock, then grabbed his boxer briefs off the floor and walked into the kitchen, where he found Nicole at the stove making a grilled cheese. She wore his faded ACL Fest T-shirt that hit her midthigh.

She glanced up. "Sorry. Did I wake you?"

"Yeah." He eased up behind her and slid his arms around her waist. She smelled like sex, and he nuzzled the back of her neck.

"I woke up starving and couldn't go back to sleep, so I decided to make a snack," she said.

"I had cheese for that?"

"Provolone." She flipped the sandwich, and the toasted side was perfectly golden brown. "American melts better but this is good, too."

His stomach started to rumble. "You mind sharing?"

"Not at all."

He got a couple glasses from the cabinet and filled them with water as she slid the sandwich onto a plate and cut it in half. Her hair was loose and messy around her shoulders, and the sight of her moving around his kitchen put a pang in his chest.

She glanced up. "What?"

He walked over and kissed her nose. "Nothing."

"Really, what? You're giving me a look."

"You're beautiful."

"Right."

"You are."

She held out half of the sandwich. "Careful, it's hot."

"Thanks."

She set the plate beside her water glass, then hitched herself onto the counter.

Emmet took a big bite. The cheese was gooey and warm. "Damn, that's good. Salty."

"It's the butter. I used a ton."

He took a long sip of water, watching her over the rim as she ate. He liked that she felt comfortable enough in his home to get up and make a snack in the middle of the night. He wished she would settle in even more and leave some stuff here. Half his clothes were at her apartment, but she hadn't left anything at his place besides a toothbrush.

He set his cup down and walked over, placing his palms on the counter on either side of her. She immediately tensed.

"I've been thinking," he said. "You're off this Sunday, right?"

"Yes," she said warily.

"I am, too." He brushed a lock of hair from her face and tucked it behind her ear. "Why don't we spend the day together?"

She looked surprised. "I'd love to," she said, setting her sandwich aside. "But I'm supposed to go to Port A to visit my grandmother."

"Can I come?"

Her eyebrows arched. "To visit my grandmother?"

"Yeah, I'd like to meet her. Is this the one with all the cats?"

"That's Grandma Doris. This is Helen. She's in a nursing home." Nicole paused. "You really want to come with me?"

"Sure, why not?"

"There's not much to do there but bring her lunch and play dominoes."

He smiled. "I love dominoes."

"*You* love dominoes?"

"My granddad taught me when I was a kid. I'm really good."

She lifted an eyebrow.

"Seriously, I'll kick your butt."

"Well. *That's* unlikely." She grinned. "But it would be fun to see you try. All right, if you really want to come with me—"

"I want to."

"—I was planning to head up there Sunday morning around eight. That work?"

"Sure. Then in the afternoon, we could swing by my parents' if you're up for it. I want to go by to look at my dad's boat." He watched her reaction. "I'm thinking of buying it."

Her face brightened. "Oh yeah?"

"Yeah. He's looking to get rid of it. It's really old, but the engine's still decent, and it's got some years left."

"Sounds fun. I love boats."

"I know that."

She smiled slightly and eyed him over her sandwich. Her interest in boats was one of the main reasons he wanted to buy his dad's. Nicole loved being on the water, and he figured it was something they could do together when they had time off work but not enough time to leave town. Their hectic schedules weren't likely to let up anytime soon. If anything, they were about to get worse.

"And I'd like for us to hang out." Her expression turned serious. "I've missed you these last few weeks. Your schedule's been crazy."

"Yeah, I know." He put their empty plate in the sink, and when he turned back, she was watching him with those bottomless brown eyes that saw everything.

"There's that look again. I can tell something's bothering you," she said.

And she was right. Something *was* bothering him. For weeks, he'd been battling this relentless anxiety that wouldn't go away. But he couldn't talk about it. How could he explain the hot, suffocating feeling he got every time he knew she was heading into some semi-dangerous situation? It was a constant struggle for him to treat her like everyone else. She was always front of mind, especially if she was in any sort of danger. It was distracting as hell.

She had predicted that this thing between them would lead to problems at work, and she'd been right. The whole situation was becoming untenable. He was trying to make some changes, and when he had a solution in place, he'd tell her everything. But not yet.

"Everything's fine." He kissed her. "So, it's a date Sunday? We'll spend the day together?"

"It's a date."

He moved from her mouth to her neck to the sensitive place below her ear. Her skin smelled so good, and he could never get enough of it.

"I know what you're doing," she said, tipping her head back. "You're changing the subject."

"You don't like this subject?" He kissed her throat.

"You know I do."

His pulse gave a kick, and he slid his arms around her, pulling her to the edge of the counter. He kissed her and felt her loosening up, getting into it. She wrapped her legs around his waist, and he moved her flush against him. He loved her skin, her taste. He loved everything about her. He slid his T-shirt up and settled his mouth on her breast, and she arched against him and made that low moan that had become his favorite sound.

"Nik?"

"Hmm?"

"Let's go back to bed."

CHAPTER

THIRTY-TWO

NICOLE OPENED THE door to the police station and nearly bumped into Joel Breda.

"Oh, hey." She held the door for him as he stepped outside. "Long time no see. What are you up to?"

"Not much. It's been a while."

"It has."

Joel wore an LBPD golf shirt and jeans, and she couldn't remember the last time she'd seen him here at the station house. He'd been consumed with the task force for months.

She shielded her eyes from the sun as she looked up at him. Like his brothers, Joel had an athletic build and those swoony blue eyes. But he had a quieter, more serious way about him, maybe because he was the oldest.

"How's the baby?" Nicole asked.

He smiled. "Good. Real good. She's sleeping through the night now."

"Well, that's awesome."

Joel looked over her shoulder, and something in his expression made Nicole turn around.

Miranda was crossing the parking lot with little Janie in one of those strap-on baby carriers.

Nicole gasped. "Oh my gosh, there she is! Look at her."

Janie's pudgy arms stuck out, and she wore a little pink cap to protect her head from the sun.

"Sorry I'm late," Miranda said. "We had a slight mishap with the car seat, but it's all good now."

"What's wrong with the car seat?" Joel asked, frowning as he stepped forward to help Miranda unhook the carrier.

"I couldn't get the latch to work when I switched cars. No biggie." She leaned up and kissed him. "I got it fixed."

Joel hooked the straps over his shoulders and kissed Janie on the head as Miranda smiled at both of them. Then she turned to Nicole.

"Hey, Nicole. How's it going?"

"Great," she said, nodding at the baby. "I can't believe how much she's grown since I last saw her!"

"Yep," Joel said, kissing her head again.

"Has Brady started the meeting yet?" Miranda asked.

"Actually, he bumped it to one o'clock," Nicole said. "Didn't you get the text? I think you were on the thread."

"I missed it." Miranda took out her phone.

"Yeah, we're waiting on Owen. He's wrapping up a witness interview. Said he'd be in soon."

Nicole watched as Joel gazed down at little Janie and then looked at his wife. It seemed like they were having a moment, so Nicole wanted to give them some privacy.

"I'll catch you inside," she told Miranda. "Good to see you, Joel."

"See you around."

Nicole went into the station and paused to let her eyes adjust to the dimness. The waiting room was empty for a change, and Denise was on the phone. She caught Nicole's eye and put the caller on hold.

"Good, you're here," Denise said. "He wants to see you before the meeting."

"Brady does?"

She nodded. "He's in his office."

Nicole stepped into the bullpen and shot an apprehensive look at Brady's closed door. She glanced around, but everything seemed to be business as usual. A couple of uniforms were sitting at computers typing, and Adam was on a phone call.

Nicole tapped her knuckles on Brady's door.

"Come in."

She leaned her head in. "You wanted to see me?"

He pushed back his chair and stood, and Nicole's apprehension ramped up.

"Have a seat. And close the door, would you?"

She pulled the door shut and sank into a chair, quickly scanning his desk for clues. There was nothing on it but a blank legal pad and a plastic cup filled with dark green sludge. Nicole managed not to make a face.

The chief sat down. "So." He nodded at her.

She nodded back. There was something somber about him today, and dread filled her stomach.

"So . . . I bumped into Joel outside," Nicole said, looking for small talk. "Haven't seen him here in a while."

Brady nodded. "Good segue."

"Segue?"

"This involves him." He cleared his throat. "We're making some changes around here."

Nicole watched Brady, holding her breath.

"I'm retiring."

Her eyebrows shot up. "You're—what?"

"It's time." He leaned back in his chair. "You ask my

wife, it's *been* time. And now my cardiologist agrees with her." He folded his arms over his chest. "I'm due to have double bypass surgery at the end of next week."

"Oh my gosh, Chief. I didn't realize—"

"No one did." He waved off the rest of her comment. "I haven't been talking about it, except with Sharon. She's had me on one of these no-meat diets—bunch of salads and smoothies—but that's not enough. Evidently, it's stress-related. Anyway, we don't need to get into all that." He sat forward and rested his elbows on the desk. "The point is that Joel is coming on as acting chief."

Nicole sat there, wordless, trying to absorb all this news. Chief Brady was *retiring*. Joel Breda was replacing him.

"Joel's a good pick," Brady said.

She cleared her throat. "I agree."

"My guess is he'll end up in the job long-term, but that's up to the city council." Brady sat back again. "And that's not the only change we're making around here. With all the growth, we're doing some reorganizing, adding some positions, including two new investigators. And we're creating a new role. Head of detectives." He paused. "We want to offer you the job."

She blinked at him. "Me?"

"That's right."

"And by 'we' you mean . . . ?"

"Joel and I talked it over. He has confidence in your leadership skills, and so do I."

She swallowed. Her heart was thrumming now. "But what about Owen? He's been here longer than I have."

Brady nodded. "Owen's a great detective. But we think you're better suited for the role. This involves people management, mentoring. And you'll be our point person dealing with victims and families. We think you'd be good at it."

"Thank you."

"Your work on Red Highway was impressive, Nicole. And the Aubrey Lambert case—you really knocked that out of the park. People noticed—and I'm not just talking about us. The feds noticed it, too. If it weren't for your input, we never would have made the breakthroughs that neutralized an ongoing national security threat. So kudos to you. You earned this opportunity."

Her cheeks flushed at all the praise from her taciturn boss.

"Thank you, Chief. I'm flattered." She shook her head. "I just wasn't expecting all this. What about Emmet? He's been here longer than me also."

"Emmet's leaving."

She stared at him. "He's . . . what?"

"He's joining the task force, taking Joel's old spot." Brady frowned and looked at her. "I thought you knew."

Nicole swallowed. "No."

"Well. I assumed he'd told you, given your personal relationship. Anyway, that's between you two." He cleared his throat. "My concern is the job offer. Head of detectives, and it comes with a salary bump." He paused, clearly seeing she was too shocked to formulate a response at the moment. "Think about it and get back to me."

"I will."

He stood up. "But don't take too long. My last day is Friday, and we'd like to have things buttoned up ahead of that."

She got to her feet, dazed, and Brady held his hand out. She shook it.

"I need an answer by tomorrow."

"Yes, sir."

E MMET FOUND NICOLE on the beach at sunset. She jogged along the waterline with the late-day sun in her eyes, her attention focused on the distant lighthouse behind him.

He saw the second she noticed him. She stopped running and pulled out her earbuds. Then she bent at the waist, catching her breath as he walked up to her.

"Hey," he said.

"Hey." She straightened and looked him over, no doubt noticing that he'd been home to shower and change since work.

He bent down and kissed her, and she pulled away.

"I'm sweaty."

"So?"

He smiled and kissed her again. Then he turned, and they started walking toward the dunes where he'd parked his truck beside hers.

She glanced at him. "How'd you know I'd be here?"

"Your running shoes were missing, so I figured."

She removed her baseball cap and wiped her forehead with the back of her arm.

"I heard you talked to Brady." He glanced at her.

Her jaw tensed. "Yep."

"So, what do you think?"

She laughed. "About his job offer? Or the fact that I had to learn about my relationship from my boss?"

Emmet stopped and faced her. He'd known he was in trouble as soon as he'd talked to Joel.

"I'm sorry. I fucked this up, didn't I?"

"Yep."

"I'm really sorry, Nicole." He took her hand. "I didn't mean for you to hear it from Brady. I'd planned to talk to you, but I was waiting until they told me I officially had the job."

She didn't shake off his hand, but she gazed out at the water.

"I apologize."

She looked at him, and the hurt in her eyes made his chest ache.

"Can we sit?" He nodded at a piece of driftwood near the dunes. "Please?"

She walked to the log and sat down. She stretched her legs out, crossing them at the ankles. He sank down beside her and stretched his legs out, too. He had on jeans and work boots, and his feet looked huge compared to hers.

"So, I guess this is why you've been totally MIA lately?" She looked at him. "You've been auditioning for this task force thing?"

"Partly. I was trying to keep up with work, too, so it's been a lot of juggling."

"I wish you'd told me. I would have tried to talk you out of it."

"Why?"

"*Because*." She scowled up at him.

"Nicole, we both know something had to change. We've talked about this. Our PD isn't big enough for both of us. I can't treat you like everyone else. I tried, believe me. And same goes for you. One of us had to go."

Frustration flared in her eyes. "But you can't just up and *leave*. I'm not okay with you making that kind of sacrifice for me."

"It's not a sacrifice."

"Emmet, get real. This is your job. Your calling."

"No, it's not."

"Yes, it is. I know you."

He took her hand. "I know *you*. And I've been watching your career for years. As a detective, you're a natural. You're great with people and interviews, and you think creatively. You're so good at it, it's scary, Nicole. I'm not like that. I'm more tactical. And I've talked to a lot of guys on the task force, and it's a much better fit for me."

She shook her head. "But the task force is dangerous. Just—*shit*." Her voice cracked and she looked away.

He squeezed her hand. He'd known this would be a sticking point.

"Everything's dangerous," he said. "Being a cop is dangerous. Or a firefighter. Or, hell, even a schoolteacher. I mean, I could get hit by a bus tomorrow—"

"That's a bullshit answer and you know it. We're talking about a job where you have to wear Kevlar to work. And do raids and takedowns. And work crazy hours. It's going to be a strain, Emmet. Just ask Miranda and Joel how easy it's been for them."

She looked out at the water, and he studied her profile. He wished now that he'd come to her sooner so he could have messaged this better.

"I know it's a lot," he said. "It's not always going to be this way. But for now, we've got to find a way to make our relationship work. Do you want us to have to drop what we have together?"

"No. Of course not. But this feels too drastic, Emmet. You love your job."

"No. I *like* my job. I love *you*."

S HE LOOKED UP at him, stunned.

Not that he loved her. She'd sensed that for a while now. But that he was prepared to say it. And not just say it, *act* on it. Rearrange his life around it. This was happening so fast. For years they'd been friends and then everything suddenly turned upside down.

He leaned forward, his eyes locked on hers, gauging her reaction.

"I love you, too," she said.

Relief washed over his face. "Good. I was starting to worry there."

"No, you weren't." She poked him with her elbow. "You know damn well how I feel about you."

"I've been *hoping*. You never said it."

She leaned over and kissed him. But then she pulled back.

She looked out toward the water's edge, where a couple of kids were digging in the sand. A fisherman stood in the surf, and sunlight glimmered off the waves as a pelican swooped down.

Nicole's pulse was racing, and not just from her run. Emotions swirled inside her.

No man, with the exception of her father, had ever sacrificed anything important for her. And she'd never wanted to feel that kind of heavy obligation to anyone.

Emmet bumped his shoulder against hers. "What's that look?"

"Honestly?" She turned to him. "I'm scared, Emmet. You're talking about sacrificing your job for me. What if you resent me later?"

"That's what I'm telling you. I don't see it as a sacrifice. It's a change, yeah, and that's stressful, but this is positive for *us*." He took her hand again. "I want this to work between us."

She gazed up at him, and the intense look in his eyes made her heart squeeze. No one had ever looked at her like he did.

Or laughed with her, or argued with her, or touched her like he did. She had never shared this level of intimacy with anybody, and it frightened the hell out of her.

He leaned closer. "Don't be scared."

Of course he knew what she was thinking.

"But I *am* scared. What if we don't work out?"

He smiled. "Damn. And I thought I was the pessimist.

What if we *do* work out? What if we get married and have kids together and grow old together, and we come right back to this beach like those people over there and feed the birds at sunset?"

She stared at him in shock.

"You should see your face right now." He grinned and pulled her against him. "All right, maybe I'm rushing you."

"This is all so much. I'm freaking out, Emmet."

"Hey. Don't." He kissed the top of her head. "It's just me."

"I love you. I only wish the rest of it wasn't so complicated."

"It isn't, really. We'll take it one step at a time. It's taken us ten years to get to this point, right? We're not in a hurry. We can do this at our own pace."

She pulled back and looked at him, and the sincerity in his eyes hit her. She trusted him. He had her back, and always had. She didn't know what the future looked like, but they could work it out together.

He leaned down and kissed her. It started out soft and tender, but then it shifted, and his hand slid under her shirt. His mouth moved from her lips to her chin to her throat.

She eased back. "I'm all sweaty."

"You're perfect."

"I need to go home and shower."

He jumped to his feet and pulled her up. "Good idea. Lead the way."

Continue reading for a preview of

THE LAST CLOSE CALL

Available now!

CHAPTER
ONE

Evie waited until the third ring to pick up.

"Are you bailing?" Hannah asked.

"Sorry."

"Evie, you *promised*."

"I'm not up for it tonight." She stripped off the sexy black tank top that she'd ridiculously put on earlier—because Drew liked it—and grabbed her terry cloth robe off the chair.

"What happened?" Hannah asked over the din of conversation, and Evie pictured her sister in the crowded sports bar where they had planned to meet.

"Nothing."

"Not *nothing*. Spill it."

Evie tied the belt and sighed. "I saw him tonight."

"Who?"

"Drew. He came by to get Bella after work."

Or at least, he'd claimed he had come from work. Given

the beer on his breath, he had probably been to a happy hour with "the team" first.

"Oh, Eves. I'm sorry."

She padded barefoot across the hardwood floors that she and Drew had happily picked out together. After checking the lock on the patio door, she peered out at the dim yard. Her daughter's swing swayed in the breeze, and her Big Wheel sat abandoned on a carpet of crunchy brown leaves.

"I know that sucks," Hannah said. "Why don't you come out with us? You'll feel better."

"I'm already in bed."

"You are not. It's barely nine o'clock."

Evie returned to the bottle of merlot by the fridge and topped off her glass.

"Come on," Hannah persisted. "We're playing darts. Blake says he'll even let you win."

Evie smiled. Her sister's boyfriend was a gem, a genuine *nice guy*. But she didn't want to be a third wheel again.

"Really, I'm not up for it."

"Well." She heard the resignation in Hannah's voice. "You're still coming Thursday, right?"

"Absolutely." She took a hearty swig at the thought of her sister's Thanksgiving potluck, which was sure to be an awkward mix of friends and coworkers. Evie had offered to bring a pie, but Hannah had assigned her mashed potatoes in a transparent attempt to make sure she didn't cancel.

"What time are we eating again?" Evie asked.

"Um . . . I don't know. Four, probably?"

So eight, then. Which was fine. Evie would be there all evening, which would cut into the ice cream binge that would inevitably accompany her first holiday in six years without Drew.

And Bella's first holiday ever without her mother.

Tears burned Evie's eyes, and she took another gulp.

"So get this," she told Hannah. "He took my silver locket." Fury tightened her chest as soon as the words were out. "You know the one he gave me for Mother's Day? He stole it right out of my jewelry box."

"Oh, come on," Hannah said. "You probably misplaced it."

"No. I did not."

"Evie, the man drives a Porsche. What would he want with a silver locket?"

"He knew it would needle me." She headed down the hall and paused at Bella's room to switch off the light, ignoring the lingering scent of baby shampoo as she closed the door.

"Do you want me to come over?"

"No, I'm fine. I'm just being, I don't know, *emotional*."

"Hey, you're allowed to be emotional. Your ex is a prick. How about we walk the lake tomorrow? We can catch up."

Evie stepped into the bathroom and confronted her reflection in the mirror above the sink. Messy hair, sallow skin, dingy bathrobe. She opened the medicine cabinet and eyed the contents. The prescription sleeping pills called out to her. But she had more willpower than that. She closed the cabinet.

"What time?" she asked Hannah.

"Let's do nine. I'll meet you at the bridge."

"Are you sure? Nine sounds early."

Evie was fine with it, but Hannah's body clock didn't work that way. She hadn't had kids.

"All right, let's make it ten," Hannah said.

"Ten at the bridge."

"It's a date. Love you, Eves."

"You, too."

She set the phone down and stared at her reflection as she took another sip. A four-mile loop around the lake would do her good. Maybe she'd stop at the grocery afterward and get some fresh produce. She could make soup. Or maybe a pie for next week. She stepped into the bedroom.

A man in a ski mask stood in the doorway.

Her wineglass crashed to the floor as she registered everything at once—the wide shoulders, the black clothes, the heavy boots.

His hands were empty, but the latex gloves he wore turned her throat to dust.

"Don't scream, Evelyn."

Her heart seized. He knew her *name*.

She thought of her cell phone in the bathroom only a few feet away. She could lock herself inside and then—

He stepped into the bedroom and pulled the door shut with a terrifying *click*.

Evie's mind raced, even as time slowed to a crawl. She had to survive this. Whatever happened, she had to survive for Bella.

What did he *want*? Her heart thundered as her eyes returned to those gloved hands.

God help me.

She inched toward the bathroom, stalling for time.

"How"—she cleared her throat—"how did you get in here?"

The hole in the mask shifted—a flash of white teeth as his mouth formed a smile.

"I've been here."

CHAPTER

TWO

Eight weeks later

T HE LUCKY DUCK was half empty, which was just how
Rowan liked it.

Johnny Cash drifted from the speakers. A young couple
occupied a high-top table in the corner, and several regulars
sat at the bar, chatting up Lila as she pulled a pint.

Rowan's favorite booth was taken, so she grabbed one
near the window beneath a neon **Shiner Bock** sign. Lila
darted her a questioning glance, and Rowan gave her a nod
as she slid into the torn vinyl seat.

She grabbed the plastic menu behind the condiment
bottles and looked for something decadent. She was starving, she suddenly realized. For the past five days, she had
subsisted on cereal and microwave popcorn.

As she skimmed the choices, Rowan tugged the scrunchie
from her hair and combed her hand through it. She probably should have showered or at least put on a clean sweatshirt before coming here. Oh well. Too late now.

"You finally came up for air."

She looked up as Lila slid a Tanqueray and tonic in front of her.

"*Thank* you," Rowan said. "You read my mind."

Lila sipped a ginger ale—her hydration beverage of choice when she was working.

"Busy night?" Rowan asked.

"Not really." She shrugged. "Good tips, though."

"Has Dara been by?"

"*Yes*." Lila's eyes sparkled, and she tossed a springy brown curl over her shoulder. "She was here earlier. With a date."

"Oh yeah?"

"They left after an hour, so you'll have to get the scoop. Are you eating?"

"Yes, but I can't decide."

"Try the nachos," Lila said. "We've got fresh guac today."

"That sounds good."

A couple walked into the bar and claimed a pair of stools on the corner. Lila eyed them as she nursed her drink. "I have to get back. I'll give Sasha your order."

"Thanks."

Lila returned to her post, and Rowan scanned the faces around the room, trying to guess people's stories. It was a game she played whenever she came here alone. All the singles tonight were regulars. Ditto the two guys shooting pool in the back. Her attention settled on the couple at the high-top. Based on their age, they might be students at the University of Texas, maybe seeking a night away from the crowds on Sixth Street. But they had a seasoned look about them. The woman's makeup was perfect. And they both exuded the stiff body language that screamed *first date*.

Rowan watched them subtly from her booth. Head tilts. Intense eye contact. The woman arched her brows as she sipped her margarita through a straw, displaying just the right amount of interest in whatever the guy was saying. He rested a hand on his knee and looked confident—but slightly nervous—as he expounded on whichever first-date topic he'd selected for the evening.

A chime emanated from Rowan's purse. She pulled out her phone and read a text from the Austin lawyer whose client Rowan had been working for all week.

Got your email. Omg TY!!

The words were followed by three halo emojis, and Rowan felt a swell of pride.

Anytime, she texted back. So glad I could help.

This attorney had sent her three referrals over the past six months, and now there would likely be more on the way. Rowan's anemic bank account was finally getting a boost. It couldn't come soon enough. Her December credit card bill had just come in, and she hadn't even wanted to look at it.

"Rowan Healy?"

She jerked her head up as a man stepped over. Tall, broad-shouldered, dark hair. He wore a black leather jacket with droplets of rain clinging to it. Rowan darted a glance at Lila. Her friend didn't look up, but she lifted an eyebrow in a way that told Rowan she'd sent this guy over here.

"Who's asking?" Rowan responded, even though she had a sneaking suspicion she knew, based on his deep voice. Not to mention the super-direct look in his brown eyes.

"Jack Bruner, Austin PD." He smiled slightly. "Mind if I sit?"

She sighed and nodded at the empty seat across from her.

He slid into the booth and rested his elbows on the table. He looked her over, and she managed not to squirm.

"You're a hard woman to reach."

Ha. He had no idea how true that was.

"How'd you know to find me here?" she asked.

"Ric Santos told me you hang out here."

She couldn't hide her surprise at the mention of Ric. She hadn't known they were friends. But she probably should have guessed. Law enforcement was a tight-knit group.

She gave him what she hoped was a confident smile. "Look, Detective, I appreciate you coming all the way out here, but I'm afraid you've wasted your time."

"Just listen."

Two words.

A command, but not. When combined with that slight smile, it was more like a statement. Something she was *going* to do, even if she didn't realize it yet.

Rowan felt a surge of annoyance. But again, she gave him a nod.

Sasha appeared at the table and rested her cocktail tray on her hip. "Can I get you something to drink?" she asked the detective.

"A Coke, please."

She nodded. "Rowan?"

"I'm good, thanks."

She walked off, her cascade of blond hair swinging behind her.

Rowan settled her attention on the detective.

"I'm with APD's violent crimes unit, as I mentioned on the phone," he said.

With every call, he'd politely identified himself and given a callback number. Rowan had called the number once and—equally politely—left a message with her response. But he'd stubbornly ignored it.

"I'm working on a case," he said, "and I could use your help."

Rowan nodded. "Like I told you before—"

He held up his hand and gave her a sharp look. *Listen.*

"It's a serial offender," he continued. "Eight sexual assaults." His dark brows furrowed. "This guy's careful. We've only recovered one DNA profile, the second attack in the series."

"If you've only got one profile, how do you know it's the same guy?"

"Because—"

Sasha was back already with a flirty smile. She placed the detective's soft drink in front of him, and he nodded his thanks.

"Because we know," he said after she left.

Rowan looked the man over. He had an athletic build, but not the steroid-infused look she was used to seeing with young cops. Then again, he wasn't that young. The touch of gray at his temples told her he was maybe ten years older than she was, probably late thirties. Or maybe it was the wise look in his eyes that told her that.

She sipped her drink and waited for more.

"A while ago we had the sample analyzed by a genetic genealogist," he said. "Spent a lot of money and time on that. They ran into some kind of wall, and the results were inconclusive, they said."

"What's 'a while'?"

"Come again?"

"How long ago did you have it analyzed?"

He hesitated a beat.

"Four years."

Rowan's breath caught. In terms of DNA technology, four years was like four decades. A lot had changed in that time—new techniques, new tools, new profiles in the databases.

But she tried to keep her face impassive as she folded her hands in front of her.

"I appreciate your effort to track me down," she said. It told her a lot about what kind of detective he was—precisely the kind that had prompted her to shift careers. "But unfortunately, I don't do police work anymore. You could say I'm retired."

"That's not what Ric told me."

She gritted her teeth. Damn it, she'd *known* doing him a favor would come back to bite her.

"Ric said you're selective, not retired." He paused, watching her. "He told me you gave him an assist recently and that your help was invaluable."

"I know what you're doing," Rowan said. She was immune to flattery, even from smooth-talking detectives who liked to play head games. "And I can appreciate the pressure you guys must be under with a serial case. But I'm not in that line of work anymore."

He leaned forward, and she eased back slightly.

"Let me be straight, Rowan." His eyes bored into hers. "I need your help right *now*. Not next month or next year. Not whenever you get bored with what you're doing and decide to come out of retirement. I don't care if I sound desperate. I'm on a ticking clock here."

Her stomach tightened at his words. And his prediction that she would backtrack on her career change irked her.

But he held her gaze across the table, and she felt that inexorable *pull* that had turned her life upside down too many times to count.

She took in the detective's sharp eyes and the determined set to his jaw. She admired that determination—she had it, too—but she had to resist this time.

At this very moment, she had an inbox full of requests from prospective clients who were willing to pay top dollar for her work. *Positive* work. *Rewarding* work. The kind of work that made her get out of bed in the morning with a sense of purpose. She'd spent three years building her reputation as one of the best in her field, and the last thing she needed to do was put all those clients on hold and get sucked back into the vortex of police work.

A buzz emanated from beneath the table, and Jack Bruner took out his phone. His expression remained blank, but she caught the slight tensing of his shoulders.

A callout. Someone was dead or bleeding or in some emergency room somewhere.

He pulled out his wallet and tucked a twenty under his untouched Coke. Then he took out a business card and slid it across the table.

"My cell's on the back. Call me if you change your mind."

He scooted from the booth, and she felt small as he towered over her. He held out his hand.

Against her better judgment she shook it.

Ready to find
your next great read?

Let us help.

Visit prh.com/nextread

Penguin
Random
House